MADAME GRAY'S VAULT OF GORE

Compiled & Edited by Gerri R. Gray

A HellBound Books LLC Publication

Copyright © 2021 by HellBound Books Publishing LLC
All Rights Reserved

Cover and art design by
HellBound Books Publishing LLC

No part of this book may be reproduced, stored in a retrieval system, or transmitted by any means, electronic, mechanical, photocopying, recording or otherwise without written permission from the author This book is a work of fiction. Names, characters, places and incidents are entirely fictitious or are used fictitiously and any resemblance to actual persons, living or dead, events or locales is purely coincidental.

www.hellboundbookspublishing.com

Printed in the United States of America

Also by Gerri R. Gray:
The Amnesia Girl
Gray Skies of Dismal Dreams
The Graveyard Girls
Blood and Blasphemy
The Strange Adventures of Turquoise Moonwolf
Madame Gray's Creep Show
The Toilet Zone: Number Two

Contributor to:
Ghost Hunting the Mohawk Valley
Beautiful Tragedies
Demons, Devils & Denizens of Hell 2
EconoClash Review
Deadman's Tome Cthulhu Christmas Special
Mixed Bag of Horror: Vol. 1
Night Picnic: Vol. 3
Coffin Bell: Vol. 2
Dig Two Graves: Vol. 2
Jitter: Issue #7
Phantoms in the Moonlight
Merry Evilmas
…and others.

HellBound Books

CONTENTS

INTRODUCTION 7
Madame Gray
ACTS OF VENGEANCE 11
Frederick Pangbourne
SLOTH 27
R. L. Meza
EL PADRINO 45
Drew Nicks
A MATTER OF TASTE 54
Gerri R. Gray
ETERNAL REMAINS 72
Travis Mushanski
OUT BENEATH THE JACK O'LANTERN SKY 81
Tylor James
THE BALLAD OF FAIRY FAY 91
Stephen McQuiggan
TROPOSPHERE 99
Jon Douglas Rainey
CREEPERS 110
Max Carrey
BLACK SKY 125
Carlton Herzog
FOIE GRAS 142
Eamonn Murphy
THE ARTIST 164
Alexander Nachaj
A DEADLY CABIN TRYST 175
John Mara
SKINNER 185
J Louis Messina
A HOG KILLING 205
John Robinson

EIGHTH DEADLY SIN	229
James Harper	
THERAPY SESSIONS	251
B.M. Tolkovsky	
DUST AND SHADOWS	266
Carlton Herzog	
THIRD TIME'S A CHARM	278
Frederick Pangbourne	
BABYCAKES	301
Bryan Miller	
CRUSADE	310
Jason Krawczyk	
THE NAME-US GAME COUNTERPOINT	321
Cecily Winter	
QUIETUS	332
David-Jack Fletcher	
AMBER MAY AND THE NECROTIC WAY	346
Matt Martinek	
HOUSE BOUND	354
Edward Ahern	
WITH A DEVIL'S STRENGTH	362
Dr. Chris McAuley	
PSYCHOSIS	369
Shannon Lawrence	
THE BLEEDING BOX	385
Bryan Holm	
THE THORN TREE	398
Michael Highgrove	
Other HellBound Titles	421

INTRODUCTION
By Madame Gray

Welcome, horror fans, to the second volume in HellBound Books' *Madame Gray* series. I hope you're not the squeamish type, for you'll discover, as you venture deeper into the cobwebbed depths of my vault, that no story is too bloody, too freaky, or too taboo for this anthology. Here, the twisted, the monstrous, and the unholy reign supreme.

In this spine-tingling collection of original tales, compiled by yours truly, you will ascend to the summit of supernatural terror, descend into the bowels of hell, and bathe in blood-drenched tales of revenge. Prepare to encounter an artist who gives new meaning to "finger painting," and an unusual portrait that will leave you feeling a bit antsy. (Let it never be said that Madame Gray doesn't appreciate fine art.) You'll also meet a faithless faith healer whose laying on of hands invokes something other than the Holy Spirit; a rotten little girl and the ghoul who digs her; and a man who feeds his swine of a brother to the pigs on their farm. For those with an appetite for the atrocious, we have foie gras, Hungarian goulash, and fetus tartare served up on the menu. Then there's the weird and disturbing birthday party for a baby that never ages. (They just don't bake cakes the way they used to.)

And fear not, my fiendish friends, there are also plenty of beheadings, dismemberments, consummate flayings and cannibal treats for those possessing a healthy (or should I say, an *un*-healthy) appetite for gore. From eye-gouging ghosts to carnivorous clouds, from boxes decidedly best left closed to a murder of murderous crows, my vault is well stocked with some of the darkest tales imaginable—each one designed to test your nerves and make you sleep with the lights on.

Each of the contributing authors to this anthology possesses a distinctive writing style that invites the reader into their stories. Their approach to the horror genre is refreshingly unique, and the gory goodies they offer up are guaranteed to chill your blood, revolt your senses, and fill your sleep with nightmares. Their names might not be household words (yet), but these talented writers have proven themselves to be masters of horror in their own right. And one never knows, among them might be lurking the next H.P. Lovecraft, Edgar Allan Poe, Anne Rice, or Stephen King. Never underestimate the power of indie writers!

So buckle up your seat belt and brace yourself for a sanguineous excursion into my vault of gore, where delights of fright await in abundance. You may take solace in the knowledge that the twenty-nine stories that lie ahead are but works of fiction (hopefully for all our sakes), but take care not to slip on those coagulating crimson puddles on the floor.

By the pricking of my thumbs, something gory this way comes!

Madame Gray
Friday the 13th
August 2021

MADAME GRAY'S VAULT OF GORE

HellBound Books

ACTS OF VENGEANCE
By Frederick Pangbourne

"It won't be much longer now," I soothingly reassured her from my end of the eight-foot dinghy we shared. Lynda said nothing and continued to stare blankly at me.

I couldn't blame her for not speaking. She'd been through a lot these past few days. We both had. The incident at the island was enough to push anyone over the edge of both sanity and reason, making them become distant things of the past. Leaving nothing short of madness to remain. The fact that we had been adrift on this small boat for nearly three days now didn't aid in our dire situation or her declining mental condition.

I sighed and looked away from her to the blue, cloudless sky and the endless stretches of ocean all about us. The sound of the water lapping at the boat's side the only noise. Looking back to the horizon behind her, I saw that the boat was drawing nearer. Perhaps now its occupants would be able to see us. I removed my shirt and carefully stood in the dinghy. Once I was confident of my balance, I began to wave the shirt back and forth high over my head.

"I think it's heading straight for us," I told her as I continued to frantically wave my shirt like some surrendering flag. "It looks like a fishing trawler."

I looked down at Lynda and still she said nothing. Simply staring with that dazed look in her eyes. It was at that time the trawler let off a bellowed blast from its air horn in the closing distance. I laughed and waved my arm harder. "They see us, love!" I shouted out with glee. "They see us! It won't be long now!"

Lynda, unresponsive to my exclamations, remained silent.

Now that they had spotted us, I sat back down and donned my shirt. My skin, red and raw from the days beneath the Pacific sun, protested in pain as the material brushed against it like sandpaper.

My body felt a renewed wave of exhilaration pass over it as I anxiously awaited the ship's arrival. I figured it would be a good fifteen minutes before it finally reached us. "Yup, it won't be much longer now," I repeated, hoping that my words were reaching her and looking down to the bloodied axe resting at my feet. "It won't be long now."

* * *

It was on a clear Sunday afternoon when we departed the main island of Hawaii, via seaplane, from Na'alehu and ventured due south seventy-six miles to the island where Professor Victor Janson and his wife Ruth awaited our arrival.

Victor's invitation was well received back at our apartment in San Francisco. He had stated in his letter, which contained two round-trip tickets, how it had been ages since the four of us had last gotten together and that the villa they had rented could easily accommodate us all. Lynda and I took his unexpected request to visit them as the perfect opportunity to turn the trip into a much-needed vacation for the two of us. Neither of us had ever been to the Hawaiian Islands, so the destination proved ideal. Especially since our flight was already paid for. Victor ended the letter with a vague suggestion of some discovery in his research, which required celebration.

Victor was an old friend of ours. He and I studied together years ago when we both attended USC, before I dropped out and Victor stayed on and eventually transferred, becoming a Theologian professor at UCLA. He had taken this year's recess from the university to conduct his own personal studies within the seclusion of a small villa on a tiny island. The island was referred to by some of the mainland's southern population as Wahi li'ili', which roughly translated to 'tiny place.' The tropical island was just over three miles in circumference and the only other occupants were a remote fishing village at the opposite western end of the island. Supplies were flown into the village every week and Lynda and I had caught a ride with the supply plane for a small fee.

The pilot knew of Victor's villa and had stated that since there was a dock at the beach leading to the house, he could easily land nearby to drop us off, and then resume his course to the village. For our departure, however, we would catch the plane at the village on its next supply run on the following Sunday. The villa was also not equipped with a landline but relied on a ham radio for communication with the world outside of the island. We had to transmit from the plane's radio prior to departing, giving Victor a rough estimated time of our arrival. His replied transmission assured us he would have someone awaiting our appearance.

As the plane circled about the eastern portion of the island preparing to make its initial landing, we could see the beige tiled roof of the villa prominent amongst the clutter of green palm trees that surrounded the house. A dock stretched from the white beaches out into the clear blue ocean. It was on the dock that we spotted a lone figure making its way across the structure's wooden planks and to a small rowboat.

The boat and its occupant met us as at the plane as it came to a stop on the clear waters off the island. What little luggage we conveyed, only two large duffle bags, was loaded onto the small dinghy and we were taken back to dock as the seaplane was again in the air and heading to the western end of the island. The operator of the boat, who laboriously worked the oars, was a young, muscular man named Noe. He was a native to the island and a resident of the fishing village. He stated that he made deliveries and did various chores up at the villa for the Jansons in exchange for addition income. Though he spoke English, he kept his conversation to a minimum as he rowed us back to the island.

Once we had arrived at the dock, Noe assisted us with our luggage and directed us to a path leading to the white, single-story villa that rested on a hill overlooking the ocean. Though we protested, Noe insisted on carrying our large duffle bags as he led the way up the twisted footpath, which proceeded to wind up into the dense jungle terrain. The refreshing ocean breeze that had caressed us earlier had abruptly come to a halt as we climbed the path into the impenetrable vegetation that strangled the very breeze from the air about us. Sweat had instantly formed and dampened my clothing, reminding me of the tropical climate in which I now found myself.

Once outside the villa, Noe paid us his respects prior to departing on an old, rusted blue bicycle with a small market basket fixed behind the seat. I slid the man twenty dollars for his efforts just before he set out on a sloping dirt road that lead from the villa and back to his village.

"I hope your trip was pleasant?" A voiced inquired behind us.

We turned to see Victor standing in the screened porch. The white of his teeth was visible through the obscured screening as he smiled.

As he emerged from the screened enclosure and came down the porch steps, we moved to meet him. Victor was thin, and his skin darkened by the tropical sun. He wore a pair of cargo shorts and an unbuttoned, flowered, short-sleeved shirt. His thick dark hair was in disarray as if he had just rolled out of bed, his face unshaven.

"Look at you!" I exclaimed and took a step back to observe him. "You'd think you've been shipwrecked here for years now."

"If only that were true," he chuckled as he took Lynda's bag and walked us into the house. The spacious interior was basic yet comfortable. Tiled floors, cinder block walls and an array of crisscrossing wood beams above us where two spinning ceiling fans were running. The furniture was modest and nicely decorated the house. I spotted the ham radio on a small table in a corner, a map of the islands tacked on a corkboard in front of it.

"This is beautiful, Victor," Lynda said as she leaned over the kitchen sink and peered through the window above it. "Where's Ruth?"

"She's down at the village. She's picking up some fish for dinner tonight. She left less than an hour ago. She'll be back soon."

"So, what have you been up to all alone out here? You were vague on what your studies comprised," I asked as we were placing our bags in a spare bedroom.

"I wouldn't know where to start, Daniel, but I can assure you it is an amazing find. I'll discuss it with you later over dinner."

"Well, I guess it must be of some great importance if you needed to coax us out here."

He grinned. "Have you ever heard of the name Dagon?"

I shrugged and shook my head. "No, I can't say I ever have," I confessed.

"You will," he replied and slapped my shoulder.

Later that evening, the four of us feasted on grilled yellow tuna steaks and vegetables that Ruth had brought back from the village. Two chilled bottles of white wine added to the meal's excellence. We dined on the open back deck of the villa and were graced with a spectacular scene of the ocean below and the display of red and orange hues from the setting sun that splashed over the rolling waters. A gusty warm sea breeze blew in from the vast openness that laid out before us, adding to the evening's perfection.

After lengthy conversations and the occasional laughs of our past and present experiences, the night slowly drew to an end. Ruth and Lynda cleaned off the table and then continued their own private conversations in the kitchen as they cleaned the dishes. It was I who finally, after a brief period of comfortable silence, poured another glass of wine and asked, "So, what is this Dagon that has you all the way out here conducting your studies in secrecy?"

He smiled and exhaled heavily then leaned across the table. "Daniel, what I've discovered here surpasses anything I've ever worked on at the university."

I was now also leaning forward. "How so?"

"There was some construction going on at the main island several months ago. They were digging up an area of untouched earth near a power plant in order to expand the facility. It was during this excavation that some relics were unearthed."

"Relics?"

"Yes. Remnants of the ancient tribes that had long ago

lived amongst these islands. I'm talking sometime around the eleventh century if not earlier. Long before any white man set foot on these shores. They asked me to examine some of the objects they had discovered. Most of them were ceramic pots, bowls, and various jewelry, things of that sort. Nothing of any real significance. However, what was also uncovered amongst these other items were tablets made of Koa wood. Etched into these tablets were the religious rites that these ancient tribes practiced."

Victor poured himself another glass of wine as he continued. "They dedicated these rites to an ocean deity that they worshipped."

"Dagon," I added.

"Precisely. Since I could not legally remove the tablets, I was able to make rubbings of the etchings. That is what I've been deciphering these past months and what I've learned is extraordinary. Do you realize that the Philistines supposedly worshipped this Dagon during biblical times? Its name is mentioned in the first book of Samuel in the Old Testament. They have exalted this fish god before Christ, Daniel."

"So ancient people worshipping pagan gods. What's so special about that? That has been going on since primitive man discovered fire."

"Correct, but it appears as if this water god has continued to be idolized in the utmost secrecy for centuries and by numerous civilizations across the globe. I've uncovered that in certain areas to this very day, it is still being worshipped in untold practices. I believe that those tablets are the first real evidence of its existence and I plan on proving that this deity truly exists."

"How?"

"I've translated the etchings of these ancient tablets with much difficulty and have come to discover that they are an evocation of these deep ones. A rite of summoning this Dagon."

I chuckled and leaned back in my chair. "Victor, are you serious? You've been out in this heat too long."

"There is a festival being held in the village tomorrow night. I'm sending the women down there to attend it while you and I put my theory to the test."

I scoffed at his intentions and was about to again laugh until I saw just how serious he was. "Victor, why? What do you propose to gain by this? Why do you need me?"

"It will prove that an ancient god of the deep, an Old One as it's referred to, exists still in modern times and has remained hidden throughout the ages, revealing itself to only those who are aware of its ageless existence and willingly accept it as their god. I now know of its existence, Daniel. And as for you, I can use some assistance that I dare not ask Ruth or anyone else to take part in. Please."

I exhaled and finished my wine in one long gulp. For him to financially back our flight all the way here, there must be something tangible to his studies. I struggled with the reasoning behind this whole preposterous circumstance. Was there perhaps some partial truth to what he rightly believed to be real? I reluctantly nodded. "Okay."

The next afternoon Victor unfolded his plan and mentioned the festival taking place in the village at the island's far end to our wives. It was as if he had rehearsed his speech a hundred times over prior to us arriving. Shakespeare himself could not have written a more persuasive proposal. The women accepted the invitation with little rebuttal, if any, and were soon swept up in enjoying a girls' night out on the island, free of their spouses. He had even arranged their transportation by having Noe escort them there and back. If I were wearing a hat, I would have tipped it to his clever and persuasive performance.

It was just after 6pm when Ruth and Lynda departed the villa. Almost instantly, Victor began rearranging the back deck of furniture in preparation to his pagan rite. Once we had cleared the deck of all obstructions, Victor then produced a large piece of chalk and copied an intricate design from his personal papers onto the wooden floorboards. Any help that I offered was politely refused as he took all preparations needed onto himself regarding the drawings. Once the bizarre symbol was completed, he encircled it with a ring of white sand from the beaches below.

"There's an axe in the hall closet. Would you mind bringing it here?" he asked as he rose from the floor after connecting the circle of sand. "I'll be right back." And with that, he departed from the deck by a staircase at the far end.

The idea of an axe being needed brought unpleasant feelings to mind as to what this ritual would entail. Nevertheless, I proceeded down to the hall closet and removed a fire axe from inside. I had only to wait on the deck for a moment before Victor came lumbering up the stairs with a small goat cradled in his arms.

"Please tell me you're not going to kill that thing," I weakly inquired.

"All rituals in appeasing the gods require a sacrifice, Daniel. The original texts called for a human sacrifice. I'm giving Dagon the next best thing without committing manslaughter."

I set the axe down and leaned it against the wall. "Victor, this is going too far. You asked that I give you a hand in all this and I have, but I'm not killing an animal."

Victor sighed heavily as he set the goat down and secured the length of rope about the animal's neck to the deck's railing. "If that's the way you really feel, then I'll do it." There was a twinge of frustration in his voice. "Could you at least collect the blood? I'll need you to fill up a container and pour some into the center of the circle when I instruct you to. I won't ask anything else of you."

"Victor-" I pleaded as he walked past me and back into the house. He returned with a small bucket in one hand and a stack of papers cradled in the other arm. He thrust the pail into my hands. "Please, Daniel. We don't have all night and this mess needs to be cleaned up afterwards. This is all I ask."

Taking the bucket, I stood aside as he set the papers on a barstool nearby and lifted the axe from against the wall. He was breathing hard and sweat beads were forming on his forehead. Upon this observation, I noticed my own breath was also coming at a quickened pace.

"Okay," he said. "After I kill the goat, you collect the blood. As you're doing that, I will begin the readings. I'll point to the circle when I need you to pour the blood. Understood?"

I nodded and took a step back. How in God's name did I get myself mixed up into this gruesome predicament? I should have just stood my ground and followed my initial feeling and plainly refused his request. But I did not refuse, and you know the saying: In for a penny, in for a pound.

Victor threw one last glance at me then lifted the axe above his head. He briefly paused for a moment and looked down upon the small goat that was casually looking about its surrounds, then swiftly brought the axe down hard on the back of its neck. The blow failed to completely sever the head, cutting through the neck's vertebrae yet leaving the head attached by a portion of the remaining flesh beneath. Gouts of blood gushed from the brutal wound across the deck and down the edge into the jungle below in a crimson cascade.

Despite the sickening feeling for the atrocious act just committed, I rushed to the dead animal and held the pail to the flowing stream of blood. Dropping the axe, Victor had moved to the barstool and lifted the first sheet of paper from the pile and read aloud: "I offer this sacrifice of blood to the Old Ones beneath the waves and from the stars, the great father who slumbers in the dark and deep ocean depths and watches from the sky. Azathoth, Umrat-Tawil, Yog-Sothoth! We call upon you Dagon, father of the seas, and oceans, hear my call. Nyarlathotep, Hastur, Cthulhu! Arise, Dagon! Arise, Lurker of the dark deep!"

As he continued his rite, I rose after I filled the bucket with the goat's blood and weakly stood just outside the circle and awaited my upcoming cue. Victor carried on with the archaic passages, his voice growing in a passionate volume as he spoke. Then, after he had gone through half a dozen sheets of paper, he pointed to me and then to the circle. Reaching my hand over the drawing within the circle, I slowly emptied the pail's contents. The blood splattered on the wood planks and formed a puddle in the circle's center as I emptied the bucket. The scarlet liquid unnaturally never seeping over the sand barrier.

At first nothing happened and Victor continued with the rite, paying my actions little attention. Then it appeared as if thin wisps of steam began to rise from the puddle of blood. I rapidly blinked my eyes, hoping to eliminate any possible hallucinations, but the white wisps continued to twist up from the blood, which was now expanding across the drawing and filling the circle. I looked up to Victor, hoping he too was witnessing what was now transpiring, but his attention was devoted to his scriptures as he read on. When I drew my eyes back, the circle was filled completely with the blood, which refused to cross the sand barrier. I could only watch in amazement as the crimson liquid now changed color and turned to a blackened hue. With the alteration in color came the foul stench of rotting fish. I stepped back from the pungent odor and turned my head in disgust. Victor, too entranced by his readings, continued with the incantation and seemed oblivious to the fetor that surrounded us.

As I watched the steaming puddle with undivided attention, something new formed. A shape was rising from the foul liquid. At first, I could not tell what I was looking at. It was as if the puddle within the circle was now a deep pool that somehow sunk beyond the deck's structure to some unknown depth. As the shape rose higher, it was now clear that it was in the form of a human. A human in the sense that it possessed a head, shoulders, arms and a torso. As human as it may have appeared, the head to the shape was obviously abnormal.

The higher the shape was lifted from the black pool, the more it became defined. It was tall with muscular arms. The skin seemed scaled as the liquid dripped from its body. The head was fishlike and crowned with frills that extended to the back of its thick neck. The eyes were huge and bulbous. Its large mouth hung agape in a frown like that of some prehistoric Chordata.

I could do nothing but stand rooted to the floor. My emotions swayed from a terrifying fear to one of equal jubilation as Victor's faith in his unproven theory was proving true. The man had succeeded in summoning a god.

As I stared at the shape in paralyzing enthrallment, I could do nothing as my mind tried to process what we were witnessing. It was when the shape stepped from the circle that my emotions swayed rapidly toward impending dread and terror. I took a step backwards, my legs quivering beneath me. As I watched in horror, the shape stepped from the circle and started reaching for the axe leaning on the railing. I turned to Victor who was still unaware of what was taking place.

"Dagon, it is I who has summoned you and it is I who shall serve you," he stated in a drained voice as his emotional conjuration was now concluding.

With the axe now clutched in its clawed, webbed

hand, the shape stepped towards him. Victor repeated his vow again and with more confidence. As if in reply, the shape swiftly lifted the axe and brought it down upon its evoker.

I opened my mouth to scream but no sound formed. Victor shouted and held up his hand in some futile defensive action to the weapon. "WHY!" The axe met his hand with damaging force as it sliced down between the index and middle finger of his outstretched hand. The blade bit through the hand and continued past the wrist and deep into the forearm, embedding itself between the radius and ulna bones. Victor let out an ear-piercing scream as blood spouted across his face and chest. For Victor, the violence was just starting. The axe was pulled roughly from his arm and came down in a succession of violent blows upon him. Each strike biting into his flesh and smashing through bone. Pieces of meat and bone fragments flew into the air in an eruption of gore as the axe continued its unrelenting assault.

I could not say how long it stood over Victor, chopping him into chunks of raw bloodied meat, but soon nothing remained that could be distinguished as a human being. It was then that another voice screamed. One that was not my own.

"WHAT HAVE YOU DONE!" Ruth screamed from the kitchen doorway to the deck. I looked away from the carnage and to her. Why had she returned? The look of pure outraged horror on her face was beyond conceivable words. "MY GOD! WHAT HAVE YOU DONE?"

Again, I could do nothing but watch as the shape now moved towards Ruth. The axe still in its hands. I trembled uncontrollably as I watched it ascend upon her in the same brutal attack. She managed a partial scream before the axe blade found its way into her face, cleaving it in two. Again, the continuous and savage assault ensued. Her body crumbled to the floor and, as with Victor, soon became nothing more than a pile of bloodied flesh portions and bone shards.

From inside the house, I now heard more screaming. How long the wails went on for I could only guess, as I was oblivious to everything around me. Madness tugged at my mind, attempting to unhinge it. When the shape stepped over the pile of meat that was once Ruth and entered the house, I realized that it was Lynda who was screaming. It was in that moment of recognition that I pulled myself from my state of terror-stricken paralysis and moved.

As I entered the house, I slipped on the pools of blood that drenched the floor and fell into the pile that was Ruth. I squashed pieces of her beneath me in a sickly wet noise, sending other chunks sliding across the kitchen floor. I looked up in time to see Lynda running out the front door with the shape lumbering quickly in pursuit. I shouted out her name and scrambled from the mound of gore and gave chase after them.

Despite being drenched in blood and slipping crazily across the floor, I soon caught my footing and was making ground. Lynda had fled out the front of the villa and had entered the trail leading to the beach. I glimpsed the shadow of the shape moving through the vegetation in tow. It wasn't until I emerged from the jungle and onto the dock at the beach that I had finally caught up with the pair. Lynda was making her way to the dinghy. I called out her name again and when she turned at my voice; she tripped and landed on the dock's wooden planks. The shape was now on her, the axe lifted high to begin another sanguinary assault on one of the insignificant humans that had foolishly pulled it from its ancient slumber. I charged the shape from behind and leaped at it just as Lynda screamed.

* * *

The trawler was getting nearer now. I could make it out in more detail. Could see two figures walking about its deck. I smiled and looked back to Lynda. Her glazed eyes staring, her face a blank expression. Yeah, the whole ordeal had, with no doubt, pushed her over the edge. She would never be the same. That was obvious now. The trawler let out another blast of its air horn, and I looked back up. It would soon be upon us.

I sighed heavily and turned to Lynda. "I hate to do this to you, love, but I'm going to have to hide you away for a minute. Everything will be okay. I promise." Reaching over, I lifted her severed head and set it beneath one of the bench seats. I gently wedged her in there so she wouldn't roll out prematurely. She had been through so much that I had to make sure she was safe. These men in the boat wouldn't understand. I am just now beginning to grasp what had transpired back there on that island. In that blood-soaked villa. Being alone out here with Lynda these past few days gave my mind time to sort through the disheveled and disturbing emotions that filled my damaged mind. I know now that there was no Dagon. No cosmic deity of the sea had climbed out of that blood-filled circle that day and hacked my companions into ground meat. No, the only thing that emerged from that circle and the accursed rite that Victor called out was pure madness. Dagon did not have to manifest into living flesh to enact his ruthless retribution on those foolish humans for imposing upon its rest. No. It had only to release me from the world of sanity and I would be the instrument of its reckoning acts of vengeance. Setting and leaving behind a gruesome and violent example for all those foolish enough to attempt that forbidden deed again.

"Ahoy! Are you okay?" one man called from the boat with a thick accent. It was now cutting its engines and drifting alongside of our small boat. I lifted my arm and waved. I glanced at Lynda beneath the seat and smiled. My other hand was maneuvering the axe at my feet. From somewhere deep within the cold, black ocean depths, it called out to me again. Its vengeful blood lust was not yet satisfied. Dagon demanded more sacrificial blood to appease the violation against it. The boat was now next to us and one of the crew, a skinny black man, was lowering himself onto the dinghy. I wrapped my fingers around the bloodstained axe handle. It was time to carry out its vengeful wishes once more.

SLOTH
By R. L. Meza

"Lord, heal Thy servant!"

A wave of exaltation moved through the congregation. Voices shrieked praise and sighed adoration; bodies swayed and undulated beneath a sea of arms, hands thrust skyward with trembling fingers splayed. Pastor Brewer leaned over Carl, and his large hands descended onto Carl's thighs as the pastor exclaimed, "Let him walk with you in the light!"

The hands repositioned, alighting on Carl's shoulders, squeezing. Strings of incoherent babble wound through the chorus of voices behind him, and Carl pictured the waggling tongues, the eyes rolled backwards beneath fluttering lashes, the convulsive thrashing. He shifted in the wheelchair. His ass itched something awful, but Carl didn't dare scratch it before the eyes of the congregation. Pastor Brewer's hands moved to either side of Carl's head, his fingers ruffling the thinning brown hair that Carl had combed over his balding scalp before church that morning. Carl glared up at Brewer, and the pastor tipped him a wink. "Rise, brother," said Pastor Brewer, "Stand up and walk!"

The fingers digging into Carl's scalp clutched, then—with a final, dramatic push that caused Carl's head to rock back on his shoulders—released him. With exaggerated effort, Carl rose, careful to lean the bulk of his weight on his arms to emphasize their shaking and waiting until the last possible moment to stiffen his knees and release his hold on the wheelchair. This time, he had remembered to disengage the brake, and gave the chair a subtle push as he stood. It rolled backwards into the aisle, eliciting a gasp of awe from the congregation. Carl straightened, wobbled for a few seconds to build suspense, then took a step forward. The two hundred witnesses gathered in the church exploded in a joyous riot of excitement, and Pastor Brewer beamed out at them from the stage, nodding with his hands outstretched, repeating, "God is good."

God is good, God is great, now pass around the collection plate, thought Carl. Sure enough, a subtle flick of the pastor's head signaled the ushers to begin circulating the ornate metal plates. The roar of triumphant voices subsided, replaced by the rustle of paper, the scratching of pens, and the clink of coins. While the plates moved down the rows, Pastor Brewer detailed the purpose of their donations, using the projector to shuffle through pictures of struggling communities with dirt floors, hungry-eyed children and skeletal livestock. Carl had retrieved his wheelchair from the aisle and taken a seat on the periphery of the front row. He squinted up at the screen above the stage, trying to determine what impoverished part of the world would not be receiving a new hospital, church or school from Pastor Brewer. It was usually some corner of South America that the pearl-clutching members of the congregation would never venture to check on the status of their charity.

Pastor Watson ascended the steps of the stage to thank

the visiting pastor for his engaging sermon, and Brewer led the congregation in prayer before slinking off the stage to a chorus of applause. Carl sat through the first verse of "Shout to the Lord," then exited with the wheelchair through a side door. He found Brewer behind the church, leaned against the white double doors of the van that they had driven cross-country, the smoke from his cigarette drifting past the golden cross, purple ribbons, and italicized scripture emblazoned on the van's side. Brewer called it the "Jesus Express."

"Help me load this thing," Carl said, struggling to collapse the wheelchair.

Brewer snorted. A smile tugged at the corner of his mouth. "I didn't heal you just so I could keep doing all the work myself."

Carl grumbled, pinched his hand in the wheelchair and cursed. "You didn't heal me at all, you sonofabitch."

"What did I say?" Brewer cocked his head to one side, eyebrows raised. He stepped aside to avoid the wheelchair as Carl tossed it through the van's open doors and said, "Now get in, before the fish heads come out and see us together."

They drove forty miles across the Arizona desert before reaching the next town with a large church, found a motel on the outskirts, and paid for the room in cash. The room's air conditioning was no match for the summer heat. Drenched in sweat, they lay atop the twin beds, stripped down to their underwear. Fortunately, Brewer had managed to schedule a guest sermon for Wednesday evening, so they would not be forced to boil in Arizona for another full week, although Carl still complained at every opportunity about Brewer's choice to travel southwest instead of heading north. Brewer bore this burden with the silent patience of a man who knows he's made a poor decision.

For five weeks, Brewer and Carl had driven across the

country from New York, performing their guest sermons, collecting donations, then moving on to the next town or city before too many questions were raised. It had been Brewer's idea to take the show on the road, although the wheelchair had been Carl's contribution. Carl had found the wheelchair in an alleyway outside his apartment, a homeless man crumpled in the seat. He hadn't realized the homeless man was dead until, drunk and in a foul temper, Carl had seized the handles of the wheelchair and dumped the limp form onto the filthy pavement. After nudging the corpse with his toe, Carl had shrugged and brought the wheelchair home. Brewer had watched from their threadbare couch in the corner of the dilapidated apartment they shared, his eyes shining beneath a curtain of unwashed blond hair, as Carl wiped the wheelchair down with rubbing alcohol. When he had finished, Carl collapsed into the seat and completed a lazy turn of the chair that positioned him in front of the television. With a click of the remote, Brewer had switched off the television and said, "I know how we can make some quick cash."

* * *

Wednesday night, and the Jesus Express pulled into a residential neighborhood that bordered the town's massive church. Carl hopped out with the wheelchair in tow and slammed the double doors behind him. As the van turned back onto the main road and continued on to the church, Carl checked the empty street in both directions, then unfolded the chair and sank into the seat. He wheeled down the street and rounded the corner at an unhurried pace, making his way towards the towering structure of glass and steel on the horizon. By the time he reached The Church of the Son, the congregants had begun to arrive, climbing from their vehicles and coalescing on the front steps with warm greetings and pleasant chatter as they entered through the tall glass doors.

Carl pasted a smile onto his clean-shaven jowls and extended his arm for the impending handshakes, the way a knight might brandish a lance for a joust. He gave a fake name—something more biblical than "Carl"—along with a vague and appropriately boring backstory. Tonight, he was Daniel Jones, "just passing through" on his way to stay with his sister in California. There was a doctor there who wanted to run some tests, maybe fix his legs. Anything was possible, if it was God's will, in the Lord's hands, praise him, bless me, *halle-fucking-lujah*... Carl felt his smile start to wane and was grateful when a middle-aged woman offered to push his chair up the handicap ramp. His arms were unaccustomed to exercise and ached from the short journey to the church.

"Lord, heal Thy servant!" An hour later, Carl was before the congregation, head bowed. Brewer's hands descended on Carl's legs, and he said, "Let him walk with you in the light!"

The hands shifted to Carl's shoulders, then his head. "Rise, brother."

Carl frowned. He felt a strange, sharp twinge in his spine, as though the nerves there had been plucked like a guitar string. Distracted, he missed Brewer's cue and jumped when he felt the clutching fingers return to his scalp. "Rise, brother," Brewer repeated, lips stretched tight as he forced the words through his strained smile, one by one. "Stand up and walk!"

With an imperceptible nod, Carl attempted to slide his arms forward for the quaking arm routine and experienced a spike of pain from his left elbow. The limb refused to budge from its position on the armrest. Brewer watched him, the corners of his smile twitching. The smile did not reach Brewer's eyes.

Nervous, aware of the silence in the church, Carl cleared his throat and seized his left wrist in his right hand. When he pulled, white-hot pain lanced from his left elbow to his shoulder, then seared up his neck to his left ear. Carl grimaced at the sudden ringing in his ear, and when the eardrum burst with a loud *pop*, he cried out in surprise. His left arm remained on the armrest, motionless, while his right hand drifted to the trickle of warmth on his neck, the fingers coming away red as they floated before Carl's eyes, his blurred vision doubling the fingers from four to eight. Brewer bent close to Carl's good ear and hissed, "You're blowing this. Get it together."

"I..." Carl tried a new tactic. Abandoning his efforts with the left arm, Carl braced his right arm on the chair's armrest and leaned forward in the seat. When he tried to stretch his legs to the ground, however, his scuffed leather dress shoes remained fixed in place, and for a moment, Carl considered the unlikely possibility that Brewer had somehow developed a sense of humor and glued the soles to the foot plates. Carl shook his head, remembering as he unlaced the shoes that he had brought himself to the church—that Brewer would not have had the opportunity to tamper with the chair. Besides, it was obvious from the flare of Brewer's nostrils and the crimson flush creeping into the man's cheeks that none of this was going according to plan.

Even with the shoes fully unlaced, neither of Carl's feet would move from the footplates. When he scooped a hand beneath his right knee in an attempt to lift it, his efforts were rewarded with a blinding pain that shot upward from his heel to his hip and set fire to his lower lumbar. An agonized moan escaped through Carl's gritted teeth. He heard the shuffling of feet and a low murmur of voices at his back. Carl tried to channel the tension from his growing panic into a unified movement, pictured throwing the weight of his body towards Brewer's outstretched arms and lurched forward in the chair. But Carl had already released the wheelchair's brake in preparation for his climactic rise, and his momentum yielded nothing more than a slight turning of the wheels and a metallic rattle from the frame.

A surge of fear engulfed Carl, and perhaps his terror was visible, because the smile on Brewer's face finally faltered. "Ladies and gentlemen…" Brewer's voice caught. He cleared his throat and said, "God is good. I am going to take this man, commune with the Lord in private prayer…"

Brewer gripped the handles of the wheelchair and spirited Carl from the auditorium without further explanation, leaving a speechless congregation in his wake. Carl saw their puzzled expressions—the gaping mouths and knitted brows—reflected in the glass doors as Brewer whisked him into the hall and hurried to the church's rear exit. Curses tumbled from Brewer's lips the moment they were no longer within earshot of the church, and when they reached the van, Brewer abandoned Carl in the chair and moved to the driver's side door before realizing that Carl was still seated. "Get up, asshole. I can't believe you pulled that shit. We're going to have a talk when we get back to the room."

Brewer's eyes flicked up to the church, searched for movement. "Get in the fucking van, man. What are you doing?"

"I can't…" Carl's throat felt constricted. Overwhelmed by anxiety, tears sprang to the corners of his eyes. He tipped his head back and willed them away.

"The hell you can't!" Brewer stalked towards him, took the wheelchair by the handles and lifted. Rather than spilling onto the asphalt as Brewer intended, Carl drooped forward like a marionette with its strings snagged, his weight tugging on the various body parts anchored to the chair and eliciting a ragged scream that caused the blood to drain from Brewer's face. For the first time, Brewer showed real concern—beyond the worry of being discovered—and the flicker of fear in Brewer's eyes scared Carl worse than the pain.

They struggled and swore for ten minutes before they managed to get Carl, still attached to the wheelchair, lifted through the double doors of the Jesus Express. It was early evening, and Brewer stopped at a hardware store on the way back to the motel, muttering about picking up some tools to disassemble the chair. He tossed the bags into the back of the van, and Carl's eyes wandered over the contents—a hammer, a box cutter, screwdrivers, wrenches, and wire-cutters. A pair of scissors had poked through the plastic.

"You think we're going to need all this?" Carl eyed the serrated blade of a handsaw.

"I don't know, man, but I'm sure as shit not going to haul you inside with that thing and ask a professional," Brewer said, lighting a cigarette and exhaling a cloud of noxious smoke through the van's open window.

They made one more stop at the liquor store, then returned to the motel. After unloading the bags, Brewer returned with the night desk clerk in tow. Together, they wrestled Carl's wheelchair from the van and—when the desk clerk lingered—Brewer slipped the man a joint and a twenty-dollar bill, grumbling his thanks. Carl winced as Brewer pushed the wheelchair across the pitted gravel parking lot to the door of their room. "Christ, are you *aiming* for the potholes?"

Brewer only ground his teeth, jostling Carl as he grappled with the wheelchair's transition from gravel to pavement. Fortunately, Brewer had thought to use one of the bags of liquor to prop the door open and, as he hustled through with the wheelchair, Brewer nudged the bag aside with his foot and allowed the door to swing closed behind them, shutting out the evening's oppressive heat. Carl felt a gentle tug on the wheelchair, followed by a second harder pull that caused the chair to pivot and slam Carl's foot into the cheap wood paneling of the television stand. "Ow, man. What the hell?"

Carl looked over his shoulder and caught a glimpse of Brewer. His blond hair was no longer combed in a neat side part. Tufts stood on end, as though a large bird had pillaged Brewer's scalp for nest material. Color had crept into his cheeks, an alarming shade of crimson that spread to his forehead in blotches, and Brewer muttered a series of phrases under his breath in rapid succession, the words blending together into an incoherent language that Carl might expect from the wagging tongues of the babbling devout, but not from a faithless, level-headed guy like Brewer. Three words emerged from the verbal nonsense, and Brewer repeated them with growing fervor, saying, "Let me go. Let me go, let me go, *letmegoletmego*—"

"Brewer, what the hell is going on?" The wheelchair rocked up on one wheel, then came down with a rattle. Brewer cried out, and Carl thought he heard pain mingled with the frustration in his voice.

"It's got me, Carl," Brewer said. The wheelchair rocked up again, came down harder, and pain shot through Carl's nerves, making him shout. "It won't let me go. I can't let go of the handle."

Carl craned his neck and saw Brewer's white-knuckled hand clenching the handle of the chair behind him. "Calm down, now," Carl said, surprised by his even tone. Inside, he felt a sickening chill crawl up his spine. "Get the tools and get us over to the mirror so I can see what's going on."

There wasn't much to see, Carl discovered, once Brewer had positioned them before the cheap full-length mirror affixed to the peeling green paint of the motel wall. Externally, Carl's hand on the wheelchair's handle appeared normal, unless he attempted to remove the hand from the chair, in which case—aside from a slight stretch of the skin at his wrist—nothing happened. Brewer's eyes were wide, rolled in their sockets, as he dug through the bag with his free hand and retrieved the box cutter, still in its packaging. With a curse, he fumbled in the bag and placed the scissors in Carl's free hand, saying, "Here, help me cut this open."

"For what, man? No."

"Fine." Brewer pinched the package between his legs and used the scissors to cut a ragged line through the stiff plastic. He wiggled his fingers through the hole and withdrew the box cutter with a hiss as the thin edge of the packaging sliced the back of his hand. *Click-click-click.* Brewer extended the blade of the box cutter and pressed it against the seam where his flesh met the plastic handle of the wheelchair.

"No," Carl said. "Hang on, now, this is not happening. Let's just have a drink and talk this through."

There was a brief flicker of sanity in Brewer's eyes, and he paused to retrieve the bottle of whiskey from its paper bag on the television stand. Using his legs to secure the bottle, Brewer twisted the cap off, then took three long swallows of the amber liquid, his Adam's apple pumping beneath the pale skin of his throat. Then, to Carl's chagrin, he sloshed the whiskey over the hand on the wheelchair handle and gave the bottle to Carl.

Brewer brought the box cutter to the place where the meat of his thumb met the plastic, just below his wrist, and pushed the blade in. Carl groaned, but Brewer's eyes were bright and focused. Blood leaked from the wound, and the box cutter shook with the intensity of Brewer's grip as he forced the blade along the length of his thumb. Then, without warning, Brewer dropped the box cutter and cried out. Carl felt a warm spatter across the back of his neck, saw a bloodstain spreading on the carpet below the chair, and said, "What—shit, what happened? Brewer, you okay?"

"Yeah." Brewer was sitting on the edge of the bed, panting. His head rested on his outstretched arm, the left hand still holding the chair. "I slipped, cut my…"

Brewer's eyes fixed on his hand. He wiped at the cut with the bedspread, leaned in to inspect it, then probed the wound with his fingertips. Brewer pushed the wheelchair closer to the mirror and retrieved the box cutter from the floor. The fixtures mounted to either side of the mirror illuminated the back of Brewer's hand with a sickly orange light as Brewer brought the box cutter across his hand in an arc, blood spilling from the parted flesh. Carl swore and felt a surge of nausea. He longed to take the box cutter from Brewer, but his attempt to twist in the wheelchair was met with an electrifying agony that traveled the length of his spine, as though a rigid rod had replaced the vertebrae there. Brewer snatched the bottle of whiskey, poured it over the crescent carved into his hand, and wiped it with the bedspread. Already pale, his wide blue eyes appeared to sink further into his skull, distant ice chips set in dark sockets.

Carl squinted at the wound, and his eyes caught a glint of light. Brewer saw it too and pinched the skin of the seam, teeth bared in a grimace, as he yanked the flesh back from the tendons, muscle, and bone beneath. *Not bone*, Carl saw, the orange light reflecting off the exposed metal rods embedded in the organic network of Carl's hand. Before Carl could protest, Brewer sank the box cutter's blade into the back of his left wrist and opened a yawning red mouth there, pried the flesh apart with his fingertips, and released an anguished cry.

Carl barely heard it above the thudding rhythm of his own pulse. "Brew, put the fucking blade down. You're going to kill yourself. We have to get you to a hospital."

Brewer laughed, a high, reedy sound that made Carl

jump. He repositioned the angle of the box cutter and dragged the blade through the skin at his elbow once, then a second time, perpendicular to the first cut. Carl stared at Brewer's reflection, rapt, as Brewer bent his arm. Metal winked in the orange light, steel protruding from the red cross carved in Brewer's elbow. Before Carl could protest, Brewer brought the box cutter higher and slashed across his bicep, a series of rapid strokes that streaked the mirror with blood.

"Yes," Brewer said, his face a white mask—a twisted rictus of manic triumph. "Bone. Good, yes."

In his peripherals, Carl saw Brewer pull the hammer from the bag of tools. The wheelchair lurched away from the mirror as Brewer dragged it to the television stand. He shoved the television aside, and it fell to the floor with a loud crash. Carl considered shouting for help, even opened his mouth to do so, before the hammer hovered in his field of vision and Brewer whispered in his ear, "Yell for help, and I'll brain you. Then you can get yourself out of that chair once I'm gone."

The threat was enough to silence Carl. In his growing panic, he had forgotten his own plight. Carl watched in the mirror's reflection as Brewer shifted the television stand, squatted and stretched his arm across the stand's width. After another long draught from the whiskey bottle, Brewer raised the hammer and brought it down in a powerful swing. Carl heard a crack, and Brewer grunted in pain. "Shit," Brewer said, "I should have bit down on something. Think I broke a tooth."

He swung a second time—*crack*—then a third. A crunch of bone from Brewer's humerus signaled the hammer's success. Carl heard retching, and the sour smell of vomit joined the copper odor of blood in the motel room. Carl reached for the whiskey, threw the cap across the room, and guzzled from the upturned bottle, felt the burn of alcohol in his throat and a spreading warmth as the whiskey flooded his empty stomach. He wiped his mouth with the back of his hand and, at the sound of a jingling belt buckle, realized Brewer had busied himself with a new task. Brewer had cinched the belt tight just below his shoulder, and was lowering the handsaw's serrated blade into the mutilated flesh of his bicep, leaning backwards to stretch the cuts wider and seat the blade against the splintered bone.

"Use your wallet or something," Carl said, "to bite on." He watched Brewer nod, set down the saw, and remove his wallet from his back pocket. Brewer poked the wallet into his mouth, bit down, and positioned the saw at his arm again. After a deep breath, Brewer began to saw. Seconds passed like hours, with only the sound of the saw grinding against bone, and Carl suspected that the hammer had only fractured the humerus, not broken it in two as Brewer had anticipated. Suddenly, the grinding gave way to the ring of metal on metal, and Brewer screamed.

He continued to scream, ignoring Carl's frantic questions, flailing just out of sight. The wheelchair was shoved forward, back to the mirror, and the box cutter was in Brewer's hand. The blade disappeared into his armpit, the illusion so complete that it could have been a trick blade, if not for the freshet of blood that gushed from the wound, the severed artery pumping precious liters onto the ugly motel carpet. There was a loud thump, a final tug on the wheelchair's handle, and Brewer collapsed to the floor.

Carl felt a suffocating terror close his throat. He tried to maneuver the wheelchair away from the mirror, but Brewer lay in a heap behind the wheels, blocking his progress. "Brew?"

Silence.

"Don't do this to me," Carl said. He felt warmth spilling down his cheeks and realized that he was weeping. "This whole thing was your stupid fucking idea. Don't you leave me here alone. Come on, man, please…"

"Help!" Carl wasn't aware of his intention to scream until he heard his voice escape the confines of his throat, a reedy exhalation of air, stripped of its powerful timbre—a sound like wind whistling through the picked bones of skeleton. He cleared his throat, tried again, shouting, "Help! Help me, someone, please!"

Brewer had requested the room at the far end of the building to avoid unwanted attention. The Desert Rose Motel was a linear structure, with the clerk's office, janitorial storage, and vending machines all clustered at its head, the rooms marching along after in single file, parallel to the parking lot. There had been only one other car in the parking lot upon their return to the motel that night and Carl suspected that it belonged to the night clerk. Through the thin, tattered curtains, Carl could see that it was dark outside.

Carl's eyes widened in a comical expression, his mouth forming an "o" as he slapped the side of his head with his free hand. The phone—*of course*. He leaned back in the wheelchair and cast a glance over his shoulder at the landline positioned on the nightstand between the two twin beds. The coil of its yellowed cord dangled over the single drawer. There was probably a Bible in that drawer, Carl thought, left behind for desperate folks like himself should they need to call for a different kind of help. Carl laughed, a hoarse bark that startled him. He waited for a snide remark from Brewer, then remembered that his friend was dead.

Using his free hand, Carl rolled the wheelchair forward a few inches, gripped the right hand rim, and tried to roll the chair in reverse. The wheelchair pivoted, the left wheel fixed in place while the right wheel bumped into Brewer's limp torso. Carl wheeled forward once more, reached as far behind as the stiff rod in his spine would allow, and seized the wheel so hard that his hand threatened to cramp. He heaved at the right wheel, cranking it with all of his strength to force the chair backwards, but the wheel struck Brewer's corpse and refused to move any further. It spun, useless, against the blood-soaked fabric of his button-up shirt.

Howling in frustration, Carl slammed his weight from side to side, the pain feeding his fear, his fear stoking his rage. The left wheel of the chair came up, then squelched back down into the expanding stain on the carpet. Carl thrashed, no longer focusing his efforts in a specific direction, because he only wanted out, and Brewer's litany from earlier echoed in his mind—*letmegoletmegoletmego*. It was only as the left wheel rose into the air, as the chair began to tip with Carl still trapped in its seat, that Carl realized Brewer's words were not just in his mind, but that they were issuing from the heap of cooling meat that blocked the wheelchair, a sibilant hiss of escaping gas that grew in volume. The wheelchair tipped on its side with a clatter, and Carl could hear Brewer behind him, the movement of his swollen tongue like the chuckle of drain water through old, rusted pipes. "Rise, brother," the voice chortled, close to Carl's ear.

Carl lunged away from that awful voice and clawed at the carpet with his free hand. The sudden movement flooded his senses with agony. Dark spots bloomed in his vision, and before Carl lost consciousness, he saw movement behind him in the mirror's reflection.

* * *

The death rattle of the air conditioner woke Carl, and he moaned, unable to straighten his neck. Dim light filtered through the curtains, a faint preview of the day's approaching heat. The air in the room was a stifling, steaming bouquet of blood and vomit with other darker smells creeping to the forefront: the sickly sweet odor of decay and the pungent reek of excrement. Carl shifted in the chair, and the smell intensified. In his terror, his bowels had released. Their contents rested, heavy and moist, in the right leg of Carl's pants. Carl tipped his head back and squinted at the door, cursing at the absence of the "Do Not Disturb" placard. Brewer must have left it hanging on the knob outside.

Brewer. Carl's eyes flew wide, rounded with fear. He tried to make himself small in the wheelchair, although it connected the two of them, and listened for signs of movement. A car passed on the highway and somewhere in the distance a dog barked; otherwise, the room was quiet. Carl bit back his fear and screamed for help, continued to shout and yell and curse until his voice was nothing more than a weak whisper. When that failed to bring rescue, Carl wept. The wracking sobs made his pain worse, and each muscle spasm was like being dragged through shattered glass. The dark blooms returned to his vision, and Carl stopped crying, unable to bear the thought of lying unconscious again with Brewer's corpse.

The phone on the nightstand was no longer an option—there was no way Carl would be able to crawl, affixed to both the wheelchair and Brewer's dead weight—but Brewer had purchased a cheap burner phone for their road trip, and if he still had the phone in his pocket… Carl swallowed, and his throat made an audible click. Since the air conditioner had released a final *clunk* and fallen permanently silent, the temperature in the room had started to climb and the long-sleeved, white button-up that Brewer had insisted Carl wear for the service was now nearly transparent. Drenched with sweat, it clung to his chest. Carl's head was wedged sideways against the floor, sticky where it touched the congealing blood on the carpet. The smell of death was overpowering, the decay within Brewer accelerated by the boiling heat, and Carl fought the urge to vomit. His eyes landed on the saw, discarded at the foot of the bed.

Reaching, Carl retrieved it and maneuvered the handsaw to the place where his left buttock was fused with the vinyl of the wheelchair's seat. It took fifteen minutes and an accidental cut to his thigh for Carl to saw through the seat. The vinyl parted and the liberated weight of his thighs and buttocks sagged to one side. Spurred on by his success, Carl sawed through the backrest in half the time. His torso sank to the carpet, level with his hips once more, and the stabbing pain in his lower back ebbed to a dull throb. Carl was relieved to find that—while both feet were still affixed to the footplates and his entire left arm remained immobilized—detaching the seat and backrest had granted him increased flexibility at the waist. He tried to straighten his legs but his knees remained firmly locked at a ninety-degree angle.

"Come on," said Carl through gritted teeth, wiggling in the wheelchair until he had almost managed to turn onto his back. His knees howled in protest, but with an excruciating twist of his spine, Carl was able to reach behind with his right arm to where Brewer lay in a silent heap. Carl craned his neck to orient his groping hand for the dreaded search and saw that Brewer's face was less than a foot from his own. Brewer's mouth hung open, one vacant blue eye staring through the parted curtain of his hair, his lips peeled back in a death grimace. This close, the carpet's filth was rendered in startling detail, scattered with crumbs and flakes of garbage, bristling with hairs. The chipped edge of Brewer's front tooth rested against the motel carpet. A long red hair clung to Brewer's lower lip, and Carl stared at the hair in a dazed stupor, wondering who it had belonged to—the maid, perhaps, or one of the room's former occupants. The hair stirred, and the foul breath behind its movement assaulted Carl's senses, caused his stomach to clench and sent adrenaline pulsing through his system.

"Hu-uh." The sound worked its way from deep within Brewer's throat, wet and guttural. Brewer's exposed eye rolled in its socket, and Carl gaped at his terror-stricken reflection in the expanded pupil. Brewer blinked, and Carl heard the sticky whisper of his eyelids as they scraped closed over the surface of Brewer's dry cornea. When the lids opened, the dark well of Brewer's pupil shrank to a pinprick, a black speck on an iris as dull and lifeless as blue clay. Brewer fixed his eye on Carl and said, "Hu-uh. Hu-uh-uh-ll."

Without thinking, Carl lashed out with the handsaw. The serrated blade split the flesh of Brewer's scalp and bit into the skull beneath, caught there. Shaking, quivering with pain from his efforts, Carl yanked on the saw to free it, leaving a long, bloodless gash in Brewer's forehead. A pale flap of skin peeled back from Brewer's skull, revealing the flash of bone and—deeper, beneath the furrow made by the saw's teeth—a glint of metal. Brewer chuckled, leaned closer, his nails digging into the carpet beside Carl's ear.

"Hu-uh," Brewer said and pressed his damaged skull against Carl's forehead. Carl tried to jerk away, planted his palm against Brewer's spongy, bloated cheek and felt the skin slough away between his fingers. There was a tingling in Carl's scalp, a twinge where his spine met his skull, and Carl dug his fingers into Brewer's cheek, desperate to push Brewer away and escape the fetid heat of the corpse's breath and that thick tongue that continued to writhe, to try and speak. Carl felt his nails grate on bone, then slip on metal, but he could not part his skull from Brewer's. They were fused, an amalgamation of flesh, both living and dead, joined by the wheelchair's sinister, creeping steel.

"Hu-uh—allelujah, brother," Brewer croaked. "Stand up and walk."

EL PADRINO
By Drew Nicks

Everything had happened so fast. One minute he and his friends had been heading towards the bridge back to Brownsville. It was spring break and booze, cheap entertainment, and lovely ladies were easier in Matamoros. They'd been good to one another and watched each other's backs. With recent extreme escalation in drug related murders and kidnappings, they knew there was safety in numbers.

They'd been at the foot of the bridge when The Kid realized he needed to drain the lizard. He told his friends to go on ahead. They nodded, laughed and stumbled on forward, saying they'd be waiting for him on the other side. Turning away, he looked for a less well-lit area. He found a small saguaro patch nearby. He barely made it. The second his fly was open and his dick was out, he evacuated his bladder like a dam knocked asunder.

Click

He felt the cold steel pressed tight against his neck. His heart slammed into his throat, but he couldn't take his hands off his dick, lest a new stream spray across his pants. He didn't know if these were gangbangers or *federales*. He didn't know which was worse.

"Alright *muchacho*, hands up and turn around! I'm not afraid to shoot you right here."

He was about to comply when he asked, "Can I put my dick away first?"

This caught the harasser off guard. After a short laugh, he responded, "Sure. I don't want to see your whitesnake, gringo."

He put his dick away and, with arms extended in the air, he turned to face the harasser.

Standing before him were four men garbed in police uniforms. Each had a tin star attached to his breast and each star had a name attached to it. The one who held a gun to his head was a short, squat man with hair like a Brillo pad. Feverish green eyes stared at The Kid, and the star read "Sergio." Upon closer inspection, he noticed the uniform was short on his powerful, hairy arms.

"What am I under arrest for?" he asked. "I'm an American citizen who really needed to pee."

Sergio laughed a deep, bellowing laugh. He smiled heartily and struck swiftly with the pistol. The sound of The Kid's wheezing filled the air.

"I don't have to tell you, gringo. Just get into the fucking truck and we'll sort this out at the station…"

Breathless and agitated, he stood and instantly felt two sets of arms wedged beneath his armpits. Stars danced in his eyes as he saw the dirty unmarked truck. He had questions but, before he could voice any of them, a rifle butt slammed into his ribs. His world went black.

* * *

The truck stopped suddenly and all four police climbed out. The Kid looked out through the grimy windows. Though he could only partially make out streetlights, he could hear the party that accompanied them. His ribs ached and he listened to the officers arguing amongst each other.

"We should wait to hear from El Padrino. This is the one he wanted, no?"

The gruff voice of Sergio took over.

"Yeah, it's him but I don't know how long El Padrino will be. An hour? Three? We take him back to the ranch then we sort this out."

The Kid unlatched the truck door and fell face first in the dry earth. The police were too busy arguing to notice.

When The Kid stood, a sharp pain shot through his chest.

Probably a cracked rib.

He glanced back at the arguing police. He knew it wouldn't be long before they noticed he was no longer captive. Through the saguaro patches, variously strewn boulders and surrounding darkness, he thought he was perhaps a mile from town. The sounds of reverie still carried across the plain.

He began to walk and, when he heard the police, started to run. The sound of rushing feet propelled his legs faster. A bullet whizzed past his head. He stopped dead in his tracks.

"Freeze! Stupid gringo!"

The Kid held his hands high in the air. He was so close to the main strip that the smell of tequila and sex hung in the air like a fog.

"Why you try to run, gringo?" Sergio asked.

Before The Kid could answer, he felt his knees buckle from the whack of the rifle butt.

"That was a very stupid move," Sergio said, standing tall above The Kid with his head silhouetted by the moon. "Now we have to do this the hard way."

The Kid's vision disappeared as the burlap sack was thrust over his head. There were a few gruff grunts and, seconds later, he felt himself being placed back into the truck.

* * *

The bag had a strange odor. He couldn't quite place it. It almost had vague undercurrents of cinnamon. Whatever substance it held, its aroma was fresh. It made his head swim. Nausea filled him.

Through the loose knit of the burlap he could see zooming lights. He knew they had to be passing cars, but an inkling made him think of beasts of Aztec lore.

The truck was stifling. Though the cool desert air should have provided some respite, the fetid body heat of five men covered that. Even through the bag he could smell the body odor and anger. His captors continued to argue in Spanish. He couldn't understand their words but their tone indicated frustration.

Why didn't I learn Spanish?

Wooziness overcame him and he bowed his head forward. The vomit was coming. A reassuring pistol whipped him in the back of the neck.

"If you puke, gringo, I'll kill you right here!"

The Kid knew this was true and tried to staunch the bile creeping up his esophagus. He was beginning to wonder if there was any way he was getting out of this situation. The reality was looking bleak.

* * *

How long has it been? An hour? Two? It felt like days when he felt the truck come to a halt. The weight shifted and the doors groaned as his captors climbed out. He felt hands on his shoulders as he was lugged from the backseat. Suddenly, the bag was removed. He saw a kaleidoscope of colors in the sky. Vivid greens and blues melded with oranges and reds. A dilapidated building stood before him. From the crumbling roof, a column of yellow smoke rose steadily towards the heavens. Two steel pots flanked the darkened entryway. Each pot burned brightly from their tumbleweed fuel.

And in the entryway stood a horrific and sinister creature. Its horned head nearly touched the top of the doorframe. Malevolent green eyes stared at The Kid. He shook his woozy head and the apparition vanished.

"Move gringo!" said Sergio; a rifle butt accentuated his order. "We're going in there."

The Kid nearly screamed but the sound caught in his throat. He knew his time was drawing near. Knew that the second he entered that ramshackle building he would not be leaving alive. He would have to watch for his opportunity and not lose any chance.

They walked single file in a procession across the ranch. The Kid was in the lead with a rifle pushed firmly into the small of his back. He glanced around for any outs. This ranch was isolated. There were no homesteads in any direction. Barren plains stretched towards the horizon.

He saw his window of opportunity slipping from his grasp. Unless, of course, he could reason with these people. He thought perhaps he could convince one of these folks that his life wasn't worth it. Judging from their ages, he theorized that at least one of them had a family. An emotional string to tug on.

"Get in, gringo!"

The Kid crossed the threshold into the shack. Darkness and evil seeped from its walls. Large clumps of black mold clung to the ceiling and floor. The closer The Kid looked, the mold seemed to breathe. Air bubbles formed and pulsated on the slick obsidian surface. In the center of the room, which could be called a living room, was a large, heavily stained plywood table. At each corner of the table were thick leather straps. These straps showed their heavy usage. Tears in the leather were numerous, though not structurally faulting. It seemed no one ever escaped.

"That's where you go, gringo," said Sergio, pointing at the table. "You lay down and we wait for El Padrino."

The Kid didn't want to lie down. Had never wanted any less to lie down in his life. Again, he thought about protesting, until his dear friend, rifle butt, smashed into his spine. He couldn't breathe or think straight. He felt himself being lifted.

Please no straps!

They strapped him down. The leather tightened like a constrictor.

Think! Think!

Two of the men left the shack, lighting cigarettes as they did so. The Kid's heart beat so fast he was sure everyone could hear it.

He stared at the ceiling. Right above him, a bubble of mold pulsated and burst. Ropey strands of fungus fell in dollops along his face and chest. He wanted to yell out to whichever vengeful spirit had allowed this to happen to him. It was then he began to realize that God wasn't going to help him. There was no God here.

He looked around and saw the cauldron. The black pot simmered and steamed. Various items floated around the top of the murky broth. When the jawbone danced to the top, The Kid screamed. The response he received wasn't positive.

"Shut up, gringo!" the man shouted, as the pistol smashed into The Kid's teeth. The Kid tasted blood.

From the front of the shack, he heard the rumble of an engine. *This must be El Padrino.* He could smell death in the air.

Murmurs filled the air. The Kid recognized the voices of his captors, but sure enough, he could hear another voice. A voice infinitely softer and of a higher pitch than any of Sergio and his goons. The Kid tried to picture a face to attach this voice to but no images would conjure in his mind. He wondered if a man with a voice that soft and sedate was as cruel as his underlings.

When the group returned, The Kid realized it wasn't just one voice he'd heard but two. The Man was quite tall, over six feet at least, and he possessed very sharp features. His nose extended just a bit too far from his face. His eyes were a vibrant green, like a pool of overripe algae. His hair was jet black and styled into a mullet. Despite the soft tone of his voice, The Kid could tell The Man demanded fear and respect.

The woman was the more shocking of the two. The Kid expected this operation, whatever it was, to consist entirely of men. The woman herself was exceptionally beautiful. She was short with bright blonde hair. Her brown eyes held a twinkle of sensuality and her movements were lithe like a cat.

The Man, the one they called El Padrino, approached The Kid slowly. His head moved from side to side as he sniffed the air. It unsettled The Kid watching this man move like a curious coyote. Suddenly, The Man stopped and anger spread across his face. He turned to his goons and screamed at them in Spanish. The Kid attempted to adjust his position enough to see their reactions but found he could not.

The Man appeared without warning overtop of The Kid. He cradled something in his hand. Before The Kid could think or say anything, The Man blew a handful of strange powder in The Kid's face. It hit him instantly. His vision blurred and colors became lively. The Man's face distorted drastically. His sharp features turned animalistic. That face now resembled an enraged vulture. Beady green eyes stared upon its chained prey. Antlers slowly pushed their way through wrinkled skin.

When The Man/Creature spoke, smoke billowed from its mouth. The Kid couldn't understand the words it spoke. Just then, his body quivered twice and paralysis overtook his limbs.

His eyes watched the scene playing out around him. The Man and the woman conversed in their odd language. The Man's underlings stood and listened. They too had morphed. To The Kid's eyes they resembled demons from Bosch's "Garden of Earthly Delights." Playful, yet no doubt malicious. Rictus grins spread tightly on their dark parchment skin.

Whatever The Man had blown into his face now seemed to be taking full effect. Blackness formed at the edges of his vision. His tunnel vision was overtaken by a kaleidoscope of colors. Strong purples and boisterous greens filled his mind's eye. A moment later, his world went black.

* * *

When The Kid came to, he had been dragged outside. Though his limbs were still paralyzed, he could feel the coarse earth sharply digging into his legs. His neck had free range of motion, so he lifted his head to gaze upon the sky. It was a dark night and a blood red moon hung high in the sky surrounded by the blackest stars. He looked side to side at the men who dragged his limp body. They wore heavy black robes covered in strange symbols. A beastly smell of sweat and raw meat wafted from their bodies. When The Kid looked ahead, he wanted to scream. He saw the makeshift altar and The Man brandishing a machete. An animalistic snout protruded from beneath his hood. Beside The Man, the pot simmered and steamed. The jawbone floated in its murky broth, accompanied by a few severed fingers.

The Kid felt himself being lowered on the altar. Every

ounce of his being wanted to fight but the paralysis fought back. He was as helpless as a kitten.

In this blackest of nights, he hoped God would help him. The machete blade glinted in the moonlight. He watched as the blade came down towards his throat and he knew God was away on business…

A MATTER OF TASTE
By Gerri R. Gray

"And in local news, more human remains have been found in a Port Devlin sewage treatment plant for the third time in less than a week. Authorities report that two feet and a thumb were found Friday morning at the same facility where a man's leg and pelvis were found on Tuesday. Last week, a suitcase containing partially eaten female breasts and other body parts was found in a wooded area by hikers, and the week before that, a Chinese food takeout box containing an ear and a spleen was found in a trash bin by a dumpster diver. Police suspect foul play was involved and are investigating. Anyone with information is asked to contact the sheriff's office or the Crime Stoppers twenty-four hour hotline. All calls will be kept confidential. Now, back to the soothing sounds of classical music..."

Roberta Pickering, a woman of impeccable taste and breeding, shook her head in disgust. *What is this world coming to,* she asked herself before turning her thoughts to more important matters, namely the unpacking and putting away of her Chateau Baccarat wine goblets. Being the *bon vivant* that she was, she'd never dream of sipping her Romanie-Conti from anything less exquisite than imported French glasses costing $150 apiece.

Being married to a retired hepatologist with a fat Louis Vuitton wallet, she could have easily afforded to pay the men from the moving company to unpack all of her boxes, but she preferred doing the job herself rather than trust her treasures in the grimy, careless hands of modern day Neanderthals.

As she was placing the last of her crystal goblets on the top shelf of her tall Chippendale display cabinet, the loud growling of a stomach and the nauseating stench of halitosis prompted her to turn around. She gasped as terror sliced through her corpulent body like the claws of a beast, causing her to drop the goblet onto the herringbone parquet floor of the dining room. Her mouth opened wide and from it burst forth a shrill scream. It was loud enough to drown out both the classical music from the radio and the sound of lead crystal exploding into an array of expensive fragments.

To Roberta's horror, standing not more than five feet from the stepladder upon which she stood was a strange and unsavory couple that, for all intents and purposes, appeared to have crawled out of a garbage dumpster.

Intruders!

The man, a disheveled ogre with an acne-scarred face and slick-backed hair resembling a drowned rat, stared at her with deranged eyes. His shirtless upper body was a crazy quilt of nefarious tattoos with a large Grim Reaper dominating the front of his torso. A black spider web design covered both elbows, while lurid portraits of infamous serial killers dotted the landscape of his arms.

Sensing her fear and disgust, he twisted his cold sore encrusted mouth into a menacing grin revealing two frightful rows of yellowish-brown teeth, which, for a reason beyond Roberta's comprehension, had been filed into sharp points. With his lips parted, the smell of halitosis intensified in the room and assaulted Roberta's delicate senses. She struggled to keep the puke from rising in her throat.

The woman at his side, a musty little scarecrow with heavily tattooed arms and bleached hair hacked into a messy mullet, giggled like an overgrown urchin. Her excessively twitching eyes were rimmed with copious amounts of smudged black eyeliner, giving them the appearance of a rabid raccoon. Clad in a long, tattered tank top, ripped fishnet stockings and mud-caked Doc Martens boots, she looked every bit like a middle-aged reject from a punk rock concert.

"Didn't mean to scare you, honey," she said, smacking a wad of bubblegum like a cow chewing its cud. Her husky smoker's voice resonated with a twang that, to Roberta's ears, was simply lacerating. "We saw you just moved in and figured we'd mosey on over an' welcome ya'll to the neighborhood. You know that little ol' red house behind your backyard? That's our love shack."

The color drained from Roberta's face. She was shocked to learn that any living creature, apart from vermin, would call that dilapidated, paint-peeling shack their home. Peeking out from a cluster of oaks and sugar maples abutting the rear of her new property like some leprous, inbred thing, it was a hideous eyesore—a blight upon its surroundings. Roberta had made her husband Gordon promise to have a contractor erect a high wall to block the offending view, as well as to keep out "all those horrid little animals" that she so detested. Just the thought of wildlife evacuating their bowels on her manicured lawn made her shudder with revulsion.

"I'm Raelene Borza and this here's my ol' man, Earl," the blinking woman continued, gesturing toward her husband with her thumb. "Some folks call him Gator, on account of his teeth, but ya'll can call him anything ya want. Jus' don't call him late fer dinner."

Earl emitted a grunting noise that Roberta guessed was a laugh. With his eyes transfixed on her ample breasts, he began to run the tip of his tongue along his lips and a bit of drool glistened at the corner of his mouth.

Roberta grimaced and felt her skin crawling.

Raelene giggled. "Don't you pay no mind to big Earl there, Miss Roberta. He's just a horny old hound dog with an eye for big purty ladies."

Roberta felt goosebumps populating her arms. "How did you know my name?" she inquired, eyeing her uninvited guests with suspicion. "And how did you...*people*...get in my house?"

"With a key, of course," Raelene giggled, amused by the sudden expression of panic that flashed across Roberta's face.

"You...have a key to my house?" Roberta hurried down from the stepladder and held out her hand, palm up. "I'll take that key if you don't mind."

Raelene's giggling abruptly ceased and her face went serious. "But I do mind. Earl and me came here with the very best of intentions, we did. But now you're givin' me the feeling like you don't trust us or something. Or maybe you think you're better than us lowlife crackers, Miss high-and-mighty in your Estee Lauder lipstick."

Grinning like an amused gibbon, Earl let out one of his laugh-grunts.

"I asked you, politely, to hand over that key," Roberta reiterated. She was fighting to maintain her composure; however, her voice revealed a tone of irritation. "Now, I would appreciate it if you-"

Raelene slowly turned her head from side to side. "Now, Roberta, don't you go and be like that. It ain't very neighborly of you. And you don't wanna be un-neighborly now, do you?"

"The key!" Roberta shouted, no longer able to contain her outrage.

At that moment, Gordon Pickering limped his way into the dining room, leaning on a sterling silver handled walking stick. He was well past middle age with graying temples framing his bespectacled, yet kindly, face. And like his wife, he was encumbered with corpulence.

"Is everything all right?" he asked, his voice unruffled. "I thought I heard someone scream."

"Oh Gordon!" Roberta cried out with relief as she ran to her husband's side. "Thank heavens you're here! These people," she pointed to Earl and Raelene, "they're from that red hovel behind our property. Did you know they have a key to our house? And they're refusing to relinquish it! Do something!"

The smile reappeared on Raelene's face as she cast her blinking eyes on Roberta's rotund spouse. "Your wife spooks real easy," she stated, nodding her head in Roberta's direction.

"Yeah, real easy," Earl echoed Raelene's words, twining them with a menacing tone. He still had not shifted his gaze from Roberta, who was, at this point, visibly shaken by his unceasing and peculiar stare.

Raelene proceeded to introduce herself and her 'old man' to Gordon and explained that they came over to welcome him and his wife to the neighborhood.

"It's a pleasure to make your acquaintance," Gordon chirped. His double chin quivered as he cordially extended his hand to the grotty couple despite his wife's glare of disapproval. If her looks could kill, he surely would have been pushing up daisies on the spot. "A pleasure indeed! I'm Doctor Gordon Pickering, but please feel at ease to call me Gordon."

"We ain't never had no doctor for a neighbor before," said Raelene. "I feel like this is our lucky day. You a veter-narian or somethin'?"

"Actually," Gordon began, his face wearing a rather amused expression, "I'm a hepatologist—that's a liver specialist, in case you were wondering. But I'm retired now; happily retired I might add. I haven't practiced medicine in years, at least not in the conventional sense."

"Well, all's I can say is retirement sure seems to agree with you," Raelene cooed flirtatiously. "But I bet you miss havin' all them young, sexy nurses around you, all ready, willing and able to do what you tell them." Her voice suddenly took on a mocking tone. "Yes, doctor. Right away, doctor! Anything you want, doctor!"

Gordon cleared his throat. "Ah, yes, well…" Sensing his wife's growing irritation, he decided it best to change the subject, and fast. "Borza—now that's a name one doesn't hear very often. Polish?"

"Hungarian," Earl replied before letting out a foul-smelling belch, which caused Roberta to turn her head away in disgust. Never before in her life had she encountered a couple as uncouth as Earl and Raelene. Everything about them made her cringe.

Not to be outdone by her spouse's indecorum, Raelene winked one of her raccoon eyes at Gordon. "Tell me, doc, are you and your ol' lady swingers?" she enquired, trying to make her raspy voice sound as alluring as possible.

The room fell uncomfortably silent for a few moments, the only sound being the vexatious smacking of Raelene's gum.

Roberta's eyes widened in disbelief. Her insides churned with revulsion. "Certainly not!" she angrily fired back, recoiling with indignation at the offensive suggestion. "I'll have you know that Gordon and I are respectful members of society! We would never lower our standings in the community by indulging in such sordid activities! Now if you don't hand over that key to our house, you'll leave us with no other option than to call the police!"

Dropping the key into Roberta's upturned palm, Raelene snickered, "Take it easy, girl. Here's your old key. I was just havin' a bit of neighborly fun with you, that's all. There ain't no crime in that." She turned to Gordon. "Now ain't that right, doc?" Turning back to Roberta, she grumbled under her breath, "It's not like we don't have other ones."

"You have a delightful sense of humor," Gordon observed, much to his wife's dismay. "As we used to say in the hospital: laughter is the best medicine...unless you have fecal impaction, in which case an enema would be more effective."

Raelene tossed her head back and let out a loud cackle that elicited a grimace from Roberta. "You're a real cut up, doc. I bet you left all your patients in stitches. Get it, stitches?"

Gordon smiled while Roberta rolled her eyes, unamused by Raelene's pathetic pun.

"You know what?" Raelene continued. "How 'bout you and your ol' lady come on over to our place tonight, after supper, of course. We can chew the fat and get to know each other better over a couple of brewskies and..."

"We don't drink... *brewskies*," Roberta interrupted, her nose high in the air. "And neither do we chew fat. Really, do we look like a couple of Eskimos to you?" But before she could utter another word, Gordon stunned her by accepting Raelene's invitation. Her stomach did a flip-flop as she heard him announce, "My wife and I will be over at eight o'clock sharp. You can count on us to be there."

A look of impish glee spread across Raelene's face like a rash and Earl's demented grin widened, resembling that of a shark. Slack-jawed, Roberta glowered at Gordon, who seemed oblivious to his wife's obvious distress.

"I just know we're all gonna have us a real fun time,"

Madame Gray's Vault of Gore

Raelene said, as the music on the radio was interrupted by a breaking news bulletin reporting the gruesome discovery of yet another body part in the local area. "And you're just gonna love Earl's taxidermy collection."

"Taxidermy?" Roberta sounded repulsed.

"Yeah. Earl likes to play with dead things," Raelene explained with disturbing delight. "Ain't that right, Earl?"

Still grinning, Earl nodded his head and then licked his lips as if the very thought of it aroused a feeling of hunger within him. "Eight o'clock," the toothy brute grunted as he and Raelene made their way to the back door. His parting words, "We'll be waiting for you," sounded more ominous than welcoming.

"Don't worry, honey," Raelene said over her shoulder to Roberta in a dubious attempt to calm her neighbor's frazzled nerves. "We ain't gonna hang you from a meat hook in the basement, then cut you up like a frog in a high school science class. Unless that's the kind of thing you're into."

And with that being said, the Borzas left the Pickering house, laughing.

A huge wave of relief surged through Roberta as her jiggling frame rushed to lock the door behind them. But, no sooner had she secured it, her short-lived relief gave way to burning anger.

"Have you taken leave of your senses, Gordon!" she shrieked. "I can't believe you actually expect me to spend the evening at that run-down house of those horrible people, those... those moral defectives! Have you completely lost your mind?"

"Now, Roberta, there's no need for expostulation."

"No need for expostulation?" A sickened look appeared on Roberta's face. "Those people turn my stomach, in case you hadn't noticed. I swear there's something creepy, something—*abnormal*—about those two. Call it woman's intuition, if you like, but I get the feeling that they're somehow connected to all these body parts popping up in the area."

"Don't be silly, dear. Earl and Raelene, they're just…well, uncultured."

"Uncultured you say? Why, they're the epitome of riffraff! They're mangy mongrels! Vermin!" Her expression quickly transformed into one of petulance. "What on earth ever possessed you to accept their invitation? Are you trying to send me to an early grave, Gordon? Really, I can't understand how you weren't thoroughly appalled by their appearance and behavior. They wouldn't know good taste if it caught rabies and bit their faces off!"

"I was simply being neighborly," Gordon explained, before injecting into his wife's bejeweled ears one of his mini-lectures on the sad state of social affairs. "The problem with the world today is that everyone keeps to themselves. No one bothers to get to know their neighbors anymore like they did back in the good old days. Everyone's either too busy or too scared to even stop and say hello. Now, I'll admit the Borzas aren't quite the champagne and caviar crowd we left behind in New York, but I'm sure…"

"That Raelene has *got* to be the most repulsive woman this side of the Mississippi," Roberta cut in. "Those rags she tries to pass off as clothes and all that hideous black stuff smeared around her eyes. And that trailer trash hairdo, which I'm every bit sure was crawling with lice, looked like a large rodent gnawed the top of it. That woman is a walking social disease." Roberta's eyes blazed. "And did you see the way that repulsive thing she calls a husband kept gawking at my breasts and licking his lips the entire time? Talk about drooling perverts. I wouldn't be one bit surprised if he turned out to be a psychotic serial killer with corpses hanging from meat hooks in his cellar!"

Gordon shook his head and chuckled. "You're allowing your imagination to run wild again, Roberta. You watch too many of those true crime documentaries on television. They have you suspecting everyone of murder."

"That may be so, but I still think those Borzas are abnormal," Roberta reiterated as she began sweeping up the pieces of her shattered wine goblet. "I really don't feel comfortable going over to their filthy little dump to 'chew the fat' with them as they so nauseatingly put it. You know I don't respond well to squalor, Gordon."

"I'm well aware of that, dear," Gordon said. He gently took his wife's hand in his and offered up a loving look. "But it's not right for us to judge others. Remember, it says in the Bible that we must love our neighbors. And our enemies, too. And to paraphrase the late, great Oscar Wilde: not everyone is good, but there's *always* something good to be found inside of everyone. Remember that little old lady who lived in the park—Mrs. Sniffen—the one who sent you into a fit of rage because she wore white shoes after Labor Day?"

Roberta nodded her head as her mind called up an image of the homeless, gray-haired spinster in her frumpy frock and moth-eaten winter coat.

"You must admit, dear, she turned out to be such a sweet thing despite her faux pas. And did you not grow to love her after I convinced you to have her over for Thanksgiving dinner?"

Roberta smiled. "Now that you mention it, she *was* delightful."

"Savor the memory, dear. Savor the memory."

As she basked in the recollection, a serene look came over Roberta's face and the pupils of her eyes twinkled in their blue irises like the stars in heaven. "You're absolutely right, as usual, dear. I'm sure, despite their distasteful outer appearances, the Borzas are very good people—deep down inside. You know, honey, I'm actually kind of looking forward to this evening now." She gave her husband a peck on the cheek. "I'd better start getting to work on the canapés."

Gordon nodded his head, approvingly.

Roberta finished up her sweeping and then merrily set about assembling the ingredients for her hors d'oeuvres. As she worked her culinary magic, she began to hum a happy tune, oblivious to the dark clouds gathering ominously outside the kitchen windows like witches at a Black Mass.

* * *

Roberta gazed down at the Ballon Bleu de Cartier watch on her wrist. It was eight-thirty. The better part of the past half hour had been spent on a rickety, stained sofa in the fetidness of the Borzas' tastelessly decorated habitation, watching them scarfing down the canapés. She took great pains to hide her disgust as her horrendous hosts stuffed their gullets, their gobbling accentuated by a soundtrack of gluttonous grunts and smacking lips. The last time she had witnessed such a blatant disregard for table manners was during feeding time at the zoo. She turned to look at Gordon, who was sitting next to her, smoking his pipe in silence, and wondered if his stomach, like hers, was twisted with revulsion.

Outside, the wind was fierce; one might even say raging with unrelenting fury. The sudden banging of a tree branch against a filthy windowpane made Roberta jump like a startled cat, the sight of which aroused a giggle from Raelene.

After consuming the last of the canapés, Earl wiped his mouth on the back of his inked arm and once again demonstrated his talent for boisterous belching.

"So…" Gordon began, in an attempt to engage in

polite conversation, "What line of work are you in, Earl?"

"Exterminating," Earl replied.

Gordon took a puff on his pipe. "Ah, pest control. It must be quite a satisfying job."

"Earl's one of them independent contractors," Raelene added. "Killin' things is what he's best suited for." Her eyes suddenly glazed over and she said, as if in a trance, "Did ya'll know that the large intestine is like five feet long while the small intestine is two or three times as long? Ain't that a hoot?"

An icy chill shot up Roberta's spine.

"Yes, I knew that," Gordon answered. "And it is most definitely a hoot."

An awkward and slow-as-molasses minute passed before Roberta spoke. "Isn't that just horrifying, all those disgusting body parts turning up all over the neighborhood?" She stared into Earl's eyes, accusingly. "It's obviously the work of some deranged thrill killer."

Gordon placed his hand on Roberta's knee. "One of my wife's many obsessions…" he paused to clear his throat. "I mean *hobbies*, is watching true crime documentaries. She fancies herself to be quite the amateur forensics expert."

"The twisted mind of a serial killer is fascinating, yet somewhat predictable," Roberta continued. "The more people they murder, the more emboldened they become, believing themselves to be untouchable. And that's when they become careless and make a mistake. You see, their overconfidence often proves to be their undoing."

Raelene laughed. "That might be true for some, but there's plenty that don't never get caught. There's a whole bunch of killings that ain't never been solved, and ain't never will neither. The way I see it, if a body's dumb enough to get themselves murdered, then they got what they deserved."

"A most illuminating theory," Gordon remarked

before turning to Roberta. "Wouldn't you say, dear?"

"Yes, most illuminating," she agreed.

"Well now, since ya'll brought up the subject of hobbies," Raelene grinned, "Earl and me wanna show you ours. It's in the cellar. Come on, we'll take you down there."

Roberta wrinkled up her nose. "Thank you, however, I'd rather not. I've never found taxidermy to be a tasteful practice."

Gordon gave his wife a subtle nudge with his elbow and flashed her a frown. "Be polite," he whispered into her ear. "We mustn't offend our neighbors, dear. Remember how Mrs. Sniffen turned out."

Roberta looked at her husband with pleading eyes. "I know, Gordon, but I just can't. My stomach is way too delicate. I'll just wait here while you go."

At that moment, Earl produced a loaded gun, which he had kept hidden between the grubby cushions of his chair. He pointed it at Gordon and Roberta. "You're both goin' down to the cellar if you know what's good for you," he ordered, baring his unsightly, sharpened teeth. "Now get your fat asses movin' unless you wanna eat some lead right here in the livin' room!"

"Earl ain't joshin'," Raelene cautioned. "You'd best do what he tells ya."

"Well, I *never*!" Roberta exclaimed in her most indignant tone.

Gordon gently squeezed his wife's trembling hand. "Let's not panic, dear. I think we should do as the man says."

"I'd listen to your ol' man if I was you," Raelene advised. "Now, hurry it up, you two! Earl gets real mean when he gets impatient."

With Earl's gun aimed at their backs, Roberta and Gordon followed Raelene down a set of creaking wooden stairs leading to the basement. As they descended, the ghastly stench of rotting flesh assaulted their nostrils. It grew stronger with each step they took. Roberta covered her nose and mouth with her hand to keep from barfing.

Upon reaching the basement, Raelene announced with pride, "Welcome to Raelene and Earl's Odditorium."

"*Earl* and Raelene's Odditorium," Earl corrected.

Roberta gasped as her eyes were met by the shocking sight of dozens of human taxidermy mounts, each one assembled from various body parts stitched together into freakish forms and posed in a variety of different ways.

As if inspired by the gaffs of old carnival sideshows and dusty dime museums, there were multi-headed monstrosities, Frankenstein-ish grotesqueries that combined both male and female pieces, and nightmarish creations that were part human and part animal. There was even a psychotic version of P.T. Barnum's infamous Fiji mermaid consisting of a stuffed and mummified lady's torso flawlessly stitched to the back half of a Beluga sturgeon. Arranged in a row on a shelf near a gore-smeared autopsy table were the decapitated heads of women and men, all with their mouths sewn shut, and some with their eyeballs surgically removed. Bloodstained bone saws and meat cleavers decorated the grimy walls and, above this real-life chamber of horrors, a pair of ominous meat hooks dangled from a beam, foreshadowing the unspeakable atrocities about to unfold.

"I hate to say I told you so," Roberta said to Gordon, "but at the risk of sounding crass in front of the neighbors, I feel compelled to say I told you so."

"As always, your intuition was right on the money," Gordon admitted.

"Shut up!" Earl boomed, waving his gun from side to side. "Which one of you whales want to be the first to die?"

"I vote for the snooty bitch." Raelene pointed to Roberta, who was now clinging tightly to Gordon's arm like a terrified child. "I hate snooty bitches! Now the doc, on the other hand, I kinda like him. He's got a good sense of humor, so I say we kill him last."

"Hear that, doc?" Earl laughed. "You're gonna have the pleasure of watching your ol' lady get gutted like a hog. Soo-weee!" An alarmed look suddenly swept across his unshaven face and he began to teeter like a drunkard. "Raelene, get them zip ties and…"

Earl began to cough and gasp for air. Frothy drool foamed down his chin onto his chest. His eyes bugged out, giving his reddening face the appearance of a large insect. He dropped his gun and then collapsed to the floor, his body shaking like an epileptic in sharp spasms, his teeth chattering and the color of his face changing from red to blue.

"Earl!" screamed Raelene as she dropped the zip ties and rushed to her soon-to-be-a-cadaver husband. But all she could do was watch, horror-stricken, as he thrashed about and spilled his bodily fluids onto the basement floor. "You're a doctor! Do something!" she screamed at Gordon. "I think he's dying!"

"I wholeheartedly concur with your assessment," Gordon remarked in a composed and doctorly fashion. "He most definitely is dying."

Raelene grabbed the gun from the floor and pointed the barrel at the Pickerings. "Looks like I'll have to finish what Earl started!" she growled, her eyes wild like those of a rabid dog. "Get ready to die, bitches!"

She was about to squeeze the trigger when an intense cramp seized her gut, causing her to double over in excruciating pain. Her heartbeat became erratic and a strange tingling sensation overcame her toes and fingers, causing her to lose her grip on the gun. It landed on the floor with a dull clank.

"I feel… so sick… what's… happening?" Raelene coughed out her words, frothy drool beginning to appear at the corners of her mouth. Her body was now twitching like a ghastly jumping jack and her face convulsed with terror. "Those canapés," she gasped, "you spiked them... with... something... you bitch!" Her eyes were now starting to bug out like Earl's. "What the hell... did you... put in them?"

"*Really*, Raelene," Roberta said, sounding flabbergasted. "I couldn't *possibly* divulge a secret family recipe! It's a matter of tradition, a matter of taste."

Gordon wrapped his arm around his wife's shoulder and both stood in silence and observed as the crazed taxidermists drooled and spasmed and gasped their final breaths. It was by no means a pretty sight to watch, yet an enthralling one nonetheless. Their deathwatch continued for several minutes before Earl's leg jerked as if kicking an invisible bucket and the rising and falling of his chest subsided. A short while later Raelene followed suit.

Springing into doctor mode, Gordon crouched down and palpated Earl's carotid artery and then Raelene's. Unable to detect a pulse in either, he pronounced them dead with a detached nonchalance.

Looking down at the Borzas' lifeless bodies, Roberta made the sign of the cross and eulogized, "Quiet neighbors make the best neighbors."

"Amen," said Gordon.

* * *

Rays of morning sunlight spilled through the windows of the Pickering house, filling each room with a mellow, golden glow. In the kitchen, clad in one of her designer muumuus, Roberta hummed a happy tune as she stood before the stove and stirred a large stew pot filled with meat and vegetables.

Still wearing his silk pajamas and bedroom slippers, Gordon sat at the kitchen table, spreading pâté on a Ritz cracker. "I think our little get-together with the neighbors last night was just the thing we both needed," he declared. "And, I must add, those canapés of yours were a real knockout!"

"Thank you, honey," Roberta said. "They always are, if I do say so myself."

Gordon let out a little chuckle. "And to think, you were so worried about the Borzas. That Raelene turned out to be quite a sweet girl, even sweeter than our dear old Mrs. Sniffen—and *she* was well aged! And what a good heart that Earl had. He wasn't nearly as tough as he appeared on the outside."

"Thank goodness for meat tenderizer," Roberta remarked. "It makes all the difference!" She glanced out the window facing the backyard. In the distance the smoldering timbers and pile of charred bricks that were once the abode of the Borzas brought a gleam to her eye. "What a glorious morning it is! And the view from this window is so much better today."

Gordon sunk his teeth into the pâté-covered cracker and immediately shut his eyes, pausing to savor the lusciousness. "This pâté of yours is out of this world!" he exclaimed. He gobbled up the rest of the cracker with gusto.

Roberta began to blush. "That's quite a compliment coming from a liver specialist!"

"Who would have ever imagined that crackers on a cracker could be so delectable?"

"Raelene was right," Roberta laughed. "You *are* a cut up!"

"It's all in how you hold the scalpel, dear," Gordon replied. Licking his lips in anticipation of flavor, he spread some pâté on another cracker. "I'm a lucky man to have a magnificent cook like you for a wife. I mean, who else but a culinary maven like yourself would have ever thought to make a Hungarian goulash using actual

Hungarians?"

Roberta beamed with pride. She sprinkled some more paprika into the pot on the stovetop, gave it another stir and then took a taste. Her eyes lit up. "Mmmm. I was so wrong about the Borzas having no taste." She spooned a bit more goulash into her mouth and her taste buds danced with heavenly delight. "They're actually *quite* tasty!"

ETERNAL REMNANTS
By Travis Mushanski

The gym bag sat abandoned on the front door bench. While there was nothing unique about the bag, there was an ominous aura wafting from within its depths. But even within it, one would never find more than a change of clothes, travel-sized bathroom necessities, and an extra charging cable for Edward's cell phone. It was nothing more than a go bag, but he hated that cursed thing more than life itself.

How long had he been staring at the bag? He traced the cold, dark room with his eyes. Nothing… Not a sound. He slid out of his slumped position on his leather recliner and twisted his neck in quick jerks from left to right, releasing agonizing cracks. Edward reached past an untouched glass of bourbon on his end table to grab his cell phone. Hours had disappeared.

There was a faint jingle of keys as the lock tumbler twisted into itself. A burst of warm air brought life into the entryway as Angela glided through the doorway. She brushed a lock of golden hair behind her ear and flashed Edward an excited smile.

"Hey baby! Why the long face?" Angela questioned as she traced his line of sight to his go bag. "Oh come on now Edward, you can't be serious!"

"Ya, I know, I know." He shrugged his shoulders and pulled himself to his feet. "Shit hit the fan with the new amalgamation software at the Winnipeg University Hospital and Gary is lost without me. He has no clue if it's a software or system issue."

"Winnipeg!" Angela tossed her purse onto the floor. "Oh my God, Edward." She put her hand to her face. She could stifle her tears so long as she avoided his gaze. "I seriously wish you were cheating on me. I think that would make more sense to me than you leaving at ungodly hours just for work."

"Oh shut up. You know I would never cheat on you!" Edward wrapped his arms around her and added, "No one but you could handle this devilish beard and you know it!"

Angela chuckled and corrected, "More like grizzly, if you ask me." She smiled and kissed Edward on the lips. "When do you leave, anyway?"

"An hour ago," Edward replied with a guttural sigh. "It's a five-hour drive, and I'd like to get in before midnight." He reached over and slung his go bag over his shoulder. "'Be an electrical engineer,' they said. 'It'll be fun,' they said!" Disappointment radiated from Angela's eyes and Edward's smile faded. "I'm sorry babe. I'll make it up to you I swear!" He leaned in and kissed her again.

"You better," Angela said as Edward walked past her through the front door.

He stopped suddenly at the threshold and looked confused for a moment. He patted his pants as if looking for something long lost. Hidden in the inside pocket of his jacket was a jet-black skeleton key with runic engravings spiraling its handle. Edward pulled it out and waved it nonchalantly for Angela to see.

"I almost forgot," he chuckled to himself. "No sense in taking my workshop key with me to Winnipeg."

Edward handed the key to Angela, who accepted it with a bewildered look. "You keep it for me. You know how I'm prone to lose things. Just…" He paused and ran his hand through his hair. "Just stay out of there, okay? I've been working on some things and it's nothing you…" A smile crept into his face and he brushed her cheek with his hand. "Just don't go in my workshop."

Angela stood for some time staring at the skeleton key, shifting its weight back and forth between her fingers. It was engraved in a language she had never known; a language no one has ever known. *What door in this house, my own house, would have a key like this?* she thought.

The thrall of the key was so great upon Angela that her consciousness began merging with it. The world grew dark and the universe began to open itself upon her mortal soul, but the connection was broken when her cell phone went off in her purse. She hung the key on the wall-mounted coat hook where it swung, beaconing her to caress its face once more.

"Hello," Angela answered her cell as she walked into the kitchen. She tossed her purse on the kitchen counter. "Oh, hi there Stacy!"

She reached up to the liquor cabinet above the stove and pulled out a bottle of Apothic Red wine.

"Oh not much," she spoke and poured herself a glass. "Just walked in the door with enough time to see Ed fleeing past me again. Ya. Another big job he's got to get to," she said, sarcastically.

The tannins of the cheap wine made her cheeks pucker.

"So tonight is gonna be a bottle of wine and a hot date with Skip the Dishes." She laughed out loud into the cell phone. "An affair? With who? Sure he's gone a lot, but he's still the love of my life. Mark from my office? Are you serious? We are just friends. Sure, he's cute and all, but still..." She giggled as she refilled her glass. "You know me. I could never! Come on Stacy, now you're just being mean. You act like he chains me up." She laughed off the conversation that was quickly getting darker in tone. "I'm not a prisoner in my own home." She could feel her face beginning to blush from the wine. "No, no not tonight. I'm just going to relax and enjoy a quiet evening alone for once. But listen..."

A creek in the floorboards made her eyebrow rise. She peeked around the corner into the hallway only to find a chilly emptiness to the house.

"Ya sorry. What I was going to say is, with Ed gone, maybe we should hang out tomorrow. Have us a little girls' night out. Or maybe just a glass of wine and a decent meal." She laughed again. "I haven't had shots for years," she reminisced. "I haven't puked my guts out in years either. Ya I should go too. Get some food ordered before I finish this entire bottle of wine on an empty stomach. Sounds good. I'll call you tomorrow," Angela ended the call.

A loud crashing sound made her jump with fright. Her wineglass and phone smashed against the kitchen floor as she grasped her chest. Her heart desperately tried to burst free but she held it in tight. She was in a daze, desperately trying to fill her lungs with air. She dashed towards the front door but doubled over in pain when her foot struck a chunk of cast iron on the entryway rug: the skeleton key.

"Are you fuckin' kidding me!" she screamed at the key. "What the hell! I thought the whole house was coming down." Groaning in agony, she cradled her foot.

"What the heck is your deal?" she said to the key. Her hand slid across the skeleton key's face and found it warm to the touch. Curious, she drew it close and ran her fingers along its runic engravings. Their meaning was beyond her grasp. A surge of energy wafted from its cast-iron surface. It was familiar. A warm caress after a life-long journey.

Dream we must for evermore,
For time's cruel hand has twisted and pulled.
As we woke the stars on high,
Our bodies of flesh and gore turn within,
Never be free of thy inky ether.

A gurgling sound clawed its way through the silent house. Angela had been sitting on the floor with her arms wrapped around her knees staring into the runes on the black skeleton key. She blinked herself back into consciousness as the unnatural sound washed over her.

A thought jumped into her mind's eye: *Edward's studio.* She instantly knew the sound had come from the basement studio, which she hadn't known about before walking in the front door that evening. *How did I not know about Ed's studio,* Angela thought, *in my own house?*

As she stood, she realized the key was now lighter than a feather, but more than that, it seemed to be pulling Angela to her feet. Pulling her across the kitchen, and then into the inky blackness of the basement stairway.

As she descended the stairs, the blackness gradually subsided by a flickering orange glow. In the faint glimmering light, Angela reached out to touch the wall that she no longer recognized. It was cold and wet to the touch. Mixed matched stones and mortar now lined the stairway walls and floor that had always been painted drywall. She peered into the distance and saw the first of what would be many wall-mounted torches. They blazed defiantly in the blackness. She shivered and held the skeleton key to her chest. Its heat pulsed throughout her body.

Onward she marched as the stairs spiralled impossibly deeper into the earth. Angela could not tell at what point they began to spiral as the transition was too slight.

So too was the sudden transition into the chamber at the bottom of the stairs. One moment she was turning into the darkness, and the next she was in the middle of a chamber lit with multiple torches. The room was barren except for a great ancient wooden door opposite of where Angela now stood. There was a faint metallic smell in the air that was subtly floral, yet struck Angela as being not quite right.

She reached out to touch the great door but pulled her hand back inches from its surface. There was a throbbing pulse reverberating from deep within. The doorknob was icy to the touch as Angela twisted the knob back and forth. It was locked tight and refused to open, yet urged her to push beyond.

The keyhole below the knob reminded Angela of horror films where the protagonist would peer through the keyhole, inevitably triggering a jump scare. With caution she leaned over and did it regardless, but all she could make out was a faint light deep within a room of shadows.

The skeleton key began to grow colder as she held it tightly to her chest. *Edward's studio,* the words swept through her mind with continued interest. *What are you hiding, Ed?* The key slipped gracefully into the keyhole as if it were greased and oiled daily. The slightest flick of her wrist caused the door to unlock with a silence-breaking *cachunk!*

A wave of rotting stench flew past her on a breeze of hot humidity. Angela covered her face with her hands to fight off the stench billowing out of the room. She stepped blindly across the threshold and could feel wetness splash against her ankles. She slipped, falling back against the stone wall, where she slid to the ground.

She groaned in pain but as she looked around the room, the groan changed into an ear-piercing scream.

She tried to cover her face with her wet hands, but the coagulating blood pooling throughout the room stung her eyes. Angela forced herself to see the madness with blurry vision. The entire room was filled with mutilated corpses, chopped, hacked and torn apart without discretion. Arms, hands, torsos and heads were scattered in mounds in various states of decay. The torchlight reflected off the cloudy lifeless eyes of the faces permanently frozen in their horrified death masks. No, not "their" death masks. They were "her" death masks. Every single corpse was Angela.

"I told you not to come down here!" came a growl from the other side of the doorframe.

Angela panicked at the sound of the voice. She spun to face the thing in the doorway, and stared up at Edward, who should have been an hour into his drive to work. His eyes were blood red with rage and his cheeks streaked with tears. He held a stained butcher's knife with a white knuckled grip.

"Baby. Oh, thank God, baby!" Angela wept as she forced the words out. "Let's just go back upstairs, we can figure this out." Despite the knife in his hand, Edward was her last grip on reality as the terror crashed into her like waves against a cliff.

"I wish that we could, baby." He wiped the tears out of his eyes with the hand he held his knife in. "I love you so much."

"Let's just go then." Her eyes were bulging with panic as she reached out her hand for Edward to take. "You don't have to do anything…"

"Don't have to do anything?" Edward repeated in a mocking tone. "The worst part is we have to do this every single time," he mumbled to himself. He took in a deep breath and sighed. He pointed the butcher knife at Angela.

"You did this. YOU did all of this."

"No, that's not true, Edward!" she cried as she forced herself backwards into one of the decomposing piles of rotten flesh. "W-what could I ever do to deserve any of this?"

A murmur began to vibrate throughout the chamber, and then grew into a whisper. The corpses twitched and jerked in memory of their final movements in life. The eyes of severed heads searched blindly in the pale torch light for a focal point. Mouths groaned through decaying black lips.

Nooooo, a grating cry came from the back of the corpse pile. The cry pulsated throughout the death chamber. Angela clamped her hands over her mouth to stop another scream from escaping.

You are we, a guttural voice came from a mound of rotten flesh. *And we are you,* came the retort of a union of voices behind Angela.

"What is going on?" Angela tucked her body into the fetal position.

Soon you will become one with us! You will soon see. The room erupted into a chaotic blend of chanting, groaning, and hushed murmurs.

"It's the curse, Angela," Edward explained through his sobbing. At some point he had fallen to his knees but had yet to pass the threshold of the chamber door.

A sudden hiss and squeal flashed through the room as if the mounds of flesh were trying to recoil in disgust. *Betrayed!* Blood flowed through their open eyes. The room pulsed with a sudden hate-filled desperation. *Retributions must be made!*

"You cursed both of us, Angela!" Edward yelled at her. "I make one little..." he paused to wipe tears out of his eyes. "You cursed me to repeat this nightmare forever!"

No... a softer comforting voice grew out of the chaos.

The madness retreated for a moment as the new voice began to speak. *You are not cursed, my precious child.*

A warmth washed throughout Angela's body. She looked up to find the origin of the ambivalent voice but saw nothing beyond the ebbing madness.

You have traded your very heart to punish the one who has wronged you. Look into yourself and you will see.

Angela tilted her head to see the twisted face of her husband. Twisted in both hate and despair, in love and resentment. She looked into his eyes and smiled a twisted, crooked smile. She didn't remember everything, but pieces of the truth flashed before her eyes.

Bruises. Blood. Suffering. A child unborn.

Her eyes blazed with defiance through a mask of blood and tears.

Edward rose painfully to his feet and crossed the threshold wading through blood towards his wife. With tears in his eyes, he raised the knife over his head. Her mutinous eyes tore a hole through his soul as the curse was fulfilled one more time.

Don't worry… You are with me now. He can't hurt you anymore….

Hours later, Edward returned to the leather recliner, exhausted and broken. He had poured himself a glass of bourbon but left it on the table, untouched. He leaned forward to stare at his gym bag he had just returned to its place at the front door—a prop that was a constant reminder of the never-ending cycle. His vision blurred as his eyes retracted behind thick, gray cataracts. He disappeared into himself if but for a brief moment.

OUT BENEATH THE JACK O'LANTERN SKY
By Tylor James

Halloween, 1959

Johnny took a sip from the bottle, then passed it to the skeleton sitting in the passenger seat. The skeleton took the whiskey into his pudgy hand. He crammed the bottleneck under the plastic chin, tilted back his head and gulped.

Johnny smiled, stepping on the gas. The Ford F-100 purred like a satisfied pussycat.

"Hell with this, man." Bill tore the visage of death from his face, chucked it onto the cab's floor, and drank uninhibited. Bill's right boot stepped on the skull mask. A crack spread from the tip of the cranium down to the chin. "Shit." Bill wiped his lips on the arm of his leather jacket, handing back the bottle.

"Thanks," Johnny said, pleased to see the bottle half gone. He raised it to his lips and took only a sip, then offered it to his brother. Bill snatched it harshly in his thick, pink paws. He drew deeply, Adam's apple bobbing like an arrhythmic metronome, then placed the diminishing whiskey between his thighs, letting it rest against the crotch of his dungarees. "Think I'll keep the booze on my side, little bro," he snarled, running stubby fingers through his greasy hair. "You're too muchuva puss to drink like a man."

Johnny kept silent at the wheel. Rolling hills dipped and lifted like waves upon an autumn sea. The honey golden sky deepened to tangerine, then bloomed pumpkin orange. Gravel dust clouded in the rearview mirror, dancing and pluming beneath the jack o' lantern sky.

"The hell you got that smile on your face for?" Bill growled.

Johnny glanced at him and liked what he saw. Bill's glassy orbs shimmered. Something vague floated in his sclera—an awareness beginning to wane and flicker like a candle flame in the wind. With any luck that flame would soon gutter at the stub until dead.

Johnny thought of smoke and of the dark night ahead of them.

"You think you're a man, do you?" Johnny countered, his smile stretching into a grimace. Sorrow and hatred addled his mind, an intoxication exceeding Bill's in intensity.

Bill leered. "I *know* I'm a man, Sally."

"Prove it." Johnny nodded toward Bill's crotch, where the bottleneck stuck up like an erection. "Bet you can't put that bottle away before fallin' dead as a doornail. I had a whole bottle of J.D. to myself last week and wasn't nearly as drunk as you are now. You think you're tough stuff, big brother, but you ain't."

Bill's hazy eyes sharpened into switchblades. "Why, you mouthy, little fugger! I oughtta take this bottle and break your face with it. Talkin' to me like dat..." Bill shook his head and snorted. "Shit. You deserve what's comin' to ya."

Madame Gray's Vault of Gore

"And what, pray tell, is comin' for me?" Johnny chuckled at the irony. Though he didn't know it yet, Bill was like a gazelle telling off a lion.

"I was gonna keep it from ya," Bill replied with a belch. "Cause what a person don't know don't hurt 'em, but since you's playin' nasty, I'll tell."

Johnny gripped the wheel until his knuckles paled. He knew what Bill was going to say. Knew, yet didn't want to hear it. Didn't want to stoke the sorrow, pain and hatred already roiling his stomach and wringing his heart like a wet sponge. Johnny's grimace resembled the cracked skeleton mask lying face-up on the floor.

"She didn't want it at first, but after I got it in 'er, she did all right." Bill's fat stomach bounced with laughter, recounting a tale Johnny knew all too well. "Hell, she even moaned a little, right after she was done screamin'."

Johnny exhaled through flared nostrils, turned and looked Bill in the eyes and laughed along with him, as if he'd just heard a good ol' knee-slapper. His innards curdled, now on the cusp of vomiting.

Bill's mouth hung open, his blubbery lips lubricated with stupidity just as much as whiskey. Thus, the brothers laughed—one of them convulsing with drunken hysterics, the other performing giggling theatrics with fastidious eyes, sharp and steadfast as a razor's edge.

When the outburst settled, Johnny said, "Whatever you say, big brother. Now shut that fuckin' mouth of yours and stuff it with that bottle. Walk your talk, or prove to me what I already know."

"Wuss that?" Bill guffawed. "What you know?"

"That your little brother can drink you under the table."

"Sheee-it." Bill wrapped his lips round the bottle, squeezed his eyes shut, and tilted back his head.

Johnny listened to the wet gulping inside Bill's throat, sucking down 80 proof liquor. The sun was a giant orange sinking into the horizon. The shadows of an occasional barn and farmhouse stretched long and dark and Johnny dreamed with those shadows.

He had told Bill they were going to a Halloween party. That part was true, but it wouldn't be held at the old dance hall on the outskirts of Emerald, like he'd claimed. Nor would their usual gang of Ronnie Harding, Jasper Clemens, or Don Wasserman be accompanying them. Tonight, he and Bill would be attending a small party of three, and the only dancing they'd be doing was with Death.

Bill belched. His head lolled left and right, eyes fluttering, speaking in some abstract Drunkanese: "Heyafugger! Justa wakemeup when weh gedder…"

The bottle fell from his hands and thudded to the cab floor. It rolled around, occasionally scraping against the skull mask. Bill groaned, his head rolling all loosey-goosey on his neck. Then his eyes rolled too, into the back of his head. Like a grotesque volcano, vomit exploded out of Bill's throat, cascading over his lips and chin like lava and slopping all over his shirt, legs, and floor.

Johnny stared out the windshield, jaw clenched tight. The rancid odor of Bill's stomach expulsion filled the cab. He rolled down his window. Crisp cool wind ruffled his blond hair. Lost in the contemplative shadows of his loathing, he hardly felt it.

The jack o'lantern sky, gorgeous as it was, hardly existed.

All he saw before him was that pitch-dark night about a week back. He'd listened to Susan sob on the telephone, her voice choked with tears, attempting to relate the monstrosity. Johnny had told her to stay put, he'd be right over, and hung up the phone.

Susan owned a small cottage, bordered on all sides by rolling ocher fields that appeared golden in sunlight. But it was night when he arrived. There was not a star in the sky and the hills were waves upon a dark sea frozen in time. He lit the hearth when he came in, finding the cottage utterly cold and dark and Susan crying there in the gloom.

She was soaked from the rain, her clothes in tatters. The polka dot blouse hung open. White buttons dangled cockeyed like broken wrists. A rip had ruptured one side of her indigo skirt, exposing a pale hip, which panties used to cover before they'd been savagely ripped away.

Johnny helped remove the sopping wet clothes and dressed her in a bathrobe. He fashioned her a mug of hot sun tea, then sat beside her. Her voice was hoarse, relating the incident in a zombified tone. Her fingers picked idly at the tag dangling cup-side.

She'd been at the Starman Drive-In, she explained, with her girlfriends. Vanessa's new boyfriend, Ronnie, had driven them there in his spacious Cadillac. It was a creature-feature playing that night: *The Giant Gila Monster* and *The Killer Shrews*. The movies were silly, she said, hardly scary at all. She told her friends she'd be right back, was going to buy popcorn from the rickety concessions stand on the east side of the field.

She bought the popcorn. On the way back, walking through the dark field that flickered in bright flashes beneath the enormous screen, hands grabbed her and pulled her far, far away from the cars, down into the dip of the hills where the grass was wet with midnight dew.

She couldn't see his face, but smelled whiskey-laden breath and knew it was Bill Evans, that lousy *creep*. She hauled off, slapping him across the face.

When he punched her in the stomach, she dropped the popcorn and doubled over. Bill laughed while she gulped at the air. Finally reclaiming her breath, she used it to scream. No one heard and no one came and she was screaming, screaming, screaming.

The breath rushed out of her again when Bill slammed his size-thirteen boot between her shoulder blades, forcing her down where grass tickled her cheeks and damp earth flooded her nostrils. Then his coarse hands, ruthless and dreadful, ripped off her underwear. His heavy bulk pinned her with oppressive gravity, then he forced his way inside, pumping away like a rabid piston while she gasped, writhed, and clutched the grass with her fists, ripping out the roots.

Tears blurred her sight into grim watercolors. Her mind slowly dissolved into a dream-state where all she could think about was the popcorn she'd paid for and never ate because it'd spilled into the grass, the bag crunched beneath Bill's feet just like she was now being crunched beneath the brute slab that pushed upon her, violating her body and soul, making her *bleed* down there, and the sounds he made, *oh God*, that grunting pig making those awful noises in between the rhythmic slapping of flesh and she dropped the popcorn she paid for all over the ground, only got a few kernels of buttery goodness on the tip of her tongue before, before, before . . .

Johnny screamed, his face flushed red, his knuckles white. That rage in his heart bloomed into an explosion. He couldn't stop screaming, stomping down on that accelerator and tearing ass down the dirt road, gravel spraying up into that lovely, hallowed sky.

He threw back his right fist into Bill's slobbery, drunken face, while keeping his left firmly upon the wheel. He launched his knuckles into Bill's nose, cracking the bridge. Blood flowed thick down his lips to pool with the vomit dribbling out of Bill's slack mouth. Johnny kept throwing back his fist, relishing the feel of warm blood on his knuckles, and the sound of bones and teeth cracking so loud it overpowered the roar of the engine.

* * *

The sun melted into the horizon, now drenching the sky deep crimson. Johnny stared at his hands, then reverently held them up to the sky. He could not tell where his hands ended and the sky began.

Then he and Susan kissed, and her mouth was soft and warm. A memory from childhood suddenly flashed through his mind. Something he hadn't thought about in ages came rushing in like a wild river through a broken dam.

Mother on the floor—her eyes alabaster orbs, foaming at the mouth, shrieking demonic incantations. Father standing over her with his precious bottle of Johnny Walker (he liked it so much he'd named his youngest son after it), his lips launching spittle as he shouted, "You crazy *bitch*, I can't stand it no more! You're done. You're so fucking *done!*" Johnny thought Daddy was going to lop his Momma upside the head with the bottle like he'd done a few times before. Instead, Daddy scooped her up, loaded her into the back of his jalopy and drove her to the insane asylum where she would remain the rest of her life. Meanwhile, Johnny was left at the house that evening with his big brother Bill, who laughed and punched Johnny's arm for crying about Momma being sick, being *real* sick, and was Daddy finally taking her to the doctor?

Bill stole one of Daddy's Lucky Strikes, smoked most of it, then stubbed out the butt directly beneath Johnny's left eye. He shrieked as embers ground and burned into his upper cheek, and he smelled the sour, acrid redolence of his own skin burning. Johnny ran crying to the kitchen sink. Splashed cold water on his face. It burned even more. Bill convulsed with laughter, amused by his little brother's agony. When Johnny settled onto the couch with a wet cloth beneath his eye, silent and brimming with tears, Bill sat at the table, smoking another Lucky, taking nips from various liquor bottles hanging around the house. *He looks just like Daddy*, Johnny thought, *he looks just like Daddy and I hate him, hate him, hate him.*

"Darling?" Susan asked. "Are you all right?"

Johnny gazed into Susan's broken eyes, where flecks of blood-red sun gleamed like burning embers, and he smiled because he saw a bit of himself inside her. "Yes," Johnny nodded. "For the first time in my life, I think I am."

Susan kissed him on the small, crescent shaped scar beneath his left eye.

* * *

An autumn breeze ruffled their hair and clothes and skittered dead leaves across the lawn. They lounged in rocking chairs upon the front porch of Susan's cottage. They smiled at one another. It had been hard work, and the hours they'd spent on the task had devoured the waning sunlight. Still, they couldn't have been happier.

It was the first time in many days Johnny saw Susan smile. For this, he was grateful. There was a light and vibrancy in her gaze, and this was a welcome change from the numb glaucoma that had settled like gray mist into her eyes on the night she'd sobbed and told him.

With glasses of Moscato in hand, they toasted to love and life eternal. Dusky blue twilight deepened into the sacred dark of Halloween. A full moon arose over the undulating sea of dead crops, gently sweeping the harvest with its ivory satin shadow.

Crickets began to sing. Stars twinkled in their snow-white luminescence, reminding Johnny of the long, cold winter to come. He didn't forbid it, like he did most years. He was looking forward to cozy nights with Susan, snuggling and drinking hot cocoa, watching snow fall from within the comforts of the cottage.

"I love you," Susan whispered, squeezing his hand.

Johnny sipped from his glass, admiring her beauty in the moon-shadowed night with the jack o'lantern's red-orange glow flickering upon her face. He was surprised to see tears in her eyes, forming into transparent, jeweled beads to slip her cheek.

"I love you too," he replied, feeling a bit like crying himself.

It'd been a trying evening. He'd have much work ahead of him tomorrow too: disposing of Bill's corpse, and cleaning all that foul blood and emesis from the cab of his pick-up. Susan might have work cut out for her too—answering perfunctory questions about Bill's disappearance to the police. She'd have to put on her best face of clueless nonchalance. A Halloween mask of its own, Johnny supposed.

Susan gazed into the jack o'lantern's glow. Johnny smiled, relishing in her obvious delight. They'd carved the lantern together, right there on the porch, covering the floorboards with a tarp so as not to get it messy and stained with gunk.

Most pumpkins were bright sherbet inside, filled with almond-shaped seeds. This was an entirely different kind of gourd, however, and it served for a veritable Halloween masterpiece.

It sat upon the bottom step, facing them.

"There are few things I've seen," Susan said, squeezing Johnny's hand tight, "as beautiful as this."

Johnny grinned down at their handiwork. The scalp of blood-matted hair sat askew over the smashed-open cranium—a job done with chisel, hammer, and an abundance of determination. Ghastly pale cheeks glowed faintly with three tea candles they'd set down within the hollow of Bill's skull. Gouging out the eyeballs had been elementary, of course, as had been ripping out the tongue (it'd looked no more than a strip of raw meat from the butcher's shop up in Deer Park, Johnny thought), but removing the brains had required formidable effort and time.

The brain, with all its folds and grooves, was a surprisingly dense organ. Susan had sliced it into sections with her largest kitchen knife, before Johnny could go about ripping out the contents. "Gray matter is no matter at all," Johnny had joked, stabbing, slicing and tearing, often ripping out chunks of slimy, warm brain with his red-slicked fingers.

They held hands across the space between chairs. The flickering glow emanating from Bill's sagging open eyes and mouth provided a romantic ambience. Once morning came, they would dutifully toss out the head with the rest of the body, burying it in the nearby Morton Woods. But at least Johnny and Susan would always have this special memory for the keeping—of the Halloween they had spent together beneath the jack o' lantern sky, and how, when the sky died away, they re-lit the night with a jack o'lantern of their very own—a symbol of their love and dedication, and the fact they would do *anything* for each other, no matter what.

On that last chilly night of October, their hands fastened together with the bond of blood. They leaned in close, and within the lantern's red-orange glow, kissed deeply.

THE BALLAD OF FAIRY FAY
By Stephen McQuiggan

Death came easy to women such as her. It seemed to smell them out from their decrepit childhoods as if they were indelibly stained by their poverty, their parents' separation, their inevitable descent to the workhouse. Fairy Fay they called her, when Death closed the book on the few squalid chapters of her life. Fairy Fay she was dubbed by the press, because the name she was born with was too common to carry the sensationalism of her murder. They took everything from her, fed on her corpse like jackals until her very bones became a myth.

Polly she once was; mother of Charles and Henry, wife of Thomas Turner—a God-fearing man, proud of his piousness and keen to hammer home his sermons with his fists. Polly left him and her boys when she found a more sympathetic lover, the only one that ever gave her peace of mind: gin.

She became a seamstress, or at least that's what she told the constables on the many occasions she awoke in their care. It was more demure than admitting to prostitution, even if she did offer them a free knee-trembler to let her go on her way.

That her profession killed her before her liver had a chance to was not a total surprise, but the manner of her passing, brutal even by the standards of her time, was what the public latched onto, egged on by an increasingly hysterical and hypocritical press.

Gang-raped by a band of young men who could not be bothered with the niceties of commerce, some said; ripped asunder by a fiend, posited others. Her face mutilated with a rusty old clasp knife and a blunt object (a stick, hazarded the coroner, or perhaps a hairbrush) inserted into her, tearing her perineum and staining her moldy old stockings scarlet with her polluted blood.

Her past was raked up, found sketchy and wanting of true infamy. She was resurrected as Fairy Fay, a construct of jaded reporters with a penchant for the mythic. Her ghost, a benevolent and healing spirit it was said, was often seen on the shit-strewn streets after the midnight hour—usually by other drunken, fallen seamstresses. Ignored in life, Fairy Fay became a Guardian Angel of whores in death.

She was an inspiration too, a call to arms for others of a more hygienic and genteel disposition. Others such as Mary Jean Crozier, who often found herself laying her little gilt bible to one side, her mind drifting off from her father's preaching, to wipe away a discreet tear at the thought of poor Fay's earthly suffering. Even now, the papers were still full of it—how a madman stalked the city, gutting the unfortunate who were forced to ply their sinful trade in the anonymous fog.

Chattering about it in hushed voices at the Tea Circles, or writing strongly worded letters to the Alderman, had little effect despite what Mary Jean's father might say; neither did prayer, God forgive her. It was Fairy Fay herself, not the sorrowful remembrance of her, which led Mary Jean out onto the streets when the servants were still abed and Father at his Club. Fairy Fay, whole and unblemished once more, glistening with Christ's pure mercy, sent especially to her to lead her to the wretches doomed to die in the sewers and the slums by a hypocritical class long immured to the Lord's teachings.

Her father would have apoplexy if he knew, but Teresa the maid was fat and indolent and could not be waked at the best of times, and Martha the housekeeper was in her dotage—a simple thing then for Mary Jean to follow Fay's silver glowing trail out into the silent gaslit streets, to wander in her holy footsteps down to the hovels that mushroomed along the river's filthy banks.

She ducked into an alleyway by the apothecary, wrinkling her nose at the stench of the puddled effluent that stained her skirts, just as a figure emerged in the mist ahead, the moonshine gleaming like a warning on the crown of his imperious hat. Holding her breath, she tried to merge with the shadows that clung to the dank brickwork at her back, tried to disappear as completely as Fairy Fay, who had winked out of her bright existence the instant the man had appeared.

The tapping of his cane echoed her heartbeat. As he approached, Mary Jean's head was suddenly filled with the lurid drawings of the penny dreadfuls she had spent so many hours poring over, except this time, in the clarity of her mind's eye, the hapless female with her guts asunder and lying in a murdered heap was her.

The moon illuminated his face and Mary Jean stifled a gasp of recognition—Mr. Carmichael, pillar of the church and founder of the Abstinence Committee, a regular and temperate voice at her Father's table. Even from her hiding place she could smell the whiskey on his breath and see its ruddy glow in his cheeks, its mischief in his gait.

Why on earth would Mr. Carmichael be down among

the dosshouses, imbibing the devil's buttermilk at such an unholy hour? Surely not to redeem the loose women he railed against so passionately over his venison pasty...but then that could only mean he was actively soliciting their brazen company.

She heard her father's voice chastising her for such a wicked thought. "You spend so much time obsessing over those wanton harridans, Mary Jean, you start to think like them and see Evil in even the kindest deeds." Perhaps, but with a killer on the loose, and so many vigilantes roaming, Mr. Carmichael was taking a chance with more than just his reputation.

Carmichael stopped and Mary Jean feared her heart would too. He took out his pocket-watch with an unsteady hand as the moon sucked the color from his face, rendering it cadaverous. The monotone light made the scratch marks on his cheek look like rents in a mask—a mask that covered up some dark abyss, some eternal emptiness beneath. In fumbling the watch back into his waistcoat he let it slip. It spun hypnotically on the cobbles before resting, glinting like a fallen star.

Carmichael seemed not to notice. Sniffing the air, as if savoring the sin of his environs, he turned his head this way and that, his blurry eyes passing over her, before he was moving on once more. As she listened to the tap-tap-tapping of his cane, Mary Jean debated whether to return homeward. It simply wasn't safe to be abroad on such a night, amid men with such paucity of moral fiber.

If she were to be seen, why, Father would put her out of doors to be sure, or send her away to her Aunt Montague's, or pack her off to the missionaries—a threat he often made when displeased, though one that caused a secret smile beneath his gruff whiskers. As the sound of Carmichael's cane faded into the thickening night, Mary Jean stepped back out into the street.

She snatched up the pocket-watch, marveling at its

solidity in this realm of vapors, tracing his embossed name with a fog-puckered finger before slipping it into her bag. She turned to go back to find the street was now lit by a divine glow. Fairy Fay, her angelic face scoured by sorrow, beckoned to her, silently beseeching her deeper into the slums.

Fay led the way, eclipsing the shabby lanterns with her holy light, her glow louder than the drunken piano that barked from the tavern by the wharf. It was a wonder that its patrons didn't come shambling out to give up their sins on their scabby knees to the source of that eye watering brightness. Fay floated on, a will-o'-the-wisp filled with the Holy Spirit, flittering through the murk, as Mary Jean hitched up her skirts and followed as fast as she could.

The twists and turns of the labyrinthine hovels left her confused and giddy; if her guiding light were to flicker out now, Mary Jean would be as lost as the poor wretches she was here to save. A feral cat, more rib than fur, spat a warning at her passing, though the derelicts sprawled in the gutter were oblivious to her presence.

Mary Jean marked her footfalls with a prayer, a staccato psalm, and Fay burned ever brighter as if fuelled by her pious passion. Down into the darkest byways she went, down to where the rats feasted on decaying dogs and were in turn devoured by the starving denizens who eked out their existence here. The moon hid its face behind a cloud in shame to see a gentlewoman here, just as Fairy Fay dimmed then faded completely into the inky shadows.

"Care for a tumble, Sir?" The voice seemed to be the voice of the darkness itself and turned Mary Jean's blood to slush. "Give us thruppence and you can play with my tuppence."

The moon now deigned to cast its rays down into the alley, revealing the mounds of ordure and litter, as a scarecrow silhouette stepped out from a slanted doorway. "Oh, sorry, me lady, I thought you was...ere, be off with you, this n' no place for the likes of you!"

Fairy Fay materialized over the hag's shoulder, her dim glow a halo, allowing Mary Jean to see the shrieking creature properly; oh, but she was a pitiable thing, all decked out in rags, her emaciated face fattened only by the filth that clung to it.

She tottered forward, the stench of her almost enough to make Mary Jean gag. How any man could part with so much as a solitary penny to couple with such a beast was beyond her comprehension, unless that man was less than a beast himself.

"Unless you be lookin' for a wee go on Ol' Sadie yerself? I'se never done it wiv a woman afore, but gis a shillin' and you can tickle me quim, dearie, wot ya say?" She smiled, three teeth standing proudly like tollbooth sentinels in her pale gums.

Mary Jean struggled to regain her pity—this thing, this *woman*, this Sadie, was probably around her own age but her sinful life had devoured her as readily as her poverty. She wore her conscience on the outside for the whole world to judge, is all.

"Did you know the Blessed One," she asked, trying to bestow compassion in her voice, "the one they called Fairy Fay, the one who stands behind you now, weeping in her mercy?"

Sadie cackled, her breath a green smog polluting the thin, sharp air. "You can call me Fay if you wish, my sweet, but I'll still need the coin first."

Mary Jean fumbled in her bag; it made no difference, for Sadie would know Fay soon enough. The divine fallen angel (soon to be elevated by His grace once more) was standing by the old crone's shoulder; if only she would turn around, see her, and be shriven.

Sadie leaned in closer, her grimy claw flexing for

money, drool dripping from her jowls in anticipation, but Mary Jean pulled out a dagger instead—taken from Father's study, the one he boasted had been christened at Waterloo—the only payment she could offer to unrepentant sinners. Sadie had barely time to curse before her jugular was severed. Mary Jean winced as the drudge's blood sprayed in a hot gush over her face.

Then, straddling the slumped whore and following Fay's mute direction, she began to carve and cut; the better to free Sadie's soul from her filthy, fleshy prison. She took a hairbrush from her bag and, with a final frantic flourish, used it to penetrate what was left of the diseased and sickening hag.

When she was done, she slipped Carmichael's pocket-watch out of her bag and hid it amid the folds of Sadie's rank old rags. Satisfied, she allowed herself to bask in Fay's radiance (*Oh, she shone so bright in these moments of release!*) as she surveyed her work. Then Mary Jean began the long trek home, her bloody hands hidden in expensive gloves, knowing that, even as the police whistles sounded, she would never be stopped.

Fairy Fay was looking out for her, guiding her in all things. There were so many more souls to release, to set free, it might take years, a *lifetime*, and she was so tired. Yet, even as the darkness enveloped her, the night swaddling her as one of its own, there was something inside Mary Jean that burnt with an intensity too bright to be ever classed as infernal.

Mary Jean would have to douse that flame down to an ember once more, and sit meekly as her father preached the Good Word, feign shock as the news of tonight's deeds broke. But only for a little while, she thought, following Fairy Fay through the foul back streets, for one day soon her fire would consume them all.

TROPOSPHERE
By Jon Douglas Rainey

Falling upwards. Her intestines feel like they're being pulled out through her mouth as Ally blindly flails her arms and legs in the open air. Her eyes are gone, having been sucked out, and equally painful is the burning sensation where her flesh used to be. She wants to scream but can't catch her breath.

She tries anyway.

* * *

Ally jerks her head forward as she wakes up in a panic. The seatbelt straps tighten around her waist and chest. She catches her breath in one loud gasp as if she had been unconsciously holding it while she slept. Fragments of her dream linger and her mouth is dry with the aftertaste of despair. There have been times in her life when her dreams seemed more like premonitions. She dreamt of her parents' car accident before she was told of their deaths. She dreamt of giving birth to Tommy before there were any signs of her being pregnant. Those dreams were more powerful than most. What she just experienced felt like one of those rare premonitions, but Ally didn't want to believe that because whatever was going on in that situation felt like anguish. She pushes it out of her thoughts, unbuckles the seat belt and assures herself that everything is okay. She sees Tom is no longer in the driver's seat and Tommy, who is ten now, isn't in the backseat. She wonders how long she's been in the car alone.

Outside, she sees that they are parked along a barren stretch of road with nothing but the hot desert in all directions. Aside from the mountains in the distance she sees only cacti, creosote bushes and sand. No insects. No reptiles. No small animals. Not even a bird.

Finally, through the rear window, she finds them standing side-by-side with their backs to her. A wave of uncontrollable anger sweeps over her as she exits the vehicle. The dry heat hits her hard as she rises out of the car too quickly and has to hold on to the passenger door to keep her balance. "I'm sure it's great to be able to piss whenever and wherever you want, but you boys are starting to abuse the privilege."

Tommy turns half way around and yells in an excited tone, "Mom, come here!"

Tom doesn't turn around at all.

Suddenly, she feels intense heat and finds herself squinting from the sunlight. She looks skyward and sees that a white cloud just finished passing over her and now the sun burns brightly down upon her skin. A few clouds float around on an otherwise clear day.

"Honey, could you come here, please?"

Ally turns her gaze toward the road and sees Tom looking back at her. She closes the door and starts walking toward him. She can feel the heat from the black tar beneath her sandaled feet and the dryness of the air in her lungs.

"I'm often asked how long it takes to drive through Nevada," she says. "And for now on I'm going to reply, that depends on how many penises you're traveling with."

"Ally," Tom snips while nodding toward Tommy, as if penis is a bad word. "This isn't a pee break."

Ally slides in between them, slipping one arm around Tom's waist and resting the other on Tommy's shoulder.

"Do you see it?" Tom asks.

She follows his gaze. About forty yards out in the desert, she spots the front end of a gray convertible with its passenger door open.

"Mom, are you blind? It's right there."

"I see it, kiddo. Calm down. What's the story here?"

"That car was driven by a young couple," explains Tom. "They passed us about an hour ago and disappeared ahead of us. Haven't seen another vehicle since. We pulled over not five minutes ago when Tommy spotted their car again way out there as we passed it."

"Have you seen any signs of the young couple?"

"No. And I called out to them a minute ago. Someone would have heard me."

Tommy enthusiastically adds, "They may need our help."

"That's what I'm going to find out. Alone. I don't want you or your mother walking around out there. The desert is full of dangerous mammals, insects and even some birds that can be aggressive. Out here, everything is a predator and if one of us should get bit by anything, whether it's big like a coyote or small like a snake, or even a spider, then we will be the ones who will need help. And we're a long way from getting any."

Ally says, "Well, if it's that dangerous then none of us should go. Let's call the police, give them a mile marker number and go. I have to use the bathroom. A real bathroom."

"I can't just drive off and enjoy our weekend with

your parents, wondering the whole time whether or not we left someone out here to… permanently vacate. It's not the kind of lesson I would want to teach Tommy. Because in this family, if we think someone might be in distress, we don't turn our back, we step up and act. That's who we are." He nods toward Tommy again.

When he talks like this, she finds it hard not to love him. Ally looks at the barren desert around them and back to the mystery car. "You're right. That's why we're all going. I think six eyes will be better than two for finding anyone who needs help and safer for spotting anything that can bite us."

Tom thinks for a few seconds before turning to Tommy. "Tommy, you stay in between us, okay?"

"Yeppers."

"Okay, let's be careful."

They step off the road and make their way through the desert foliage toward the car. All of them constantly scan the ground as they move in a straight line, seeing nothing but plant life and sand. After just a few minutes of walking under the hot sun, all three of them are sweating profusely. They reach the convertible and see that the front end is dirty and beat up from driving through the desert. They can also see that the car is sunk down where the ground is lower than the area around it. Tom notices that none of the tires are flat as they spread out around the car. With the top down, they all clearly see a purse and small suitcase in the back seat. Nothing is on the front seats or on the floor spaces. Tom notices that the seat colors don't match because the driver's side seat cover is missing. He leans down for a closer inspection. "The gear shift is in fifth gear and the keys are turned forward in the ignition. That means the car had to be going pretty fast when it went off the road. Nobody down shifted, so it looks like the car just kept going until it bottomed out here. Probably blew the engine."

"Footprints," Ally says, dryly. But the sight of small footprints leading away from the passenger side and trailing off in the desert somehow make the situation all the more real to her.

Tom leans close to Tommy. "Tommy, you inspect the car while we follow the footprints. I don't want you in the car. I want you to examine the outside for any kind of damage to the car or tires. That would be very helpful. Okay?"

"I want to follow the footprints with you," protests Tommy.

"Tommy, this isn't an adventure. This is serious and I need you to do as you're told. Understand?"

"Okay."

Tommy starts to walk around the car, searching for clues while Tom and Ally follow the footprints. They walk for about fifteen yards when Ally suddenly stops and grabs Tom's arm. "Stop. This can't wait." Ally jogs back to Tommy and by the time she reaches him, her clothes are soaked with sweat. She leans down to face him. "Honey, actually, I don't want to walk too far in this heat. Why don't you follow the footprints with dad and I'll check the car?" Tommy smiles with excitement and starts to run toward dad. Ally yells toward Tom, "Honey, Tommy's going to go with you and I'm going to PEE-K around the car!"

Tom shrugs his shoulders. "Really? At the scene of a possible accident?"

"There's going to be two accidents if I don't do this right now."

Tom turns away, waiting for Tommy to catch up to him as Ally runs around to the far side of the convertible. She lifts her skirt and pulls down her panties as she squats down, concealed by the car and begins to pee.

Tom notices that the footprints stop just a few feet ahead. They just end. The ground doesn't show any signs of disturbance or give any clues as to what happened to the girl. A sudden draft that brings a chill up the back of his neck gives his whole body goose bumps as he realizes that, aside from the desert vegetation, his family appears to be the only living things out there. No signs of coyotes or rabbits. No lizards, snakes or spiders. He can't even recall the last time they drove past some road kill. It's as if the land had been picked clean—like meat off the bone. Same with the young couple in their convertible. The boy seems to have been picked clean from the car while driving on the road. And the girl appears to have made it on foot for a while before getting picked clean too—right there, where he's standing now.

Ally finishes peeing and maneuvers her underwear up and skirt down, before rising from the side of the car. The first thing she notices is that Tommy is gone. "Tommy? Tommy!" She runs around the car, frantically looking around in disbelief.

Tom immediately turns around and is also shocked by the absence of his son, who was only a few yards away just a moment ago. "Thomas Junior!"

Panic and dread consume Ally as she stumbles over some weeds and almost falls but regains her balance and continues looking around some large cacti. "TOMMY, ANSWER ME!"

"Tommy, answer your mother right now or you're in big trouble!"

Ally had never heard Tom sound so afraid in the twelve years that she's known him. She turns to Tom with heightened desperation. "My God. Where is he?"

"I don't know, he was right here," Tom motions toward the ground where his son's footprints just stop. He feels nauseous at the thought of a sinkhole pulling his son down into the earth. He notices that the ground and bushes around his son's footprints aren't disturbed in any way. Perplexed, he shakes his head and looks around again when movement catches his attention. He looks up and sees a white cloud in the sky, but nothing else. Not even a bird. He starts to look away when the cloud suddenly moves. The white cloud is the size of a large house as it moves rapidly across the sky in the distance. There is no wind to propel it and furthermore, the cloud seems to move with purpose. He can hear Ally say something to him as he watches the cloud move toward the mountains in the distance before suddenly changing direction and picking up speed. His wife continues to say something but all Tom can hear now is the sound of his own heart beating loudly in his ears. The cloud dips down to twenty feet above the desert, then changes direction and starts to quickly move parallel with the ground, directly toward his wife, who is now screaming at the top of her lungs. Tom looks Ally in the eyes and is surprised to see that she isn't screaming about the moving cloud. In fact, she can't even see the cloud as it approaches from behind her. She is looking at Tom. No, not at him, he realizes. Above him.

Tom feels shade cover him as he looks up to see a second white cloud, also the size of a big house, positioned over him. The cloud seems multi-layered, with the deeper layers moving in all directions within the outer layers. Only the faint sound of blowing wind is made as a tornado shaped wind tunnel starts to form in the cloud's center, directly above Tom. The wind tunnel quickly accelerates into a powerful vortex that instantly widens and twirls downward with incredible speed. Tom instinctively raises his hands in defense as the twirling mass opens up just a few feet above his head. A vacuum sound is heard as the pressure within the vortex sucks the shirt from his body, followed by the flesh from his face, arms and hands. His eyeballs get sucked out of their sockets and Tom tries to scream only to have his lungs cave inward as oxygen is suctioned out through his mouth. With streams of blood twirling upwards out of his eye sockets, his body lifts off the ground and completely disappears into the vortex. The twister shortens and works its way up back into the cloud again without a trace of Tom or the attack.

Ally stops screaming and tries to grasp the situation. She knew the moment she saw that cloud swiftly positioned itself over Tom, that it was something more. In a moment of clarity, her fear succumbs to the knowledge that her son must have been sucked up too. And in that horrific moment of realization, she hoped that her son was taken whole, due to his smaller, lighter frame without being peeled first by the cloud-thing's wind straw. The moment of clarity ends with her acknowledging how vulnerable she is out in the open. She turns to run for the family car.

That's when she notices that she is standing in the center of a large, circular shadow across the ground. She instantly realizes what Tom must have been staring at and she looks up just as the cloud hovering above her spins a vortex in its center. The vertical flow widens and spirals down toward Ally with lightning speed. She screams and jumps to her side, falling hard on the ground next to a large rock and tall cactus. She rolls toward the inside of the rock's crevice and tries to wedge herself underneath it. A loud whooshing sound is heard and she sees the open end of the vortex pulling sand up from all around her until she is forced to close her eyes. She feels her body getting sucked out from beneath the rock when the tall cactus gets torn out of the hard ground next to her and soars up the vortex. A deep, thundering rumble bellows out of the center of the cloud and the vortex immediately shrinks in size. The twister suddenly spins in the opposite direction and the cactus is spit out toward the ground below. The cloud rumbles again, louder.

Ally is already on her feet and running for her car. As

she runs, she looks back and sees the two clouds gaining on her. She turns her focus back to the car as she gets closer to the road. She fixates on the passenger door handle and refuses to look away from it as she runs. The uneven desert dips downward and her right foot bends at an awkward angle, snapping her sandal strap. Her sandal flies off, but she keeps going. Her eyes do not divert from the passenger door handle, even as a large shadow passes over her. There is only the door handle and nothing else. She hears the terrible sucking sound above her head and her hair rises upwards just as she reaches the car, lifts up the door handle and jumps inside the passenger seat. Ally closes the car door and sees one of the vortices sucking desert sand up right next to the car. The vortex swirls up and disappears.

Ally jumps in the driver's seat and tries to turn the ignition, but the keys are not in it. As she realizes Tom must have taken the keys with him, she screams in frustration and slams her fist down on the console. She hears the keys go flying up and land back down on the console. Tom did leave the keys! As the two large shadows circle around the car, she sticks the keys in the ignition and the engine roars. She throws it in gear and slams her foot on the gas. She swerves back and forth along the road until she finally gets control of the wheel, driving straight down the centerline. Looking out the side windows, she can see the two large shadows of the clouds moving along the desert, keeping up with her. She continues to accelerate her speed and eventually the shadows fall back. The speedometer reads one hundred and ten miles per hour for several minutes until she loses all sight of the clouds and their shadows.

She decreases her speed as the adrenaline slowly fades and is replaced with an overwhelming sense of aloneness that she has never known. Tears start rolling down her face and she licks her lips, realizing how dry her mouth is.

She looks around the car for something to drink. The tears fall even harder as she looks at the empty seats, unable to believe that her boys are gone. She thinks back to her dream—NO—her *premonition*. If only she had woken up and immediately pulled her husband and son back within the safety of the car. Had she accepted the dream as a warning, she could have saved them both. Instead, she dismissed it, and the all-encompassing feelings of regret and loss consume her. She cries harder and the sound of her deep sobs fill her ears for several minutes until she forces herself to stop by holding her breath. She listens for the sound of something she thinks she heard beneath her sobbing.

The sky echoes with a deep rumbling. The steering wheel vibrates in her hands as the sound of thunder bellows from above. She looks out the back window and sees a massive shadow, the size of a stadium, covering the road and both sides of the desert behind her. The shadow and the rumbling are getting closer. Ally hits the side button on the door and her window goes down. She reaches out of the window and tilts the driver's side rear view mirror upward. In its reflection, she sees a cloud ten times the size of the last two, soaring upon her with its multi-layers rolling within each other. She floors the gas pedal. The cloud's shadow passes over her through the windshield, then moves over the hood of the car and continues along on the road and desert at her sides. She glances at the speedometer—one hundred and forty miles per hour. She leans forward and looks straight up through the windshield and sees the rolling underbelly of the cloud. A loud rumble rattles her eardrums and the car. She almost loses control of the wheel and continues to keep the gas pedal floored as the enormous cloud creates a giant vortex that twirls down toward the swerving car. Ally hears a loud vacuum sound and feels the front end of the car lift off the ground. She holds onto the steering wheel as the car tilts straight off the ground and disappears up into the vertical flow.

Ally is pressed against the seat, staring forward into the swirling mass as the vertical car spins in circles, up toward the cloud. As the twister shortens, the base of the cloud, where the vortex meets, starts to open wide. Even though Ally is being spun in circles, she can now see that she is being sucked into a gigantic mouth filled with hundreds of bluish white fangs as big as refrigerators. The giant fangs continuously roll within the flying predator's mouth, like grinding gears.

As the vortex shortens, bringing the car and Ally closer toward its massive, roving jaws, she panics, kicking hard with her feet and yanking on the seat adjuster at the same time. The backrest extends straight back and Ally soars out of the seat and through the car like a rocket. She crashes through the rear windshield and drops out of the shortened vortex as the car continues to spin upward. The enormous flying mammal abruptly turns at an angle, spins its vortex in the opposite direction and forcefully spits the car out. The sound of thunder crackles from its belly, loud enough to shake the tops of mountains in the distance.

Ally's arms and legs flail as she falls fifty feet above the desert. Her body spins around and she grasps at the air so desperately that she breaks all the nails on her left hand, digging them into her own palm. Despair and fear overwhelm her as she opens her mouth to scream. Nothing comes out as the air is sucked from her lungs. Clothes and flesh tear away as Ally gets sucked up into those massive churning teeth.

* * *

Nearly an hour later, while en route to Las Vegas, all six members of the Kirpatrick family will step out of their

RV and walk a short distance into the desert to investigate a strange sight: a vehicle that is sticking vertically out of the ground, like a big metal splinter. There will be no clues as to what happened to the vehicle's prior occupants and no answers as to how their car wound up nose-dived in the middle of nowhere.

Two things will prove to be fatal for all six members of the Kirpatrick family: The first will be that not one of them will realize the land around them has been picked clean—like meat off the bone. The last will be that only after it's too late, will all of them realize what lurks above the three large shadows that will make their way across the desert floor, circling closer until they get right over top of them.

CREEPERS
By Max Carrey

The frost traveled through the air in erratic motions, as if each flake of snow were a creature swimming along the wind, though they melted against the burly hide of Blue Beast, the old ice hauler work horse of Jack's, with flared nostrils and steady hooves. He'd earned his name when he was colt. A barn's roof had caved in under the massive weight of a heavy winter, and within reason he should have frozen to death, yet he was resolute and unwilling to die despite the gnaw of frost biting at him, turning him blue.

Jack was just about as weathered and as much a beast. His meaty hands were rough and calloused, and his ankles were covered in bloody blisters from tight boots to keep the cold from snapping off toes. On the bottom of his boots were metal plates with cleats, creepers, to better ensure that he would not slide all the way down the mountain.

He'd seen it before. The man was barely recognizable. A pile of snapped limbs like a ravaged tree with branches piled high for the fire.

No, there was no rushing the land, no pushing it against its will. Fearing too much weight upon an already heavy horse, he let Blue Beast pull the sled and the tools, and he carried their camping pack. Leading them along the rim of trees, they steadily climbed up the slope toward the mountain's crest, against the harsh unrelenting wind and several feet of snow.

They'd already done greater hauls at the lower level ponds, packing the icehouse for the town to use during the summer months. But this job was different as Jack was hired to retrieve several blocks of ice that were nestled nearly among the clouds. The pond at the mountain's top was purer water that his wealthy employer gave as prescription to his ailing wife.

Jack was the only man brave enough, and perhaps stupid enough, to take on such work, though he didn't do it for the money but for the land's sake, fearing that the man would become desperate enough to hire machines to rip through, grind down the mountainside and pollute the precious water beyond repair with their crude instruments.

He was in awe of nature, and it seemed befitting, as he looked somewhat like a grizzly bear, not just because one of his several coats was made of one, but from his hunch. Though he was delicate enough on his creepers, he lumbered about the woods like half a man. So the half-man half-bear and his horse trudged up the hill.

The air was thinner the higher they went, and the dry cold stung Jack's eyes. Flesh threatened to stick to flesh, and the wind whipped around so fiercely that the air trapped in his nostrils was bitter, sharp as a knife upon inhale. Blue Beast grunted against the bit in his mouth, working at it restlessly with his jaw.

As they neared the top, those last few feet were simply the earth and snow trying to envelope them in its freezing craggy embrace. The incline was so steep that their muscles strained against the innate downward pull.

But Jack and his horse did not succumb to it, for they dug in with their cleats and crested the mountain. They flung themselves onto the leveled ground, and gulped air back into their hollowed out chests.

The trees up there seemed to whisper amongst themselves, as the chill whistled through their frozen branches. Shards of ice hung suspended on everything it possibly could, and the freshly fallen snow dusted the ground soft as a cloud, although the pond out in the clearing was firm enough to have the stark, bluish tint of the sky reflected off it.

Jack unpacked his tools and left Blue Beast to wander as he pleased, for he never trotted off far. Then he anxiously approached the wide expanse of ice, kneeled down and placed his gloved hand atop the cool slab. He imagined he could feel the rushing water beneath it and the life that still stirred somewhere within, though not even a faint vibration could be felt.

Twisting his auger to drill a hole into the unblemished chunk of ice felt almost cruel. He would do his best to keep the precious land unscathed as much as he could, as it had a lonesome beauty all its own, but he had a job to do. So after several holes were drilled and the measurements compared, he had found the best places for harvesting and planned to take three blocks, all of even cut to keep the sled balanced.

Slowly he planted his creepers into the ice and mentally prepared himself for the sawing, as it was like no other exertion to be had. After he'd inhaled and exhaled a satisfactory breath he began.

The pond saw ate away at it, as shards of ice sprang from the fearsome metal teeth, and once Jack established his momentum he picked up the pace. He would pull the saw almost completely out of the ice then plunge it all the way down, heaving with all his weight, until the handles hit and his knuckles along with it. Cracking, maybe the ice, maybe his bones, it didn't matter, for the job would be done.

His brow was wind-whipped dry and his lungs emptied, for as soon as he had cut around all three blocks he collapsed against Blue Beast to catch a weary breath. But a strange sensation hit him as his senses picked up on something he couldn't place his finger on. Something was different than all the other times before; he could feel it.

The dying sun had already arched over them, and was beginning its slow decent downward. He listened carefully to the howling gusts, and caught a hint of a noise that carried along the air, an echoing weep. It quickly grew, startling Blue Beast, who leapt up whinnying and began to pace nervously. Jack tried to calm him by stroking the bridge between his eyes, but Blue Beast could sense the fear that crept through his master and continued to neigh and kick up the ground.

Jack searched the fields with his eyes, but saw nothing and began to panic, for the wail was one of gnawing persistent pain, undoubtedly animalistic, as it also resounded like a predator letting the new game know it was *his* territory.

Jack's breath knotted in his chest, held in anticipation, and his spine tensed straighter, making him appear much more human than half-man half-bear. He was simply a man, vulnerable to the raw power of nature and all its children.

The weeping stopped suddenly, though Jack's anxieties continued to bloom. As much as there was a curious longing to see what'd made the sound, something told him he didn't want to know.

He tied Blue Beast to a tree, fearing for the first time that his horse would try to run away. But they had encountered the wild before, and there was no point in leaving only to have to return again later, so he decided to grab the ice and depart as quickly as possible.

Damning himself for his stubborn ways and refusal to surrender, he pulled his handmade contraption from his tool bag and hurried to the pond. It was a long iron tube that he sent through the hole the auger had made, and upon releasing the latch the inner hooks came out and dug into the bottom of the ice, grabbing onto it firmly.

Jack readied the rope that he would tie to Blue Beast, who would then haul the ice out, but the wind kicked up abruptly, roaring and violently ripping through the land. The stiffened trees began to sway, and their icicles to crack.

Jack dodged a falling spear of ice, and it shattered beside him. Blue Beast whinnied and pulled on his restraints so severely the rope cut against his hide. His hooves kicked out into the air, his eyes bulged from their sockets and foam flung from his mouth. Icicles fell, coming dangerously close to puncturing him.

Unable to watch his faithful companion be killed or exhaust himself to death trying to be freed, he rushed forward to help. Reaching Blue Beast he threw caution aside, but was gravely mistaken, for a hoof caught against his ribs. His body crunched and he staggered to the ground. An additional heartbeat of pain sprung to life in his throbbing chest.

Blue Beast cried against the strain of the ropes; every fiber was stretched to its limit, yet it wouldn't give. Blood trickled from his muzzle, which surged Jack forward and, taking his knife, he frantically sawed until the rope was cut. It lashed through the air as Blue Beast became a darkened streak among the flood of white, galloping over the mountain's edge, and then suddenly gone.

Retching, he cast himself down in defeat. The knot of pain stuck like an invisible knife in his side, and everything he did tweaked. The ground began to shake underneath him, at first with a slight tremble, but swiftly it turned violent. The fearsome wind blustered the snow, and it began to shift.

Jack sought cover beneath a tree. His fingers dug into the rough bark, and he bore down on his creepers desperately as the ground started to slide out from under him. Like a wave the earth tumbled and crashed, an avalanche spilling over.

Once the rumbling had slowed back to a quiver, he tore himself from his spot to look down the mountain. A lonesome panic cascaded throughout his body, relieving him of any warmth he had left. He was as cold on the inside as he was out, with that dry stinging chill. The air tasted sour on his tongue, though he gulped it down frantically. He was alone. The avalanche blocked his descent.

He stirred suddenly, ripping through his supplies, busily making plans while he waited for the passage to clear. He only had two days' worth of food and a mixture of half-hay and half-chaff for Blue Beast. Jack hung his head low, for if he'd only listened to that old horse perhaps he'd be beyond the avalanche too, but at least Blue Beast was safe. Jack wished he had pulled out the chunks of ice from the pond before leaving him all alone, because maybe then he could've had fish to eat.

His gaze flitted around the ice-shattered forest atop the mountain, at the quiet pond, within the heights of the skies that were beginning to darken, and found no animal. When the avalanche had blasted through the land, no other creature stirred or sounded in the air. Yet surely *something* was there, for its pain-filled howl had come before the snow shifted. It was as if its cry had signaled the wind, and Jack was beginning to wonder if the *thing*, whatever it was, had trigged the avalanche. What a powerful beast it must be, though he didn't have time to think much on it, for night was coming swiftly.

There was no use in trying to light a fire, as the wind would put it out, so he focused his attentions on securing his food by tying it head height onto a tree, just in case there were scrounging animals nearby that he wasn't aware of. Then he tied down the sled and laid upon it, covering himself completely with his bearskin jacket, and hoped for sleep to come quickly as he didn't trust the darkness, especially if he was to be alone in it.

The tranquility and quiet had left nature, making way for the raw respect of its formidable power. All within a moment everything had changed. Suddenly it was a prison, of one.

Jack tried to ignore the gnawing ache of his side, where Blue Beast's hoof was imprinted in purple and green bruises. He tried to muffle the wind by plugging his ears, yet he still heard it whispering, and after many long hours of it, he believed it was mocking him. Sweat beaded down his brow, mixing in with the tears he tried to fight off. He had not slept for even a moment.

Night came, the temperature dropped even lower, and shadows dispersed themselves over everything. He was huddled upon his sled, holding his knees to his chest, as his eyes whipped around maddeningly. The trees looked like monster's teeth against the blackened sky. The natural hum of the earth pulsed, and he felt it weighing down upon him, and his tired mind imagined sinking into the snow and being swallowed up by it.

Time ticked on slowly, painfully slow. Darkness shrouded the land so thickly it obscured even the stars above. Jack felt detached from the rest of the world, and was as helpless as an abandoned baby. He shivered and looked for the eyes he felt staring at him, but believed it was just the darkness licking at his senses, playing tricks on him, and teasing him for his fear.

He clenched his eyes shut, determined to not let his mind slip down the mountain to join the avalanche below. A puff of hot breath grazed against the nape of his neck, but he remained steadfast, refusing to be toyed with. For there was nothing there, he was sure of it.

The pain in his ribs, though great, had subsided somewhat to make way for a numbing. But his veins pulsed with a strange new rhythm, as if trying to speak to him. *Those* eyes, it said about the ones he could not find, *those eyes*. Soon it lulled him into an expected pace that drifted him off to sleep.

Starting awake he immediately flustered to take in the sights around him, panting nervously. He found it morning; the wind had left, and all was still, though he was still alone as well.

His joints were stiff and he groaned against them. Unfurling, he stood and stretched his sore body. His churning stomach sung with the tenderness of a broken ribcage and gnawing hunger. Looking to his food pack he gasped, for it was ripped open and emptied of its contents. Massive slashes were dug into the tree he'd tied it to, and upon studying them, he realized they had been done by the sharp claws of some kind of animal, although they looked like no other markings he'd ever seen before.

Squeezing his fists together until his fingers cracked, he screamed from deep within his belly. He'd always thought the land would provide, that it would take care of him, if only he respected it, but there was something cursed about the top of that mountain and he wholeheartedly believed that he'd caught it.

Left with only his tools, he took his saw and hacked angrily at one of the trees, gashing into its trunk to peel away the bark. He scrounged the fallen pieces and hungrily put them to his mouth. They were difficult to chew, bitter and sourly fragrant. He forced himself to eat, digging his teeth into the inner flesh of the bark, trying to tear at its meat, desperate to satiate his hunger.

He scrapped fragments of ice from the pond to melt upon his tongue. He wouldn't die, he refused…but s*omething* was here with him and it was watching him unravel. *It* was real, and not the imaginations of a stressed mind. So he took up his pond saw and entered the trees, looking for answers.

His footsteps were surprisingly awkward, as if he weren't used to traversing the wild mountains. Yet for the first time in a long time, perhaps in his whole life, he was completely out of his depth. Something strange and unexplainable was happening. The air was unnaturally still, even the trees held their whispering as he walked among their branches.

The freshly fallen snow concealed any tracks, and so the clawed thief must have ravaged his supplies during the night. He damned his soul, for he'd known to keep wary of the darkness. But as his thoughts drifted to the swelling blackness from before, the more his veins itched within his flesh, and it only heightened the belief that all was not as it seemed on top of the mountain. Surely, something was different. Something had made its way there, and was slowly revealing itself to him.

Jack's breathing was ragged, puffing out white smoke as his lungs tightened into a knot the further into the woods he went. His wandering eyes never alighted upon a single clue or hint of life outside of himself. It was beyond abnormal; it was grotesquely unnatural.

Once he'd made it to the other side of the mountain he found that the avalanche encased its entirety. He was completely trapped, and it caused his heart to fall lower in his chest. But he quickly went rigid with the snapping of twigs.

Twisting about, Jack frantically searched for what had made the noise, but saw nothing. Screaming and crying, he burst out in a blustery array of emotions that replaced the violence of the wind that had left him in silence.

The sky was darkening again, as he'd spent practically the whole day searching for a way out that didn't exist, and for an animal that he couldn't find, because it didn't want to be found. It was wickedly playing with him, he was sure of it. Its wailing hadn't triggered the avalanche; it had commanded it. This *thing*, was evil... he could sense the surety of it vibrating in his bones.

Trying to ignore the surging stabs of pain shooting through his body he turned and ran. The blurring sight of trees, snow, and ice disoriented him, yet he pushed on, stumbling over his exhausted feet. He tried to outrun the oncoming darkness, even as it began to lick at his heels.

His nostrils flared like an animal's, his body burned with the over intake of air, which sent mind imagined stars to explode in his vision. He could feel the eyes on him once more, as the sensation was stronger in the dark, and it urged him onward.

Jack burst through the line of trees out into the clearing. His creepers slipped on the pond, he fell forward, and cracked his skull against the ice. Then he was completely enveloped in the swirling blackness, as his blood trickled down his forehead to stain the pure cool white beneath him.

He was prone and vulnerable, twitching every now and again in a shudder of pain. The mountain and the trees rustled about him, and those eyes watched him patiently.

Days later his spirit reentered his body, stirring him from his sleepless slumber, Jack curled his stiffened limbs into himself. The frost burned, bit, and numbed his flaking flesh, and he began sobbing, crying out against the aching throb that beat against his skull.

He was still alone, seemingly enough.

Desperate to rid himself of thirst, he began to frantically lick at the pond, though his tongue stuck and ripped in places where his drying saliva hadn't wetted the ice enough. He gnawed at the bark, but it turned to acid in his stomach and he vomited, unable to keep it down. So his belly stayed empty, as he grew hungrier.

Jack trembled within the soggy layers of clothing, fiddled nervously with his tools to keep the blood flowing in his fingers, and waited, holding out for a single hope to appear.

Night crept upon him, and his terror-filled screams rang in the air, as no salvation came. Again and again and again, it repeated, as he lingered on. Though his legs could no longer carry him to the edge of the mountain, he knew somewhere deep inside that a passage had not opened and the avalanche stood firm.

The unseen eyes that belonged to the wailing howl he'd heard on his first day there continued to haunt him. At first he snarled and snapped at it like a cornered dog, but surprisingly the need to keep the undetected evil at bay began to disappear. He no longer cared if its eyes were on him. It was such an engrained feeling that it became a part of his being, something to be expected, and strangely, wildly, he depended upon it. Suddenly at night he prayed to it, to release him of his woes, yet it did not listen. It simply kept watch and waited, and Jack dutifully did as well.

Even more time passed, and the trees were scraped bare of their bark for food that didn't settle and were spat up mounds. It lacked the succulence of meat, and the tear of juicy flesh that his belly craved. He ran his scaled tongue across the ridges of his teeth, and even began to bite down upon it, though it did not taste of the sweetness he longed for.

Dips and long strips of ice were dug out of the precious pond for drinking, and Jack could be sure that no special healing properties were contained in it, for it gave him no extra strength and did nothing to heal him. It wouldn't save his employer's wife, and it wouldn't save him. It would hold him for as long as it could, but it wouldn't last much longer.

His wounds seeped, and his flesh had sunken in

around his ribs. A yellow tint clouded his once-whitened eyes. Ice clung to him, blistering his ashen skin. A couple of his teeth were scattered upon the ground at his feet, broken by all the bark, by the harsh gnashing and grinding of his jaw.

He was gaunt, fading away into nothing, lonely, up on top of that mountain. But really it was the *thing* that ate away at his mind that took the greatest toll on him. Jack was barely recognizable as a man, or a bear, or a being made of frost. He was something else entirely.

The wind that had fled, so many days ago, suddenly began to creep back into existence. It pushed away the stillness, and suffocated the silence. The trees whispered once more, keeping their voices hushed enough so that he couldn't make out their words, but he guessed they spoke of the eyes. Whatever creature those eyes belonged to, for he ruled the mountain now. He commanded it over nature itself.

Snapping twigs in the distance did nothing to spook old Jack. He was used to finding no culprit among the sounds. So he sat, as exhausting as that was, and inhaled the wind, wishing he could sap its power and take it for his own.

Something was carried along the air. It was slight at first, barely noticeable, but once the gust picked up pace it blustered past him, filling his nostrils. It was a smell he'd never experienced before. It was familiar, but so vibrant that what came with it were all new sensations. He could smell a cold sweaty tang drying among the snow, and it touched his nerves, causing his fingertips to alight with pressure as if he were grazing his hands along a heaving body. He could hear the diminishing pulse of a heartbeat, practically see the frostbitten man to whom it belonged, and taste his sweetness.

Jack's muscles awakened and he roared as an unnatural vigor consumed him, for the hunger he felt was too overwhelming to ignore. He was Jack no longer.

Though his slight frame appeared weak, he stood without hindrance and rolled his joints to loosen them. His bones cracked, and the wounded ice of the pond did as well as he dug in his creepers, springing off with animalistic agility.

He weaved through the trees with blurring swiftness and plunged down the side of the mountain, trailing the scent of meat. Gliding along with ease he came to the base of the blocked passage, raised his nose to sniff at the air, then let the wind lead him the rest of the way.

Among the scattered piles of rustled up earth laid a man, so bitten from the frost he was practically blue, though underneath he still ran warm with blood. His leg was broken, a hunting rifle was held within his grip, and a finger rested upon the trigger.

The trapped hunter's eyes were wide with fear, for although what stood before him looked somewhat like a man, this man no longer had any humanistic trait left in the way he carried himself.

He was not there to help the hunter, and the hunter knew it.

He licked his lips, and a toothy smile spread across his ashen face as he flung himself forward.

The hunter yanked his rifle up. A shot fired, yet it only hit the air.

Teeth tore out a throat that gurgled helpless cries as still-living flesh was swallowed down an eager gullet.

* * *

It was many weeks before a search party could properly break through the avalanche, for it was a perfect ring of ice around the entire length of the mountain. All the snow that had cascaded down piled itself into a wall that froze solid, and it was nothing like anyone in the town had ever seen or heard of before. But the harsh winter was beginning to thaw and so they were finally able to chip enough of it away to make a passage.

They had known something suspicious was afoot with Jack the ice hauler, for the wealthy man who'd hired him came to report him for stealing his money without providing what he'd paid for. Yet when Jack's legend of a horse, Blue Beast, came trotting into town, somehow still alive though he appeared half-dead, he was then reported missing.

The search party traversed the land with difficulty, even though it was much easier ground than back when Jack had first encountered it, but they were not accustomed to climbing such an unforgiving incline. However, after a two days' journey they made it to the top, though what greeted them when they got there was anything but a victory.

Human bones were snapped and scattered among the gleaming, stark white snow, with no remaining muscle, tissue, or single droplet of dried blood left on them. Even the marrow was drained clean.

Giant clawed slashes were dug into the ice and the men, who were sickened and spewing their guts, figured that some sort of evil beast had torn the ice hauler to pieces.

They hadn't known about a lost hunter, for if they had, perhaps they would have tried better to identify the bones. Maybe collect them and rearrange them into a skeleton. See if it had the hunch that so many people spoke of that made Jack look like half a bear. But even if they wished it, they had no time for anything other than fear, for the feeling of eyes upon them sliced through the wind to burrow into their flesh.

A painful wailing howl echoed in the air, natural but somehow also unnatural, and it startled them. The search party stammered and stumbled about, yet their terror only increased as another painful hungry wail joined the other to travel along the length of the wind.

BLACK SKY
By Carlton Herzog

Keenly and closely, we watched you and drew our plans against you. The way you might study the transient creatures in a drop of water. You dismissed the idea that any other creatures possessed an intellect as cool and cruel as your own. Now your blood is our wine, your eyeballs our *hors d'oeuvres*, your hearts our meat, your mucus our limpid gravy. So much sweeter than mice and worms.

Before my glorious resurrection, I had no such appetites. I existed as a pair of watery eyes suspended below droopy lids. I was filthy. Scabs and sores scaled my skin. Bugs licked my greasy sides. Crabs ran up and down my scrotum. Warts proliferated on my anus. The plump portions of my rump were squashed flat from sitting. A life of Metamucil, a few drops of piss, and pencil-long toenails.

I was a rotting carcass with carious teeth, shackled to a wheelchair, and waiting to die. Mine was a philosophy of decomposition built on three of the four pillars of wisdom: life is suffering, human existence is absurd, and the nothingness before my birth is equal to that after my death.

To dwell on such negatives would have only compounded my despair. So, I practiced the fourth pillar of wisdom: distraction from the other three. Every day, I would dutifully climb into my squeaky wheelchair and make the trek from bed to window—a task, for me at least, as treacherous as Herzog's climb of Annapurna. There I would, binoculars in hand, survey my tiny rectilinear universe to its limits, reprising Jimmy Stewart's role in Hitchcock's *Rear Window*.

One might conclude that an apartment complex courtyard and the windows of same would offer meager entertainment. After all, this was Japan, and we Japanese are uniformly polite, calm, and shy people. But the place had a gloomy atmosphere of breathless and unexplainable dread made manifest by the madness of its residents.

It was if an all-moving darkness with no substance of its own moved people to grisly acts of violence. Over the years, one man bashed his wife's brains in with a showerhead; a woman threw gasoline on her husband and then ignited him with a road flare; another woman dismembered her husband with his own samurai sword and strew the parts in the courtyard; a Shinto monk stood outside the gate and stabbed passersby in the eyes and throat. A young boy beat his father unconscious with a baseball bat, slit his throat with a straight razor, and unceremoniously chopped off his head with an axe; a young girl who aspired to be a cosmetic surgeon poisoned her parents, then cut off their faces.

Yet, the complex rarely had vacancies. Government subsidized housing seldom does. Existing at the bottom of the food chain, the poor are compelled to live in places that more well to do people would avoid like the plague.

Despite its notoriety, the complex was home to any number of seemingly benign activities. The most notable were those of *Garusukouto Nippon Renmei*. Led by Ahmya Serazawa, the troupe would march, practice martial arts, and recite their loyalty oath and sing. On special occasions, they would dress as *Tengu*—the Heavenly Sentinels. That entailed a red-faced mask with a prominent nose, red robes, and a feathered fan. I learned that the *Tengu* were minor demons—half bird, half human—in service to Makkuru, Lord of the Sky.

At first, the girl scouts infused a much-needed vitality to the place. Take, for example, their ritual feeding of the crows with nuts, fruit, bread, and cake. The practice grew out of Ahmya's antics as a clumsy four-year-old who was prone to drop food in the yard. Her maladroit hands always fumbled whatever she handled, be it candy, nuts, chicken nuggets, or sandwiches. When she did, the crows would swoop in to recover it. Day after day, they would perch on the phone lines and wait for her. As she got older, she graduated from accidental to deliberate largesse, going out of her way to feed them on a regular basis. This led to their penchant for gift giving—miniature silver balls, black buttons, blue paper clips, red Legos—in short, anything shiny that could fit in their mouths. Trinkets male crows would bestow on their mates.

To an able-bodied person, the daily repetition of those activities would be mind numbing. Not so for me, the caged and toothless bird. I longed to be free of my apartment, my body, and even my humanity. I wanted to be a crow, tracing parabolas below the billowing clouds and hearing the semaphore of other wing beats echoing on the wind.

But those were more innocent times. In the weeks that followed, they changed their brand from its iconic green and khaki uniforms to something more sinister. Now they wore black uniforms and matching black sashes and berets. They called themselves *Karasu No Jungo* (Order of the Crows). They could have passed for Latter Day Hitler Youth. Or something more insidious, for instead of Nazi propaganda, the girls, black buckets in hand, would throw bits of raw meat to the assembled horde.

One day, the murder of crows dropped from the sky and alighted in a circle around the girls. I watched the tableau below me with horrified fascination. Aside from the gothic visuals, I could hear the girls talking to the crows. I distinctly heard them answer in the high-pitched rasp of crow vocal mimetics. Only these weren't mimetics. They sounded like the rehearsed call and answer of a church service, or in this case, an Avian Black Mass.

The words were not modern Japanese. Nor its lineal antecedents, such as *Yamato Kotoba* or *Kano*. They had a primordial, inhuman meaning known only by those imps in black and their corvid congregation. Eldritch words invoking eldritch forces antagonistic to all things human, perhaps.

The linguistic oddities were mirrored and multiplied by the physical ones. There seemed to be an overlap in the facial structure of the two distinct species. For their part, all the girls—including the exchange students from Norway and Sweden—had black hair. Coincidence perhaps, I thought, or a conscious decision to dye their hair for congruity. Much like the ubiquitous, long black fingernails I could see. Fingernails that had more in common with claws than hands.

But it was their faces that made me shudder. I could swear that their canines were enlarged nearly to the point of fangs. More than that, their noses had the curvilinear sharpness and sheen of a corvid beak. Their eyes seemed to have no whites. Dark abysses in predatory faces.

Likewise, the crows had necks and jaw lines consistent with the ability to chew. Whenever the crows opened wide to catch a chunk of flesh, I could see teeth and protruding fangs. These were not mere crows, but *karasu no monsuta*. Monster crows.

Once the feeding was over, Ahmya gave the benediction. After that, her land and air battalions dispersed—the girls to their respective homes, the crows to their nests. From there, Ahmya, who lived in the apartment below me, came to visit. She sported a black beret atop thick black curls fashioned into ringlets. Handmade merit badges on her sash ran the gamut from *Tokubetsu Dairinin* to *Heddo Curo*. Special Agent to Top Crow, respectively.

She opened her little black pouch to show me her latest acquisitions. This time around, her gift-giving crows had bestowed on her a pearl-colored heart and a tiny piece of metal with the word *Besuto* engraved on it.

Normally, these visits, at the behest of Ahmya's sympathetic mother, lifted my spirits. They told me that I was still a person to be valued and loved in some small way, despite my unappealing condition. This time, however, I felt as if tentacles longer than the night itself were slowly and inexorably wrapping themselves around me. A feeling made more pronounced by our ensuing discussion.

As she showed me another gift—a metal screw—she asked, "Did you know that my crows have teeth? They look like the kind I have seen in pictures."

"What kind of pictures?"

"You know, pictures of sharks. The ones where the teeth look like rows of pointy triangles. If they wanted, they could chew me up just like that."

She gave her fingers a loud snap and continued, "But they won't because they said I and the other girls are honorary members of their murder. A murder of crows. They love me and I love them. One time, Mrs. Kempo was yelling at me because some garbage fell out of the bag when I took it to the curb. The crows dive-bombed her. Scratched and bit her. Nobody believed the crows bit her. But I saw it with my own eyes. That was when their teeth were smaller. But they have gotten bigger just like mine—see? I'm a vampire now."

I looked at her wide-open mouth. She had a double row of jagged teeth complemented by two incipient fangs. Her nose had the same hard curvilinear arc as a crow's beak. I said nothing but knew beyond a shadow of a doubt that I had traveled far from any road without leaving my small apartment.

After she left, I used my landline to call my old friend, a prominent ornithologist and professor of Wildlife Science at Tokyo University, Ito Uzumaki. I gave Uzumaki a detailed description of the physical changes to the girls and the crows, as well as the bizarre interactions between the two.

Professor Uzumaki, largely skeptical of my claims, nonetheless, acted as if they were plausible.

"During my undergraduate days, I studied the Cretaceous era fossil record of the toothed songbird *sulcavis geeorum.* Its teeth had serrated edges suitable for cracking open hard exoskeletons of insects, crabs, and snails.

"Although *sulcavis* provided the only physical evidence of toothed birds, the historical records of Europe mention them with disturbing frequency. In 1714, the Romanian historian, Tzvetan Todorov, in his *Diable Corvus*, described an attack by toothed crows on a remote human settlement after the inhabitants had destroyed the crows' nests. According to Todorov, the mob of enraged crows descended on the village and tore pieces of flesh off children, presumably in retaliation for the murder of the hatchlings in the nest.

"Some of the crows had more than mere teeth. Fangs were also part of their arsenal, fangs that were used in a vampiric fashion to drink the blood of their victims.

Todorov's monograph contains a sketch of one crow brought down by an arrow. It had a larger than normal beak, punctuated by two down turned fangs in the front, as well as an oversized mandible containing two rows of sharp serrated teeth."

The story, as well as the physical description of the crows' dentition, bore a striking similarity to other stories from Russia, Norway, and Germany. In every instance, the human population felt threatened by the crows and attempted to exterminate them. That opened a Pandora's box of trouble, for the crows found ways to make life miserable for their attackers. They would befoul the water supply. They would murder cattle, cats, dogs, pigs, and poultry. They would carry off tools and clothes. In the dead of night, they would assemble on rooftops and caw for hours.

"So, you believe me?"

"Without hard evidence, I can't do that. Take a picture and send it to me and we'll go from there."

"What about all that stuff that happened in Europe?"

"It's all anecdotal, unsupported by evidence. Get real. Those stories smack of legends and tall tales."

"I think these crows might be dangerous."

"Then call *Karaspatororu* (Crow Patrol). The people there are trained to deal with the urban nuisance of crows."

"You think I'm crazy, don't you?"

"I think it's possible that your disability and confinement make you see things that aren't there. That's not insanity; it's just that you're bored, and your mind has sprouted wings and taken flight as compensation for what your body cannot do. Or what you say is true, and the seemingly exotic events are controlled by laws unknown to us. Whatever the case, once Crow Patrol gets rid of the crows, you'll sleep better."

I considered his words. I decided that I would do

some more observing before I alerted animal control. After all, Ito could be right: my confinement could be causing delusions and hallucinations.

A few days later, a stray pit bull wandered into the courtyard. I had never seen him before. At the time, Ahmya was tending to her mother's flowers while the crows kept a watchful eye from the ledges and phone lines. The pit ambled toward her.

Ahmya saw him. She did not seem troubled, even though his hackles were up as he came toward her. She began talking to him. And what she said sent a chill up my spine: "Well, you're just in time for dinner. And as luck would have it, you're the main course."

The pit bull, perhaps sensing something wicked was coming his way, began to growl and snarl at her. Still, Ahmya didn't move a muscle but smiled at him and spoke in that arcane language she had used with the crows.

Then he charged her. Before he reached her, the crows launched from the ledges like ballistic missiles, beaks first, and impaled the pit bull, covering him in a sea of black feathers. More crows followed in a coordinated assault. Every now and then, a few crows would fly off with bits of dog, chewing the bloody morsels as they flapped away.

The real horror of the moment came when several crows flew over to Ahmya and dropped bits of dog meat before her. She reached down, picked them up, and then popped them into her mouth, lustily chewing and savoring the stringy, bloody bits.

The crows picked the dog's carcass clean of flesh. Others, with a taste for bones, set to work gnawing on femurs and ribs.

As for Ahmya, she finished her snack and then returned to tending the garden as if nothing untoward had happened.

When my visiting nurse, Emiko, arrived the next day,

I asked if she had seen the pile of dog bones in the courtyard. She said that she not. I had her wheel me to the window. Sure enough, the bones were gone.

That spooked me. Did the crows dispose of the massacre's evidence? Or did a neighbor decide to remove the chewed up remains? I wasn't going to wait for an answer. I called Crow Patrol and explained the situation about the crows. I punctuated the urgency of the matter by asking, "If they can tear a pit bull to pieces what might they do to a person?"

Shago Saito came out the next day. He had once been a promising PHD candidate in Tokyo University's Evolutionary Biology program. But a drinking problem had proved his undoing. So, for now at least, he functioned as Takayama Province's Crow Patrol.

When he reached the Hekkido Apartments, he inspected the grounds. He took note of the things that would attract crows and other wildlife to that area. Then he went up to my apartment for a statement.

Agitated and frightened, I said, "I tell you those crows have teeth, and they ate that pit bull right down to the bone. That's not all. The little gang of freaks that used to be Girl Scouts now worship those crows and feed them meat. And I even saw one eat raw dog meat. What kind of weird pagan shit is this?"

Shago smiled. "I'm not surprised. This is not the first report of a crow attack or crows with teeth. All birds have the genes for teeth, but normally those genes lie dormant. As for the kids, I have seen worse. This current generation goes out of its way to find itself. Have you ever seen a Nipponese cyber-punk? Talk about fucked up, what with those plastic tube hair extensions. Apparently, the weirder the better."

"Okay. But why are those genes suddenly turning on now?"

"Calm down. Crows are a syanthropic species. Like

rats and cockroaches, they have adapted themselves to human ecology. If I'm a crow, then living near humans offers many advantages as opposed to life in the wild. There's a ready supply of food in the form of garbage. The area is well lit so I can see owls that would otherwise sneak up on me. And it's warmer."

"Right—but why teeth?"

"Have you ever heard of the Red Queen Hypothesis? It holds that competing species are locked in an evolutionary arms race. So, each side must run faster and faster just to maintain the status quo. Humans and crows are competing for the same space. But humans don't want peaceful co-existence with crows; they want to exterminate them. So, to maintain the equilibrium, crows are evolving better weapons. Everything you have described—teeth, fangs, their own language and not just mimicry, human familiars, larger size—is all consistent with that hypothesis."

"And talking crows?"

"Crows are the smartest birds in town. Crow brain size in relation to body size is better than that of primates, like chimpanzees and gorillas. Think of them as smart feathered apes. They have over 250 distinct crow calls, and at least two dialects, one for family and one for the collective. Crows use and make tools. They make tools to get other tools to get food.

"What are you going to about those chatty birds?"

"I'm going to install a scare horn. Since you're home all the time, I'm going to give you a remote activator. Whenever the crows congregate, you click it. The bullhorn will sound, and the crows will scatter. After a while, they'll get the message and find another place to roost. I'm going to do the set-up and then speak to the complex manager."

"Sounds good to me."

"And if Tippi Hedren and Rod Taylor show, then head

for the hills."

I gave him a bewildered look.

"Alfred Hitchcock. *The Birds.* Inexplicable avian apocalypse. Forget it. After I have installed the acoustical scarecrow, wait for them to gather, then give them a blast on the bullhorn."

Shago left the apartment. He went to the center of the courtyard and installed the bullhorn. I heard a curious, and somewhat devious, Ahmya confront him.

"Whatcha doin'?"

"I'm setting up an acoustical scarecrow. My job is to make the crows go away. The man in the wheelchair is going to help me do that."

"The crows aren't going to like that. This is their kingdom."

"Honey, I don't care what they like or don't like. They're just birds. This is a place for people."

"Okay, if that's how you want it."

"Don't get cute with me. Run along, I've got work to do."

The next day I woke to the smell of feathers. I turned and saw crows on my nightstand, my dresser, and my wheelchair. From my vantage point, I could see that my only window was still closed.

A crow flew over with the clicker and landed next to me on the bed. It dropped it onto the sheet. Then clear as a bell, it said, "No."

That "No" was multiplied a hundredfold as the crows filling my apartment echoed that curt sentiment in a chorus of scolding "Nos." I pulled the covers up over my head. I was terrified at what the crows might do.

But after a time, silence fell over the apartment. I peered out from under the blankets to see that all the crows were gone. The clicker itself had been shattered into pieces that lay on the floor.

I asked myself, *How did they get into the apartment?*

I considered that Ahmya might have let them in since she knew the spare key was under the mat.

I watched Shago show up a few days later. He was doing a follow up to see if the acoustical scarecrow had functioned as he had promised. He was surprised to see all the crows congregating in the complex. He inspected the bullhorn then manually activated it. All the crows took flight but instead of leaving the complex they flew in great dark circle around the complex and then, without warning, spiraled down in a vortex of black feathers straight at Shago. Within minutes, nothing was left to say he had been there, save his truck parked in front.

I was flabbergasted. I was afraid. So much so I called no one.

Over the next few weeks, Ahmya and her girls held their Black Mass in the courtyard. Each time, the congregation looked a bit different. Specifically, the girls looked more like crows, and the crows looked more like people.

Having consulted with her avian protectors, she decided to pay me a visit.

"Kenzo, you are doing the right thing by not helping the humans. You will be rewarded for that."

"You speak of humans as if they were a different species. Like you're not one of us."

"I am a *Tengu*—a Heavenly Sentinel: part bird, part human. And soon the human part of me will be gone, as it will for the rest of my girls."

"How is that possible and why?"

"The Elder Gods have stood by long enough. Man's time is over. Why? Because his chemicals killed the bugs that birds rely on for food, and in doing so created an apocalypse for us. The Elders decided to step in and give this world over to its rightful rulers: the birds, who are the direct lineal descendants of the dinosaurs."

"And why shouldn't they? The birds outnumber man

ten to one. They rule the air. Soon they will rule your cities. We will foul your water, ruin your crops, clog your cooling towers, crash your planes, smash your windshields, and devour your cattle and children. Without your factory-farmed food and machines, you will be reduced to throwing sticks and living in caves."

I stared as she opened her mouth wider than I thought possible for a human. Her teeth glistened with the sheen and sharpness of steel, as did the two menacing fangs that protruded on either side of those buzzsaw-like teeth.

"I am a cripple. I have harmed no one. But if you must kill me, then I ask only that you make it as quick and painless as possible, for I have been tormented enough these many years. Death would be a welcome release from a life of physical and mental torture."

"Brother, you must be patient and trust me. No harm will come to you. To the contrary, you have always been our friend. Be at peace and wait for your moment. It comes."

As time passed, the local news began reporting the disappearances of children and pets. At the same time, the crow ranks swelled in the province. With Shago missing, the Takayama province elders took extreme measures. They enlisted the aid of the *Kuro Tako No'On Nanodo* (Black Kite Girls). So named after the black kite raptors they handled.

Although the Black Kites had adopted falconry as a purely intramural activity, they refined it to such a high degree that they were routinely called in to eliminate various urban squatters such as crows and rats as well as wild cats and dogs.

Like the Order of the Crow, the Black Kites regarded their wards as sacred creatures and their own mission divine. As such, they approached falconry with the same lethal efficiency of a military hit squad, going so far as to train themselves in the combat arts.

When they discovered that their birds had grown teeth, and in some instances, bookended them with prodigious fangs, the Black Kite's zeal for their work grew geometrically. But unlike their corvid counterparts, their agenda was fundamentally pro-human.

On the day when the Black Kites were to make their debut at the complex, I was sitting at the window watching the daily ritual. Although I was afraid of both the crows and the girls, I was also compelled by a morbid fascination to continue observing them. After all, there was nothing else to get my mind off the constant pain. So, why not break macabre and be a ghoul if only from a distance?

This day I would not be disappointed by the high and bloody theater that would unfold before my two rheumy eyes. The Black Kites, ferried to the apartment complex by the local police, gathered at the fence. Inside, they could see Ahmya and her congregation gathered for another Black Mass. What they didn't see was the thousands of crows that had followed their caravan from City Hall. Hundreds circled above, while hundreds more settled on perches near the complex.

There was an eerie silence to the ambush. Normally, crows let fly with scolding caws when a predator approaches them. This time they remained still, the only movement being that of their following black eyes, eyes that numbered in the thousands as the murder became a multitude. The stage was set for wholesale massacre.

The self-assured Black Kites strode into the courtyard with their hooded birds. Neither they nor the officials with them believed that any outcome was possible, save the extermination of the crows before them.

Halfway into the courtyard, the Black Kites released their birds. When they did, two things happened: First, the crows attacked, dragging the hapless falcons to the ground, and tearing them apart. Second, the girls from the

Order of the Crows charged the Black Kites.

I expected it to be an exchange of kicks, hair pulling, scratching and spitting. Instead, I watched as the Crow Girls clawed off the skin of their enemy, then sank their fangs into carotid arteries. Blood sprayed in all directions, accompanied by loud screams.

The Crow Girls didn't simply murder the Kites. They drank their blood and ate their flesh. And did so with the rapacious gusto of any jungle predator following a kill. Such was their bloodthirsty nature and the razor-sharp efficiency of their new teeth.

The stunned police and Crow Patrol tried to intervene but were waylaid by squadrons of bloodthirsty crows. As the crows had done with the pit bull and later Shago, they tore the city officials apart and ate them down to the bone. By the time it was all over, the only living things in the courtyard were the crows and the Crow Girls. Everything else had been torn apart and eaten. Now all that remained was for the crows to gnaw down the bone remnants.

Over the next few days, I began my own metamorphosis. My MS symptoms appeared to be going away, so much that I stopped taking my pain medications and muscle relaxers. I found that I could even walk short distances without debilitating pain and shortness of breath.

I considered that the crows might have had something to do with it. But before I could give the matter more thought, something truly remarkable and life altering happened.

I went to bed on a Saturday night as a man and awoke Sunday as a crow. I marveled at the miraculous transformation for a moment, but unlike Gregor Samsa, who turned into an unhappy bug, I relished in my new body, and flew out the open window to join the murder waiting for me below.

I alighted in front of Ahmya.

"Welcome Kenzo. Or should I say, as it now says in the *Book of Beasts*, Mallasu. You may know me as Akkitasu, demoness of the gateway. Now attend me, as I assume my true form."

With that, Ahmya morphed into a majestic three-eyed crow.

"All glory to Makkuru, Lord of the Sky, who gave us teeth that we might chew the flesh of man and savor his flesh. Even now He looks down on us from his heavenly aerie and smiles at what we have accomplished. My fellow flyers, my winged warriors, my trusted titans of the air, we are no longer the hunted but the hunters, no longer the slaves but the rulers.

"Soon we will gain dominion over the earth. As it was when our ancestors, the mighty dinosaurs ruled the land and seas. We will be joined by all our skyborne brethren, from the eagle to the lowly hummingbird, from the owl to the osprey. All endowed with biting teeth to tear apart and feed upon our two-legged oppressors.

"Some of you believe we should be kinder to man because he is intelligent. But Makkuru says man's idiocy trumps his wisdom. He is ruled by emotion. He gives battle to everything around him. Unlike other creatures of the earth, he does not keep the balance. He goes from place to place, devouring all the resources. The only way he can survive is to spread to another area. He is a virus, a disease, a plague upon this world. We are the cure."

I, Mallasu, now possessed of human intellect, endowed with the aggressive vitality of my new form, and filled with the bliss of heavenly metamorphosis, spoke— along with all the rest—my assent in that eldritch avian tongue. Then, without another word, the murder that was now a multitude took flight, and with claw and fang and appetite for all things human, spread blackness across the skies, broken by ribbons of rainbow colors as the setting sun glistened on our ebony feathers.

That, Madam President, is the new order of things. Accordingly, you will tell your people to lay down their arms and swear allegiance to Makkuru, Lord of the Sky. Anything less will result in your annihilation. We await your decision.

FOIE GRAS
By Eamonn Murphy

Tom Powell tried to sit up and couldn't. His stomach muscles clenched with the effort but he didn't move. He tried again and realized there was a strap across his chest, holding him down.

Where am I?

He shifted his shoulder and moved his left arm. He could raise it about three inches but after that something stopped it. Seconds later, he knew the same was true of his right arm and both legs. His heart beat faster and he resisted the urge to yell.

Tom blinked. He was flat on his back in near darkness. There was a faint light source somewhere. The room smelled clean, antiseptic, like a pharmacy or a hospital. He could vaguely discern a sound not far away: low murmurs and a faint clinking as of cutlery. Cautiously, he turned his head to the left. His head wasn't restrained! He peered into the gloom and slowly discerned shadowy shapes about ten feet away.

There was a solid block about three feet high, like a bed, and he saw that someone was laying on it, flat on their back, like him. Around that object stood three tall figures.

Tom felt a surge of relief. *I'm in a hospital. Something's happened but it's all right.*

The scream spoiled that idea. It came out of the person on the next bed as if ripped from his or her throat. It was a scream of pure agony.

Tom trembled and stared harder, trying to see what was happening. One figure stood over the bed and had a hand on the patient's torso. He raised it to his mouth. There was something in his hand. Something that dripped. He put it in his mouth.

The victim carried on screaming.

Tom began sweating and struggled harder against his bonds but to no avail. He shouted, "Help! Somebody help! They're killing him!"

The screaming went on, drowning out Tom's own shouts. He yelled louder in a blind panic. As far as the confines of his chest strap and limb restraints allowed, which wasn't much, he thrashed. He drummed his heels on the hard surface beneath him and strained at his bonds until his bones ached, all the while shouting as loud as he could. After some minutes, his shouts turned to sobs. Making less noise himself, he realized that the screaming from the next bed had stopped.

Tom's chest heaved as he gasped for breath. He closed his eyes. When he opened them, someone was standing over him. In the darkness, the figure was just a shadow but it seemed tall. Then a hand moved down towards his chest.

The hand held a scalpel.

Tom screamed again.

* * *

"Tom! Tom! Wake up! Wake up!"

A figure stood over him. He threw a punch to defend

himself. She swayed back to avoid it.

"Tom, it's me! For God's sake, you're having a nightmare again!"

His whole body stiffened, every muscle locked, ready for fight or flight. Finally, he recognized his wife. He exhaled a deep, shuddering breath. Looking around, he could see he was in his bedroom at home. This week's book was on the bedside cabinet and a photo of his late father smiled down at him from the wall to his left. The wardrobe and chest of drawers were in their proper place and so was he. Safe at home in their little house in Chipping Sodbury, a cozy English market town. No mad surgeons in the room. No threat.

"Fiona." He jerked upright. "I nearly hit you. God, I'm sorry." He panted breathlessly and his stomach ached. The same ache that had been bothering him the past few days. At least the bump on his head was no longer sore.

She shifted herself and lay beside him. "Don't worry about me. What about you? This is...well, it's every night now. Every night since that weekend." She turned and looked into his face. "Something's wrong. Something's very wrong."

He said nothing, knowing what was coming.

"Maybe it's guilt."

She was back to that. He sighed. "I have nothing to feel guilty about."

"No." She turned her back to swing her long legs out of bed and stood up, her chestnut curls dropping to halfway down her back. She was forty years old now but had kept her slim figure. Some of her plump, jealous girlfriends said it was because she had no children. Not for the first time, he realized she was a beautiful woman. He needed no other, despite what she thought.

"Where did you go that Saturday night, Tom?"

Here we go again. Ten days before he had gone for a couple of pints in Bristol with an old mate from his bachelor days. As ever, they met in the afternoon, had three pints of beer and meal to soak them up, then headed home at around seven before the rowdy crowds descended on the town. It was a dark November night and he had driven home the usual route. He remembered setting off. He remembered waking up at dawn, thirsty and starving hungry, with a big bruise on the back of his head, sitting in his car on a quiet country road.

He had no memory of the time in between. It was a complete blank.

"I keep telling you, Fiona, I can't remember." He sat up and shouted the words, "I can't remember!" The pain in his stomach worsened at the sudden movement. He lay back down, grunting and gritting his teeth.

"No," she said. "So you say. But you've had nightmares ever since." She turned away. Bending over the chest of drawers, she took out her clothes for the day and walked to the door. That meant she would not change in front of him.

Before flouncing out, she fixed him with a defiant stare but he saw the tears in her eyes. "She can't have been that special if you don't even remember it."

"Oh, Fiona."

She slammed the bedroom door, leaving him alone.

His stomach clenched again. He managed to get out of bed. Looking in the mirror at his muscular body, he reflected that he had kept his shape too. Of course, he needed to stay fit for his job.

Another spasm hit and he gritted his teeth in pain. It was bad enough to make him decisive.

"Damn it. I'm calling the surgery."

* * *

"I hate going to the doctors," said Tom.

"Don't we all." The older man next to him was lean

and almost gnarled looking but had a gentle smile and an easy manner.

Tom's local surgery was in the nearby town of Yate at a modern new medical establishment in the shopping center. He sat in the waiting room on a plastic chair, one amongst eight rows of ten plastic chairs divided by an aisle down the middle. The reception desk was over to the left, by the entrance, and a corridor to the right led off to the treatment rooms. A pinging noise alerted him to look up at the television screen on the wall before him. "Joan Wilkins to Room 4" it said, and an elderly lady to his right tottered to her feet and shuffled off down the corridor.

"What's the problem?" The old man looked sideways at Tom. "You look fit enough."

"I am. I'm a PE teacher by trade, so I have to be. Doesn't stop you getting ill." He grunted as his guts twisted again.

"So?"

"Stomach pain. Had it for a week now. Can't ignore it any more."

The old man grimaced. "That's the worst. Bowel investigations, you know. Fingers inserted where fingers shouldn't go."

Tom winced. "I hope that won't be necessary."

"For your sake..." The television pinged again, interrupting the conversation.

"Edward Jones to room nine."

The old man stood up. "That's me. Good luck, mate." He walked away, using a cane for support.

The public address system called Tom to the treatment room ten minutes later. The doctor sat by the desk, frowning at a computer screen. He pointed to another chair beside him and Tom sat down.

"I'm Doctor Bartlett." He was a short, stout man with thinning hair and a carefully crafted black beard that tried and failed to hide a double chin. He scanned the computer monitor and frowned. "Hmmm. Well, you don't bother us much Mister Powell. Haven't seen you for years." He swung his swivel chair to face the patient. "What's up?"

Not long after, Tom was flat on his back on the black couch with the polythene curtain pulled around in case anyone walked in, not that it would have mattered much. The only part of his anatomy exposed was his belly. Doctor Bartlett poked and prodded at it and asked if this or that hurt.

Tom winced. "It all hurts, doctor. My guts feel as if someone's been beating them with a truncheon, but there's nothing to show on the outside."

"How are your stools?"

Tom had known that was coming. "Okay but it hurts to go. Hurts my stomach when I...you know...push."

"Hmmm." The medic peered at the lower end of his patient's torso. "You've had some surgery in the past, yes?"

This remark baffled Tom. "No. Never."

The little man's face twisted with irritation. "Well, you obviously have. There's a thin line that's paler than the rest of the skin. Scar tissue."

Tom sat up. His eyes were wide; his heart beat faster. "No. No, I tell you. I've never had any surgery anywhere."

"Look, there's no point in concealing information, Mister Powell. I can see…"

"I have never had any surgery!"

"Calm down." The doctor took a step back as Tom turned so that his legs were back on the floor. "We are not here to be abused."

Tom took a deep breath. Like most people, he had seen news reports about hooligans attacking NHS staff and been disgusted by it. He stared at the floor and let the red mist clear.

After half a minute, he spoke again. "Seriously, Doctor, I have had no surgery of any kind, certainly not on my stomach. I've always been fit as a flea. I'm a PE teacher for God's sake. Check my records."

"I trust my own eyes, Mister Powell. There is scar tissue."

"But…" Tom pressed his lips together and closed his eyes. "If I haven't had surgery, it's not scar tissue. It must be something else."

Doctor Bartlett emitted a dismissive noise then returned to his computer and began to type.

Tom adjusted his clothing. "What happens now?"

The medic ignored him for a few seconds and continued typing. Then he swiveled the chair around. "You *are* in pain, and you're clearly not a hypochondriac. Therefore, I am referring you to the hospital for an X-ray and a scan to find out what's happening inside. I'll make it urgent. You should get a letter the day after tomorrow, and the appointment will probably be next week. Do you need a sick note for work?"

Tom managed a smile. "No, thanks. I won't be doing a lot of bending and stretching myself but I can still make the kids do it." He worked at the local academy and enjoyed it.

"Okay. Well, take it easy and come back if anything changes."

Tom stood up. Clearly, Doctor Bartlett wasn't prepared to make a fuss about the scar tissue again. He had better things to do than argue with patient, but no doubt he would put it in his report to the hospital. For now, though, Tom relaxed. He had taken action and put himself in the hands of the good old National Health Service. They would sort him out. His stomach was still griping but he felt better already knowing that the matter was in hand.

He nodded to the doctor and left, wondering if he

should have mentioned the dreams.

Nah. Bad dreams were nothing. Too much cheese, probably.

* * *

They gave him an appointment the following Tuesday afternoon. The letter for it came on Friday, two days after he saw Doctor Bartlett. They were not pleasant days. Work was fine but there was a chilly atmosphere at home. Fiona barely spoke to him. It couldn't go on, and Tom decided a confrontation was better than this protracted ill feeling.

"Sit down," he said when his wife stood up after dinner. It was seven o'clock and the early evening news had just finished playing on the television in the kitchen diner. They always ate dinner between six and seven while watching the news. The local program often attempted a tenuous connection to the national news but today had closed with some rubbish about flying saucers, stuff more suited to the summer silly season than late November. The reporter delivered the story with an amused smirk.

In happier days they might have retired to the lounge after dinner, to read or watch a film but now Fiona retreated to another room used as an office to read, or sulk.

She glared at him.

"As they say in the soap operas," growled Tom, "we need to talk."

She snorted. "What is there to talk about? I don't want to listen to more of your…"

"Lies?" He gripped the table, his knuckles white. "When have I ever been a liar, Fiona? When have I ever been less than straight with you?"

Her dark eyes were as cold as space. "Two weeks ago.

When you didn't come home to our bed."

"I didn't go to any other fucking bed, either!" he yelled. "Why can't you get that through your thick skull? I slept in the car!"

He hadn't meant to shout.

She looked at him. "You said you couldn't remember."

He banged the table. "I can't remember, damn you! But I woke up in the fucking car so presumably I slept in the fucking car! I sure as shit didn't sleep with whatever hot blonde model you've imagined for the last fortnight!"

His stomach suddenly clenched. It felt as if someone had punched him in the guts and he bent over and groaned.

Fiona's eyes widened. "Are you okay?"

Tom tried to straighten up. He sighed. "No. Not really. Something happened that night and I don't know what but it sure fucked me over good. It's left me with stomach cramps and an unhappy marriage. So, no. I'm not okay."

She sat on the chair beside him. After a few deep breaths, she spoke again. "You didn't play away that Saturday?"

He managed a weak laugh. "I'm a natural-born monogamist, honey. One woman at a time is all I can cope with. I didn't play away. I never would."

She had tears in her eyes but was calmer. "Then… what happened?"

Tom shook his head. "I don't know. But I bruised my head, didn't I? Sometimes concussion can cause temporary amnesia." He laughed. "So can beer but I didn't have nearly enough for that."

She nodded.

"I didn't crash because the car was fine. Maybe I had an altercation with another motorist and came off worse? That might explain the sore guts too." He shrugged helplessly. "I don't know. But I *do* know that I didn't spend the night in anyone else's bed." He took her hand. "You believe me, don't you?"

She smiled. "I believe you." She kept his hand in her and stood up.

"What now? *Coronation Street*?" She was a lifelong fan of Britain's longest-running soap opera and he put up with it. At least, now and then, it had some humor.

Fiona shook her head. "Bedtime, darling. We have some catching up to do."

* * *

The next day, Tom had his usual fortnightly pint with his old friend. Despite their pleasant evening and morning, Fiona had been edgy.

"Do you want me to pick you up?"

He shook his head. "Don't be silly. You hate driving in Bristol. I only have three pints and a big meal with it. I'm safe to drive." She grunted. "And I'll be straight home. You can count on it."

"Please do."

Tom had been married long enough to know what to do. He stepped over to the kitchen sink where she was washing up the lunch dishes and hugged her.

"Straight home. Whatever happened…" He stopped. As he didn't know what had happened, it was outside his control and he couldn't say it wouldn't happen again. "Lightning doesn't strike twice," he said firmly. "I'll be back."

"Okay, Arnie."

He stepped back and made a crab pose like a bodybuilder, showing off his PE teacher muscles. "And I got mine without steroids."

She pursed her lips and moaned, "Oooh, go quick before I haul you back to bed."

Laughing, he plucked the car keys from the hook by the door. "See you soon."

His friend was already at their regular table in the pub at their regular time, three o'clock on Saturday afternoon. Late enough to miss the lunch crowd and early enough to avoid the yobs. An easy-going Welshman, James Jones had settled down into a steady bachelor routine of working long hours, gaming and watching television in his time off and eating too much. Over the last few years, he had developed a taste for fine dining and went to some expensive restaurant as a treat once a month. Apart from that, he lived a simple life in a studio flat near the center of Bristol and cycled to work.

That Saturday he had a *Daily Mirror* and two pints of *John Smiths* bitter in front of him. As Tom came over, he pushed one forward.

"All right, mate." He pointed to the newspaper. "You see this? Your little corner of England made the national papers."

"How?"

"UFOs!" James slapped the page. "Multiple sightings of lights in the sky over the last couple of weeks in South Gloucestershire. *The Mirror* gave it a double-page spread."

"By their top correspondent Phil Space," said Tom. "I saw it mentioned on the local BBC program. They come out with this crap every so often when there's not much real news."

"Yeah, I know." James folded the paper over and pushed it to one side. "Funny doing it for Gloucestershire though. Normally it's Wiltshire and corn circles."

"Which are all made by hippies with planks and string," said Tom. "I went to the pub where they hang out and heard all about it."

"Well, maybe there's something in it." James was unmarried and had plenty of time to spend on the Internet.

Madame Gray's Vault of Gore

He had become interested in multiple conspiracy theories of late, and Tom had a good time mocking him. "I mean Roswell and all that. And plenty of U.S. Air Force pilots and other reliable people have made reports."

"Rubbish."

James waved an arm to indicate the universe. "You believe that, in all the vastness of space, we are alone? Us grubby little humans. The only life form in ten billion galaxies, or whatever it is now."

"I don't know, and I don't care. How's work?" James worked as a security guard on the local council and had to deal with members of the public, many of who, judging by the stories he told, were quite mad.

"Usual."

"Any great dinners lately?" James's posh food habit amused Tom.

James leaned forward. "Yes. I had foie gras." He smiled. "You know what that is?"

"Yeah." Tom shrugged but his lips contorted as if he'd just swallowed something awful. "Up to you what you eat, mate. I saw a documentary about it once, watched geese being force-fed. It made me sick. Foie gras?" He dismissed the notion with a violent chopping motion of his hand, nearly knocking his pint over. "I wouldn't have it."

"You eat meat," riposted his friend. "Those pigs and chickens don't die of old age, you know."

"No. But they're not tortured either."

"They're just animals, you know. They eat insects and things the same as we eat them. It's nature. Don't feel guilty about being at the top of the food chain."

That argument didn't wash with Tom. "As I said, you eat what you want. But I'd prefer it if you didn't boast about this one."

"Okay. Okay." James took the hint, and their conversation resumed their usual pattern of work, films and fond memories of mad bachelor days. The time passed, and afterwards, Tom made it back home to a glad Fiona with no trouble. It was a good day.

* * *

"To be honest, Mister Powell, I'm baffled."

Tuesday afternoon had come around and now Tom sat in a comfortable chair in a small consulting room at Southmead hospital. He felt tired. The dream had come back on Monday night and he stayed awake until dawn, too tense to drop off again. He wondered if he should see a psychiatrist.

They had done the X-rays twenty minutes earlier. Five minutes ago, Tom had lain on a couch while the specialist prodded his stomach with stubby fingers. It had hurt.

"What...what do you mean baffled?" Tom was wringing his hands as if washing them. He had always been fit and proud of it. He hated illness. The prospect of something going wrong with his body scared him.

Mister Farraday was a tall, balding man of about fifty; slim and slow moving, dressed in an expensive shirt and smartly creased trousers; a smooth professional. He pointed to his computer screen, which showed the dark X-ray images of Tom's innards.

"The X-ray shows nothing," he said. "There is some slight inflammation of the small intestine but nothing serious. Of course, the X-ray wouldn't show bruising." He turned to look at Tom. "Have you been in a car accident lately? Anything that might cause trauma to the region?"

"No." Tom shook his head. At the same time, he wondered if that was true. After all, he had woken up in the car with no memory of the night before. But the car was intact. Surely that ruled out an accident.

"Been in a fight? As I say, your symptoms are like

trauma. I can tell when I touch the area that it hurts."

"Nothing like that."

"How does it feel to you?" The consultant leaned forward.

Tom winced at another twisting pain in his abdomen. "To be honest, doctor, it feels as if somebody opened me up and stirred my guts with a paddle, like Mel Gibson in *Braveheart*, then sewed me back up.

"Ouch." Farraday turned back to his computer, touched a key, making the X-ray image disappear. "I'll put you in for a laparoscopy. That means we'll introduce a camera through a small incision and have a look around."

"Do you have to?" Tom grimaced and squirmed in his chair. "I'm sore enough already."

"I'm sorry, I think it's necessary."

Tom shrugged. "When will it be?"

Farraday played at the keyboard and studied the screen. "There's always a queue for these things but… Ah, not too bad. We can fit you in next Wednesday if I make it urgent, and I will." He gave a wan smile. "The worst thing for doctors is not knowing what's going on. Once we have a diagnosis, we feel much more comfortable."

"Will you be doing the operation?" Tom had acquired a certain amount of faith in Farraday's confident professional manner.

"I will." The consultant stood up and held out his hand. "Don't worry, Mister Powell. We'll sort you out but these things take time."

"What do I do meanwhile?"

"Take painkillers." As Tom began to protest, the doctor held up his hand. "I know, I know. You healthy chaps don't like pills but trust me; it's the best way. If you have pain, take a painkiller. Paracetamol has almost no side effects. Don't take aspirin. That can cause trouble with stomach problems. If you need anything stronger, call your GP."

"Okay. Thanks, doc."

As he walked down the long concourse of Southmead Hospital, heading for the exit, Tom wondered again just what the Hell had happened to him that Saturday night.

* * *

On Wednesday morning the UFO story was upgraded from *The Mirror* and a local joke item to the BBC national news. Tom had a bad night's sleep because of his stomach pain and got up late, so he only heard it over the radio on the way to work. It wasn't the headline but the Beeb was taking the matter seriously.

"There have been several sightings by reliable witnesses," said Michelle Hussein on Radio 4's *Today* program. "Many people also took pictures with their phones and have sent them in. You can see them on our website. We have Professor Brian Cox on the line now." A pause. "Professor, what do you make of this?"

Tom was a big fan of the learned former pop drummer, but just then he arrived at the school car park, running late. No time to listen to Brian. Reluctantly, he turned off the radio and went to work. No doubt it would be on the six o'clock news later.

It was and with pictures to back up the words. Tom stared at the television in awe.

Even Fiona was agog. There had been sightings in England, the States and China. They sat on the sofa looking at clear images of two disc-shaped crafts in the sky over Wiltshire. The UFOs moved slowly as if careless of being seen. Expert witnesses opined that the pictures were genuine. There were so many of them now that they could hardly be anything else. The government launched military aircraft but as soon as they came near, the flying saucers—there was no other word for them—headed up into the stratosphere.

After the news, there was a special program on the subject in which scientists and cosmologists rehashed the old arguments about the possibility of life on other planets.

"Possibility?" Tom was too old for shouting at the television but still indulged now and then. "Possibility? It's a certainty now."

Some American military experts thought the flying saucers might be Russian. The Russians denied all responsibility. The Pentagon response: "Well, they would say that wouldn't they?"

While Fiona watched *Coronation Street* (the most extraordinary event in human history being insufficient excuse to miss soap opera), Tom went online. Most of the comments were variations on amazing, the ubiquitous adjective of the age, with far too many exclamation marks. Some made wry comments that the first alien contact should be with the United States according to the movies. Other wags responded that the Martians had landed on Horsell Common in Surrey.

Eventually, Tom went to bed and finally, despite his excitement, he slept.

* * *

Something was wrong.

Tom started into wakefulness filled with deep unease. A dream again? He couldn't remember anything. He slid his left hand across the sheet to touch Fiona. She wasn't there. Not unusual. Often she would get up in the night to go to the toilet, waking him. There was light coming from somewhere, probably the hall. Everything was normal.

Drowsily, he turned on his side. She would be back. He closed his eyes, then opened them again.

Something *was* wrong. The light wasn't coming from the hall, but outside. Was it a full moon? The bedroom curtains weren't thick, and they passed some nights in a sort of twilight. Tom preferred complete darkness but let Fiona have her way in this. Such concessions are part of married life. Even so, he didn't recall that the moon had been full.

He heard something as well: a distinct humming noise. The fridge? It seemed to be coming from outside, though. Police helicopter? No, they were louder and usually about on Friday or Saturday nights, not Wednesday.

Tom was too tired to bother much about anything but this collection of oddities troubled him. And Fiona seemed to be taking a long time in the toilet.

He was just dozing off again when a hand touched his shoulder. He smiled and turned to look at her. "Welcome…"

He stared into a long narrow face. Blue skin. Huge brown eyes with no whites.

A dream. He was dreaming again.

There was a buzzing noise, and his entire body quivered, convulsing on the bed as an electric current coursed through him. He screamed and blacked out.

* * *

Tom woke slowly. He groaned. The back of his neck ached and his head was hanging forward, his chin pressed against cold metal. There was something against his throat as well, he realized, and he had a terrible headache. He let out a long, slow moan. His throat felt dry. It must have been a Hell of a night.

He squeezed his eyes more tightly shut but it didn't help the pain in his head. He would have to get up and get some Paracetamol. Unless Fiona…

He jerked his head up with a start. Fiona! She had been missing. He twisted to look to his left. It was pitch black. He couldn't see a thing but felt sure he wasn't in his bedroom. The space felt bigger somehow. There were faint groaning noises coming from everywhere around him—left, right, behind and in front. Someone cried out weakly.

"Help."

No one answered. Tom wasn't sure he could speak.

He wasn't flat on his back in bed, but upright. He tried to look down but there was a silvery metal shelf at neck level and he couldn't see beyond it.

Then Tom realized that he couldn't feel his body. Not at all. He swallowed and felt the spit go down his throat, but there was no sensation beyond that point.

Blind panic.

I'm a disembodied head on a tin shelf!

No. That wasn't possible. He wondered if he could shout.

"Help!" His voice was weak and cracking because his throat was so dry. If he could shout, he had lungs. He wasn't just a head.

Someone else cried out, wordlessly this time, and the general background noise increased. There were grunts, groans, sighs. It sounded like a barracks at Reveille.

A strong, clear voice interrupted the hubbub: "SILENCE."

Tom was looking straight ahead because anything else hurt. It was still dark but he perceived something moving in front of him, coming from below, a darker rectangle against the darkness. It seemed to be about the size of a sixty-inch television screen.

A dot of light appeared on it and expanded. It was a screen. Tom gazed at a rectangle of blue light. Looking around as best he could, he saw that there was a row of them stretching away to right and left, about ten meters apart. Peering into the distance, he could discern four to his left and five to his right, as well as the one in front of him. This gave him some impression of the size of the room. It was like a public hall—perhaps a hundred meters wide. He had no way of telling how large it was in any other dimension.

The screen flickered and an image appeared. It was a face. Not human. Blue skin. Huge brown eyes with no whites. Two holes where a nose should be and a thin slash of a mouth. Tom panted in sudden panic as he remembered the face he had seen from his bed.

The lips moved and sound came from all around them.

"You are prisoners. Remain quiet. Listen."

Someone over to Tom's right began to chatter incomprehensibly. Then he screamed.

"Remain quiet," repeated the blue face on the screen. Tom bit his lip. He didn't want to experience whatever had ripped the scream out of his fellow victim's throat. He focused on the screen and tried to suppress his panic. *Listen, Tom. Listen.*

The voice spoke calmly. "You are prisoners. You will be prisoners for the rest of your lives, and you have only one task." The blue alien paused. Was that a smile twitching the corners of its mouth? "Eat."

Eat? Tom wondered if he had heard correctly. Why should they eat? What use was that to anyone? Tom had seen plenty of science-fiction B movies and knew that humans kidnapped by aliens were put to work in uranium mines or some such. That's what the Daleks did to Peter Cushing. *Eat?* It made no sense.

Over to his right, someone else screamed in frustration, then screamed again, in pain, as the aliens used some punishment on them. Tom guessed that it was electricity. He tried to feel his body but there was still no sensation. For now, he just had to wait. His face flushed with rage as he planned violent revenge for this humiliation. Tom Powell was a fit, strong man. A proud man. No one treated him like this. No one.

And where was his wife? Where was Fiona?

The alien on the screen spoke again. "Be silent. I will explain your purpose only once. Listen, and you will, perhaps, understand your fate." That twisted half-smile again. "It may console you."

The image changed to a diagram of the human body with the internal organs displayed. Tom had seen the like before in biology textbooks. An arrow, like a cursor on a computer screen, hovered just over the left shoulder of the male portrayed. When the voice resumed, the cursor moved to point out the relevant organs.

"Your species gets energy from food, as do we. When you eat, the food passes down into your stomach. There it is processed by powerful acids, which begin the digestion process. From the stomach, it passes through the pyloric valve and into the duodenum, the beginning of the small intestine. From there, it goes through various other processes, but they are irrelevant. The stomach turns food into a substance you call chyme, a semi-liquid mass of partly digested food."

The cursor stopped at the small intestine and the alien spoke again. "We have been watching your species for some time now. The first visits were almost seventy years ago. Earth years. Initially, we were curious. Then we considered communicating with you but you are so primitive it is not worth our while. Then we wondered if you could be useful and took some samples for closer examination. The samples were usually returned but had no memory of their extraction—just a hole in their lives and some bad dreams. Their attempts to get publicity for their plight were...amusing."

That's what happened to me! The bastards took me. Examined me. Put me back. Tom twisted his head in agitation. *I'll kill them. I'll kill them all.*

"The experiments were largely a waste of time, but we discovered something, almost by accident." The diagram of a human body vanished and the face of the alien appeared again. Its weird lips twisted in a smile. "*Chyme is delicious.*"

Nobody screamed. The revelation stunned everyone into silence.

"Your job," the alien resumed, "is to make chyme. So you will eat. You are the advance guard for your race. For now, we have only one large ship here and can transport just a hundred of you back to our planet to supply the finest restaurants. For now, chyme will be a luxury." He smiled again. "You will do great work and make us rich. Lights."

As he said the last word, the room was suddenly illuminated. Tom blinked in shock then squeezed his eyes shut. When he opened them again, he could see all too clearly.

The metal shelf below his neck extended forward about six inches. It also carried on to his left and right for quite some distance, and by twisting slightly, he could see more human heads all neatly in a row, two meters apart. He estimated that there were about twenty on either side of him. Just above his head, a four-inch pipe ran along the row of imprisoned humans.

The screen had gone and Tom also had an unobstructed forward view. A row of people faced him. At first, they appeared to be disembodied heads on a tin shelf, as he felt himself to be. Then he saw that there were bodies beneath the shelf.

Just bodies. They had no arms. No legs. They were torsos and not even complete for they ended at the waistline. Another metal shelf supported the torsos. From that, below each human, a tube descended into a transparent horizontal pipe that extended in both directions. It rested on the floor of the chamber.

Someone was walking up the row opposite and fastening a device to the faces of the people. "Tom!"

He recognized the voice. He peered ahead and scanned the faces of the row opposite. She was over to his left.

"Fiona!"

There was a figure standing behind her. It slipped something over her face and fastened a strap at the back of her head to hold it in place. It looked like a gas mask but there was a plastic tube coming out of the mouth area. The figure moved in front of Fiona and fastened the tube to the pipe that ran overhead.

Tom heard a movement behind him. He shouted in vain protest as something slipped over his face. He twisted his head uselessly as the strap tightened.

Armless, legless, tied up and powerless he opened his mouth to scream. The pipe attached to his head flexed, and his mouth was full of something. He gagged and chewed desperately. It was food. Some paste that tasted of meat and vegetables combined. It kept coming, and he kept chewing and swallowing, breathing through his nose, almost choking. It seemed to last for hours.

Finally, the food stopped. Tom blinked away tears and focused on Fiona across the aisle. Fiona. His wife, whom he had promised to love and protect.

He had failed.

This was their fate now. They would be force-fed to make luxury food for a superior species.

No arms. No legs. No possibility of escape. Tom felt utter despair.

Oh, Fiona. Our goose is cooked.

Tom remembered James and his foie gras. *Top of the food chain?* He laughed bitterly then almost choked as another dollop of mush that came down the tube into his mouth.

Our goose is cooked!

THE ARTIST
By Alexander Nachaj

His name was Steve or Jeremy or something like that. She couldn't remember and didn't really care. All that mattered was that he had good hands, clean fingernails, and no inhibitions about driving the two of them back to her place in the suburbs.

"Feel like a drink? I can make you another Blue Hawaii," Jenny offered, standing by the mini bar in her living room. She was twenty-five years old, tall and slim like a model.

He sat on the sofa, dressed in ripped Parasuco jeans and a V-neck sweater. He was busy twirling the keys to his Chevy around his finger. "Nah, that's just the stuff I order at the club. Makes for a good conversation starter, you know?"

"Worked on me," she said, playing along with a wink.

"I'll have a rye on the rocks."

"Canadian Club?"

"Perfect."

She poured them each a whiskey and came back from the kitchen with ice. As she handed him his glass, she noticed him looking around the room.

"What do you do for a living?" he asked. "Or are you a student?"

She stood in front of him, sipping her whiskey. "I'm an artist. Like my mother."

"Cool," he said. He glanced at a red ochre painting of a sunset on the wall. "That one of yours?"

She shook her head. "No. It was hers. She taught me the ropes, but my work isn't ready for the world yet."

"Ah," he said, quickly losing interest. He was staring at her crotch, his hand moving to her thigh. He reached around and squeezed her ass.

"Your body is amazing," he said.

She put down her drink and leaned in, her hands going for the buttons on his shirt.

"It's your body that interests me. Take your clothes off."

He didn't argue. He quickly got naked. As he sat there in the buff, she scrutinized him from head to toe. She played with his cock in a perfunctory manner before settling on his fingers, examining each one up close and pressing them against her own.

"You into hands?" he asked, perplexed.

"Fingers," she said.

"Shit. That some kind of fetish?" Before she could answer, he reached down to cup her breasts, but she slapped his hand away.

"Not like this. I want you to shower. Get started. I'll meet you in there."

"Awesome," he said as she showed him to the washroom. When she heard the water running, she got ready and returned to the washroom completely nude.

She pulled back the shower curtains. Steve, or whatever his name was, stood there, rinsing off his suds. Seeing her like that, he grinned.

"All right," he said, making room for her to step in.

"Let's do this."

She stepped in with a grin of her own. After closing the curtain, she revealed the hunting knife she had hidden behind her back.

Steve's eyes went wide as she slashed his neck. The skin gave way like butter against the well-sharpened blade, her deft aim slicing the artery. He clasped the wound with a hand, too confused to fully grasp the situation and fight back. Blood spilled over his fingers in thick gushes. He fell backwards against the wall, sliding to the bottom of the tub.

She kicked away his hand, letting the spray run free. Blood showered the wall, the curtain and their naked bodies. She crouched before him, mesmerized by the ephemeral beauty of the red patterns forming on the tiles before being washed away by the warm water.

* * *

The hardest part was getting him out of the tub. Once that was done, she wrapped him in the shower curtain and dragged him by the feet to the basement. His head made a loud thud as it hit every step on the way down, cracking his skull before they reached the bottom.

She unwrapped him on the concrete, taking a moment to appraise the red trail left in his wake. There was still time to collect some of his blood as it leaked from his neck and skull, but that wasn't why she took him. She took her bolt cutters and went to work, cutting off the index and middle fingers of his right hand, appreciating the smacking sound they made as they fell to the floor. After she gathered them up, she went to the adjacent room that acted as her studio.

The floor of the dimly lit room was covered with blue tarps. An easel stood in one corner, the first dotted splotches and thick strokes of a red sunset taking shape.

On the table sat various jars with different shades of red. Each was filled with blood mixed with varying quantities of ash and cocoa to give it the desired texture, shade and consistency.

She unwrapped her brushes. A dozen of them lay there—fingers of varying lengths and sizes, the tips of which she dipped into the paint. Some were long and twisted, others becoming gnarled from age and decay. Most of them had been kept in brine between sessions to retain their texture, but even then, they wouldn't last forever.

She put the two she had taken from Steve next to the others and measured them alongside one another. She was pleased to see that the middle finger was the desired size and girth she was seeking, but his index was similar to the one she had collected from her previous week's guest.

"Fuck," she muttered, tossing the finger into the trash alongside a bundle of entrails and other leftovers she hadn't been bothered to burn yet. Behind her, she heard the chains rattle.

Straightening up, she went to the big cage in the opposite corner of the room and removed the tarp that covered it. Inside was one of her most prized possessions. His name was Tom and his naked body sat there wrapped in chains and covered in his own excrement. His eyes and tongue were missing, along with most of his fingers and toes. An IV ran from his arm to a blood bag hanging from a nearby rack.

She noticed, with some dismay, that the bag was less full than she was expecting. Apparently, Tom hadn't touched the plate of mashed beans and leftover meat she had left for him earlier.

Crouching before his cage, she peered at his eyeless face.

"You have to eat," she said. "Or I get back to cutting things."

Tom sat there, huddled up and shaking, apparently resigned to whatever fate she had in store.

Selfish bastard, she thought. She took the bag and emptied it into one of her jars. There was likely enough blood to finish the piece, but without the right brushes it was hopeless to accomplish what she wanted. That meant another trip to the club, and another guy.

Jenny sighed. Her mother had taught her that artists, true artists, required a certain level of conviction and focus, but this was taking too long. Sooner or later someone would notice a pattern and trace the trail of missing men back to her home in the suburbs. She had to make sure the next one was the final one or risk giving up the whole project.

I won't let you down, mom, she told herself as she dipped Steve's finger in the paint and tested her new brush.

* * *

She met him two nights later at a club on the Main. He was like most of the other men she'd approached along that stretch: Young, healthy, and kind of full of themselves.

His name was Paul. His hands were large and rough like a carpenter's. She expected him to be in the trades, but he was a resident physician at St. Mary's Hospital. When they stood side by side, he towered over her, intimidating her slightly. She realized he'd be a pain in the ass to get out of the tub, and was about to go looking for another guy, but when he leaned in and asked if she lived nearby, she knew he was the one.

He drove them to her place in his Honda, parking a couple houses down and walking up. Inside, she showed him to the living room and offered him a drink.

"Rye on the rocks," he said.

Curious, she thought. Paul was the second one to make that same request. She wondered if men thought it made them seem classy.

After returning with the ice, she handed him his glass and took her seat on the other end of the sofa. The two of them made small talk, but unlike most of the men who had sat there, he didn't seem all that pressed for getting it on.

As he went on talking night shifts at the hospital, and the level of conviction it required to stay focused, Jenny sighed loudly. She would probably have to do a bit of work with this one. Get him excited before there was any hope of leading him into the shower.

She took off her sweater, flashing him a stretch of stomach. She giggled and slowly fixed her shirt, waiting for his move, yet he didn't press the opening. Odd.

Fine, she thought, sliding closer and putting her hand on his bicep.

"So," she said, running her fingers across his bare forearm.

"So," he said, giving her an odd look, like he couldn't decide what to do next.

"Anything on your mind?" she asked, trying her best to sound devious and suggestive.

He put down his glass. "Actually, yes. How did it go?"

"How did what go?" she asked, making her way across his chest and down towards his crotch.

"You know, with Jeremy."

That gave her a moment's pause. She tried to place the name. "Who?"

"Jeremy."

She pulled her hand back and gave him a fake smile. "I don't know any Jeremy."

"Of course you do," he smirked. "You went home with him the other night. From the club."

Jenny slid back. *No*, she told herself, *his name was Steve... or had it really been Jeremy*? If so, she couldn't believe it. What were the chances these two knew each other?

Paul smiled and moved closer. "Yeah, he's a good buddy of mine. Last thing he told me was he was gonna spend the night at some chick's place. Even sent me a photo of her." He dug out his phone and showed it to her. On the screen was a picture of her standing in line at the washroom of the club. From the angle, it looked like it had been taken incognito from a few feet away in the crowd.

Jenny all but gasped. She had always taken precautions when people tried photographing her, preventing any evidence of tying her to the men she met, and yet Jeremy had snapped one of her before she even laid eyes on him. That didn't make any sense. Had he been watching her that night?

Change of plans, she told herself. She stood up and walked over to the bar, her eyes looking for something she could use as a weapon. She had some things hidden around the house, such as a crossbow in the dining room and a hunting knife in her bedroom, but the only weapon in the living room was tucked under the couch where Paul sat.

"Good old Jeremy," said Paul, continuing despite her obvious discomfort. "He's usually easy to reach, but I haven't heard from him since."

Jenny began to panic. Paul was dangerous. That much was clear. She should have listened to her instincts sooner, but it wasn't too late. She had to act quickly.

"Me neither. He left before the night was over," she said, making her way towards the hall. Paul, however, anticipated her move and stood in the way to block her.

"That's funny because I saw his car parked out front on the way in. That Chevy of his might be an old beater, but man, he loves that car more than he loves chasing a piece of ass. I can't imagine he would leave it here and bus it all the way back to the South Shore."

Paul gave her a sidelong look and Jenny knew the game was up. She tried to run, but he swung one of his big arms around her. She felt a sharp, stabbing pain in the small of her back. When she glanced down, an empty syringe was being pulled from her.

"Hyoscine with a dash of Rohypnol," he said, pinning her against the wall. "Never leave home without it."

* * *

Jenny squirmed and tried to break free, but Paul pushed her back against the wall. She noticed her vision was beginning to blur and she had trouble keeping track of her thoughts. Either it was her growing panic or the stuff he injected into her was working fast.

"If Jeremy had gotten his way with you, I wouldn't need to be doing this," he said, sounding frustrated. "You were supposed to end the night in five different dumpsters, so what happened?"

Jenny stopped fighting and made like she was giving in. The moment Paul eased off, she scratched his cheek, her nails digging through the skin. He cried out and tossed her aside. She clipped the corner of a table and collapsed to the floor.

"Stupid bitch. You think I came here to play?" He kicked her in the back. She rolled over, closer to the couch. Quickly, her arm went under, looking for the knife she kept tucked into the frame. Her fingers found the handle, but he grabbed her by the feet and pulled her out. "You're not my type, but I can still make you feel pain."

Paul turned her over and punched her unceremoniously in the face. She felt the cartilage in her perfectly upturned nose crack and blood gush down her nostrils and into her mouth. She turned her head and coughed, red ooze spattering across the carpet.

"Let's try this again," he said, grabbing her by the neck and lifting her off the ground. She gasped as he slammed her against the mini bar, knocking over the bottles. He looked at her bloodied face and scoffed. "Where is he and what happened to him?"

Jenny held his eye as she grabbed a bottle and brought it round towards his head. He blocked it with his hand. The glass shattered, spraying them with whiskey and cutting up the lower part of his palm. She meant to stab him with the remains of the bottle, but he was too quick, and she was too dizzy.

"Now you've made me angry." He took the broken bottle from her. "I'm far less polite when I'm angry."

She spat blood at his face. In return, he stabbed her in the forearm with the bottle, twisting. Blood pulsed from the wound, swelling up like a gory well.

Jenny screamed.

"You gonna tell me what I want to know?"

"Yes," she coughed, crying and fighting against the agony. If anything, the pain was the only thing keeping her conscious. "Basement. He's in the basement."

Paul's expression changed. It went from fury to something almost like vindication. He was evidently pleased that his suspicions had played out.

"Show me, now."

* * *

Jenny hobbled to the basement with Paul staying only a step behind. To stop her from bleeding to death on him too soon, he had torn a strip of her shirt to use as a tourniquet around her arm.

They went down the rickety stairs and Jenny showed him to the other room. After flicking on the lights, Paul looked around, surprised.

"What the fuck is this?" he asked as his eyes landed on the half-painted canvas and the jars of paint. "You some kind of artist?"

"Something like that," she said. "I take after my mother."

"Whatever. Where's Jeremy?"

"There." She nodded to the cage. It was covered with its tarp.

Paul leaned in. "What is that?" He kicked the edge of the cage and stepped back as chains rattled around inside.

"He's still alive?" Paul asked, suddenly eager and moving to pull the tarp away. When he did, he came face to face with the wretched, filth-covered being inside. Tom moved to the edge of the bars, his hollow mouth begging for water as his eyeless sockets blinked.

The big man stood still in utter disbelief at the sight of the eyeless beggar before him. Whatever Paul was expecting to see in there, this wasn't it.

Jenny didn't hesitate. With the last of her strength, she went for the bolt cutters on the table and swung them with all her might at her guest's head. They clacked against his skull with a sickening thud. Paul tumbled forward against the cage, his weight bending the side of it before he fell to the floor.

Jenny stood over him with the bolt cutters and swung the heavy pair into his face, again and again, until it was little more than bloody pulp and mashed bone and her energy was spent.

Before passing out, she grabbed a handful of fingers from her table. She managed to hold the larger of them up against Paul's hand. Comparing them, she felt tears forming in her eyes.

They were the wrong size. The wrong fucking size.

* * *

Another night, another guy.

She drove up to Laval, hitting a club far from her usual haunts. It was harder than before, with her arm in a cast and her face messed up to all hell, but she managed to bring home a desperate exchange student from France named Mathieu. Not wanting any repeats, she hailed them a cab for the trip back to her place. When it was over, Mathieu lay dead on her basement floor, one finger less than when he arrived.

She worked all night and the following day, finishing her canvas with the finger brushes and blood paint. When it was completed, she stood back and studied her work. Her finger traced the passionate crimson brush strokes and felt the brittle texture of the paint, letting her live through the emotions and the sacrifice that had gone into it all over again.

It had been a struggle, to say the least, to complete the work the way she wanted, but what great artist never struggled with their craft?

"What do you think?" she asked Tom as he rattled around in his cage.

Tom was an easy critic. He nodded wordlessly.

Jenny chuckled. It didn't really matter what Tom thought. She'd finish him off with a screwdriver to the neck one day or another. Instead, she thought about her mother. The woman who had raised her, brought her up and shown her the vision and commitment required of a true artist. Though the cancer had taken her too soon, Jenny was proud to be able to finish what they had started together.

A DEADLY CABIN TRYST
By John Mara

The headlights of a rented Range Rover cut the fog and dodge the potholes of a muddy road that dead-ends nowhere. Jerked along by some unknown force, the Rover delivers its cargo, Astor Fillmore, to the family's New Hampshire cabin, there to settle an estate—and a deathly score.

"Finally, we're here!" Roxanne says from the passenger's seat. "It's about goddamn time." In the vanity mirror, she fortifies an ample coating of red lipstick and black eye liner.

Ancient oaks, sentinels of a forgotten time and place, flex their craggy arms to announce an unusual arrival. "Let's get the hell outta here." Roxanne rubs goose bumps.

"No way, Roxie. This place is the down payment on that Malibu bungalow you love. My wife'll never know."

As her own down payment, Rox treats Astor to two eyefuls of cleavage. Then, she finishes a letter sent from Fate:

. . . As sole heir, then, of the Fillmore family estate, you are the beneficiary of the impending sale of the family's property. I

will meet you there for the passing promptly at 8 a.m. on Saturday, November 15.

> *Very Truly Yours,*
> *Mortimer Goodman, Trust Officer, Concord Bank & Trust*
>
> *P.S. You will find the cabin in good order, Mr. Fillmore. Leave the caretaker a handsome tip!*

Eyes closed, Roxanne is at Malibu Beach, deliciously alone in a hot bikini, until a slam of the rear door ruins the ocean view. The cutting wind—or some ungodly force—starts Astor and his aluminum suitcase toward the cabin.

Across a blanket of dead leaves, Roxanne follows with an Italian suitcase that matches her weight and nearly her height, even with the high heels. The dreary mist allows only the silhouette of a log cabin. But, in a kind of spectral parting, a swirl opens the curtain of fog to reveal a lonely grave. The mossy burial site is free of leaves, and draped over its worm-eaten marker is a bouquet of red roses, their beauty past. "Astor? What the hell is that?"

"I'll tell you inside."

* * *

"Wow! Good order indeed!" Astor says as the aluminum luggage gouges a dent in the pine floorboards. Back when Elvis was king, Astor's father built the cabin for weekend family getaways—and the occasional tryst.

"Shit, I'm trapped in a dismal coffin here," Roxanne says and shudders at the panorama of wide pine that makes up the floor, walls, and ceiling of the cabin's one great room. With only an overstuffed chair and a couch, the room is more a wooden cavern. "Ach, it even *smells* like a dreary tomb." A wool sweater tames the clammy miasma that clings to her arms.

"A warm fire will do the trick." In a grand flagstone fireplace, Astor sparks a fire with the mountain of wood the trusty caretaker has left behind. "Besides, there's no electricity." Lighting tapered candles, he ducks under a flying hair dryer.

"Ahhh, that's better!" Astor rubs his short arms over the crackling fire. "Yikes! Even better!" Roxanne runway-walks from the cabin's one bedroom. A bathrobe flashes open to tease at the negligee painting her slender frame.

"The bedroom's made up nice, but it smells like a ten-cent cigar."

"So the caretaker's a smoker," Astor shrugs. He pops a bottle of Tuscan wine and arranges the platter of grapes, Brie, and Stonewall Kitchen crackers from an open suitcase. Then, sinking into the couch, Roxanne nestles in the arms of Astor's silk pajamas. "This place isn't so bad now, is it?" The lady-killer bathes his porky, drooped jowls and crooked nose under the waterfall of red hair that cascades over Roxanne's shoulders.

"Who the hell is that?" Back stiffened, Roxanne bolts straight up. Above the fireplace mantel, the fire's rising glow illumes a life-sized portrait of an elegant woman dressed in a white evening gown, with bejeweled gloves on her graceful arms. She wears a silver tiara. Her smile, though, is more of a sneer.

"Those haunting eyes! They're boring a hole in my skull!" Roxanne pulls her bathrobe together and wanders the room. "They follow me wherever I go!"

"Now, now Rox. Have a seat." He tugs on the bathrobe. "More wine?"

"Don't Rox me! No more wine, Romeo. No more nothing." She double-knots the bathrobe. "Is that your…mother?"

"No. That's my father's wife." He swirls wine. "My

mother was a girlfriend he had on the side."

The flickering flames paint a scowl on the portrait's face.

Astor's eyes are someplace far away. "It was Gramma that raised me in Malibu. May as well been shipped there in a ten pound FedEx box. Haven't been East since."

"And the burial site?"

"It's the grave of Mrs. Fillmore here." He waves the wine glass at the portrait. "She walked in on dad and his cheap…" Astor's eyes meet Roxanne's. "My mom."

"What happened?"

"I was teething in California by then. Story goes, Mrs. Fillmore's body was found here along with two puddles of blood. It was a grisly mess when all the shooting stopped."

"Two puddles?"

"The bodies of my dad and his girlfriend…ahem, my mom…were never found." The rising wind rattles the windows, flutters the candles, and flares the fire. Mrs. Fillmore's eyes turn charcoal black and wander as though crazed.

A shotgun mounted in the mantel's shadow catches Roxanne's eye. When she tracks bullet holes in the far wall, long nails dig into the back of the couch. "That does it, fella. Gimmee the goddamn keys."

"Hey, it was a long, long time a-" A pattering sound fills the air. And then something scampers in the wall behind the portrait. Roxanne stands frozen, eyes popped.

"It's nothing but field mice, no doubt." Astor forces a plastic smile. "More wine?" His voice rises two octaves. The fire grows wild. Fed by something other than the caretaker's oak, its shards throw grotesque, dancing shadows around the room.

A rustle—as though a siren call to action—comes next. The patter behind the portrait radiates slowly around the walls. The unbroken thrum shivers Roxanne's spine.

Then, where the walls meet the ceiling, dust begins to fall. Specks at first, a wave builds as the thrum grows. Munched fragments and coarse sawdust cover the baseboard more and more on every spin of Roxanne's bug eyes. "Ca...car...carpenter ants!" her breathless lungs allow.

"Don't worry Rox." The wine in Astor's glass quakes. "Carpenter ants don't bother humans."

"You make friends, pal! I'm history!" Roxanne's legs remember how they work. Through the door's windowpanes she sees someone vanish into the shadows behind the gravesite. The door refuses to open, barred from outside with a pinewood plank. She tries the double-hung windows next, but they're secured—from intruders, no doubt—with one-inch screws. "We're trapped like raaats!" echoes off the pine. A hammering heart joins the acrid Brie burning in Roxie's throat.

Back in the great room, the woodless fireplace is in a roar, and the carpet is stained blood-trail red under a shattered wine glass. Astor swallows hard, his saggy eyes transfixed on the portrait. "It can't be." But it is: the painting's black, roving eyes take flight! Soaring from their sockets are a few dozen winged carpenter ants. They avoid the waving arms of a man unnerved and land in Astor's nest of curly black hair with a threatening buzz. The droning throng smells fear.

The winged demons, antennae raised, probe Roxanne too. But they quickly return to mark Astor with a scent. In time, the devils leave the swain lying in a chubby knees-to-chin ball and then pass through the eye portals, a reconnaissance flight complete.

"What now?" Roxanne says after she unfurls Astor.

In response, the excavated pine galleys disgorge bands of raging carpenter ants. Legion upon legion follows the foraging trail of the forward scouts, each wave strengthening the scent. An army on the crawl, they march. A force in the air, they fly. They move in a thoughtless, robotic motion—directed by a feeding instinct—and the gloved arm of Mrs. Fillmore. The sneer on her face turns plaintive smile, and a slender finger points to her target: Astor. An inferno rages in the fireplace below as though it's the gateway to hell.

Even more seething hellions are borne of the portrait's womb-like mouth, nostrils and ears. The secret lovers are in the grip of an undiluted terror they've never known. Encircled by the chittering throng, they stand huddled and helpless, their nightclothes soaked in sweat.

Then, in the middle of Mrs. Fillmore's chest, the blue hole of a shotgun blast takes shape. Blood drains from it and saturates the evening gown. Her face turns ashen but the smile remains.

From the gruesome hole, an ant takes flight with membranous, double wings. Blue-backed and larger than any of her multitude, she is surely the egg-laying queen of the brood. The legion of obeisant servants below grows silent as she circles the portrait in tribute—and then glides around Astor with a foreboding buzz.

"Stay away from me!" Roxanne shoves Astor and slowly, very slowly, backs away from the ambush. The squirming phalanx opens a path in its midst, and she—one of three dominant females—gains clemency.

At his ear, Astor hears the queen's feint squeak; it may as well be a reverberating cannon shot. All in the mob uprear their little haunches and the sentence is announced: Death! Death! Now executioners unleashed, a murderous trap springs on Astor. Storm troopers climb first and take purchase on his pant legs, first outside and then within.

A hopping madman with eyes agog, Astor scrambles out of the pajama bottoms and flails at the pack. The yowling gang steps back, but then the largest of the loathsome critters counterattack in a snarling panic to avenge their brethren. In a frantic assault, the angry herd stampedes, slithers up Astor's legs, and covers his torso, three deep.

Pressed in the corner, red hair gone wild, Roxanne's mouth is an O of fright. Her blank eyes dart everywhere. She tries to scream but is dead silent. Tries to run but is frozen. The wind howls outside. The fire rages on—as Mrs. Fillmore brightens.

The ravening horde blankets Astor in a pulsating shroud. He writhes in the noxious darkness within. Their mark subdued, the beasts dig mandibles and pierce stinging tentacles into Astor's savory, plump skin. A quivering hand emerges from the orgy and its sweep reveals maniacal, bulging eyes. His jugular found, blood spurts everywhere and the extraction of bodily fluid begins. Some of the worker ants start to haul the precious, succulent food supply back to their colonies.

In a desperate plea for life, the black shroud emits a chilling scream. Astor throttles the multi-headed hellbeast as though it were a single, ferocious monster. But the vermin maul and rip his chest and back, flaying him whole in the bloodlust.

Roxanne cringes at a muffled howl of agony, the final animal plea of a man insane, damned and delivered early to hell. Arms extended in the way of a Frankenstein monster, the wriggling, top-heavy mass starts its death march toward Roxanne. Her heart is ready to burst. Mercifully, the lunatic's nightmare ends when Astor collapses where his father fell on this night forty years ago.

Roxanne's bathrobe sleeve does little to mask the fetid odor of death. She bunches into a bony, trembling ball and awaits the rallying swarm. Resigned to fate, her bladder empties its store of Brunello. In another female redemption, though, the queen glides back through the open chest of Mrs. Fillmore. On cue, the gluttonous brutes—all except the food processors—retreat. A black curtain darkens the four walls next as the tiny heathens scale the pine boards, skitter through every crack and fissure, and find their hollowed nests.

Mrs. Fillmore's hands are at peace, and the hellish flames and vicious wind have breathed their last with Astor. In what seems a lifetime—and in a way it is—Roxanne, a putrid stench rasping her nostrils, skirts around the corpse and the sucking sound of its busy attendants.

Somehow, the front door is unbarred. Leaving the accursed realm, the taste of freedom outside fills her lungs. But right away, the lungs empty and a new anxiety seizes them: the grave is dug up and empty of its tenant. She races and takes refuge in the Range Rover—an escape hatch from the brink of hell. Then she realizes the keys are in Astor's suitcase. Then a cadaverous form glares through the driver's side window, and a madness born of unendurable terror surges in Roxanne. A soul-chilling "Noooooo!" cleaves the crisp night.

Smiling there sublimely is the ghoulish Mrs. Fillmore, hair the texture of straw, jewels tarnished, and evening gown tattered with a seeping hole in the chest. Her anemic face is gaunt and sunken, with leathery strips of ghastly skin stretched over a protruding skull. The stately tiara, though, shimmers—as does the 12-gauge shotgun.

A door swings open and topples the living corpse. Dashing back inside the cabin, Roxanne collects her breath—and gathers her wits—when the locks click the sound of salvation. Once steeled, she ventures into the great room to find the keys to her escape. Instead, she finds in the glow of a blazing hellfire—oh, the horror!—Mrs. Fillmore. Above her, the portrait frame is empty. "A Fillmore whore you are," she snarls, thin lips drawn back from her glimmering yellow teeth. She gestures to Astor with the shotgun. "And he the whoreson fruit of my husband's adultery!"

Hyperventilating, Roxanne backpedals. She hides eyes big as saucers behind trembling hands.

"Stop right there, Missie. You're on the spot where I humbled the last whore."

For the ravenous carpenter ants, the shotgun blast is a dinner bell rung. Savage droves pour forth from every woody lair, and another sumptuous banquet begins.

* * *

At 8 a.m.—promptly—a rusty 1970 Ford pickup truck on its last mile pulls in behind the Range Rover. The pickup disgorges an old timer, broken-down too. "Near time to shut the ole lady down," he says of the November breath that chills his creaky bones. Snowflakes, vanguards of an early Nor'easter, begin to fall. Warming the man is an eternally stoked cigar at the center of a bristled face. Some mysterious force governs the man; his vacant eyes aren't up to the task.

The force carries the man to the grave. With a rake, he levels and perfects the site's disturbed soil and scatters another night's gathering of leaves.

Inside, the man walks mechanically past the ever-shrinking corpses of Astor and Roxanne, the tireless carpenters still sucking and hauling their winter store of food. "Keep at it, fellas," the crusty man says with a sideways grin. "Them bones are the hardest part. Ah he heee!"

Then the withered man's demeanor takes an amorous turn. At the portrait, his blank stare meets the glistening eyes that look upon their dominion below. "Never looked better, sweetheart." Head cocked and pie-eyed, he basks in the warm glow of an affectionate smile returned.

"Things would've been different, dear, for the two of us both." He adorns the mantel with a fresh red rose. "If only I got that stinkin' bullet into Mr. Fillmore's chest before he shot you." A filthy sleeve mops tears—and years—of regret.

A double-winged flutter brings the lovelorn man back in time. The blue-backed queen soars above the portrait in a majestic salute and then alights on the self-righteous shoulder of Mrs. Fillmore.

The man hoists the shotgun from the mantel, snuffs life out of the cigar, and then bends a knight's homage to the regal pair. The caretaking done, and done well, he tramps into the nicotine-stained bedroom, there at last to take his winter rest.

SKINNER
By J Louis Messina

Skinner scratched his skinless sores, drawing blood lines across his featureless face with his fingernails. The blotches itched. His body throbbed, wincing and oozing from the boils underneath his clothes. Spreading the knives over a cloth on the table, he arranged them in order from small to large. He kept them clean and polished; they twinkled in the overhead lights.

"There's more than one way to skin a cat."

The proverb intrigued Skinner, and his thoughts roiled, hot to find its meaning. Once the fire lit beneath him, the pot began to simmer, and he searched for the phrase on his cell.

"That's a strange saying, isn't it? Who skins a cat? What do they want with the pelt? And how many inexplicable ways are there?" He picked up a bottle of antiseptic and spilled some onto a rag. "The expression has many origins. One says it's Southern and refers to gutting a catfish. I can buy that. Another says it's from a gymnastic move that looks like turning an animal inside out. That makes no sense to me. Does it you?"

Skinner addressed the man roped to the ceiling and floor by iron rings, spread-eagled, hanging naked. Sweat broke out over his body in beads, like blisters about to pop, dribbling down and pooling at his feet. His penis and testicles shriveled in the cold, and his pubic hair matted from perspiration. The smell of fear—rank, stark, sharp—filled the room. Skinner inhaled the stink and shivered, as if it were an aphrodisiac. As Skinner approached, the man's eyes widened, recording the last images of his life. His cries vibrated against the duct tape over his mouth. Skinner grabbed the man's hair and peered into his dilated pupils.

"Asked you a question, Gerald. Nod yes or no. Does that make sense to you?"

The man shook no, spraying sweat off his face. Skinner licked it off his lips and tasted the salty treat; then he dabbed the man's face with the antiseptic.

"Glad we agree. Sounds cruel to skin a cat. Personally, I'm a dog person, so it doesn't bother me much. Now, as far as how many ways, I estimate there's only two: Alive or dead. Guess which way I like it?"

Skinner turned back to the table, perusing his options. He held up a knife with a fine blade designed for delicate work. He massaged the handle and admired his reflection in the steel. He liked to see his expression, wet with anticipation, and imagined the newly severed skin hiding his imperfections, creating a new identity, a new person, one with ordinary features.

Skinner strode back and circled the man, noticing the clenched buttocks, the tightened muscles, preparing for his attack. He thought it amusing. Nothing the man did could stop the pain to come, stop him from sculpting his victim. Gerald strained against his bounds; his flesh wormed, as if struggling to transmute into something but couldn't.

"What are you, Gerald?"

Gerald hung his head and moaned.

"Doesn't matter. On with my dissertation. There are more ways to skin a man alive." Skinner tapped the knife on Gerald's body like a teacher with a pointer on a chalkboard. "Start at the legs and *splice* your way up; take off the chest first; remove the genitals. I like the face the best. Did you know you can live without a face? I have and suffer for it. Nietzsche once said: *To live is to suffer; to survive is to find meaning in the suffering.* Most of you I'll use as fodder. Best way to hide my victims."

When Skinner finished his presentation, the man sobbed, his hysterics muffled by his gag, drool dripping out the sides. Tears flooded his cheeks. He loved this. It cleansed the skin. He wanted clean skin, pristine, fresh.

"You're looking at the door, hoping for a rescue. No one's going to bust it down and save you. That's what happens in the thriller novels, Gerald. The flawed but plucky detective rushes in. But you don't want that, do you? Not after the crime you've committed. You killed your girlfriend. And she wasn't your first."

Gerald's eyes flinched.

"Oh, how do I know? I'm a Skinner, remember; I've studied you for months. You're the perfect candidate, as were the other murderers. Who knows you're here? No one. You won't be missed for days. I'll use oil drums to dispose of the little parts. We're in a sound proof room in my basement. The plastic tarp beneath your feet catches the blood. Relax and enjoy the fun. Just as you did when you murdered Janet. You took your time."

Skinner picked up a magnifying glass and studied Gerald's face. Terror had stretched it. He had pleasant, handsome features. Not movie star looks, but they could catch a woman's eye. They would seal, naturally, over his, the magic of his species. Carving took artistic skill. He'd start at the forehead, work around, and end under the chin. Sometimes it stuck, but he could pull it away without tearing it.

"There's another way I love to skin my cat." Skinner tore the duct tape off in one rip and plucked out the slobbered rubber ball inside the mouth. "I love to hear the screams."

Gerald screamed, shouted for help and mercy, to let him go, he'd tell no one, begged for his life.

"We all have an expiration date, Gerald. We're walking corpses, waiting to die. Yours is past due. Like sour milk."

"I have money, lots, you can have it all, whatever you want, just name it. Anything!"

"You and I are about to experience an amazing transformation." Skinner stood rigid, cherishing the moment. "Do you know that when someone is doing something naughty, something they don't want to be caught doing, their senses are more alert? Let's say, someone steals from a store, their heartbeat quickens, they see danger everywhere, they can hear a fly, a footstep. Or a husband watches porn and doesn't want his wife to catch him; he hears every little sound to warn him. He jumps, clicks it off, and turns. If you do something truly depraved…"

The fun began. Skinner sliced. Blood seeped and trickled around the mask. The shrieks drove him to ecstasy. He felt his erection rise and strain against his pants, aching to escape. His senses burned. The cut was a thing of beauty. He peeled off the face and went to work on the rest.

The blood spurted everywhere. The blood spurted *everywhere.*

The pelt would make a fine addition to his collection on the wall.

* * *

Wrapped in an overcoat and hat on a sunny morning, Gerald the Skinner scurried down the block, as all the people did in this new world, mollified with fear; he studied the skies, clear of clouds. Relieved—no rain in sight.

A man leaned over the balcony on the third floor. "Hey, Gerald, where you been?"

"Business up in Portland."

"Brave man."

The apartments, houses, and his building had been fortified with metal, and the windows boarded, a fortress against the deadly population. Gerald unlocked the sliding, iron barrier, and walked into the apartment on Fourth Street, Oakland, not having bothered to look up at the man. Skinner had been recognized as Gerald. His comfort level climbed with each stride. He stepped into the elevator, jingling the keys in his pocket with his hand, listening to his surroundings. He had to stop fidgeting. Gerald had displayed the cool exterior of a seasoned killer. Skinner had learned too well how to do that.

He entered the loft on the top floor. Spacious. He could live here for months before anyone discovered him. Everything looked normal. There was a normal pool table in the middle, a normal bar in the corner, a normal Van Gogh painting on the wall, a normal big-screen TV on a stand, and a man dwarfing the leather chair, his legs crossed and dangling, his hands behind his head, grinning behind thick, dark shades—abnormal.

"Morning Gerald. Take a seat."

"Who are you? How'd you get in?" Gerald removed his cell phone. "Get out now or I call the cops."

"No need." The man flashed a badge, stuck it back into his coat pocket, and reframed his leisure magazine pose. He reminded Skinner of an antique steamer trunk abandoned in an attic. "Detective Drummond of the San Francisco homicide unit at your service."

"The flawed but plucky detective?"

Drummond removed his sunglasses. "Excuse me?"

"A private joke of mine." Gerald jingled the keys in his pocket. "Isn't this breaking and entering, even for a detective?"

"Your landlord let me in. Was all the invite I needed."

Like some bloody vampire, Skinner thought. He had to navigate his words carefully or else stake the man to death.

"And to what do I owe the pleasure?"

"We found someone you know. Janet Springer."

"My girlfriend? She lodged a formal complaint against me? I only hit her a few times. Let her get a restraining order. I'm through with her anyway."

"No. She's kind of dead. Thought you might know why."

Skinner rocked his head back and gave the detective a glance of surprise, hoping to quell his suspicion. He wasn't going down for a murder he hadn't committed. But Drummond acted too casual for someone who'd come to arrest him.

"How would I know? Been in Portland." Skinner crossed to the bar, hoping to find a weapon there. "Can I get you a drink?"

"Little early." Drummond licked his lips and his eyes roamed over the liquor bottles. "And I'm on duty."

"Cut the crap, detective. Why're you here?"

"Janet was tortured to death. For quite a while. I can connect you easily to the crime."

"Then why haven't you?" Skinner had to call his bluff, see where he stood. "Take me in already."

"Where's your bathroom?"

"Find it yourself or piss in the potted plant."

"Where's the bedroom?"

"Feeling frisky? I don't roll that way. Go find yourself another lover-boy."

"You don't know, do you? Could tell by the way you surveyed the room when you entered."

What game was Drummond playing?

"Arrest me or get out." Skinner poured a shot of Jack Daniels, threw it back, and slammed the glass on the counter. "I've got things to do."

Drummond massaged his face with both hands, rose, stretched and strolled to the bar and sat on the stool. The fat on his rump boiled over.

"I've got things to do, too, asshole. I'm tracking a serial killer, a real monster."

"How delightful." Was Drummond onto him? Skinner reached for a knife under the bar, thinking he might stab the detective in the neck. "What's that got to do with me?"

"Thought you could help track him. *Skinner*."

Skinner tried not to blink. He smiled to disarm his victim. "Name's Gerald."

He had the knife and pulled it out, slowly, targeting the detective's bulging throat.

Unsmiling, Drummond looked down over the bar. "And I'd think twice 'bout going for that knife."

Skinner dropped it and withdrew his hand. Using the detective's face would only frighten kids on Halloween, anyway. Okay, he knew what he was. But he wasn't after Gerald or him. Should he confess?

"You've no proof of anything."

Skinner tried to pour another drink, but Drummond seized his arm.

"I could pull your mask off and end this charade. But I don't want to see what's left of your ugly face. Then I might have to take a drink. And you don't want that. It leads to bad things."

Skinner inhaled deeply, smelling the detective's skin. A hint of cheap cologne, and underneath, pine and dirt and something foreign, conflicted. It told him what he needed to know. Drummond was a good man. Wasn't a killer. And Skinner didn't kill good men—unless forced to.

"So, you think I'm a Skinner?"

"Know it." Drummond stuck his finger in the empty shot glass and twirled it around on the counter. "I don't have your sensing skills or super reflexes, but I'm a damn good detective. Skinners are illegal. Most have been caught, caged, and executed. I've killed a few myself. Hate vigilantes."

"Afraid we'll put you out of a job?"

Drummond's face turned mean; spittle foamed on his lips. "You're all infected. I'd kill you now if I didn't need you."

"Hunted like rabid animals."

"Yep. I also know you only kill the diseased. Like wolves thinning the herd."

"And you need me to thin the herd of this serial killer? You don't object to how I do it?"

"I did once." Drummond closed his eyes and suckled the whiskey on his fingertip. Shifting his weight in his seat, he folded his arms on the counter and leaned in. "You'd have to work with me, no going maverick. Once it's done, I let you go 'bout your business. Hell, I might even help you."

"Why not just do it yourself? You've got the whole force behind you."

"The guy's slippery. Been at it a year." Drummond pulled out a worn picture from his wallet and flung it on the bar table. "He killed this woman, brutally."

"He must've killed a lot of women by now. What makes this one special?"

Drummond's hands trembled. He eyed the bottle, moved his hand toward it, but swiped the picture and slipped it back into his wallet.

"She's my wife. Was. And the captain took me off the

case. Said I was emotionally compromised and all that psycho-babble mumbo jumbo bullshit."

Drummond had him cornered. Fight or flight?

"Why'd he kill her?"

"A warning. I got real close to catching him."

Catching killers was his business, too. Skinner decided to make an alliance to save his own skin, thinking he might lose the fat oaf later and slip into another state. He held out his hand. Drummond, gnashing his teeth, slapped it away.

"Don't touch me, sicko. It's things like you that murdered my wife."

"I like your Machiavellian flair. You've coerced yourself a partner."

* * *

Drummond broke the window, climbed through, and clicked on his flashlight. Skinner followed. The glass crunched underneath his shoes.

"Breaking into a crime scene?" Skinner said.

Drummond swung the light onto Skinner's face. "You got ethics all of a sudden?"

"You're the boss." He flicked on his flashlight. "We could've done this in the afternoon."

"Evil hides in darkness. That's what you do, right? You kill your victims at night."

"I prefer *selective individuals for disposal*."

"What, you a left wing nutjob? Undocumented slayers instead of illegal butchers?"

"Let's not squabble and get on with the investigation." The living room, a frilly area with a feminine touch, was immaculate except for a lamp and table knocked to the ground. Evidence of a struggle. Skinner moved to a bloodstained loveseat. "This where he slaughtered his latest victim?"

"He stabbed her but took her somewhere else to kill and skin her. Found what's left of her in the Golden State Park. We can't examine the body, unless we can break into the morgue."

"A Skinner gone bad."

"What's that?"

"Skinners that hunt good people instead of the creeps. An unbalance in their brains."

"And you're not unbalanced?"

"There's a fine line between good and evil."

"Let's just find the bastard and kill him."

"Your style's not far off from mine." Skinner searched under the cushions and couch for clues. "If he's using women's faces for a disguise, maybe we're tracking a drag queen."

"Think the perv wants to become a woman?"

"I think he wants to hide himself and throw us off." Skinner rolled his eyes. "I've done it myself."

Skinner knelt at the couch and placed his hands on the cushions. He sniffed them, a dog on a scent. The smells of the killer absorbed through his palms and sent him reeling onto his rear.

"I've got him inside me." Rising, Skinner tottered, dizzy, then wobbled over to a desk, drawn to it. "He went here." Inside the drawer, he found a note. "Looks like he was expecting us."

Drummond wheezed and dragged himself over. His gravelly voice resonated vulgarity. "What is it? An invite to dinner?"

"*The fat detective and his Skinner will die within twenty-four hours.*"

"So damn personal. I like to eat."

Skinner licked the note and smacked his lips. "Something's different about this Skinner. How'd he catch onto us so fast? He might have more powers than mine. A new breed."

"We better find him before he finds us, then."

"He's watching us now."

Drummond whirled, withdrew his gun, and searched the room. "Where?" He banged open a door to a bedroom and stuck his head in. "Time to kick some pervert ass!"

"I'm not sure where he is. But he's hunting us."

"We're in a circle jerk, that it?"

"Leave your personal life out of it." Skinner rubbed the nape of his neck, irritated by Drummond's boorishness. "We better stay alert, or we'll be pelts on a wall."

"How the hell do we find him?"

Skinner dipped his hand back into the desk drawer. "He left us a clue. Dead skin."

"Whose?"

"That's what we'll have to find out."

* * *

Damn the wind! It danced with the leaves, whirled debris, tossed dirt and disease, and, worse, amalgamated the smells, the good, the bad, into the darkness. It also brought the Berserkers out to forage for food.

"I'm losing the scent. Pull over here."

"We're not going into the park without backup. Nobody goes there anymore."

"That's where the skin leads me."

Drummond pulled the car to the side. "You know it might be a trap."

"No question about it. But we've got to play his game."

The park was feral, strewn with fallen, green-mossy trees and overhanging foliage, riotous with dangers. Skinner wouldn't be surprised to find hundreds of bodies dumped there, hidden in woody graves. The Berserkers lived in the parks, hunted in packs, and if they knew prey had entered their lair, they'd be on the menu. They tore their victims apart, limb-by-limb.

"Why haven't you rid the planet of Berserkers?"

"Not enough workforce. After the pestilence rains, too many people had been changed into God knows what. We lost a lot of good officers."

"Not everyone changed." Skinner crept into the park, his body and words burdened with sadness. "I was an English professor at City College. Had a wife, Evelyn. When Gates' apocalyptic weather altering machines transformed the unlucky people into savage killers, she was a victim. Now the weather goes constantly bonkers. I hear a mob threw Gates off a cliff and dropped stones onto his broken body. His weather and his monsters are evolving."

"I was and still am a detective. No demon rain touched me." While Drummond inched across the park and scratched his cheek, his other hand itched the gun in his holster, and he reminisced, as if drudging up a forgotten memory. "Checked a book out when I was thirteen. 'Fraid it's overdue."

"I'm surprised you read at all."

"Something called *Lady Chatterley*. Flipped through the damn thing to find the dirty parts. Got me through my adolescence."

"You sure about that?"

Drummond held up a hand. The wind swooshed and rattled through trees and brush, making every sound important and perilous. The high-pitched howls of Berserkers wailed in front of them, in front of them, in front of them, and then it was behind. They'd been surrounded. Trash thrashed in the wind storm and smacked and slapped them in the face, pummeling their bodies. It smelled like all the garbage in the world vomited onto them.

Drummond drew his gun and fired and hit nothing,

fired again and hit nothing.

"Save your bullets!" Skinner screamed over the hurricane. "We need to move!"

Drummond swung his flashlight. "*There!*"

They crashed through the lush landscaping, plants, maples, twisting pines, turbulent azaleas, and tempestuous cherry trees, scrambled up into a Japanese Tea Garden house, flung themselves in, and shut the door.

The place filled with the stink of rotting flesh. God only knew who or what was in there with them. Skinner hadn't puked in a long time. He was used to skinning people, the raw flesh, the flood of blood, the depths of their cries, but he never let them rot. The rain had washed away most of his humanity, morphed his brain, given him a new purpose: vengeance, and left him disfigured, but he could still feel revulsion. He gagged. Drummond made a retching sound deep in his gut, dry heaving.

"Shit! The stench's going to drive me insane." Drummond removed a flask from his coat pocket, took a swig, and covered his nose. "Let's find a way out."

"Wait. It's here. Out the back."

Drummond drained the flask and shoved it back into his pocket. He bent over and grabbed his face in pain.

"Move your ass before I spill my guts out."

Skinner stumbled forward, an awkward gait, slipping and sliding on blood-smeared tile, the muck glistening, like an oil slick in water. He passed the severed limbs piled in the corner, half-eaten, and fell out the back door into a garden swarming with plants like frightened beasts stampeding.

Drummond lumbered behind him, jerking through the suffocating undergrowth, the giant brush, weeds, and flowers. Skinner stopped and bowed and fell to his knees, looking over a clothed body without a face and covered in greedy ants, picking the body clean.

"Know this person?"

The wind ceased, replaced by a snow flurry. Skinner could never predict how bad the weather would turn. Sometimes it'd just move on and the sun would shine; other times, a tempest in the night.

Grunting, Drummond bent down on one knee, his body shaking from his mass. His breath, laboring, materialized in the frost. Skinner hugged his body for warmth.

Drummond patted down the body and withdrew a wallet. He rummaged through the emptiness and withdrew the only thing left: a picture.

"Officer Reedy? It can't be."

"Why's that?"

"He's alive. Left him at the station before I went to see you."

"The killer caught him on patrol, left his body here."

"He's a desk jockey. Never leaves his desk, except for coffee, donuts, and to take a piss."

"What does this mean?"

"Hell if I know. Makes no sense."

"Must have gotten him on the way home someday ago. Which means, the officer Reedy at the station isn't Reedy."

"Two Reedys? One was boring enough." Drummond unfurled Reedy's bloody hand. "A ticket to the de Young Museum."

"Our next clue?"

They heard growls and monkey sounds, feet and hands battering the Japanese House, throwing things against walls.

"The Berserkers found us," Drummond said, his speech slurred.

"Let's go to the museum."

As the snow mutated into a blizzard, they hurried through the park. The Berserkers, hairy, Neanderthal beasts, broke through the back door of the house, surged out, yowling, and pursued. Drummond lagged behind, huffing and puffing, turning red from fatigue and the cold.

"Need to rest."

"You need to join a gym. Keep up."

Drummond slid on a patch of ice and tried to keep his balance. Two Berserkers jumped him from behind. The detective fell face down, *thud*! *splat*! like a chopped sequoia tree, and the beasts grabbed his legs and pulled him back into the woods.

"Skinner!"

Skinner gazed into the white, swirling mist blanketing the branches into winter. Gray tones bathed the landscape in depression. Where had they taken Drummond? He hadn't heard screams, yet, so they hadn't torn him apart. If Drummond could get to his gun, he might fight them off. He waited. No other sounds carried over the roaring snowstorm. Should he run to his rescue?

On the other hand, he thought, if Drummond died, he could escape and go back to the car and resume his carefree life of death. After all, he'd been blackmailed into helping. Who cared about a foulmouthed detective and his serial killer, or whatever it was?

Teeth chattering, Skinner jogged back out of the park, remembering Evelyn. After the killers split her into pieces, he'd tracked them down and, with his special abilities, whittled them into nothing. Drummond wanted his wife's murderer, too. He didn't want to deny him that.

He'd thought of Evelyn every waking moment of his life, and with every thought of her, of ending his life in every way possible. Could saving Drummond lead to a reason to live?

Skinner headed back to where Drummond had fallen and followed the imprint the obese body had left in the snow, disappearing in the shower and sleet. He tiptoed around the trees, whispering, "Drummond?"

The trail ended, but no signs of Berserker ape feet.

They'd faded, except one: human tracks with shoes, and they broke off in another direction. He heard grunts and wails in a remote part of the park. Their foul smells struck his nostrils. Although the banquet could take them quite a while, if they had dragged Drummond far away to eat, he'd never find him in time. Should he go on without him? Solve this case on his own?

Someone touched him from behind. Skinner's heart and feet jumped. He leaped out of the person's reach with panther swiftness.

"Drummond? How'd you get away?"

"Damn lucky. Thought you'd deserted me. Wouldn't blame you. Let's get to the museum before any more monsters come out to play."

The snow vanished, and a storm gathered above, black, menacing clouds. Lightning flashed; thunder boomed. A sprinkle of rain.

"Keep under the trees!" Skinner shouted. "They'll protect us from the rain."

They stayed off the paths and ran over the slush. A few drops plinked onto Drummond's coat. When the acid burned through the material, he yelped and shook it out. Skinner wondered, had always wondered, if the next rain would turn him into something else, something less human than he was now. With frantic, calm strides, they dashed to the museum; seemingly so distant, it felt like crossing into another country.

Palm trees and brush encroached up to the building, having grown into a jungle. They clattered up the steps crawling with weeds, dodging toxic droplets, tiny bombs of mutilation, to the glass doors, and burst in. The rain bombarded down, thumping the roof. Drummond found an old broom and slid it through the door handles to keep the Berserkers out, at least for a while. The museum was damp and dark, and Skinner lurched from the intermingled smells.

Skinner spread his arms and inhaled. "The things are here."

"Things?"

Skinner scanned the room at the artwork hung on walls with the colors caressed into celestial creations, and at the sculptures molded from marble and metals, into diverse, unique, and crazy artifacts.

"Get your gun out."

Drummond, a fat, vain, and boastful knight, a veritable Falstaff, slipped out his gun and staggered through the room. Skinner stayed behind the broad body, his olfactory senses working in hyperdrive. His head pounded from the overload of smells. He thought his skull might erupt.

The things, for that was what they were, and there were many, enticed him, as aromas from a restaurant drove a starving vagrant out of his mind. They entered a room filled with embryonic statues. They looked shapeless on the surface, but underneath, an impression formed.

The impressions grew. The growth was imperceptibly clear. Heads, arms, bodies, legs, a cacophony of humans, but not human. Skinner knew he was in the trap, but he was a bee drawn to nectar. He hadn't thought to flee. Drummond stood as still as the statues, except for the gun in his hand, waving it like a flag of surrender.

A statue, clearly a man now, spoke. "The last Skinner has been delivered."

Drummond turned on Skinner and pointed his gun.

Skinner raised his hands in slight submission. The betrayal had broken over him, as daybreak vanquishes the night.

"You're one of these—things?"

"Absorbers. Used Drummond's face to throw you off the scent. It preserved his memories, and I took his shape."

"Everything a lie?"

"No. We killed his wife. I carved him up in the park and left him for dead. Gerald killed Janet, a Skinner, to get to you. Knew you'd find him. But he turned out to be no match for you. You're the best we've seen."

"Gerald was a, what? An Absorber?"

Drummond forced his hand onto Skinner's face. Skinner fought and flailed his arms, hoping to fling him off, but the partial flesh absorbed into Drummond, revealing Skinner's exposed, red, blotchy, skull face, bubbling blood.

"Gerald returns to the fold."

Doubling over, Skinner grabbed his throat and gasped for air. "Why not just kill me when you had a chance?"

The Absorbers circled him with their arms stretched to touch him.

"We want to absorb your essence, your gifts. It will make us stronger. We'll absorb the human race and make a utopian world order."

"*A Brave New World*? I'll pass, thank you."

"I don't believe we gave you a choice."

As they closed in, glass shattered in the distance. If the Berserkers had found their way in, Skinner thought they might delay his absorption. But the Absorbers hadn't appeared disturbed by the sound. If the Berserkers attacked, perhaps they'd be absorbed as well. Drummond must've soaked his assailants up like a sponge. At least they'd rid humanity of those poor souls that had been turned into raving, anthropophagus lunatics.

The hands covered him and sucked. Skinner fell to his knees, gritted his teeth in agony, and tried to pull away but couldn't. He was dying a slow death, drained into nothingness.

A fate worse than death, Skinner thought, recalling Gibbon's *Decline and Fall of the Roman Empire*. But a worse fate was living.

A bullet struck an Absorber in the head and it went down. Startled, the Drummond Absorber broke his connection and looked up. Skinner, given uncanny reflexes in the change, snatched the gun from Drummond's hand and shot him in the face. When Drummond hit the floor, the others drew back.

"Kill them all!"

Someone at Skinner's back fired again and killed another Absorber. The utopian creatures had one fatal flaw: they could die. Skinner shot a few and stumbled backwards, joining the other shooter. Looking askance, Skinner saw the person void of his face, someone who'd been skinned.

"Drummond?"

"Sloppy work. The dumbass thought I was dead. It takes more than one pervert to take me down."

It was Drummond, all right. The flawed but plucky detective had come to his rescue after all.

The Absorbers retreated and transformed into the shapeless blobs. Although the bullets had no effect, they remained harmless in this state. They slithered to the other side of the room and, like gelatinous dough, escaped under the crack in a door.

"We're not safe here," the real Drummond said. "Berserkers were on my tail. Be here soon."

"Your Absorber left your car outside the park."

"Let's go for it." Drummond felt his face and hissed through his teeth. He looked Skinner up and down, as if trying to figure him out. "They take your face, too? You look like shit."

The rain had ceased. They trotted out of the museum and through the muddy park.

"I'm a Skinner. I take out the bad guys."

"Me too. And these things are real sickos."

The primate cries echoed throughout the woods. The trees shook. Skinner and Drummond took off at a sprint.

The plants snapped and quivered. A creeper vine whipped at their feet, trying to lasso them with its tendrils. They skipped out of the way.

"I think I saw a flower with mouth and teeth," Skinner said, breathless.

"Evolution's a son of a bitch!"

Skinner felt an unexplainable gladness to see Drummond alive. The uncouth detective had grown on him, like new skin from a scab.

"I have powers to fix your face. I can catch murderers for the both of us, and we can work in disguise. However, it won't be the same one you had."

"You've seen my real face. No big loss. Probably an improvement." They found the car and jumped in. "Hell, Skinner, let's team up and stop them. I overheard one talking about absorbing some scientist, a Doctor Baker, out in Los Angeles. The degenerates are planning something perverted. I owe them a goddamn bona fide beatdown."

Skinner looked at his horrific reflection in the mirror. "Let's kick us some utopian creature ass!"

Spitting dirt, the car screeched over the gravel.

"First, I need a stiff drink."

"Did you know that term comes from hiding stolen cadavers pickled in whiskey barrels?"

"That's really fucking annoying."

Down the road, bouncing and bickering, raced the faceless men.

A HOG KILLING
By John Robinson

Sober or drunk, Roosevelt Collier, by his nature, was not a nice man. It was rare to meet a person he had not wronged, offended, or assaulted by word or deed. Directly, indirectly, face-to-face, or guilty by association, he was considered an affront to society.

Not many offensive, or defensive, hands were raised against Roosevelt, nor were words of criticism spoken within his earshot. Even kind remarks and friendly gestures could raise his ire. Often were the times he had shattered a bottle over a man's head, pulled a knife or fired a shotgun to instill his particular brand of fear and dominance. He had been jailed on a number of occasions, sometimes escorted to the city limits, or ushered off premises with futile warnings, yet nothing severe befell the tyrant.

Roosevelt was tolerated because the Collier family was one of the oldest families, and one of the founding families, of Cabris County. Having long ago fallen on hard times from bad business decisions and vice, the Colliers had remained land rich. No one in the family ever had much idea what to do with the property to improve their financial standing and by the time of Roosevelt and his seven years younger brother, Eldon, the farm's vast acres of spotty wilderness, rocky fields, and barren hills sat mostly unoccupied.

Eldon Collier, the nicest, gentlest, of what remained of the Collier clan, was not a smart man. What he lacked in intelligence and common sense, he compensated for with gullibility and superstition. It was his mile-wide, impressionable and intellectually challenged state that caused him, when Roosevelt died, to dismember his brother with an ax and feed him to the hogs.

"Too mean to die, too ornery to stay dead," is what their father, Emmett, used to say about his eldest offspring. He often told Eldon, in private, "Your Ma was the lucky one." She died of pneumonia when Eldon was ten and had escaped a good deal of Roosevelt's torments.

For all of Emmett's good qualities, his more vile attributes seemed to have amplified and multiplied in Roosevelt the way a mutt magnifies purebred traits. He and his first-born child battled with words and fists and whatever was at hand. Theirs was a history of broken bones and bloodshed, hostility and hatred. Eldon grew up a spectator, sometimes collateral damage, to the wars between Roosevelt and Emmett and the world.

When their dad's heart quit in his sleep, they buried Emmett in the back field because Roosevelt didn't want to have to look at the grave every day. "Bad enough we gotta look at hers," he had thumbed at their mother's resting place in the side yard.

For Eldon, being the sole cohabitant with his brother wasn't as bad as he had expected. Roosevelt's cruelty to him was mainly belittlement and teases, treatment Eldon had lived with his entire life. Roosevelt would push him down from time to time, trip him, give him a whack with a shovel handle, knock his dinner plate from his hands and make him clean up the mess.

Mostly, especially intoxicated, it was just a frank statement of, "Stupid," or "Mealy brain," or "Girls is smarter than you."

The brothers lived in their own world on the family farm. Eldon could never recall visitors coming to be neighborly and sit a spell with a glass of tea or lemonade and bestow the latest gossip. People only came to do business: to pay rent owed for grazing pasture, to buy a pig, pelts, or sell a calf. When Roosevelt died, it was only Douglas Hurst who paid respects, and that was solely by coincidence. Hurst brought his monthly rent of the east ten acres and a distraught Eldon told him how the mule had kicked his brother.

"Got'em in the head," Eldon sniffled.

In the face, to be most accurate.

Roosevelt resembled a rotted jack-o'-lantern left on the stoop, forgotten, from Halloween until Valentine's Day. Barely breathing, hardly a wheeze, his head bubbled with blood. His face was deflated, teeth broken. The man's jaw was lost in the stew.

When he saw the pummeled man, Hurst spilled his lunch in the corner with violent contractions of his stomach. "God Almighty!" he said between bursts of bile. "Christ, Eldon! Jesus Christ!"

Roosevelt Collier died with his little brother at his bedside, holding his limp hand.

Douglas Hurst stared at them in pity and disgust.

Hurst had offered to help bury Roosevelt, but Eldon declined. The young man wiped snot across his shirtsleeve. "I'll do it. I'll not trouble you with it."

"At least let me help you dig the grave, boy."

"No, sir," Eldon straightened his back. "I'll take care of me and mine."

Hurst left with no more fuss or offers.

Eldon wrapped his brother in the sheets he died on

and dragged his body, by the shoulders, into the afternoon sun. It was a great effort to pull the dead weight, greater than the task of dragging the injured Roosevelt into the house to the bed.

The chickens ran with complaints across the yard when Eldon disturbed their meeting with the lifeless bundle. The pigs stirred with their own rumors in their pens. White clouds gathered to shade Eldon from the late sun as he began to dig.

He chose to put his brother beside their mother. He smiled that neither could voice objections nor do a thing to stop him. The thought struck him that he could dig daddy up and move him here as well with nary a word said.

Grave digging was not new for Eldon. It was he alone who buried their dad while Roosevelt sat at home with a bottle of rye whiskey. The only help his brother had given him was: "At least three feet wide, seven long, six deep." The final product was not so precise, but it had been accomplished to a degree.

Eldon sang "The Old Rugged Cross" for company and, with each follow through of the shovel, glanced at his mummified brother. At the head, the sheets were soaked red and gave a vague impression of the pulped face beneath. Flies buzzed the corpse, found a buffet in the bloodstains, searched for more in the folds of linen.

Eldon tossed dirt into a pile. He was mid-shin deep with evening coming on.

"So I'll cling to the old rugged cross, and exchange i-"

Roosevelt's legs twitched.

Eldon leaped from the hole. He swung the shovel and brought the cutting edge down on his brother's shrouded knees. "Stop that!" He whacked Roosevelt's head and the scoop rang like a bell up to his own teeth.

He tossed the shovel. "I'm sorry, oh, I'm sorry!" He fell beside his brother, coated in a cocoon of ice cold sweat. "I didn't mean it, I didn't, you scared me's all. I'm sorry!" Tears streaked the grit on his face.

The body didn't move again.

Too mean to stay dead.

That's what daddy always said.

"Always," Eldon mumbled.

Something that mean and that dead....

"Liable to come back meaner."

Raw pink piglets squealed and ran around the sows at the trough. The two boars lazed in their pen in the shade of the overhang. The biggest rolled to his feet and grunted, gave a passing consideration to the piddlings of the last Collier.

If Roosevelt were to come back, and he sure had told Eldon some stories about the angry dead in his day, he'd be double mad as hell to have to crawl and climb his way out of that grave.

"Plumb madder than hornets."

The big boar rooted his snout in the dirt and snorted.

Eldon went to the shed. There, on the wall, he took down the ax. He weighed it in his hands, ran his coarse palms over the length of the handle.

The ceiling was too low in there to get a good swing, too much clutter to move. Plus, night was a breath away and Eldon wanted something more than the palpating flicker of an oil lamp or lantern when in such close quarters with the deceased.

He propped the ax on the porch and took hold of Roosevelt's swaddled feet. His brother's head bounced on the steps as he hauled him back inside the house. "Sorry," Eldon grimaced at each particularly hard knock.

Eldon unwrapped him in the parlor, shooed the flies that had followed them from the yard. He pushed the couch and chairs clear, moved the tables of neglected, dusty *chachkies* that had belonged to their momma. He righted every knickknack that fell over.

On the porch, he sharpened the ax with the file the way his daddy had taught him, and finished with the strop as the evening came on. The front door was open and, intermittently, Eldon stopped to listen for any sign that his brother was skulking the house.

The next thing he did was turn on all the lights. He brought every lamp he could find to the parlor and, ever watchful on the body, he clicked on each one. The pure brightness pushed to the corners the confused darkness, which had crept in and shoved it clear into the night.

Eldon stood over his brother. He gripped the ax securely.

The flies had returned with reinforcements. They made Roosevelt's face writhe, helped his brother to give a little mocking buzz of laughter.

The final Collier took his stance.

To him, the most obvious place to start was with the head.

Roosevelt was tough and muscled, and dividing him up was not as easy as Eldon expected. When he brought the ax down on his brother's throat, it bounced, nearly flying out of his hands. On the second hit the skin split and bones cracked, but the skull remained firmly attached. Three more hits, full force, made the battered head shift from its ragged moorings.

Two chops each separated the arms from the trunk. With a tired groan, Eldon divided the arms at the elbows (two chops) and wrists (one each, he was getting better).

He sharpened the ax to catch his breath. Eldon's hands quivered from the hard work. A rugged soreness had developed into his back and arms, up his neck. Pain didn't usually creep on him so soon when he spent the day chopping wood.

The smell in the house was tolerable, though not welcoming. The air was humid with sweat, blood, and active decay. Hurst's puke still sat souring in the corner.

Eldon's farm nose was iron, but had its limits. As soon as this chore was finished, he'd have to air out the house, maybe even light a scented candle.

The torso was alive with pitch black flies. They scaled the stumps, fleet footed, became bogged down in clots and clumps. The pests wouldn't leave, circling and diving as soon as Eldon's sticky hands quit their attack. He'd have to work through the crawling cloud of them.

Roosevelt's feet came off quick enough when Eldon went back to work. He busted through the kneecaps and dislodged the lower legs "easy squeezy."

For the thighs, Eldon got the rusty hacksaw from under the kitchen sink. It sliced through the meat like a hot knife counting off pats of butter. When the old blade struck bone, the bone gave readily to the point that Eldon wished he'd used the saw for the whole damn business.

Then the blade broke on Roosevelt's right thigh.

Eldon sighed, happy for the few minutes of comfort the saw had provided.

With the majority of the cutting done, Eldon snapped the last of the bone with his hands. A butcher knife from the kitchen (the one with his grandfather's initials carved in the handle) severed the last of the ties that bound it.

He gathered the head and smaller parts of his brother into pails.

Eldon pulled the sheets up at the corners and tied them over the torso. He picked it up, as best he could, his boots slick with gore even on the carpet spread over the parlor floor. He dropped the carcass into the wheelbarrow normally used for gathering kindling.

He snugged the limbs that would fit beside the body and the rest he piled on top. He slid the pails onto the wheelbarrow handles and wasn't sure where the strength came from when he lifted the load.

The wheelbarrow nearly capsized going down the front steps, and Eldon almost lost his footing, but he kept it, and himself, upright and stable through sheer will and the grace of God. "Nice and steady," he reminded himself until the wheelbarrow touched down on good earth.

Frail threads of clouds covered the silver ball of the moon like fissures ruptured in a wall. The night's luminescence turned black the smears and skims of blood that drenched Eldon and the smorgasbord he catered to the hogs.

He tossed Roosevelt's head, hands, arms, and feet to the sows and piglets. The legs he tossed in the corner of the boars' pen. While they were busy taking their first licks and nips, he opened the gate and wheeled the rest inside. He unwrapped the sheets and dumped the torso. He bundled the linen to burn with his brother's clothes and made a hasty retreat.

As the hogs went to their meal, Eldon filled dirt back into the unused grave. He packed it. It looked quite professional.

He sat on the porch and watched the hogs eat until the early rays of dawn. The sows dined heartily, the piglets had no interest. The biggest boar butted the smaller out of the way to feast on the torso. The smaller trotted off with a string of intestines and returned to nab a leg.

Once the roosters crowed, Eldon gathered the scraps. The sows and piglets gave no protest. Neither did the boars; they grunted as they lay on their swollen sides.

Eldon built a bonfire with the brush they had cleared from the fencerows. He tossed in the last of Roosevelt (mainly bones with putrid meat still clinging on), his soiled clothes, bed things, and the rug from the parlor.

He scrubbed the pails in the creek. Back home, Eldon added his own sullied clothes to the flames. He cleaned himself in the claw-footed tub upstairs.

The day was spent feeding seasoned maple to the fire and watching the road to the house.

No one came, just as Eldon expected.

In the afternoon, when the flames burned out, he sifted through the ashes. Roosevelt's parched skull inspected every move Eldon made with a hollow-eyed bemusement.

Eldon used the hammer to pound the skull, and the other bones, to shards and powder.

He stirred the bone dust and finer chunks with the ashes.

* * *

Eldon was exhausted. He slept through the day and night to the next morning, a Thursday. Thursday meant taking the truck to Jerry's Food Mart and the Dandy Rose Diner to pick up outdated produce and food scraps for the hogs. It was routinely Eldon's job since most people didn't enjoy dealing with his brother. He looked forward to it when he woke with a stinging sense of loneliness amid the forlorn pops of the old house.

He smiled once he turned onto the crooked spine of the highway. It felt good to fight the stiff steering wheel, to feel the guttural rumble of the truck around him, how it flowed through him. Eldon whistled no particular tune when he pumped the brakes. He was thankful for the day's purpose.

Jerry Sparns, namesake of the Food Mart, helped him load crates of moldy oranges and brown lettuce. It took Sparns a good half-hour to finally say, "Hurst told me about your brother. I'm sorry to hear it."

"Thank you, sir."

"He was... well.... Roosevelt's with your momma and daddy now."

"Yes, sir," Eldon nodded.

He knew Mr. Sparns was being nice; it was what people did. Eldon also knew the sad truth: if anybody was destined to burn in Hell for all eternity, it was Roosevelt.

Probably their daddy, too. Momma was the only one for sure who made it to Heaven.

Clark and Petula Davis owned the Dandy Rose. Clark watched silently as Eldon and the dishwasher, whose name Eldon did not know, emptied buckets of scraps into Eldon's sparkling pails. When they finished, Mr. Davis told him the same as Sparns, pretty much. "Sorry to hear about your brother." Before he left, Mrs. Davis came out to give him a quick hug and told him to "be careful out there on that farm all alone."

At stop signs and at the town's single traffic light, people waved, offered their best, and let Eldon know he was in their thoughts and prayers. Some of them genuinely meant it. Others didn't; they just felt sorry for him, they needed something to say. With each condolence, Eldon read the meaning: they were glad he wasn't as mean as a snake and twice as cruel. He registered their subdued elation, as if their burdens were lifted, in every kind word they offered him.

What broke Eldon's heart was he felt the same relief.

* * *

The smaller of the two boars was dead when Eldon got home.

Eldon leaned on the fence and stared at the deceased porker. The piglets screamed and raced around in the adjoining pen.

The sun was free in the sky. Eldon pulled the bill of his cap low to shield his eyes. The dead hog's throat and stomach were gnawed. Its wounds were still fresh.

The big boar slammed its shoulder into the fence. Eldon fell and the piglets' squeals rang like laughter. Dust danced as the boar stared at him sprawled on the ground through the open space of the wooden slats. Its ears twitched. It snorted and poked its snout between the boards.

Eldon crawled towards it as it sniffed the offal-tinged air.

The boar withdrew. It turned circles in victory and grunted. When it stopped, it trained its black eyes on Eldon.

"What the hell's wrong with you?" he asked the hog. "Look at what you did." The fence was splintered. A singular jagged crack had erupted where the hog had rammed it.

"You gone mad or somethin'?"

The boar's maw twitched like a rabbit's runny nose. Its eyes regarded the man, blinked.

Something stirred in those dark pits, something familiar and sullied.

"You...mad...." Eldon reached his hand between the boards to pet the beast's cold, moist snout. "Roosevelt," he whispered.

The hog chomped. It bit off Eldon's fingers at the second knuckle, leaving only the thumb intact on his right hand.

Eldon screamed as he flailed, his new stumps pumped crimson spurts like a lawn sprinkler. He cradled his mangled hand, begged for God to stop the pain and prayed for his momma to make everything all fine and dandy. The sows shrieked at his yelps, joined their piglets in a confused stampede of circles.

The hog charged the fence again. Its head broke the splintered board. Eldon sobbed on the ground in spouts of blood. When he finally stood, he stumbled, his feet and legs failed at successful retreat.

The boar trotted off, satisfied, to the shade of its den.

* * *

Eldon plunged his hand in cold water from the faucet.

The pain flared in black dots in front of his eyes and he dropped to the floor until the waves of nausea receded. A strain of warmth seeped into his face. He took a towel from the hamper, brushed cold sweat from his temples, and wrapped the brown stained cloth around his throbbing, shaking hand.

It still bled, though less, and he had enough mind to know a hospital was his best recourse. The large eye of the oven-top would never heat the cast-iron skillet hot enough to cauterize it, or he didn't think it would. He'd have to put the skillet in the oven or build a fire in the pot-bellied stove. But, the heat achieved, would Eldon have the nerve to go through with it?

He drove to the next town over to the hospital. "Combine accident," satisfied the curiosity of the doctors and nurses when they asked how it happened. The doctor whistled and the staff went to work.

Eldon was there until dark. He was medicated, sewed up, bandaged, given a prescription he crumpled into his pocket. They wanted to keep him overnight, but he refused. He walked out with a paper bag of fresh gauze, wraps and a tight drumming pain.

Weak, his dad spoke across the gulfs in the back of his head. *The poker have done it.*

"The fire poker." Eldon could have slapped himself. It never crossed his mind. He could have got that hot enough for sure to do the job.

Not 'is fault, Roosevelt piped up. *He's born dumber than a turnip. Girls is smarter.*

Eldon drove home, slow, with an excruciating headache of laughter echoing between his ears.

* * *

He skipped dinner and slept through the night. He woke once to hog snorts and piglet squeals. Sleep returned easily, though. When Eldon opened his eyes next it was with hunger pains in his stomach and the full brightness of day in bloom outside his bare windows.

A pot of pinto beans sat alongside a plate of souse meat in the refrigerator. Eldon made a hearty sandwich with the meat. Using his left hand would take some getting used to. The mess he made preparing breakfast would wait to be cleaned later.

Eldon settled on the porch steps to feed his belly. The chickens lurched about the yard as the sows finished the last of the slop in their trough. Next door, the boar paced in the beginning rank of the dead hog sharing its space.

With only a couple of pathetic bites of his sandwich eaten, Eldon's stomach decided it had had enough. He swallowed with a tumult in his throat.

The red sea of chickens parted as he crossed the yard to the boar's pen. He tossed the last of his morning meal to the hardpack ground. The hog flicked its spring-coiled tail as it investigated the sandwich. It pushed the bread aside with its snout and gobbled the thick slices of souse loaf.

Souse was Roosevelt's favorite breakfast.

* * *

Mending the fence was not easy. The pain was constant in his injured hand. Every movement, every jostle, sparked armies of intensified agony that charged forth from his stitched digits a thousand times over.

But Eldon endured. He stationed the board in place with his leg, held the nail with his right hand and swung the hammer with his clumsy left. Twice he missed the mark and hit his injured hand, twice he yelled. His blunted fingers were bleeding when he finally finished.

The boar watched. It snorted at the man's efforts. It grunted at his failures.

It laughed. And its laughter spread across the farm until the chickens chortled with the piglets and the sows whispered in their sewing circle that the man, the last remaining man on the farm no less, was useless.

Stupid.

Why, the sows seemed to conclude in their conclave, *we're smarter than him.*

Eldon banged the hammer on the fence, but his aim was off and he delivered a mere glancing blow.

The chickens cackled. He threw the hammer into their throng. They heckled him as they scattered to the four corners of the yard.

The sows squalled as Eldon ambled passed.

"Shut up!" he yelled at them. He bent for the hammer on the dark circle of earth. The hammer was dried with specks of his blood.

The boar scratched its back at the mended section of fence. The new planking creaked. Eldon pointed the hammer at the boar. "As good as I been," he told the filthy beast, "I done everything for you!"

The hog ignored him.

The man hammered at the post. The boar struck off across the pen, startled.

"We took care of each other," Eldon told it. "We did, didn't we? For all the grief you did me, I took up for you jus' like you'd took up for me at times. You'd take my whoopins from Daddy and I took some of yours, too, didn't I?"

The giant hog trotted around its pen.

"Well, didn't I?" Eldon hollered at it.

The boar sprinted towards the fence.

Eldon backstepped.

The hog slouched and sat on its haunches.

"I don't understand why you do these things." Eldon stared at his injured hand. "You put me down, you hit me. Then you whoop others for calling me dumb."

The big hog huffed.

"Then you do something like all this," Eldon waved his rosy bandages. "You got all of' em laughing at me. Why?" He leaned across the fence for secrecy. "Didn't I stop Daddy from sending you away? He talked about it, didn't he? Said he was gonna kick you out, you couldn't come back home no more. He was gonna get rid of you. I stopped him, Roosevelt. I made it so's you could stay home. This is your home jus' like it's mine. Born and raised here, the both of us."

The hog rolled in the dirt, kicked its trotters in the air.

"What do you care? Maybe Daddy should've kicked you to the curb."

The boar wobbled on its legs to stand. It rested its black eyes on Eldon.

Stupid. Not a lick of brains. Dumber than dirt. Useless.

Eldon swallowed a groan. "If that's how you want it, that's how it'll be."

* * *

Eldon endured. He abided.

He lived alone in the hollow house, collected rent money, paid bills, and tended to the swine.

Not a soul stopped to check on his welfare. Douglas Hurst, and a couple of others who rented parcels of land, reported to those interested in town that the last Collier was alive and well. When Eldon made his weekly trip for slops and provisions, he was greeted with civility and very little interest (as it always had been).

You're a waste of air, Roosevelt told him at night whenever he'd reach the edge of sleep.

A waste, their dad concurred, faint from the deeper recesses.

Eldon's brother chided him during chores: *Don't*

know up from down. With each withered lettuce leaf and rotten tomato he poured into the trough, Roosevelt informed him: *Don't know your elbow from your asshole.*

He lavished the boar with food. He watched him fatten as spring went into summer and summer to autumn.

Time ticked by. October arrived. Leaves changed colors, fell.

Days wore on.

Runt. Shoulda been brained straight out the womb, Roosevelt snickered.

Eldon blared the radio to drown Roosevelt's yammering (when they heard Tricky Dick was hospitalized for phlebitis, they all had a good chuckle).

The first real chill finally bit the neck of lingering heat. Winter was brewing, bubbling beneath the vestiges of the humidity.

Eldon sharpened his ax. He readied his knife.

The temperature dropped as November dawned.

The boar ballooned.

* * *

The days had been cold, the nights freezing. On the morning of the nineteenth, Eldon woke to the farm coated with a solemn layer of finely packed snow.

He found the pigs huddled in their enclosure, nestled serene in the mounds of hay he had provided for bedding. A single sow and a feeble piglet remained alive by that wintry day. They didn't stir when the man crunched across the vacuum of the yard.

Of course, the boar lived.

The gargantuan creature barreled through the hoarfrost and dirty snow. It sought something, anything, from its empty trough. It eyed the man who stood and stared at it. The behemoth snorted demands for a kingly meal; its declarations puffed steaming clouds in the sharp air.

Eldon flexed his fingers on the handle of the butcher knife. He climbed into the sow's pen.

The sow and the piglet didn't attempt to run. They lifted their heads for the blade as Eldon slid it across their throats, each in turn. Weak fountains of blood sprayed on the legs of his brown coveralls.

They ain't laughing now.

Roosevelt had been silent the last few days as if he'd frozen up with the weather, hiding in the furrows of his little brother's brain for warmth.

Eldon didn't bother with a reply. He watched the limp pigs give up the ghost. They laid still with no further use for breath.

You can't get rid of all your problems that easy.

Eldon climbed back over the fence.

You're gonna miss me.

The boar paced the length of its pen.

"No one's missed you."

You've not had a chance to.

Eldon cleaned the knife blade on his pants leg.

The boar waddled to the rear of its pen.

Hey, Roosevelt piped up, *why don't you get the pillow?*

Emmett, their dad, woke. *It's up on your bed, son. Put it on him like you put it on me.*

Roosevelt: *Or get the hammer again, retard. You gonna come up behind me like last time?*

Eldon climbed over the fence. The mended board screeched.

The hog went into its enclosure.

Eldon squatted to peer into the den, mindful to keep a respectful distance. The boar's eyes blinked at him.

"I've thought on some things," Eldon said. "Where'd I have been if Daddy kicked you out the door? How long before it'd been me he sent down the road?"

The hog shuffled in the gloom.

"You had an idea you might sell the place. If you did, you never said nothin' about what you was gonna do with me? Where would I go? Was I part of the plan? This is home. Don't nobody care about us, Roosevelt. The mule's been dead near two year and Mr. Hurst didn't blink an eye when I said it thumped your head. Nobody did. Nobody asked anything. Cause nobody cared. They's just glad another Collier's gone."

The cold crept beneath Eldon's clothes, slipped under his skin.

"Roosevelt... Like I said, I've thunk on some matters. I buh- I buh-... I think I been able enough just me out here. I don't think I need you no more. I think it's high time you go back to being dead."

Eldon had his injured hand gloved. He ran the wilted fabric of the fingers, and the aching stumps they concealed, over the dull gray of the butcher knife's blade.

"They waitin' on me to die, too, maybe."

The boar poked its head from the doorway.

Eldon kept his eyes on the knife. He didn't twitch a muscle.

The hog emerged fully, its back and sides scraped the wood of the doorway. It sniffed the air as it approached the man. Its snout danced slickly over Eldon's stubbly face. The beast turned its nose from his unclean odor.

Eldon patted the hog with his injured hand, scratched behind its floppy ears, petted its sides. He half-stood from his crouch and put his arm across the wide expanse of its shoulders. His left hand, the knife held tightly, slid under the pig's head, the blade turned up and poised at its neck.

The hilt of the knife touched the hog.

Mealy brains.

The boar shifted and slammed its flank into Eldon. He staggered; the knife nicked the hog's chest. It squealed as Eldon fell on his ass in the snow and pat filled ground.

The man held fast to the knife. The hog ran at Eldon. It trampled him, its hooves pressed deep into his stomach.

Eldon lashed out. The knife sliced a red ribbon down the pig's side. The monster's rear hoof dug for traction in the man's testicles. Sparks of pain ruptured in Eldon as the beast lurched free and ran.

The massive hog rammed the weak spot of the fence. The boards broke and the hog awkwardly squeezed through, wild, screaming.

Eldon spotted the butcher knife in a pile of filth. Eldon couldn't reach it, he couldn't move for the immense pain flooding throughout his body. He lay on his side and puked; the strain twisted the torment to new degrees.

His head dropped. The unfathomable ache began to lessen. The heat of sickness roasted his bones. Eldon concentrated to focus. He saw blood painted across the disturbed slush.

Inhale. Exhale.

Eldon tried to count to ten.

Inhale. Exhale.

He raised his head. His arms moved, soon his legs loosened and followed suit. Eldon struggled to his feet with a hitch of breath in his chest. Wet, nauseous pain radiated from his groin and accompanied his halting, limping stride.

It was easier to unlatch the gate than climb over, or through, the busted fence. He followed, slowly, with baby steps, the ruts in the snow across the yard and around the house. Crimson rivulets stretched to the field. He smirked to think of the bloody snow as the peppermint brittle his momma used to make at the holidays.

The hog was digging its snout in the snow thirty yards out. It pranced in circles, squealed with delight.

With considerable unease, Eldon went up the back steps. In the kitchen, the hammer waited in the sink. He quivered with pain and anger, but to have the weapon in hand, to feel it a part of him, brought a reserve of calm.

He shuffled across the yard. Each step poked the pain like a nest of angry hornets. The endless stings of anguish slowed him, but the torment, with the hammer, kept him determined.

"Roosevelt!"

The hog stopped its play and jerked its head in Eldon's direction.

"Pig-hoo-o-o-o-ey!"

It saw the man on his staggered march across the ivory field.

The boar grunted and ran.

* * *

Eldon followed the hog's tracks into the woods of the unoccupied north acres. His advance chewed the snow pack in monotone until the ice-laden trees and the creak of their limbs in their frigid winter coats enveloped him.

The tracks wriggled in loops around shrubs, smashed through the copse. Eldon swiped at sweat as he lurched in the boar's hoofsteps. He stopped for breath, for a moment to rest the pain pulsating up and down his body. Slivers of his own blood trickled zigzag brooks down his thighs.

Do you got it in ya?

Eldon moved one foot at a time.

Pathetic. Weak as some sissy. Ya always were.

Snow fell. The flakes forsook laziness for a tempest. They caught with the icicles, bowed the branches. Drifts piled higher on the woodland floor.

Eldon's breath puffed thicker in cuneiform and curlicue clouds. He forced himself onward. He couldn't think of the new ache smoldering in his toes that wormed its way to his ankles. There it met the kaleidoscopic pains from his groin. It soon dulled to numbness and reduced his lame hobble to a dying man's amble.

He persisted.

The hammer urged his leaky boots to keep to the task.

As the snow fell, the ruts the hog made were filled and the bright red splotches of blood became pink.

Eldon scratched at the tickle on his scalp with his gloved nubs. His hat was gone. He stood wondering when it had fallen off, probably during the tussle in the pigpen, he wasn't sure, when a scream drifted from the whirling distance to his ears. It was a terrible, frightful scream.

It sounded human.

Eldon knew otherwise.

He didn't know if his steps actually quickened, but he felt the urgency fuel his muscles. Eldon kept his (raw) eyes fixed straight ahead, he lifted his feet (that weighed an unfeeling ton each) and stomped them in the disappearing path. He staggered to keep his balance with every other gain achieved.

You're gonna die out here, ya goddamn idiot, his brother laughed. He was dismissed when the wind flexed its might into a white squall. The voice was lost amid the bombs of branches breaking and their muffled crashes to the smothered landscape.

The storm's barrage died as suddenly as it had been unleashed. Disoriented, Eldon had to stop to look for the hog's trail. It was still present, faintly. In the new brisk visibility, he saw the tracks vanished at the rise of a hillock.

Eldon dragged his feet in pursuit.

The hill stopped at the lip of a gully. The snow was torn and tossed. The trail ended below at the hog. Its head was twisted backward, its trotters akimbo and motionless, where its gluttonous girth had somersaulted to an end. A thickening transparent coverlet of snow and ice had already tucked the boar in for its final good night.

Eldon tried to keep upright on his descent, but it was

in vain. His boots slipped in a flurry of winter sludge and rolled, he presumed, much in the manner of the hog. Falling down the embankment didn't hurt, the snow provided a reliable cushion, it only agitated the pains he already felt.

At the bottom, an arm's length from the boar, his lungs pounded with frigid air, Eldon still grasped the hammer in his gloved hand.

The hog's frosted eyes somehow met the man's.

"Here piggy, piggy," Eldon mumbled. He caught snowflakes in his mouth.

Standing was not an option. Half frozen from the core out, he got no farther than his knees and crawled to the hog.

"I got you," Eldon's teeth chattered, chewed the words.

He raised the hammer, straining, and brought it home with all the strength he could muster. The face buried deep in the boar's showing eye. "I told you I'd get you!"

Eldon pulled the hammer free with a slurp of suction. He battered the hog's head until his heart was ready to burst in his constricted throat.

The boar's head split open, its defining features contorted and fluid. He could see Roosevelt in the tableau of meat and bone.

Still, he gripped the hammer.

"I told you..."

Inhale. Exhale.

Razors in, razors out.

"I got you."

You sure did, Roosevelt said. *Did me in,* he chuckled and his laugh gained momentum.

Stupid, his dad joined in. *I never wanted you, you know that? I pushed ya momma down the stairs to try to git rid of ya.*

"Daddy-"

But ya came along anyways, Emmet said. *Had to keep ya, I s'pose. You never was good for much. Too dumb.*

They danced, arm in arm, round and round, circling his brain. *Dummy dummy dummy!* they sang. *Stupid bastard!*

"HUSH IT NOW! Y'ALL JUST HUSH IT! SHUT UP!"

Eldon snapped his eyes wide. Relief welled at the corners of his eyes.

"Momma-"

Don't you worry, honey, she said. *They won't bother you no more. They always wanted to pick at you-*

"Always-"

They're just jealous is all. Always were.

"Momma, they-"

Hush now, she said. *Don't you worry. You were always my special one. But you look so tired, Eldon, darling. You need you some rest.*

"I do," he agreed. "I hurt all over, Momma."

Get some rest, baby. She began to sing, *I left my baby lying here-*

Eldon stared down at the hammer in his fist.

-lying here, lying here-

In a quick motion, Eldon slammed it down on his head.

"AHHH!"

-I left my baby lying there-

The claw dug under his skull.

"AHHH!"

He pulled it out. A section of his skull flipped over. Eldon dropped the hammer.

"Hoo hoo hoo hoo!"

His arms stiffened and jerked, they pushed at invisible phantoms.

-to go and gather berries.

Eldon fell with spasms. The cold rushed into his head.

"Hoo... hoo... hoo..."

His body went limp.

"Hoo... hoo..."

His eyes met the hog's rictus of horror.

"...hoo..."

The wind whipped.

Snow spiraled from the pale heavens and was tossed in winding torrents.

It began the chore of burying the dead.

EIGHTH DEADLY SIN
By James Harper

The deadly sins have no number to bind them, not seven, but many more. And why should that not be so? The degree and extent to which man shows hate and disdain to his fellow man can never be confined to a handful; the contempt one man shows to another can be seen daily as we pass each other on the street in our rush toward death: no smiles, no greetings, no warmth as we push and shove through to our doom in minded determination to meet our onrushing, ignominious end. When men bear some much hate and crime against each other, how can there not be more? Many more?

There are more than seven deadly sins. And the eighth is worse than the ones before it.

As her metatarsals broke—all of them in both feet—the woman strapped to the floor released a surprising groan while the sound of bones splintering filled the cramped room. The moan almost echoed, its reverberation deep and low.

"What the hell?"

Gordon's nose wrinkled as his upper lip curled. Taking a step closer, he watched as the ops pounded the soles of her feet with a three-pound truncheon. The woman, a black one of some indeterminate age, perhaps thirty, maybe forty, who knew, lay on the floor, her feet raised and bound to accommodate the beating.

She moaned again. From behind the glass, Mitchell Gordon turned to Daniel Kenney. "That's unusual, isn't it, doctor?"

Kenney looked up from his tablet. "Eh?" Then, a glance to the woman in the room surrounded by the GBS operatives. "Oh, yes. Yes, it is unusual, sir."

"I didn't think that the procedure we're implementing would elicit that sort of reaction."

"No, you're absolutely correct. It shouldn't."

"What's this woman's name?"

"Ah, just a second." He swiped half a dozen strokes. "Siliya. Muroyi Mukwae Siliya."

"What's the age?"

"Indeterminate. These people don't keep written records that give us a clear, consistent timeline."

"I expected—you know—a scream, a yell, a whimper. Not what we just heard."

"Their kind's shown to be very uncooperative."

"I understand. I just didn't expect—I've never seen this particular reaction is all."

Kenney's eyes continued their focus on his iPad. He pulled a candy lozenge from his faded and frayed lab coat pocket, crunching it in his mouth in a manner that made the skin on Gordon's neck roil with a chill. Without looking up, he said, "Well, you know. You can never really tell."

"Check your record for previous tacticals. You say she's been here six weeks?"

Kenney swiped upward. "45 days, right."

"What else have we presented? Rectal feeding?"
Kenney swiped down. "Yes."
"Sleep deprivation?"
"Ah, yes. Three occasions."
"Duration?"
"A hundred eighty hours each."
"Each."
"Yes."
"Klegs?"
"Um, yes."
"Black out?"
"Definitely."
"Did we waterboard?"
"Four sessions."
"Sub temp?"
"Er—just a sec. Yes, 50 degrees. Nine times.

"I'm presuming we ran through the basics. I mean, we did the rudimentary: the facial slapping, the abdo strikes, the forced shaking."

"Yes, yes and check."

"And nothing from her? No information for the client?"

"No."

"Nothing?"

"No results listed."

"She's that tough?"

"These people always are."

He released a long sigh. "I guess that's why I'm here." He glanced at Kenney's feet. "You know, I got other—better—things I could be attending to."

Gordon shook his head, exhaling.

Kenney said, "Previous reports put her in the center of the Marine op when it went south. She was in the middle of it."

"Well, I guess we're going to have to up the game. Time for a pro to take over." He stared at the floor. "I'm really tired of having to do everything around here."

The black woman began whistling on the other side of the glass. The range of sound ran from a deep low, almost baritone, to a high-pitched octave above C.

"You know, in the Arabian world they call this procedure the *falaka*."

Absorbed by his tablet, Kenney said, "Uh-huh."

Gordon returned his attention to the African woman. She opened her mouth, eyes closed as the ops continued the pummeling. A new sound emerged from her: Music. In a language Gordon had never heard, she sang a song.

Gordon elbowed Kenney, pointing. "Wha—what's that?"

Kenney squinted at her. His eyes, their sclera yellow and bloodshot, skipped about the grey concrete walls of the tiny room before returning to the woman's form.

"Yeah, I don't know. Could be coping."

"Yeah, well, it's out of the usual. I don't like the out of the usual. Where's she from?"

"From the Southern Zambia region. North bank of the Zambezi."

"Do you know what language that is?"

"No clue. Shona? Tokaleya? Could be that. Probably that. It's the local dialect."

The operatives lifted the woman by her elbows, raising her from the floor. They strapped her arms into the standing rack, a metal device that forced her to stand on her broken feet. The ops moved away. The melody of her song remained constant, a lilting, haunted threnody.

Swearing a curse, Gordon entered the ops room. Over his shoulder, he turned to Kenney to say, "Do I *have* to think of everything around here?" The woman would never leave the facility so it made no difference to him—or anyone—if she saw his face.

As he approached, the woman viewed him through slit eyelids. She continued her song as he came near.

He stood as close as the manual recommended. In a soft voice he said, "Miss, I'm Mitchell Gordon. You've been here six weeks without helping our investigation. I'm here for two reasons: One, I alone can relieve the stress you're undergoing now. I have the authority. And two, under that authority, I must tell you that you have reached the limit of your time here."

He leaned into her face. She smelled of piss, sweat and blood. And beneath that, lay an undersmell, the odor of—what? Gordon could not tell.

"Miss, you must tell me what happened in your village the night the soldiers came."

"*Woz ekhaya woz ekhaya woz ekhaya.*"

More singing. She sang, "*Woz ekhaya*" over and over in a repeating cadence. She did not vary in her pitch or tempo. The song rang in an ominous melody, one that evoked the grave as well as the night.

Then she puckered her lips to whistle. A thin, reedy tune came forth, its rhythm as different to her song as a march to a lullaby, the tune resonating in tone and rich in timbre.

She opened her eyes, meeting Gordon's. That's when he realized the underlying smell; her stare reflected it. She smelled of accepted doom.

"Enough. This is useless." Gordon moved to leave the ops room. With his hand on the door knob, he said, "I want hourly reports on this woman."

Leaving the building, he stalked the walkway to the parking lot. Reaching for his phone, he pressed the screen for a name.

After two rings, he said, "Wilson. Yes. The final villager continues to thwart our best effort."

He listened for a moment. Then: "No. No. Completely unsuccessful." Listening, he opened the door to his

Spyder.

"No. No, I think we're going to have to cede this one." Another moment. "No, what is with these people?" Another. "Yes. We're had the most turgid resistance to our methods that I've ever encountered." Starting his engine, he backed out of his reserved space to drive out of the lot into the night. "Yes. All right. I've established my position. I'll do that then. Definitely. I'll keep you informed." He hung up.

Twenty minutes later, he pulled into the wooded driveway of his Great Falls house. The lights in the kitchen told him Julia woke in the middle of her night for a pregnancy-driven snack. With a grim smile, he entered his home.

"Hi, Sweetie," she said as he opened the back door. She waved the paper plate that held the chocolate cake slice as she swallowed a forkful.

"Honey, what are you doing up?" He measured his cadence to show his concern without revealing his anger; they had discussed this—at length. "The boy needs his rest."

"I know. I know. But I was so *so hungry*." The last word emerged in the most mournful way. He remembered her saying other words with the same inflection, words that made him hard. "Besides," she said, "I made this myself from scratch. It's pretty slamming; you ought to try it."

He opened his mouth to speak when she whirled around to meet his gaze. "You know what? I read a random fact today. You want to hear it?"

Before he could respond, she said, "I read that they think the first human, the first person to evolve into what we consider human today was a woman who came from lower central Africa 150,000 years ago. They call her Mitochondrial Eve."

"Really?"

"Yeah, isn't that cool?"

He drew her into his arms, rubbing her pronounced belly as he squeezed her. "He needs his sleep." Taking the plate, he said, "Off to bed."

She pushed her lower lip out in protest. Standing in the cold light of their custom kitchen, the neon blasted her blonde, shoulder-length hair.

Before she could speak again, he pointed to the general direction of the bedroom upstairs. "Now go."

She turned to obey. He watched as she scampered away.

As he listened to the faraway noises of her bathroom ablations, he checked the email he had gotten from that afternoon. The subject line read: "Mother's Status."

After a minute, he typed, "I'll see her in the morning." Then he went to the cabinet for the Blantons.

When he awoke the next day, Julia had already left for her Week 42 OB/GYN appointment. He checked her text, then his brother's.

The next twenty minutes saw him from bed to front door as he left to drive to the hospice where his mother received end stage care. The Wyler Center, halfway between his brother's Alexandria house and his, could be reached in ten minutes, depending on Beltway traffic.

At her room, he entered to see her restrained, the straps wrapped around her wrists attached to the railings on her bed. She looked at him in bewilderment, her face devoid of recognition.

"Sir? Ma'am?" she said, her voice crackling with age. "Could you please tell me where I am? Could you help me here? Either of you?"

Shaking his head, he went for the nurse call, then thought better of it. After pressing the button, he stormed out of the room into the main corridor to the Nurse Station.

A matronly nurse anticipated his approach but waited

for him to speak first nonetheless. Her lips stretched in a thin line across her withered face; he had seen her like before many times.

"I'm–"

"Yes, Mr. Gordon, I know who you are."

"Why is my mother restrained?"

"She's escalated her behavior."

"Escalated?"

"Perhaps you better speak with the doctor about that. I'll call her now." She lifted the analog receiver.

In his mother's room, her look frantic and afraid, she cocked her head in increments as she took in nothing from every inch of her view. Cognition and lucidity long since evaporated in an Alzheimer's haze, she lacked even a rudimentary ability to function.

He smelled her feces as he approached her side. He noticed that she had more gaps in her hair, portions of her bare scalp showing through in a greater number of spots. Perhaps that explained the term "escalation."

"Mister? Miss?"

Under his breath, he said, "There is only me, Mother."

"Could you please ask them to remove these?" She pulled upward on the restraints.

In a louder voice, he said, "I'm having them come to do just that now, Mother."

"Oh, thank you." Her gaze drifted from him to the empty space behind him.

"Miss, could you please get me a glass of water?"

Gordon exhaled a laden sigh. "*Mother. I'm* the only one *here*." He went to get her request.

Then he texted Charles: "I'm getting rid of this useless Indian."

Charles's text returned. "She's Paki."

After half an hour, the doctor in charge of her care arrived. She came into the room with the cheerful attitude Gordon had always seen in her approach, a bright presence that he presumed calculated.

"Dr. Davi, I have a series of questions to ask you."

With a nod, Susan Davi directed her attention to her patient. She held his mother's wrist for a moment, then asked, "How are you feeling, Mrs. Gordon?" in a voice that sounded a decibel or two higher than Gordon liked.

"Are you the doctor?"

"Yes, Mrs. Gordon, I'm your doctor, Dr. Davi."

"She's been hallucinating."

Davi shot him a look to silence. He did not appreciate that either.

"Look, doctor, I think–"

"Mrs. Gordon, I'm going to speak with your son for a minute. Then I'll be back to speak to you again."

"That's all right. I'll just talk to this nice lady here." She nodded to the empty space on the doctor's left.

As they departed the room, Gordon said, "You see, doctor? That's what I tried to warn you about."

Dr. Davi waited until they had stepped a few paces into the hallway before addressing Gordon. "Mr. Gordon–"

"*Doctor* Gordon."

"Dr. Gordon, your mother is in the end stage of life. The vagrancies of her cognition should, in fact, deteriorate more rapidly now."

"Well, doctor, my confidence in your method and practice has also deteriorated. To an untenable point."

"That's within your prerogative, Mist– Dr. Gordon."

"I believe the quality of care you've rendered is based on your lack of—experience. So I want to see a more—seasoned professional come in."

Dr. Davi's back straightened. "You're entitled to your opinion."

"I'll make the arrangements for your replacement. I'll insist you stay on until that individual is secured."

"Of course."

An alert from the room sounded. They both dashed back to his mother's bedside. The heart monitor blared its warning as they found his mother rigid and stiff in the bed, her head tilted behind her to stare with unseeing eyes at the headboard.

Dr. Davi moved in a flurry of action. She checked the throat to determine the cause of her patient's state.

"She's swallowed her tongue. She's stopped breathing."

Grabbing a spoon from the nightstand, Dr. Davi inserted it into the mouth to retract the organ. After several failed attempts, she took her flashlight to examine the mouth and throat.

"It's detached."

"What?"

"The tongue. It's detached."

"How is that possible? *Is* that possible?"

Dr. Davi shrugged. "I didn't think so." She inserted the spoon deep into the esophagus then gently attempted to pull the tongue out from her throat. As she worked, the crash team arrived. Two men and three females, one pushing the defib cart.

Over her shoulder, Dr. Davi said, "We can't defib due to the patient's advanced age. But prepare a needle." She finished retrieving the tongue, laying it on the kidney pan nearby.

One of the crash team applied a stethoscope to the chest while another switched off the monitors. She shot Dr. Davi a grim look. "No pulse detected."

"Let me have that needle," Dr. Davi said. Taking it, she injected into the sternum.

They waited for a response. The crash tech listened again for a heartbeat. She shook her head twice.

They waited a full ten minutes before Dr. Davi said, "All right then." Turning to Gordon, she walked over to say, "I'm sorry, Dr. Gordon."

Loathing to speak in front of this many witnesses—too many opportunities for someone to get it wrong—Gordon just nodded. He'd wait for his chance.

* * *

The African woman whistled the same low, dirge-like tune, a simple haunting melody untethered to Western convention. Listening as he sat across from her in the ops room, Gordon realized he recognized it from his dreams the night before. Somehow the song had invaded his consciousness, an unacceptable development.

"Miss, we have reached what we call an impasse. I'm afraid I must insist that you cooperate as I have to draw your case to a conclusion."

Her eyes locked onto his, her expression untouched by either her condition or his comments. Her puckered lips delivered the song without break, its key and mode as unique as any he had heard. As the air in the chamber filled with the music, Gordon noticed that his people had lost focus, and had stopped their tasks to listen.

"Ma'am, that's quite enough of this." He stood to press his foot on the top of her broken arch. Closing her eyes in a wince, in the moment her whistling stopped, he knew he had her.

"Miss, I need you to cooperate." He stared at her as he stood above her. She met his gaze.

Their pupils bolted as one, she held his gaze. Then she smiled.

Gordon felt his skin go cold. Shaking his head to rid himself of the feeling, he promised himself he would make her pay for it.

Then she spoke for the first time. "What would you have me tell you, Missterr Gorrrdon?"

"Our information puts you on the scene of the attack that killed our Marines. I simply need you to tell me what happened to them."

"Is that all?"

"Yes, just tell me what you saw."

Another chill came across him as she smiled at him. She resumed her whistling; this time with high-pitched notes than ran through the air like an open industrial refrigerator door emptying its contents of atmosphere.

After five minutes, Gordon stood, walked out into the ops room, turned to Kenney, and then said, "I've had enough of this shit. Hammer her teeth."

Later, driving to his brother's for their scheduled meeting, he called to confirm. Getting the voice mail, he sighed a long exhale then said, "On my way be there in five. But, really, Charles, we need to talk."

A minute later, his brother buzzed back.

"Hey, Mitch, sorry I missed your call. I'm barbecuing out back."

"You know, we're going to have to work out the details on Mother's arrangements."

"Yeah, yeah. I figured."

"Have you given any thought to it?"

"Well, sure."

"I mean really, Charles. Have you given any thought to the funeral arrangements for our mother or are you just going to allow me to go through the motions—*like I always have to*—to get the job done?"

"Mitch. I have some ideas."

"Really? Some *real* ideas? Not some blue-sky, let's-honor-her-in-some-half-assed-way ideas?" He turned onto his brother's Taylor Run street behind the Masonic Temple. Four yards down, he slipped into Charles' driveway.

"Look, I said I have some. We can talk about them when you get here."

"I'm coming in now. I just don't have faith that, in

light of your history of bailing, of getting me to do all the heavy lifting so you can do, whatever brain-dead, flighty thing you're pursuing, you're going to actually pitch in this time."

"Mitch, I'll pitch in. I'll do what I have to."

"I hope so. I just have my doubts."

He walked from the drive to the backyard with an eight-foot wooden fence. He smelled the permanent charcoal burning from the gas-fired grill.

Charles faced him, looking at the grill, engrossed in his cooking process. As Gordon approached, he noticed him leaning on the picnic table behind him, vodka drink in one hand, grilling tongs in the other as the grill separated the two of them. He pocketed his phone.

"Hope you're hungry. I'm grilling up something special."

"Oh really?" He stared at his brother over the grill.

"Oh yeah. One of a kind, really."

"Look, Charles, I've no appetite for either your eternally charcoal grilled concoctions or your lame notions about what will be appropriate for our mother."

"You sure? Cause it's gonna be good."

"Yes." He detected, however, a unique aroma in the air.

"Okay. I know better than to try to twist your arm. Your loss."

"So what's your idea?"

Charles pulled from his glass. "Ah, we can talk about it."

"Look, Charles, I came to talk."

"Right. And we will. Right now, I'm fixing—"

"Stop stalling."

"Come on, have a look. You might change your mind."

Gordon opened his mouth to argue but thought better of it. Charles's drinking made him impenetrable. He moved to the side of the grill where his brother stood in his unbalanced stance.

As he came around, he saw what had made Charles unbalanced: His foot had been hacked off above the ankle at mid-shin. The right foot gone, Gordon saw the stump bleeding out in a generous red flow. His brother stood leaning against the picnic table as the blood drained from the open wound onto the concrete of his patio. It spilled into a pool of spreading fluid onto the cement, staining the white stone in red matter.

Gordon looked at his brother's face for understanding. Charles smiled then nodded toward the grill.

"Hope you brought your appetite." He grinned, bearing his teeth.

Shocked, Gordon followed his gaze. There, roasting on the fire, the foot sizzled like a London broil. He saw the blackened skin smoking as it broiled over the charcoal; its meat sizzled as his brother sprayed it with water from a squirt bottle.

"You know," he said as poked it with tongs, "there's plenty here for both of us. You're welcome to stay for dinner."

* * *

The air still held the ozone from the rain, the savannah pregnant with humidity as the fire team of U.S. Marines hiked out of the glade onto the eastern outskirts of the jungle village. The four of them, spread in tactical search formation had come from Zakeyo in a circular route, looking for the position of a local gang of terrorist thugs calling themselves Ramwa Chivi. Now deep into the night, they had started at dawn.

"Lang, what's this joint ahead?" Barnes asked. A dog barked in the night.

Lang studied his tablet. "I dunno. Looks to be Muruni, Snuff. Pop 350 or so. Usual deets we been seeing all day. Can't really be sure though. Could be any village in this area."

"Right. Break it, men," Barnes said. The men sat on a well a few hundred feet from a ramshackle shed on the edge of the village. Around the well, several stone structures stood, built of hand-fitted blocks without mortar; they spread out from the well in a pattern that evoked a simple rhythm. A goat bayed in the dirt-bitten yard beyond the metal-walled hut.

The men sat on the well wall, going to their devices or, in Phillips' case, smoking. Marks drank from his canteen without interest, staring off into the savannah they had just hiked from. Lang unzipped to relieve himself against the well wall.

"Make it fifteen," Barnes said. "Then we recon this village to send a report."

"Just like all the others, I bet."

"Try 'n have some optimism, Phillips?" Barnes said. "Maybe this is the joint where we locate those motherfuckers."

Phillips laughed without mirth. Marks echoed the reaction. He, too, emptied his bladder on the wall.

Marks said, "That'd be too good to be true, Snuff. Then we'd be done with this shit detail and get roll back. That kinda luck don't happen on shit detail like this."

Barnes shook his head in a slow manner. "Yeah, you right. Just stay cool so we can finish then get the fuck out."

"Bet."

"I gotchu."

From the lit yard, a woman approached. Silhouetted against the backlight, she approached in careful movements as the men raised their weapons. Barnes motioned for them to lower their arms.

"Let's see what she has to say."

She came closer, moving into the area of stones. Marks turned on a lantern. She looked as if she could have been forty, but she could have also been a hundred, her age that difficult to pinpoint. She held up her hand to shield her eyes against the 40-watt glare.

"*Uri kuitei pano?*" she said in a tone that conveyed her irritation. "*Ibva ipapo.*" She pointed to the walls where they sat.

Keeping her in his direct line of sight, Barnes said, "Lang?"

"Probably Shona, Snuff," he said, swiping his tablet. "Gimme a second."

"You men, move away from there," she said. "You have no business here. Who are you? You speak English. Are you South African?"

"American," Phillips said, rubbing his cigarette into the soil.

"American? Why are you here? Get off there." She pointed to the well wall.

Phillips and Marks refused to comply, watching Barnes for their next move. Barnes stepped toward her. "Ma'am, we're with the American Marine Corps. We're here on a scouting mission. I promise we'll be here only a short time, then be out of your way."

"You need to move out of this spot. It's a sacred shrine. It's the Pit of Souls."

"What?" Phillips laughed. "What kind of–"

"Shut up, Phillips," Lang said. "This is her home, not ours."

Marks stepped closer to her. "Listen, have you seen any of the Ramwa Chivi? Tell us that, lady, and we'll get the *fuck* out of your hair."

"You must move away from the Pit of Souls."

Barnes held his hands up, palms toward her. "Look, what's your name? Who are you?"

"I am the Muroyi. I keep the Pit."

"Oh, the pitkeeper," Phillips said with a laugh.

Lang said, "Phillips."

Marks took her elbow. "Enough of this shit. Lady, tell us about the Ramwa Chivi. We been all over this joint for the past 24 and we ain't come up with shit. They gotta be somewhere. I'm betting here."

Phillips said, "You know, Marks's got a point. If Intel says they here and we ain't seen 'em up till now, then it stands to reason they here." He lifted his weapon in her direction.

"Phillips," Barnes said. "Check your—"

The woman said, "Stay away from—"

Lang said, "Lady, stay away—"

All five spoke at the same time. Then everyone shouted.

The woman pointed to the deep stains against the wall of the Pit of Souls. "You have desecrated the holy place."

She waved her arms in a sweeping motion. The men found that they could not move. Walking up to Phillips, who looked bewildered in his frozen state, she said, "You have desecrated the Pit of Souls, our channel to the First Mother." She pushed her hand into Phillips's chest, inserting her palm as if donning the sleeve to a blouse, the hand melting into his ribcage like a burning iron through paper. In a quick motion, she pulled it out, bloodied, grasping his heart. It throbbed in her clutch.

"I give you to the Sky."

Phillips evaporated into the wind, becoming transparent before drifting into the night.

She moved to Marks. Repeating her action, she tore out his heart, saying, "I give you to the Rain." He melted into a pool of water that ran to the stone edge before seeping into the soil.

Again with Lang. "I give you to the Ground." He crumbled into dirt, a mound of earth that began to blow away in the breeze.

And Barnes. "I give you to the Flame." His body burst into fire.

As she bowed her head, she said, "Thanks to you, First Mother, for your strength and wisdom. "I return to you your children."

Turning, she marched back to her home.

* * *

Negotiating the Mixing Bowl traffic the next evening, he barked his frustration on the line with the hospital. His attention diverted, he just missed an accident as least twice in his commute.

"I don't care!" he said, shouting. "I don't care. He's been there all day without any good answer as to why and what's wrong with him."

He paused.

"What you don't seem to understand, Dr. Alvanessa, is that, while you may serve as the head administrator, I know enough people in the area, in Fairfax County and the Virginia government, to get this done through *them*. Do you get my meaning?"

He waited a moment, listening.

"Good. Get it done. Get my brother the treatment he needs." He threw his phone into the Escalade console. Entering his parking space, he dialed Kenney as entered the complex.

"Where are you?"

A moment. "Good, I'm coming in now."

They had the woman standing on her broken feet, her arms on the standing bars propping her stance. Gordon looked her over as he entered the room. Now determined to get his answers, he'd lead the questioning himself. Her mouth a ruin of shattered teeth and smashed lips, she bowed her head in a resting position as she awaited the next series of inquiry.

He stood inches from her. Looking toward the floor, she failed to even acknowledge his presence.

"Good evening, Ms. Siliya."

She lifted her head to look at him, meeting his gaze. Her swollen lips drew back in what could only be a pain-filled smile as she stared into his eyes.

"I'm afraid I'm going to have to insist on responses today. Accurate. Truthful. But, if you want me to help you, you will need to give me the information we need to help you."

Her smile broadened. Tears rolled out of the corners of her eyes. Her elbows trembled on the bars from her effort to stand.

"Really, it's on your hands. Will you help me?"

She bowed her head again, then looked up into his face. He took it as a nod.

"Very well then. What happened on the night the American soldiers came?"

The song rose from her again, at first in a low pitch, then lifting to a high, sharp octave; it filled the room with her voice. Her voice reverberated throughout the space, resonating against the walls of the soundproofed chamber.

Gordon shouted to make himself heard. "I will not tolerate this anymore! You must answer my question!"

The song stopped. The music ceased as she rose her head once more to meet his gaze. A crooked grin crossed her blasted mouth as she looked at him. He felt a wave of cold sweep over his skin as the air around him dropped in temperature.

"The answer, Missterr Gorrrdon is that the eighth deadly sin is cruelty. But the ninth… the ninth is racism."

She exploded into a shower of blood and internal organs splattering Gordon, the woman's body spraying him as her matter, the exploding flesh of her body, splashed against him. His face, his eyes, the entire front of his body became drenched in her flesh and gore as she erupted over him, blinding him in bits of skin and muscle as her ejecting body covered him in wet, bloody tissue.

Gasping, wiping his eyes, he hurried to look at her. The front of her body was now gone, destroyed in the self-detonation of her form. A ravaged travesty of what was once human, he could see the cavity of her chest and abdomen emptied of the contents that had burst over him, her spine and ribs visible in the wreckage that remained.

* * *

Furious, Gordon drove home, his shirt and slacks now useless, covered in blood and pieces of flesh. He had attempted to clean it as best he could but the extent of the damage, the literal explosion of a human body against him, had ruined his clothes.

Entering his house, he heard his wife moving about the kitchen. He slipped through the hallway toward the rear of the home to avoid her seeing him in this state.

"Hey, honey," she called.

"Hello, dear. I'll be right there. I've got to clean up."

"Okay. I made dinner."

"Uh, oh, great."

"Wait till you see. I'm so proud of the recipe I came up with. I hope you'll like it."

He removed his bloodstained shirt. Looking at it, he realized he'd have to throw it away. He examined his gore-caked slacks. Also worthless now.

Balling them into a wad, he stripped to his skivvies. He stashed the clothes in a spot she'd never see so he could later retrieve them.

Calling, he said, "I'm going to take a shower."

"Okay, Sweetie. Don't be long. Dinner's going to be ready soon."

Coming out of the shower, he toweled off before

donning gym shorts and a tee. He smelled her cooking, its odor unlike anything he had sensed before. Used to her cooking, he knew her limited repertoire; this smelled different.

Calling out, he said, "This smells different?"

He heard the joy in her voice as she called back. "Yes, like I said, this is totally new, totally unique. I'm just putting it out now in the dining room for you. I sure hope you like it."

He stepped into the darkened hallway that led to the kitchen. Still in the dining room, her back turned, he looked at the kitchen. Pots scattered about, the tiled floor covered in grease and liquid, food and flour and powder lie everywhere.

"I'm afraid I made quite a mess in making it."

"No matter," he said, swallowing the words as he spoke.

Her back to him, he saw her from behind. She wore a short white teddy, the one he had bought for her for Valentine's. But dangling between her legs, he saw something strange. A tube? It glistened in the light coming from above the table.

Stepping closer, he almost slipped on the slick floor. He saw blood on the tiles, blood splattered with entrails. The kitchen was littered with internal organs.

Turning to face him, she smiled. "Hi, honey," she said, wearing nothing other than the teddy which was open in front. Her stomach and breasts were covered in blood. From her crotch—from *inside her*—he saw the greasy rope of her intestines descend, glistening in the dim light. The long tube of her organ had dropped out from her abdominal cavity and was dragging on the floor. Her intestines and more.

"I made something special for dinner tonight."

The coil of her gut slid on the floor behind as she turned to face him. "Look what I arranged, darling. I made a special meal." She indicated the dining room table where candles lit the two place settings.

"One of a kind, really."

Across the floor in a bloody mess of entrails and afterbirth, Gordon saw a splay of internal organs. Looking at her abdomen, he saw a tiny hand protruding from the bulge of her bloated pregnancy. Gordon felt his bowels melt into water. She chewed a slick piece of meat.

"I pulled him out myself so that he could join us." She beamed at him. "For dinner."

Her smile widened as she said, "I'm thinking about calling it fetus tartare."

THERAPY SESSIONS
By B.M. Tolkovsky

James – 1/1/2021

James shifted uncomfortably on the scratchy polyester couch. He glanced around the tiny room as he waited for his court-appointed therapist to arrive. The inspection didn't take very long. The room was small, barely larger than a standard cubicle. It contained the couch he was currently fidgeting on, along with a slightly more comfortable looking desk chair a few feet away from the couch. Several framed degrees from universities he didn't recognize were clustered on a miniscule table next to the desk chair. A few boring watercolor reproductions lined the walls, but the main focal point of the office was the large bookshelf that almost skimmed the ceiling. It appeared to contain hundreds of tomes on the murky depths of the human psyche, and it made James feel a bit nervous for some reason he couldn't exactly verbalize.

He glanced up as the door opened and his new counselor walked into her office. James' first impression of her was how... *dull* she seemed. She was a middle aged, slightly overweight woman wearing a shapeless cardigan and dirt brown trousers that appeared to be about an inch too short. She had dishwater blonde hair, pulled back in a frizzy bun, and wore round, black eyeglasses that gave her an inquisitive, owlish expression. Her face was bare of makeup and she wore no earrings or jewelry that James could see.

The therapist settled herself into the desk chair across from James. She picked up a small notepad and an ink pen from the little table next to her chair, and only then did she raise her eyes and look directly at James for the first time. "It's nice to meet you, Mr. Shaw. May I call you James?" He nodded his assent. "Wonderful. My name is Dr. Olivia Green, but please feel free to call me Olivia, if you wish. I take it that you understand why you're here today?" Once again, James nodded his understanding. "Excellent. Then please allow me to tell you a little about myself before we begin.

"As you may or may not already know, the prison specifically referred you to me upon your release due to my extensive work with violent, sexual offenders. Throughout the course of my research and practice, I have successfully treated thousands of individuals like yourself and helped rehabilitate them in order for them to transition safely back into society. I can assure you that my success rates are quite high. However, in order for this course of treatment to work for you, you will need to abide by the rules and regulations to the letter. Any deviations from my program requirements and you will be immediately terminated from my practice and will return to prison to serve out the remainder of your sentence. If I am not mistaken, that would be fifteen years, six months, and seven days, yes?"

James felt a swooping sensation somewhere between his stomach and solar plexus, reminiscent of a sudden vertical drop off a very tall building. He thought of the almost daily beatings and abuse he had endured from his fellow inmates while the worthless guards turned a blind eye. "Yes ma'am, that's right. I was granted early parole after my lawyer won my case on appeal. They told me I would need to stick to some pretty strict conditions to keep my freedom, and I want to assure you that I am willing to do whatever it takes. I don't ever want to go back to that place."

As James spoke, Dr. Green watched him intently, her sharp brown eyes magnified by her oversized eyeglasses. "Yes, I read all about your appeal." She leafed through her notepad and read a direct quote from the trial transcript: "The defendant, James Shaw, shall be released immediately and without delay due to an improper collection of biological evidence and failure on the part of the police to obey the proper chain of custody when submitting said evidence for testing and evaluation." Dr. Green placed the notepad back into her lap. "In other words, you got off on a technicality because the primary detective investigating your case was sloppy. He took the semen sample from your victim home in the trunk of his police cruiser and let it sit there for over a week while he went on vacation before he remembered to take it down to the station, correct? This meant the evidence, *technically*, could have been tampered with, or ruined by biological decay from the heat, or in some way 'fixed' by the cops… and thus, here you sit today."

James felt his cheeks flush crimson. Yes, that was precisely what happened. Thank God for that idiotic detective and his conveniently timed Hawaiian vacation, or else James would still be behind bars for at least fifteen additional years. Sure, his original sentence did include the possibility of parole, but only after serving 80% of his time. And even then, most parole boards didn't tend to be too merciful to men who had raped, tortured, and killed a young woman. Especially men who were (allegedly) suspected of having engaged in this type of behavior for many years before they were finally apprehended.

Taking a deep breath, James leaned forward and met the doctor's eyes. "Yes ma'am, you're right about that. I suppose I did walk out of the joint because I got a good lawyer and a shitty investigator on my case. But I'm here today because I truly want to change. I know that I can be a better person; I just need some help to figure it out. I want a chance to live a normal life, just like everybody else. That's all I want. I want your help. Please."

Dr. Green leaned back in her desk chair, and for the first time since walking into her office, she smiled at James. "Excellent. Then let's begin."

<u>Dr. Green, Clinical Notes – 1/1/2021</u>

JS was referred to me upon his release from Alto Prison, where he served approximately 5,288 days of a 30-year sentence. JS was initially convicted on one count of rape, one count of murder, and one count of aggravated sexual assault for the torture he inflicted on the victim (female, initials GB, age 27, Caucasian, sex worker). Even with my considerable exposure to cases such as this one, the crime scene photographs of GB are… extreme. Evidence would later show that JS likely held her in the basement of an abandoned property for at least two weeks, given the advanced state of emaciation she was in. The sad remnants of her body were so covered in blood, cuts, and bruises the crime scene investigators couldn't immediately identify her gender or ethnicity. GB had been bound at the wrists and suspended from the ceiling in a makeshift pulley system JS is believed to have installed in the basement. The pain must have been excruciating.

JS is an intriguing case. The lead detective who investigated his case felt certain JS is responsible for a number of similar unsolved cases throughout the state, particularly given his ease of access to female sex workers in his former line of employment (long-haul trucker). I am inclined to agree. This type of sadistic, sexual deviancy tends to develop slowly, blossoming into true horror after a great deal of trial and error. I think individual sessions with JS three times a week should be a good start. I'll start with the usual battery of tests (Psychosexual assessment, TAT, House-Person-Tree, Minnesota Multiphasic Personality Test, the Abel Assessment for Sexual Interest, and a penile plethysmograph, of course). I think I'll even throw in a classic Rorschach test, just for fun. I believe JS is going to be a special case, indeed.

James – 1/4/2021

James found himself back on Dr.Green's couch, dreading the start of his first talk therapy session with her. The weekend had been hell. She had made him come in for more than five hours for an extensive battery of tests, including a horrific one she referred to as a 'penile plethys' test. This test involved lab assistants showing him violent and sexual images and measuring the response reaction of his... member. The less said about *that* test, the better. James was still ashamed to think about the erection some of the pictures had given him. He was a smooth talker, but that kind of data seemed pretty damn difficult to fake.

He glanced up as Dr. Green entered the office. She was clad in her usual garb (lumpy sweater, ill-fitted dress pants, frizzy bun pulled back from her face), but she seemed to be in a good mood, and James felt himself relax just a little. He could do this. He had fooled many, many police officers, guards, judges, and lawyers in his day. He could handle one harmless old spinster, even if she did like to call herself 'doctor.'

Dr. Green settled herself in her desk chair and smiled

at James. "Good morning, James. I would like to check in with you about the testing you underwent this weekend. I have had a chance to review all your results. What was that experience like for you?"

James settled himself a bit deeper into the couch. "To be honest, it was pretty humiliating, doc. Having someone in a lab coat measure your erectile response to a picture isn't the most pleasant thing that's ever happened to me. Although, I guess it isn't the worst, either." He gave a weak chuckle, attempting to downplay the rage he still felt after enduring this indignity.

Dr. Green leaned forward slightly. "I'm sorry you had to experience that, James, but it really is very helpful for me and your course of treatment." She picked up her notepad and flipped to the middle. "James, you mentioned that this wasn't the worst experience you've ever had. I'd like to discuss that further. Let's talk about your childhood. The information I have paints a pretty grim picture."

He sucked in his breath. 'Grim' was certainly one way to characterize it, if that was how you described daily ass whippings from your strung out mother and an absentee dad who was so perpetually wasted he barely remembered any of his kids' names on a good day. James remembered how powerless he felt as a child and young teenager, before he came into his own and realized the pain *he* was capable of inflicting on others.

"My childhood was horrible. I'm sure that's all in your file. Both my parents were users and my mom beat the shit out of me and my sisters almost every day. On a couple of occasions, my dad sexually abused me, too. I'm sure most of the guys like me that you work with have the same sob story, huh?"

"Mmm, perhaps… Many sexual abusers were themselves the victims of abuse, but it isn't set in stone. The cycle can be, and usually is, broken. I'm much more interested in the abuse *you* inflicted. Tell me, did you torture animals as a child?"

James reeled back. He hadn't been expecting that; she was supposed to be sympathetic to him, wasn't she? Isn't that what therapists do; sit and listen to you cry about how bad your mommy and daddy treated you and then tell you none of it was your fault? "Well, I'm not proud of it, but yeah, I did. A couple times."

That was putting it lightly. James still remembered the exhilarating surge of power and strength he felt the first time he ripped the wings off a butterfly as a child. He quickly graduated to small animals: chipmunks, squirrels, and rabbits he caught in a trap placed in the woods behind their rundown single-wide trailer. He remembered the time he put the neighbor's Chihuahua in the oven... his mother had nearly beaten him to death when she discovered the pitiful little corpse, but it had been worth it. So worth it. The posters for the missing Chihuahua (Mr. Squeaks, what a pathetic name) had remained on telephone poles around the trailer park for months afterwards.

Dr. Green nodded her head as she made a small notation in her omnipresent notebook. "Yes, indeed. Thank you for your honesty. And after reviewing your juvenile and adult criminal histories, I see you were also fond of fire setting?"

He remembered the first time he had played with matches as an eight-year-old and almost set the trailer on fire. After that, he was hooked. It culminated in him setting his little sister, Jackie, on fire when he was twelve-years-old because she wouldn't take a shower with him. The eight-year-old had been left with second-degree burns on nearly half her body. They never reported the sexual or physical abuse to the law; his mother simply told the physicians at the emergency room that the little girl had been playing with a candle unsupervised while she was trying to bathe her other daughter. Social Services got involved and Jackie was sent to live with her mother's second cousin when she was released from the hospital. James never saw her again. Last James had heard, she'd changed her name and moved out of the state. Good riddance.

"Yeah, I got caught with a few arson charges when I was in my twenties, but I got them all pled down and only did a few months behind bars."

Dr. Green smiled a Mona Lisa grin that disturbed James just the slightest bit. "Yes, you *really* do have a knack for finding good lawyers." She glanced at the small clock on the wall. "That's all the time we have for today, James. I look forward to Wednesday's session."

<u>Dr. Green, Clinical Notes – 1/4/2021</u>

Based on the testing and interview, JS definitely meets the criteria for the Macdonald triad (animal abuse, fire setting, and bed wetting). Unbeknownst to him, I was able to locate his mother, MS, and had an in-depth phone interview with her. She is quite elderly and living in an assisted housing facility, but her memory is still sharp and she was more than willing to share. She confirmed that JS regularly wet the bed until he was a teenager; she admitted to spanking him as a deterrent for this 'shameful' behavior. MS also confirmed that her son regularly molested both of his younger sisters and committed frequent acts of abuse toward animals. She declined to comment further when I politely asked her why she repeatedly allowed these horrific acts to happen in her home.

Given the presenting evidence and case history, I now firmly believe that I have a sadistic, remorseless, serial killer on my hands. JS is proving to be quite interesting, indeed.

James – 1/6/2021

"James, we only have a few minutes left today, but I want to touch on one more subject before we close: your alleged victim, GB. I must say, I've studied the crime scene photographs and they are absolutely horrific. Torture, starvation, sexual mutilation… I have to ask you: what did that feel like?"

"Dr. Green, we both know that I was granted early parole for Gretchen's case. There's no hard proof I ever met that girl, and I know my rights. I'm not going to sit here and admit to something I didn't do and go back to prison for the rest of my goddamn life."

She shook her head and waved her hand, like she was swatting away imaginary flies. "James, this isn't a trap. Legally, you cannot be convicted for her case again, even if you write a tell-all book and proclaim it to the world. You *can*, however, go back to prison if you do not cooperate with me fully during our therapy sessions. So tell me the truth: when you murdered that woman, how good did it feel?"

It had been, in a word, orgasmic. The best feeling in the world. Gretchen wasn't his first; far from it. The interstates and overpasses in this country are crawling with desperate women looking to make a quick buck to support their habits, whatever they might be. However, Gretchen *had* been the first and only one he held for an extended period. She was the only one he had really been able to take his time with: an artist and his masterpiece. James remembered the depression he felt when she finally died and the fun ended. He had been preparing to take another one when he was caught; his lawyer later told him a jogger who frequented the area had called in an anonymous tip about the noises and horrendous stench emanating from the property on her daily morning runs.

James leaned forward and stared Dr. Green directly in the eye. "Murdering that stupid bitch was the best, most pleasurable moment of my life. I would do it again and again and again if I could."

She smiled and leaned back in her desk chair. "Fabulous. Now we're making progress."

<u>James – 1/25/2021</u>

It appeared that James had been misled about therapy by his former cellmates. The convicted sex offenders he lodged with for so many years had told him horror stories about being forced to 'empathize' with their victims and 'put themselves in their victim's shoes.' James had always refused to attend the counseling, maintaining that he was innocent and therefore didn't need it. Now, he was increasingly excited about attending the sessions with Dr. Green. She had given him a homework assignment in his last session, and it had been a delight. She had asked him to write out a narrative indulging in all the little details of his time with Gretchen, and he quickly warmed to the task. He found himself writing more and more about Gretchen and his past kills, reading the narratives each night as he was falling asleep. They gave him nothing but sweet dreams.

<u>Dr. Green, Clinical Notes – 2/8/2021</u>

JS is progressing nicely. During our last session, he moved beyond his story of the abuse he inflicted on GB and began to openly discuss his previous victims, which I strongly encouraged. Even for my (admittedly desensitized) stomach, the details of his previous victims were difficult to hear, and I have been bringing them home with me, reading copies of his victim narratives obsessively each night. I awoke from a horrid nightmare yesterday, drenched in sweat, visualizing JS' army of dismembered, burned, and forgotten women, their empty eyes staring directly into mine. My partner held me for hours as the tears streamed down my cheeks and into her hair. We sobbed together, both our bodies shaking with pain and rage. Then I got dressed, plastered on my best professional face, and went to sit with a killer of women for 50 excruciating minutes.

James – 3/4/2022

"James, I want to take a moment and acknowledge your growth and development over the past year. We've engaged in some incredibly intensive therapy, and while I understand that it must have been incredibly challenging for you at times, I appreciate your forthrightness and openness with me. I must say, I've never had a patient progress quite as quickly as you. May I make a small confession?"

James used his best "aw, shucks" grin as he listened to the good doctor's spiel. If he was capable of experiencing it, he might have felt guilt at how easy it was to swindle the stupid old biddy, but guilt was an emotion he had never been burdened with, along with pity, remorse, or love. Those were things lesser mortals lived with, not him.

"Of course, doc. To steal a line from your book, you can tell me anything. No judgment here."

She gave him a warm smile. "James, I wasn't totally upfront with you when we began treatment together, and in light of your tremendous progress, I think I should share something with you. I have been following your case for a long time now, and when I heard that you were being conditionally released from prison, I pulled a few strings and specifically requested your case."

He frowned, his cheerful mask slipping for a fraction of a second before he managed to call it back. "But why did you want to work with me so badly? You must have an unlimited number of freaks beating your door down for help all the time."

"Not *freaks*, James, just misguided people who desperately need help. To answer your question, I'm not totally sure why I felt so compelled to work with you… I think I just sensed that there was something special about you. I wanted the opportunity to bring that side of you out, to show other people that true change is possible. And I must admit I believed you would be a professional challenge, and that always intrigues me, too."

James smiled. "Well doc, I can understand that. Nothing to forgive, as far as I'm concerned."

"Excellent. Now that I've gotten that off my chest, so to speak, I would like to say that I feel confident about your rehabilitation, and after completing tonight's assignment, I will be happy to sign off on the completion of your court-mandated treatment. Exposure therapy is an important part of my program, and taking you back to the scene of the discovery of Gretchen's body is the final step in your therapeutic process. Are you still feeling comfortable with this plan?"

This time, the grin that covered his face was genuine. "I'm totally comfortable, Olivia. Let's do it."

3/4/2022, 6:37 P.M.

James parked his car outside the abandoned property. He closed his eyes, remembering his last visit here, savoring the sweet details of his final moments with Gretchen. He clambered out of his vehicle and walked over to meet Dr. Green, who was standing patiently in front of the entrance to the small, forsaken house. She carried a little bag, from which she produced a large flashlight for herself and one for him. Dr. Green gestured for him to follow her inside. James smiled as he imagined swinging his heavy flashlight and caving her skull in. Patience, patience. He followed her into the building.

They made their way down to the basement. The room still bore touches of the police investigation. Despite their best efforts to clean up after themselves, the crime scene technicians had left traces of fingerprinting powder throughout the space. The white powder gleamed in the glow of their flashlights.

James walked slowly around the room, each square inch a placeholder for his fondest memories. The stairs he dragged the unconscious Gretchen down after he knocked her senseless when she hitched a ride in his truck. The corner of the room where he had constructed a makeshift table from cardboard boxes and plywood, upon which he placed his implements of torture and pain. And the ceiling...

He sucked in his breath. Could it be? Yes, the pulley system he had so painstakingly installed was still there! The chrome gleamed in the reflection from his flashlight, the ropes still suspended and dangling. He hadn't dared to hope that it would still be installed, figuring the law would have dismantled it when they swept the property. It was better than he remembered, and the surge of excitement that coursed through his body carried the flood of Gretchen's tears and blood with it, flashbacks of pure bliss. James was leaning forward to inspect the slightly frayed rope end hanging from the pulley when he felt a small stab in his upper bicep. He had enough time to jerk around and watch Dr. Green extract a small hypodermic needle from his arm before he lost consciousness and collapsed on the floor.

"James, James, can you hear me? It's time to wake up now. Your therapy session is beginning."

James slowly regained consciousness in pure physical agony. His head felt like someone had given him a nice bash with a pipe wrench. His shoulders and arms were on fire. He attempted to sit up but was met with a sickening realization: he was suspended from the ceiling, hanging from the very pulley system he himself had installed in this dank basement, so long ago. Dr. Green was seated in a chair in front of him, placidly writing notes in her notebook.

He glared at her. "What the hell did you do to me, you stupid bitch?" Without glancing up from her writing, Dr. Green replied, "Relax, James. I gave you a very small dose of gamma-hydroxybutyrate. I believe you used it to incapacitate several of your past victims, though you always called it GHB when you referred to it in your narratives with me. As a result, I thought it would be fitting for tonight's final session."

James felt a cold pit of fear begin to curdle in his stomach. Attempting to remain calm, he flashed his most charming smile and said, "Look, I think I understand what you're trying to do. You want me to put myself in my victims' shoes and feel their fear. Well, it worked, doc. I've learned my lesson. Why, just this afternoon you told me that you could see the progress I've made in treatment. I'm a changed man!"

Dr. Green finally looked him in the eye, and James felt the most tangible, primal fear he had ever experienced in his life. "James, you are incapable of change. You are a monster. Even after working in this field all these years, I never let myself believe that people were just 'born bad.' I truly thought that people were products of a combination of their nature and their environment, not one or the other. But you, dear James, completely shifted my perspective on the true depths of evil that lurk within certain individuals.

"I must, once again, beg your forgiveness. I still wasn't entirely truthful with you earlier this afternoon, when I explained why I wanted your case so badly. You see, it's a bit unethical—well, a *lot* unethical, but you were once quite close to someone who is very, very dear to me. And when I saw that you were going to be released on parole, I knew I couldn't give up this opportunity to rehabilitate you."

Out of the corner of his eye, James saw a slight, thin-framed individual step forward, though half her body was obscured by shadows. Dr. Green's face lit up with the unmistakable glow of love and adoration. "James, I would like you to meet our special guest this evening. She has graciously agreed to help you with your final phase of treatment. This is my wonderful wife and partner, Johanna. Though I believe she was still going by the name Jackie the last time you saw her?"

He opened his mouth and screamed as the thin-framed 'Johanna' stepped closer to him. Out of the shadows, he could clearly see the burn marks covering nearly the entire left side of her body. The left side of her face was sagging, and her ear and neck showed the tell tale signs of several skin grafts. She was wearing a wig, pulled back in a loose ponytail, but it did not obscure the brownish-purple burns that started at her forehead and snaked down her exposed arm and her leg, beneath the hemline of her blue jean shorts.

Johanna beamed as she stared up at James. "Hello there, big brother. Long time no see! Oh, how I have *missed you*. We have so much catching up to do, but don't worry, there's no need to rush. We have all the time in the world together, now."

James continued to scream and scream as Johanna and her lover walked over to the small makeshift table he had created so long ago, full of the same instruments he used on the unfortunate Gretchen. His screams would continue long into the night and early morning, but the newly soundproofed basement afforded ample opportunities for the final therapy session to continue, uninterrupted.

DUST AND SHADOWS
By Carlton Herzog

I stood beneath a burning sign that read: "The Fallen shall rise again in rivers of Blood." It was flanked on either side by two massive, inverted crucifixes to which were nailed two bloody Jesuses. There was a line of blasphemous statutes behind them as far as my eyes could see. The most notable of which were demons beheading archangels and Mother Mary being sodomized by two jackals.

When I walked forward, I came face to face with an enormous living nightmare. It had man-like hands and a head with a goatish, chinless face. But its pink, deep-set eyes in their ciliated orbits, and the purple feelers emanating from its skull, were anything but human.

Its bare chest had the leathery, reticulated hide of a crocodile. Long green tentacles with red sucking mouths protruded from its abdomen. As it breathed, its tentacles rhythmically changed color. It moved on eight ponderous legs. Stupendously bulky and thick, they could have easily belonged to a Jurassic sauropod

"I take it I'm dead and this is Hell. How did I die?"

It spoke in sibilant tones as a fetid, yellow ichor trickled from its mouth.

"It was spectacular. The landing gear from a Boeing 737 broke off, achieved terminal velocity as it fell and, with the kinetic force of a small meteor, drove your disgustingly obese body into the tarmac. Your head, torso and legs got pile driven straight down while your arms were sheared off at the shoulder. As for your soul, it shot out of you like projectile vomit. A truly poetic moment."

"What's my eternal punishment going to be?"

"That will be up to you. My associate Vulk will explain it."

After he finished, a green, foul-smelling mist appeared, from which emerged a bat-winged, bloated corpulence of a thing. It had an octopus head, the face of which was a mass of feelers. It had a scaly, rubbery-looking body with prodigious claws on both its hind and fore feet. Its squamous skin was greenish-black with golden flecks and striations. Hell's creaturely chaos writ large.

"I am going to give a short tour of what awaits you here. Then you will choose."

A moment later, we reappeared in a measureless cavern somewhere deep within Hell. As we stood on the blistered ground, I could hear no sounds of life. There was only the ceaseless hiss of rising gas plumes and the boom of falling rock. We walked between gaping fissures and then up an incline culminating a plateau overlooking a valley.

"See the Gluttons, mirror images of yourself. They lie all swollen and obscene in the icy paste of putrefaction. Cereberus, who guards the prisoners in that fetid slush, would only be too glad to rip and tear you apart as he does with the others. He'll slaver over you as you did in life over your food. Perhaps, he'll toss you in the Evil Ditch where flaccid souls lay piled, eating one another and their own filth.

"Over there is the flaying station. Witness the purple imps with straight razors methodically peeling the skin off the damned. Watch them rise into the sulfurous air, straight into a floating slaughterhouse. See the demons mechanically feeding them into an assembly line. Along that assembly line are demons with meat cleavers for hands, carving the flayed into rows of neatly sliced legs, torsos, and heads. Those parts are then sewn back together, but not along the strictures of human anatomy or the classifications of biological science. Rather, they become a nightmare of parts and more parts, anthropic anatomical inversions, as if a child had cut up a doll collection, then randomly reassembled it into an army of poly-limbed fiends. Torsos are given multiple heads, arms and legs."

We floated off that plateau and across the valley. Below, I could see a mass of twisted, emaciated corpses emerging from graves. Adjacent to that cemetery flowed a river of boiling blood filled with the damned. They were watched over by a regiment of Centaurs.

There seemed to be no end to the horrors. We floated over a forest where the bodies of the damned were fused with trees and devoured by harpies. That forest gave way to a mudflat imbued with grotesque spiral life forms with hints of horrific haunting faces deep within the mud itself. It was as if human bodies had disintegrated into the ooze and now existed only as abstract, abject patterns of saturated dirt.

As we moved deeper into the Valley of the Damned, I saw headless bodies glistening with an iridescent black slime and reeking of an obscene odor fighting one another. I could see, beyond them, great inky monstrosities, present in loathsome profusion, that were semi-fluid and passing through one another.

It was then that Vulk made his purpose clear.

"I can put you in any one of those abominable torments. Or, on fulfilling a simple request for Lucifer, I can restore your life and reward you handsomely."

"Tell me more."

"There is a swinging door inside the Vatican that leads here. Only two people have the key to lock and unlock it: The Pope and Cardinal Mullins. If that door were opened, our legions could leave this place and lay waste to God's Creation and, with that as a jumping off point, retake Heaven and cast God, along with His smug angels, into this fiery abyss."

"What would I have to do?"

"I would send your spirit into one of the secret concubines used by the cardinal. You need only convince him to open the door for us, or steal the key and do it yourself. After that, you need but sit back and enjoy the show."

"Dressed as a woman?"

"No—as a pleasure puppet in his harem of flesh love dolls."

"And after?"

"I'll seat you in whatever body you choose. When it no longer suits you, I'll find another to your liking. If you grow tired of life, I'll find you a place as an honored agent and advisor."

"I'm in—when do we begin?"

Just as my transition from living to dead had been instantaneous, so too was the reverse. No sooner had I posed the question than I was rocketing back through the ether.

A moment later, I was in Rome looking into a mirror. Staring back at me was the most beautiful woman I had ever seen. A raven-haired beauty with porcelain white skin, thick ruby red lips with long, matching red nails, and the firmest, fullest breasts ever. I wanted to feel uncomfortable in my own skin. But when I looked at that reflection and drank in my elegant beauty and curvy figure, I saw the power that is woman to twist and warp and bend a man's soul into any shape she pleased. Drunk on power, in thrall to my spectacular form, and thinking myself above every other person alive, I pondered whether I should ignore my black bargain and make my own way in the world.

However, those musing were interrupted by a still small voice chirping inside my head.

"I can hear your thoughts and see your actions. Only a fool would dare betray us. I can bring you back to face judgment here anytime it suits me. So, I suggest you put aside your delusions of grandeur and get to opening that gateway."

Although I was willing to complete the mission, I was curious as to how I could move so freely back and forth between the earth and the infernal domain.

"You are an unassigned soul, free to move between earth and Hell, whereas the damned already here and their demonic overseers can only come and go through the Hell Gate. Once you open it, we will overwhelm Earth and Heaven. Currently, there are 117 billion damned souls in Hell compared to the mere 3 billion blessed in Heaven. That means we can possess every human on the planet twenty times over. Humans endowed with that much demonic power and under our absolute control give us an overwhelming tactical advantage. Now get to dolling yourself up. The Old Lecher, swollen with power and a taste for antique pageantry, has sent an eight-horse carriage to your apartment."

When the coachman came to my door, I found I could both speak and understand Italian.

"Bon giorno, senorita. Il cardinale chiede il piacere della vostra azienda."

"Si. Ho aspetto havo. Andiamo dunque."

We made our way along ancient cobblestone streets

until we reached the security gate for Vatican City. The driver flashed his credentials to the one guard festooned in Renaissance attire, while the other looked me up and down, less for security and more for pure admiration of my elegant features and lines. I wanted to Basic Instinct him but thought better of it.

The carriage pulled up before a door of pure wrought gold. The valet, another late Renaissance costumed character, led me through winding ornate passages to a door. I was told to go and wait for the cardinal.

To say that the Vatican apartment was baroque would not do it justice. It was an explosion of gold, crimson fabric, and antique furniture in mint condition. It seemed so wrong for them to hoard wealth while most of the world starved. But that was as far as I got with my moral indignation. After all, I was about to open a gate and unleash Hell on Earth. Who was I to quibble about gold and whoremongering? When I considered the evil I was about to unleash and the vortex of pandemonium and murder that would follow, the Church's hypocrisy seemed meager by comparison.

The cardinal was a bald, old man with perfect teeth, pale skin and the salacious leer usually found on sexual predators. It didn't take a sociologist to know that this libidinous alley cat had abused his share of young women, and probably young boys as well, even as he exhorted his flock to abstinence. If Dante's model were true, then this old fart would eventually do a slow painful walk in a cape lined with lead for all eternity.

Vulk read my mind. "Don't worry about him. We've got something special waiting for these Vatican shitbags. Now work that old man and make him give up the key."

The cardinal got right to the point. "How are we today my little red bird? Ready for a poke or two?"

"*O si Papa!*"

"English bitch. I'm Irish by birth, so your wop tongue

gets on my nerves. Come over here and let me get a look at you. My God, you're gorgeous. And those breasts, so succulent."

"You like?"

"Oh yes, very much I like. Now get out of that dress while I slip out of my robes. I hate these things, so cumbersome and freighted with pomp and ceremony."

As we both undressed, I noticed the gold key ring around his neck. I wondered if that was the one I was supposed to swipe. Vulk, hearing my thoughts, spoke to my mind.

"That's it. The door you will use it on is in the sub-basement."

Being coy, I asked, "What's that key for, your grace?"

He smiled a toothy smile.

"It's a secret, but for you I'll make an exception. This key opens the door to Hell itself."

"You're not serious."

"Oh, but I am. Would you like to see? Yes? When we're done here, I'll show you, maybe crack the door open a bit and let you look inside. Does that sound exciting?"

Before I could reply, I could hear Vulk inside my head.

"He's going to have his way with you up here and then, sadistic prick that he is, push you through the door into Hell. Don't let him get behind you when you're down there."

I silently assented to the advice. But there was still the matter of copulating with the old geezer. It was weird and creepy being the woman on the outside but a man on the inside. On the one hand, I knew exactly what the cardinal would like. On the other, I was terrified of being penetrated.

The first few minutes were disgusting as his tongue snaked around inside my mouth and his hands groped my breasts and private parts. I wanted to jump up and run for the hills. But the longer we went at it, the more comfortable I became because it felt great.

A woman's erotic nervous system is far superior to a man's. The sheer number of nerve endings and their acute sensitivity make for an intensity and duration that no male orgasm could ever achieve. It was like the difference between cheap pot and top shelf heroin.

I could have gone all night, but the old cardinal was spent after the first ten minutes. So, he poured me a drink and we chatted. Then we dressed and headed to the sub-basement where he presumably intended my doom and damnation.

The sub-basement was as ornate as any of the other floors. The walls were filled with Renaissance frescoes and tapestries. Ancient furniture in mint condition and statuary lined the hallway.

The door to Hell was surprisingly non-descript. I expected *Abandon all Hope Ye who enter here* or something equally chilling. The only symbolism was a gold crucifix fitted to the door.

When we got to the door, I expected the cardinal to mutter some incantation in Latin or invoke some spell. But all he did was slip the key ring from his neck, put the key in the lock, wiggle it a bit, and then slowly unlock the door.

"Come closer my sweet. As I open the door a crack, you stick your head in and look around. But only for a moment lest some errant demon snatch you up and drag you down to Hell. I'll keep one hand on the door and another on you to ensure you don't accidentally fall into the abyss."

I did as he instructed with one exception. When I felt I had enough leverage, I shoved the door open, pinning the cardinal against the wall, then spun around and held it against him.

For a few brief moments, nothing happened other than the cardinal began screaming and cursing.

"Have you lost your fucking mind? Let me go, you whore!"

"I think not, your grace."

With that, the legions of the damned poured through the open door in a vortex of sound and motion. I watched the wretches rush forward in wave after wave after wave.

I heard Vulk speak to my mind's ear.

"Get out of there. The walls are going to break on either side of the door from the rush of bodies. You need to get out of Vatican City. I'll guide you to the old pagan temple on the outskirts of Rome. There my familiars will give you safe harbor as the apocalypse unfolds."

I got out of Vatican City. I hailed a taxi and made it to the rendezvous where I was met by three figures in black robes. They took me to an old farm a few miles up the road. They told me to make myself comfortable as they brought food and drink.

Then they switched on the television. I couldn't believe my eyes. Rome was being overrun by so many dead bodies it looked more like ants attacking a field. Bringing up the rear was Fenris, the Ragnarrok Wolf, the Frost Giants, and Surtur the Fire Demon.

The dead sang as they marched:
Hail Satan, come now all the fiends below,
God in his Heaven is sure to go.
Now the Fallen in rivers of Blood
Turn Creation to dust and mud.

The screen filled itself with battalions of reanimated necrotic matter enhanced with demonic claws, beaks, horns, stingers, and fangs. What the dead couldn't catch, the demons did, tearing apart the fleeing human population and drinking it dry. Rivers of Blood indeed.

I spent the next week enjoying—if one could call it that—the hospitality of the Satanic Church while everyone else was ground into the dust of the planet. During that time, the cities of England and the European Union were reduced to charred rubble. Surtur incinerated NATO's air, land, and sea responses. A week later, He did the same thing to Russia.

In America, the Midwestern Pentecostals prayed for divine intervention. And they got it in the form of an angelic brigade. But it was too little too late. Initially, the angels had some success turning back Hell's demons, but were later overwhelmed by the Titans, Fenris, Hela, and Surtur.

After that, God and His Son turned a deaf ear, much to the amazement of the Bible Belt. To save themselves from a hideous end, most Christians in the West renounced their faith and swore allegiance to Lucifer and the Powers of Darkness.

By the end of the year, planet earth was completely under Lucifer's dominion and control. His dark minions began Hell-forming the earth. They turned the world's factories and power plants into phosphorous engines that rained fiery embers and ash down across the planet. Save for hardy lichens and insects on land, and acid-loving jellyfish and red algae in the surrounding waters, there was no wildlife.

Planet earth had become a shadowland of eldritch horrors, a hatchery for loathsome abnormalities that mirrored and multiplied the ones I had seen in Hell. An uncanny living dead planet of filled with rivers of boiling blood, haunted forests, and voracious demon-like ogres. The chaotic landscape and climate of Hell replicated on the earth: burning deserts raining flame, living mud, and walking cadavers everywhere.

I found myself wondering what my place in the new order would be. An overseer in the relocation camps or an administrator for Hell and Human Affairs or even a territorial governor?

But that was all wishful thinking. After all, I had cut a deal with the Father of Lies. An entity that had rebelled against God himself, not once but twice. And here I was, a mere thing of flesh. So, I should have expected him to screw me over.

When the appointed day came for me to collect my reward, I was summoned to what was left of the White House. I was led to a penned area where my old friend Gorgoroth was feeding on cattle.

He greeted me enthusiastically. "Well, if it ain't my old pal Franky Fox. Or should I say Foxy Francine Fox. Man, you are one hot mama. If only I were human. Let me offer my sincerest congratulations on a job well done. Likewise, Lucifer, our generous and farseeing monarch of Hell, Earth, and soon to be Heaven, congratulates you as well.

"Thanks—now about my reward. I earned it."

"And a reward you shall have. Lucifer in his wisdom and munificence has decided that you will remain forever young. An immortal succubus, a thing of unparalleled beauty and a lure to men and women."

"Hold on—you want me to stay in a woman's body and be the Court Whore to the King of Hell? That makes no sense. You have no more enemies other than God and His feeble army of angels. How is a seductress of any value in that scenario?"

"Not for the divine but for the leaders here on earth. We used the stick to whittle down the numbers of men to a more manageable number. Now we mean to use the carrot. Your physical charms make you an ideal influence peddler, someone who can get mortals do as we want without our having to maim or kill them."

"Do I at least get an official title, something other than whore?"

"You will be a cabinet minister in charge of the Department of Sexual Influence and Seduction. You'll have your own staff, driver, and estate."

"Do I have a choice?"

"Absolutely not. Refuse, and you will be the main course at your own personal barbecue."

"When you put it like that, it's no choice at all. Minister of Sexual Influence and Seduction it is. Now whom do I have to fuck to get a drink around here?"

THIRD TIME'S A CHARM
By Frederick Pangbourne

Rutherford failed to look up from the files and papers sprawled out across the top of his desk when a knock came from outside his office door. Intensely preoccupied with the file's contents, even the second succession of knocks went without acknowledgement. It was only at the third series of knockings that he abruptly pulled his attention away from his work, as if hearing it for the first time.

"Yes? Come in," he said, looking up to the door and removing his thin wire-framed glasses.

The door swung inward and a young man somewhere in his late twenties, compared to Rutherford's age of fifty-eight, stepped in, pausing just inside the threshold. Rutherford said nothing at first, only squinting at the clean-shaven man in the white hospital lab coat. Under his arm he held a small stack of manila envelopes.

"Dr. Rutherford," the man said, nodding to his senior.

Rutherford smiled at the man and replaced his glasses. "Ah, Thomas. Come in, boy. Come in. Close the door behind you, please."

Thomas Patton smiled in return and closed the door behind him as requested. "I brought the files you requested."

"Yes, yes. Very good. Take a seat." Rutherford motioned to a pair burgundy leather chairs in front of his desk. Patton sat in the chair closest to the door, the files resting on his lap.

"How has the research come along? Any new insights?" the doctor asked.

"Very little, I'm afraid. There isn't much more information on the item other than that which we've already obtained."

Rutherford nodded at the man's answer, then leaned over his desk. "It's of no importance at this point."

"How so? You're not abandoning the experiment, are you?"

"No, no. Of course not. On the contrary, I believe I have found the perfect test subject."

"Recently? Where?"

Rutherford lowered his voice and smiled as he spoke. "Here. She was admitted over the weekend. I have made the necessary arrangements, and she is currently under my care."

"That's marvelous news, Doctor." Patton sat up straighter in his chair at the promising announcement. "When do you plan on putting the experiment into effect? Two months should be-"

"Tonight."

"I'm sorry. Tonight?" Patton replied with noticeable uncertainty.

"Why not?" Rutherford moved off the desk and leaned back deeply into his high-backed leather chair. "I see no reason why we shouldn't. The sooner the better."

"What about preparation?"

"I've already taken care of everything. Pardon me for not consulting you prior but I wanted to waste no time once they admitted her, and I found that she fits our needs perfectly."

"Who is she?"

"Ah, yes." Rutherford sat up quickly and adjusted his glasses as he rummaged through the opened files and papers on his desk. After a few seconds of sifting through the paperwork, he lifted a file from the others. "Here we are. Patricia Canton. Twenty-six. Her family admitted her for evaluation regarding an extreme Obsessive-Compulsive Disorder. Apparently, she still lives at home and her constant compulsiveness was too much for her parents to deal with. Their decision in placing her here has now become our benefit."

Patton stared at the folders on his lap and nodded slowly as he contemplated the doctor's proposal regarding the newly obtain subject. "It may be risky," he finally said, lifting his gaze to meet Rutherford's, "especially if… well, the item is really…" his voice trailed off.

"That, too, has been taken into consideration and I've already taken every precaution."

Patton's gaze fell back to his files, and he said nothing for several seconds. Though they had discussed the experiment for many months now and even laid out the plan to its basic intent, not to mention the extensive research into the item, he did not think that it would be carried out this quickly. Dr. Rutherford's executive position at the psychiatric hospital practically allowed him to prepare for his elusive experiment unhindered, but Patton still did not see it being carried through for several more months. The unforeseen advance in scheduling had taken him off guard. Though Rutherford's position at the hospital was held in the highest regard and was unchallengeable, his was not. His residency at the hospital was just short of three years now and, during the majority of that time, he had been under the watchful eye of Dr. Rutherford. It did not take long for the good doctor to see his potential and their common interests before taking him into his confidence and assigning him as his personal assistant to his upcoming experiment.

"I suppose so. If you truly feel that we are not rushing into this," Patton finally said, with some hesitation.

"I do not." Rutherford closed the file pertaining to Patricia Canton and placed it at the edge of the desk. "Feel free to look over her file. I see nothing that should hinder our progress, but you look it over, nevertheless. Perhaps I missed some minor detail."

Patton silently nodded and took the folder, replacing it with the ones on his lap. "Here's everything I have on the item. As I said, there wasn't much more information. I believe we have everything ever written about it now."

"Excellent. Capital work, Thomas," Rutherford said, taking the folders and placing them on the desk closer to him. "Once the day shift has left for the day, we can begin setting up the final touches to the room. I thought we would begin around, shall we say… ten this evening?"

Patton looked up from the girl's open file. "Uh, yes, that should be fine."

"Good," Rutherford replied with a beaming smile and pulled the top file from Patton's stack and opened it before him. "Now, if you'll excuse me, Thomas, I want to go over these before we start this evening. If you like, pay our newly acquired patient a visit and get a basic assessment of her for yourself."

Patton silently nodded again and stood from his chair. Without further interaction, he showed himself out. He walked several feet down the hall to the elevator and stopped prior to pushing the call button. He opened the file on Patricia Canton and skimmed through its contents as he waited for the lift to arrive. Patton took notice of her excessive repetitive actions when checking or evaluating items by counting them in three's. Given examples included tapping on closed vehicle windows to ensure they were actually closed, continually turning lights on and off before leaving a room, and checking the gas on the stove by also regularly turning the knobs off and on. All were done in a secession of three. The elevator chimed, and the doors slid open. Patton closed the folder and entered. He pressed the button for the patient rooms on the sixth floor.

The sixth floor held all patients who were deemed competent enough to be left in lockless rooms, unlike the eighth and ninth floors, which were of a higher security and held the more mentally unstable and psychotic patients. Still carrying Patricia Canton's folder, Patton made his way down the gleaming, buffed, white tile floor of the hall to room #37. Before knocking, he peered through the door's small glass window. A slender woman sat at the desk against the wall with her back to the door. The quaint room with its blank white walls was equipped with a single bed, desk, and chair and a tall locker for personal items and clothing.

Patton rapped on the door, and then entered. The woman turned quickly at his sudden appearance.

"I'm sorry. I didn't mean to startle you. I'm Dr. Patton. I work with Dr. Rutherford," he said, apologetically.

Patricia Canton was a petite woman with brown, shoulder-length hair. Her delicate facial structure enhanced her fair complexion and blue eyes. "I'm sorry." She chuckled. "I wasn't expecting anyone and I'm still trying to get used to being here."

"Totally understandable." Patton smiled. "How are your accommodations? I know it isn't the Hilton, but we try to make it as comfortable as we can."

"It's not so bad." Her eyes wandered the room as she spoke.

As she twisted in her chair and surveyed the room, Patton glimpsed an opened paperback book on the desk.

"May I ask what you're reading?" He gestured to the book.

"Oh, this?" She held the book up, revealing its cover. "Just some romance novel. I picked it up before I came here. I figured I might need something to do if there was a lot of downtime."

"Well, hopefully you won't be here that long to finish it. I've reviewed your file and I think that, if everything goes well, you may be out of here within three or four weeks."

"That long?"

"I'm afraid so. At least you'll be permitted to be at home on the weekends. It all depends on you, to be honest. Dr. Rutherford is a brilliant doctor, so just listen to any advice he has and you'll be fine."

Patricia nodded her head slowly and turned her gaze to the floor.

"Cheer up. You'll be fine. Trust me. Well, I don't want to keep you from your reading. I just wanted to introduce myself and let you know that Dr. Rutherford will begin your evaluation starting tonight."

"Tonight?" Her gaze rose to meet his.

"Yes. He feels, as well as I, that your evaluation should begin immediately. The sooner we start, the sooner you can leave." Patton forced the most convincingly sincere smile he could muster and nodded to add to his false expression. The evaluation, if it were to be called that, would be far from any pleasantness that it portrayed if proven true. "An orderly will stop by sometime before ten this evening to escort you. Any questions before I depart?"

"Why so late?"

"The doctor is a busy man and, unfortunately, that is the only time he has available today. Like I said, the sooner we start, the sooner you'll be back home. I'll see you tonight, okay? It was a pleasure meeting you." And with his parting words, Patton exited the room and made his way back to the elevator and to his own office. Behind him, he heard a door open and close three times.

Patton's own office was but a meager step above the room Ms. Canton was currently occupying. Exempting the bed, his office was furnished with a long bookshelf, a larger desk, his own bathroom, and a few of his framed accomplishments on the wall behind him. He exhaled as he fell into the chair behind his desk and craned his neck back until he was gazing at the ceiling. It was strange how in the beginning, when Rutherford had initially approached him with some reluctance and secrecy about the item he had come into possession of and the experiment he was preparing to conduct involving it, it seemed like an opportunity of a lifetime. Though his belief in the occult was somewhat skeptical, the chance to work side-by-side with a man of such renowned reputation in the psychiatric field was a golden opportunity that he was unwilling to let slip through his fingers, regardless of his beliefs. The doctor had presented him with his theory with such confidence and enthusiasm that it was impossible to reject his offer, despite the bizarre nature of the unorthodox demonstration. Now, though, shadows of doubt were growing.

Patton sat up straight in his chair and pulled himself close to the desk. Logging on to his computer, he figured the best way to utilize the allotted time before things were to begin was by going over the collected data already gained on the item. As the computer was loading, he thought of how he was now feeling a twinge of guilt. Perhaps it was the sudden advancement to their time schedule or the fact that he had laid eyes upon the newly obtained test subject and viewed her as she was: a human being and not some lab rat. He brushed the distracting emotions aside as he was now scanning through the various files regarding the item and its fascinating origin.

The hand-painted image of a small, jeweled chest of gold and black metal, adorned with various gems of great value, appeared on the screen. There were no known photographs, at least that he could find, of the object. The chest was no larger than perhaps a shoebox. The Tyrant's Casket. Rutherford had never quite mentioned the exact circumstances of how he had come to acquire the inimitable object in question, only stating that it had cost him more than his junior assistant could ever imagine and that he obtained it somewhere in the Middle East. Patton thought he had mentioned Iraq at some point. Or was it Iran? Regardless, the so-called Tyrant's Casket was an object said to be of great supernatural properties and apparently sought-after by many who believed deeply in the occult and the object's potential.

Patton sifted through several references regarding the casket and enlarged a disquisition by an early 18th century archeologist named Armand Baeza. It was the most informative piece on the object's history he had unearthed in the vast domain of the Internet. Various religious scriptures would have it that a Sumerian demon prince by the name of Andralimorthax, also referred to as The Desecrator of Flesh, was defeated in a fierce battle by the archangels, Raphael and Uriel, and imprisoned in the ornate box as punishment for his insurrection for all eternity. To ensure that the Tyrant's Casket would never fall into the hands of man, it was buried deep within the earth and the key to the tyrant's prison was hidden somewhere on the opposite end of the earth, far from man's prying grasp. And, to ultimately ensure that if the casket and key were to ever be discovered and come together, an atypical lock was created for the casket to prevent Andralimorthax from ever being released once again upon the world.

Patton lifted his gaze from the screen to the wall clock across from his desk. 7:27 pm. A couple of more hours still. He rubbed his eyes with the ball of his hand and continued reviewing files on the computer. He surfed through half a dozen more articles pertaining to the object until he found another piece that had showed some promising information. It was this writing in particular that had initially intrigued Rutherford once he was aware of his gained object's potential and propelled him to carry out the groundwork to his glorious experiment. The paper was written in 1939 by none other than the world-renowned occultist and magician, Aleister Crowley. The occultist stated that, through his own insight on the Tyrant's Casket and his vast knowledge of demonology, anyone who was blessed with the unique opportunity of obtaining both the demon's casket and the iron jeweled key to the prison would be granted with immeasurable gratitude from its hellish prisoner for being released, and inconceivable power bestowed upon its human liberator. The thought of unleashing the death-dealing tyrant back into the realm of man was unheard of and such a blasphemous notion would even create great offense to the gods themselves. Though it was foolish to even be considered, the avaricious rescuer would be exempt from the violence to follow and instead drown in riches beyond their imagination. Crowley believed that, through deep meditation and astral travel to the nether planes, he had uncovered the casket's unique locking mechanism. The answer was simply turning the key three times within the lock. The three turns representing the Father, the Son and the Holy Ghost. Thus was the sole purpose of Patricia Canton.

What they discovered sometime later during their extensive research was yet another paper discussing the opening of the casket, which gave a more disastrous outcome to the so-called liberator. Ancient scrolls unearthed in the excavated temple ruins of eastern Afghanistan back in 1958 referred to the Tyrant's Casket and painted a different picture than that of Aleister Crowley's. Discovered scrolls told of great bloodshed coming to those who were foolish enough to open the casket. The sacrilege of releasing the demon would irreversibly extract a heavy toll not once, but thrice. The number three again coming into play. This latter knowledge was the reasoning Rutherford did not attempt to open the casket himself. The fear of an infernally lethal repercussion instead of glorious rewards forced the doctor to reconsider and find other means of achieving his ultimate goal.

At some point during his time reviewing his notes on the computer, Patton had drifted off to sleep. His eyes, strained and fatigued from their time staring, unblinking, at the glowing computer screen, had unexpectedly lulled him into a light slumber. It was not until his neck, bent at an unnatural angle, caused him to breathe heavily and emit a grunted snort, thus abruptly awakening him. Clearing his throat, he sat up straight in his chair and looked about. The screen was now in saver mode, and the clock across the room read 9:21. As he was shutting down the computer, the phone on his desk rang.

"Dr. Patton," he stated, clearing his throat once more.

"Thomas, are you coming up? I've already sent for the girl," Rutherford said.

"Yes, sir. I'm on my way now."

Exhaling deeply, he placed the phone on the receiver and rubbed his eyes. They felt dry. There was no sense printing anything else to bring with him since he had already given Rutherford everything from earlier, so he opened his desk drawer and removed a small notepad. If things played out as Rutherford had anxiously hoped for, there would be much to document. Giving his office one last visual going over, he stood and made his way upstairs.

Patton was approaching the doctor's office door when

Rutherford rounded a corner, meeting him.

"I was just in the observation room making sure everything was in place," Rutherford stated as he neared. "Are you okay?"

"Yes, I'm fine," Patton replied, rubbing his eyes. He imagined he still had a fatigued look upon his face.

Once in the office, Patton took notice of a video camera mounted on a tripod facing a curtained section of the office wall. "I informed the front desk and security that we were not to be disturbed until further notice." He then made his way to the black curtained wall and pulled a drawstring at the curtain's edge, drawing back the thick wall of material. Behind the curtain, a large glass window was fixed into the wall. The glass was a one-way mirror, allowing the observer to watch the attached room virtually unseen. Patton stepped closer and peered through the glass into the observation room.

The room was small. 15'x15' and void of any décor or furnishings, save for a table with a chair situated at either end. It was primarily used to observe interviews between the doctor and patients. It was not uncommon for the video camera to be used during these sessions, providing a form of video documentation. The room, however, had now been rearranged for Rutherford's purposes. He had placed three slender tables at each wall, except the one providing the door, and both chairs removed. On each table there were different objects placed on their surfaces. The items varied for each table. Table lamps, keyed padlocks, an old cassette tape recorder, a couple of cookie jars, and amongst these common items sat the infamous box. From where he stood, he could faintly see the end of the key protruding from its lock.

Rutherford pulled back the sleeve of his lab coat, exposing his wristwatch. "She should be here at any moment. I'm going to meet her out in the hall and explain the evaluation to her. Once we step into the room, start the camera please, Thomas."

"Yes, sir."

Once Rutherford had departed the office, Patton looked to the notepad still in his hand and scoffed, realizing he had foolishly forgotten about the video camera, and stuffed the pad into his lab coat pocket. Outside in the hall, he could vaguely make out voices. The orderly must have arrived with Ms. Canton. Shortly afterwards, the door to the observation room opened and Rutherford escorted the woman in. It was then that Patton realized there was no sound, and he promptly turned on the room intercom and started the camera.

"What we are going to do this evening, Patricia, is evaluate your behavior in this room. There is no right or wrong action in here. I just want you to browse about and do whatever you like. Feel free to touch the objects on the table if you wish. Again, this is not some pass or fail test. I simply wish to get a feel of your actions so I know where to proceed in a treatment, Okay?" Rutherford's voice came from the office speaker in the wall.

Patricia nodded as her eyes took in the objects on each table. Patton could perceive by the look forming on her face and the manner in which her eyes darted from item to item that she was already holding back on interacting with each object.

Rutherford then turned and gestured to the one-way glass. "I will be behind the glass, observing everything. If you have any questions once I leave, you need but only speak aloud. I will be able to hear you, all right? I will come back once I am satisfied that I've seen enough for a proper evaluation."

Patricia only nodded again in acknowledgement as her gaze wandered over each table in eager anticipation.

"Very well then, Patricia. I will see you again shortly. Remember, there is no right or wrong action here," Rutherford said, smiling before throwing a glance to the camera behind the glass and departing the room.

"Has she touched any of the items yet?" Rutherford asked as he entered the office.

"No. Not yet," Patton answered.

"She will." Rutherford moved next to Patton and gazed through the glass into the observation room. "It will only be a matter of time. She can only restrain her compulsion disorder for so long before she gives in to its irresistible urge."

"Look," Patton said and pointed to the glass.

Patricia was drifting through the room and to the tables. Though her hands had yet to touch any of the objects, her eyes were already pushing buttons, opening and closing lids, and turning keys. She eventually stopped at the table nearest the glass and lifted her gaze from the table's items and looked into the mirrored glass in front of her. Though they were invisible to her stare, the uncanny feeling that she was watching them instead of the reverse could be felt. After a moment, her eyes fell back to the table, sweeping over the small table lamp, a Donald Duck cookie jar and the black, obsolete, Panasonic tape recorder. Her hand rose carefully, and she pushed the play button on the recorder. No sound came from the instrument as a cassette tape was absent and the spindle beneath the cover spun silently. She then hit the stop button and repeated the action twice more before opening and closing the transparent lid three times.

"And so it begins," Rutherford said aloud to himself.

After the tape recorder, she moved to the cookie jar, removing and replacing Donald's sailor cap lid thrice before her eager hands found the lamp and its dangling chain cord. Her eyes were fixed intensely on each object she interacted with, as if her repeated actions required the utmost attention. She then moved to the table to the right of the glass and continued her fixated behavior on the next group of objects.

"Out of curiosity, Doctor," Patton said, "what will you do if no harm comes to her from opening the casket? What if the legend is true, and she is… rewarded?"

Rutherford turned and faced him, his face an expression of cold stone. "I plan on intervening most extremely before her actions are acknowledged." His hand dipped into the hip pocket of his lab coat and produced a syringe half-filled with a clear liquid.

Patton eyed the syringe with dumbfounded astonishment. "What- what are you planning on doing?"

"I've invested too much in this to let some button pushing simpleton steal a divine glory that she could never begin to comprehend, Thomas. Once she makes her way to the casket, I plan on waiting outside the door and will do whatever it takes to receive my rightful recognition if the legend is true."

"You don't plan on murdering-"

"Quiet now. She's making her way to the casket's table," Rutherford interjected as he replaced the syringe back into his pocket and watched through the glass with a sinister impassioned anticipation. "Murder will be the least of my sins if this scenario plays out as I hope."

Patricia had her back to the glass as she approached the last table. The first item to her left was a simple, chrome-plated, steel padlock. The end of its tiny key protruded from the lock. Like a similar lock she had found at the previous table, she lifted it and twisted the key; the locked unsecured and she turned the key back and closed the lock. She repeated the steps again until it was completed three times. Assured that the lock was finally secured, she placed it on the table and directed her attention to the oddly decorated looking box in the center. It resembled a mini treasure chest, the size of a shoebox. Like the padlock, she found the key already inserted into the locking mechanism.

"Doctor, I beseech you." Patton found his mouth void

of saliva and his eyes unavoidably fixed on the young woman on the other side of the glass. "Do not allow this to compel you to-" Patton turned to his senior, but the man was no longer at his side. He looked behind him and saw the office door wide open.

Patton felt his breath shaken as he exhaled heavily and turned back to the observation window. With her back to him, he could not view her direct actions but the motion of her arms indicated her hands were working diligently on some unseen task.

Patricia felt the sensation immediately upon touching the small chest. She could only describe it as some invisible electric pulse emitting from the object, which ran up through her fingertips and into her arms, followed by the undeniable arousal of dread. The key turned with minimal difficulty and, to her astonishment, unlike any common lock, it continued to turn. Each full rotation in the mechanism resulted in an audible 'click'. When the lock had turned over twice, the door to the room opened and Dr. Rutherford stood on the threshold.

"Are we finished, Doctor?" she asked, facing the man and pulling her hand from the key. "I couldn't help touching everything, but you said-"

"You are fine, my dear. Finish with the casket and we will complete the test." Rutherford strained against every fiber of his being to maintain his composure and forced a smile.

"Oh, I- I mean, I don't have to, I can-" Her eyes fell back onto the box like the pull of a powerful magnet. She felt her hands tremble as her uncompleted ritual was prematurely disrupted. Her lips twitched.

"Everything is perfectly fine. You've done nothing wrong, Patricia," Rutherford reassured her as he took a step into the room. "You just need to finish with the casket, and we can stop the evaluation."

"Casket?"

"The box, goddamn it!" He suddenly realized his mounting frustration and found his one hand reaching into the lab coat's pocket, his fingers wrapping around the syringe. He forced another smile and spoke in a calmer tone. The startled look on her face reminded him to stay in character. "I'm sorry. It's just that it's getting late and we should really wrap this up, dear."

Patricia was now torn between two worlds. Both of an equal reality, yet one possessed an uncontrollable urge that overrode all else and she could not ignore its beckoning call. Despite the sudden aggressiveness of the doctor, which had taken her off guard, the so-called casket demanded her attention, which she was could no longer disregard. Still staring at the doctor for a brief moment, her face remained in an expression of dismay by his unexpected outburst as her hand slowly reached for the end of the key in the box. Her fingertips gently fell onto and gripped the key as her eyes returned to the box and she twisted it a third time with the lock resulting in another 'click'. At the third turn, the lid to the box abruptly opened ajar and discharged a hissing sound as if suddenly releasing long contained gases. A festering stench of the foulest rot filled the air.

Patton stared from the office in immeasurable tension as he watched the scenario unfolding with unpredictable results. Part of him begged to intervene and stop Rutherford's obsessively destructive endeavors; yet, despite the man's insane actions, something rooted him to the spot, unable to turn away from what he was witnessing. The very concept of unleashing an impossible dream into the manifestation of a nightmarish reality could only be viewed until they played the last act out. It must be watched.

Both Patricia Canton and Dr. Rutherford froze at the sudden opening of the infamous casket. After she completed her ritualistic act, she turned her blank gaze to the doctor. He stood wide-eyed and physically petrified. His very breath being held within his chest in longing anticipation, his one hand plunged deep into his lab coat pocket. A deep low groan then seemed to be breathed out from inside the box. The sound caused her to turn back to the object in curiosity. The horrid odor of death still lingered in the air.

From Rutherford's standpoint, he had the entire scene in full view. Once the casket had opened and the gas within released, he froze in mid-step, the unknown expectation holding him fast. His fingers were wrapped tightly around the lethal syringe, ready to dispatch her at the first sign of the glorified resurrection. When the guttural sound poured out from the casket, he flung aside all reality, as the supernatural outcome that was prophesied was now becoming his reality. It was his time to move forward and receive his new master as it stepped forth into the material plane once again. Pulling the syringe out and into full view, Rutherford found renewed strength at his expected unholy restoration, and hastened at the woman. It was the then that the room went black.

The room fell into a lightless void of blackness as the power in the entire hospital was eliminated. Before either of the three could react to the sudden darkness, the top of the casket flew open in an explosion of flames. A depthless inferno raged deep inside the casket as it roared with an audible thunder. The observation room was alight in a hellish display of red and orange that cast flickering shadows about the walls. Patricia fell backwards at the hellish explosion, the back of her head striking the edge of the table beneath the one-way glass. Despite the barrage of stars that appeared in her closed eyes upon impact, she quickly scrambled to her feet using the table she fell against as leverage. As she stood on unsteady legs, she scrambled to take in all that was happening about her. She looked to the open box and the unnatural flames that burned brightly from somewhere deep within its container. The sound reminded her of a jet engine, with its roaring intensity. From the corner of her eye, there was a movement in the dark corner of the room. She turned to see an immense shape fall upon her. Her mouth opened to scream, but it was too late.

Rutherford could only watch in horror as his moment of immortal glory was demolished in one broad stroke of fate. The sudden explosion had caused him to drop to one knee and grip the door jams with both hands to avoid falling over. The syringe fell from his grasp and landed somewhere on the floor. When he raised his head, he watched as Patricia Canton struggled back onto her feet. As the woman regained footage, he glimpsed in awestruck astonishment as a massive shape emerged from the shadows and fell upon the woman. At the last moment, the body of the resurrected became alight in flames as it claimed the woman who had released it. A wave of relief washed over him as he watched the horrendous price for freeing it being dealt to anyone but himself.

Andralimorthax presented its liberator with the most appropriate gift it could offer. A large, clawed hand fell atop the woman's head, lifting her to her toes and holding her fast while it forcefully jabbed the index and middle finger of its other hand deep into the base of her throat, just above the jugular notch of the breastbone. Gouts of dark red blood spurted out at the penetration of its fingers and splashed onto the floor. Patricia coughed and gagged in desperation as blood poured over her lips and down her chin, flowing together with that of her gushing throat wound. Her legs peddled in the air and her arms twitched uncontrollably at her side as her nervous system was overwhelmed. The two fingers pushed deeper in, then curled inward and in one powerful tug, ripped the woman's rib cage from her chest, pulling out the front portion from the torso. An eruption of gore splattered the room as her organs fell from their protective covering and fell to the floor in wet splashes. The body was then tossed aside like a discarded bag of trash.

Patton retched at the unbelievable display of revolting power and reached out to the nearest thing for support as he vomited down the front of his lab coat and onto the carpet. His hand fell upon the video recorder and his weight toppled it, causing both he and the tripod to fall onto the office floor.

Rutherford remained in a Gorgonized state of shock as he lay witness to the ease in which the demon could lay waste to the human form. The thing stood tall, its head barely touching the room's eight-foot ceiling. A humanoid body of flaming physique and muscular strength. From its upper back protruded an array of long pointed spikes like some prehistoric monstrosity. Its face was molded into a mask of seething fury, whose stare was nothing short of an apocalyptic demise. Its head was covered by some type of crowned battle helm, which opened over the mouth, and, like its back, was adorned with sharp spikes. Pinpointed eyes of fiery white peered from the helm's eye slits and a lipless mouth of thick gums displayed long, sword-like teeth. It looked up from the mess of human meat in its hands and met Rutherford's wide eyes.

Rutherford dropped to his knees at the only form of a physical god he had ever known. Seeing was believing, and there was no denying in all that was heaven and earth that what he was gazing upon was nothing short of a god. He bowed his head to the tile floor as it strode toward him, its footfalls vibrating the floor beneath him.

"I pledge myself to you, oh mighty one of the infernal pit," Rutherford stammered in desperation. "It was I who came in possession of your prison and it was I, your faithful servant, who prepared your release. Spare my pitiful life, master, and my body and soul will be yours for all eternity. Show mercy, oh mighty one."

"It is fortunate that man is ignorant of the true world around him," the demon responded in a voice whose deepness and vileness could be heard only in Rutherford's mind. "Men such as yourself, Doctor, will hope against hope just to stay alive for only a mere moment longer. Such an enduring human trait that you will no longer possess."

Rutherford turned his head up in disbelief at the baneful reply. When his head was tilted fully upward and his eyes met those of the demon prince, it also repaid him in the most suitable fashion. Gently it placed a hand atop of the human's fragile head. Rutherford closed his eyes as he prepared for his fate and, in one quick movement, the grip on his head tightened like an industrial vice while its other hand jammed its fingers up under his chin. The talons punched through the soft tissue beneath with ease, and slowly it pulled back. Rutherford screamed as he felt his jaw being pulled away from his skull. The sound of tendons popping, ligaments and muscle tissue tearing, was all too audible as the mandible came from the man's face in one final blood-splattered pull. Still holding onto the head, it flung aside the separated jaw. It watched with pleasure as Rutherford flailed about in its grasp. The man attempted to continue screaming without a jaw, but only a gargled howl escaped from the long, dangling tongue that hung listlessly from the bloodied hole in its throat. Releasing the man, his body flopped to the floor, face first, where it continued its death spasms. It finished the mortal off by delivering a fatal blow of great strength to its spinal column, the line of vertebrae instantly crushed like splintering walnut shells.

Patton watched the doctor's fate from his knees as he peered just over the frame of the window, hiding himself like a terrified child from the hulking horror, separated by just a thin pane of glass. As the prince of hell stood upright over Rutherford's body, it turned its malevolent gaze to the mirror. Patton slid from the window, avoiding its gaze, and balled himself into a fetal position on the floor, praying to a savior he had no belief in until now. It was then that the fiery illumination from the casket extinguished as suddenly as it had erupted, casting the rooms in darkness. A second later, the sound of fuses being reset came from the hall outside the office and the emergency lighting system was activated, softly illuminating the halls of the hospital.

Patton peered up from his doubled over form, oblivious to the vomit he was lying in and which caked his lab coat. The fact that he had unknowingly urinated himself had also gone without care. He felt his hands trembling uncontrollably as he ever so slowly unfolded himself from the fetal position and made his way to his knees. Carefully lifting his head, he peered through the glass. His eyes widened and his breath came in sporadic gasps as he scanned the observation room, only to find it empty of the victims of the hellish carnage. Where both Canton and Rutherford's bodies had been disposed of, there was nothing. The bodies were no longer present. The scorched residue of some blotched substance was all that remained in their mangled forms. It was as if they had simply melted away into black sludge, erasing any evidence of what had transpired. His eyes wandered from the floor to the table upon which the casket had sat. Only an unidentifiable, molten slab remained behind where the object once stood.

From somewhere in the far distance, he could hear the faint voices of orderlies and staff as they attempted to assess the situation of the power outage. Wearily, Patton made his way to his feet. His legs threatened to buckle as he up righted himself, using the wall for support. Once he felt confident enough to walk, he made his way out of the office. Shortly after he stepped in the dim lighting of the hall, the power resumed, and the bright fluorescent lights overhead temporarily blinded him as he staggered toward the elevators. A pair of male orderlies urgently moved past him as they rushed hastily elsewhere within the hospital. Neither seemed to take notice of Patton's disheveled, vomit and urine-stained clothing as he stepped uneasily closer to the elevator doors. Despite his hands still shaking, he managed to push the call button and leaned up against the wall as he awaited the lift. He realized he was suffering from shock and hoped that he could maintain his composure until he made it back to his own office, where he would collapse into his chair. His mind was beyond dismayed from thinking clearly through everything that had transpired. He needed to rest. Screw rest. He needed to fall into a deep slumber for days. The elevator chimed as the lift reached his floor.

Carefully pushing himself from the wall, he looked down at his clothing. He appeared as though he had spent the night in a nauseating cesspool. He prayed that the lift would be empty as he hopelessly adjusted his tie and closed his eyes. The lift stopped even with the floor and the doors opened. *Please be empty*, he mentally pleaded.

"Ah, just who I was looking for," a horridly too familiar voice pierced his mind.

His eyes flashed open and saw beyond the opened elevator doors was an endless black void. Before his lips could part and cry out, Prince Andralimorthax emerged from the cold melanism. The hellish face of white, pinpointed eyes and long teeth met his gaze. "Did you think that I had forgotten about you, Doctor? Only after the eradication of one more may I rightfully return to my long-abandoned throne."

"Third time's a charm," Patton whispered dreadfully as he felt urine spilling down one leg.

It was then that its clawed hand sprung out and

grasped a handful of his lab coat and shirt beneath. The mouth of a hundred swords opened wider than nature had ever intended, and Patton's face was pulled forward into it with such force that his feet left the floor. As the elevator door leisurely slid closed, muting Patton's blood-curdling screams from the other side, one brown leather shoe remained behind just outside the elevator.

BABYCAKES
By Bryan Miller

Babycakes' chubby arms and wiggling fingers, and practically his whole head, are smeared with pink frosting. A bright glob of it is mashed into one of his little pasta-shell ears, and more is slicked into the fine blond hairs that feather the skin over his soft skull. He's vibrating with the sugar buzz, but he doesn't smile. His glassy blue eyes gaze off into nowhere while a fat tapeworm of pink-stained drool stretches from his open mouth onto the plastic high-chair tray, which is a gory crime scene of crumbs and buttercream. He's one year old today, again. He has been one year old so long I forget when he wasn't.

"Come on, birthday boy," my sister Alberta says as she scoops a fingerful of sweet mush off the plastic tray to press between his slack lips.

Alberta's slurring her words so badly she doesn't make much more sense than Babycakes. That's why I put so many ice cubes in my vodkas. It keeps you hydrated, sharp. Alberta just leaves her glass in the freezer to keep her drink cold. You can't tell her anything she doesn't want to hear.

A cone-shaped silver-and-gold party hat sits crooked on her head like a glittering growth. Four staples run down one side where my brother-in-law Ricky has refastened the flimsy rubber band when it popped loose over the years. Ricky's party hat is on straight. He's stuffed into his chair watching TV. Ricky hardly ever speaks, even less than Babycakes if you count grunts and cries. Alberta would tell you he stopped talking after the tragedy with little Wanda. Truth is he never had much to say before that either. He drives long haul, and even when he is here, he's barely here. He's paying no attention whatsoever to the party. In Ricky's defense, he's been to this party fourteen or fifteen times before. I can't recall exactly; I've lost count. I should know since this is partly my fault.

"All done, Babycakes. Back to your playpen."

Alberta sways a little when she lifts him up out of the highchair, which she's brought into the living room for the occasion. Her feet aren't too steady crossing the room to put him in the pen. I told her, that's why you need to put ice in your drink.

Babycakes just stares through the plastic slats. His little blue jumper is frayed at the ends like hand-me-downs even though it's only ever been his. I bought it for him for his birthday eight or nine years ago.

He got the nickname Babycakes on account of the way he demolished his very first cake on his very first birthday. Before that he was just Dustin. That's his real name, but nobody uses it anymore. Back when he was still Dustin was a frightful time. From the day he was born, Alberta couldn't leave him alone, not even for a second. If I so much as carried him into another room, she'd go into a high panic. She wouldn't let him out of her grip, not even for me or Ricky. Like she thought if she ever let go of him, he'd just disappear.

Alberta hadn't really been right in the head since little Wanda pulled that fryer full of hot oil off the stovetop onto her head. All that grease sizzling onto her face and down into her clothes, her diaper. Alberta was the only one home at the time. This was before I moved in when I quit my shifts at the Dollar General to go on disability on account of my carpal tunnel. Ricky was off delivering a load of snowmobile parts to North Dakota. The nurse at the hospital finally got my name and number out of Alberta so I could come and calm her down. When I arrived, she was shrieking in the waiting room outside the surgical unit where the doctors were failing to save little Wanda. They had to stick Alberta with a sedative to calm her down so they could treat the raw-red patches on her arms and neck where she'd burned herself carrying the caramelized little girl.

After they got her to sleep that night, I drove back to the house, where the front door still hung open. Somebody had to clean that kitchen. The linoleum flooring blistered out in a crescent moon shape around the oven. The worst part was the smell. Not just fryer oil, but something very specific frying. Like pork rinds and hair. They never replaced the tile. That ring is still there in front of the stove. At first, nobody mentioned it because to address it would be to mention little Wanda, which would set Alberta off. By the time Ricky should have replaced it himself, I'd gotten so used to standing on it while I cooked my breakfast that I didn't think to bring it up. It's amazing what you can get used to after awhile.

Alberta thought it was some kind of miracle when she got pregnant three years later at thirty-nine. If you factor in my lump of a brother-in-law, I'm inclined to agree it was a miracle. But sure enough, she swelled up big. She stopped drinking vodkas altogether for the whole nine months, even on the weekends.

Then came Dustin, and the nervous attacks. From the

moment she brought the baby home, she stopped going into town. Ricky and I had to do all the shopping. She started cutting her own hair. Forget leaving the house, you could hardly get her to leave whatever room Dustin was in. It was a chore just convincing her to take a shower. It was like my sister was convinced if this new baby got her out of her sight, just for a minute, somebody'd take him from her.

I'm the one who suggested Alberta go see Enid Carmody, who was known in town to practice a certain kind of country medicine. The Baptists and the Catholics have a different name for it. Enid's just an old hippie lady with some folk remedies. That's what I would have said at the time. I only sent Alberta out past the county line to the Carmody house for something to calm her nerves. St. John's root or tree bark tea. That's all I had in mind.

Enid Carmody's cure seemed to have done the trick. Alberta came back from her trip out to the county smiling easy. I asked her if Enid Carmody had given her some hippy-dippy herb tea, and she said no, and I asked, "Well did she smoke you up with some reefer, because you seem awful relaxed?" Alberta just told me Enid had given her the answer.

A few weeks later, come Dustin's first birthday, my sister was as laid-back as I've ever known her to be She didn't take hardly any vodka at all. She let me play with the baby in the living room like a normal aunt while she baked his cake. "I got pie at the Kroger for the rest of us," she said. "This cake is all for the birthday boy." We brought the highchair into the living room, next to the couch, in the corner where the artificial tree goes in December. Ricky even laughed a little when Dustin started stuffing sugar and butter into his mouth by the fistful. Alberta cooed over his little baby cheeks all covered in cake, her little cake baby, her little Babycakes.

It was only later that Alberta explained to me that

Enid Carmody gave her the ingredients for the special cake so that now he would always be her baby and she could keep him safe at home forever and ever.

Forever is longer than you'd think. That's what's on my mind now as Babycakes starts pounding his head against the bars of the cage, which is what his playpen is if you consider he's never going to leave it. He wipes one sticky hand on the brown shag carpet. Alberta is passed out. You can tell Ricky is still awake because his beer arm keeps moving, but otherwise he stays still. When I scoop Babycakes up out of his playpen, his head thumps against my chest and leaves little frosting masks printed on my blouse.

Babycakes makes growling sounds while I rinse him off with warm water in the bathroom sink. Even under all the sugar that scent is still there on his skin, like spoiled milk and dead leaves. For the first few years he had that powdery baby smell. That faded eventually, and for a while he smelled like nothing at all. Then I started to notice the fungal tang. That was around the same time he started to lose interest in his toys and his eyes stopped focusing on anything in particular.

When I get all the frosting off Babycakes, I carry him into his bedroom to put him in a fresh jumper and lay him down in his crib. It's the same every night for Babycakes, who will always be a baby as long as Alberta drives out to Enid Carmody's place every year and picks up the ingredients for his special cake.

I tickle Babycakes' stomach. He doesn't laugh. He doesn't even move. He just grunts. Poor Babycakes, who's never going anywhere.

* * *

A whole year of slow days roll by fast when they're all pretty much the same. Funny how that works.

Babycakes' first birthday comes around again before you know it. I heard Alberta take the car in the morning, presumably out to the county to the Carmody house, only the whole afternoon goes by and I don't smell any baking when I wake up from my nap.

In the living room, Babycakes sits stock-still in his playpen. His eyes are dirty mirrors. At least he's not grunting. The only sound in the living room is Ricky's weed-wacker snore over the hiss of the muted TV. Alberta is passed out, face down, on the couch with her mouth hanging open. The TV's flickering light gleams off the mercury fillings in her back teeth. One hand dangles next to her room-temperature vodka glass. I've told her so many times you have to put ice in there to stay sharp.

I give my sister a nudge to rouse her and remind her she needs to bake that cake. Alberta wipes the back of one hand across her dry lips and asks if I can do it this year.

I'm not much for cooking, but it's Babycakes' birthday and I forgot to buy him a present again, so I can hardly say no. First thing's first. I fill a glass with ice, making sure to clink it extra loud to make my point. Then I top it off from one of the plastic Svedka jugs. The ingredients for the cake are in a brown cardboard box on the counter next to the sink. They don't look so witchy. A plastic baggie of little black seeds, another of some dried herbs that look like pipe tobacco, an empty coffee can half-refilled with strange flour the color of river water.

I sing some old George Strait songs to myself while I mix the flour in a bowl with sugar, eggs, and milk. Cold as my drink is, it's hot in the kitchen. Or maybe it's that I had one more vodka today than I counted. Or that my whole face gets hot when I think about Dustin, how he used to be, and Enid Carmody, and how I had to go and open my big fat mouth, which is what our mother used to say when she drank her G&Ts. She'd say, "Girl, you don't have to open that big fat mouth and let every bad idea up there come out of your head." That hurt my feelings at the time, but the more I think about it, the more I think maybe it's true. The feeling is so strong I have to grip the edge of the countertop for a second to steady myself while I stare down into that box of ingredients.

An hour later, the cake smells okay coming out of the oven. I wipe some yellow frosting over the top. When I bring it into the living room, Ricky and Alberta are awake again. The box of party hats sits next to the couch, unused.

I put Babycakes in his highchair to present him with his dessert. He listlessly squelches frosting between his fingers and spreads the cake around with sugared fists. Alberta gets exasperated and starts scooping up mashed cake from the tray and poking it into his mouth. Babycakes obliges until his blue eyes go heavy and he starts swooning in place. He's eaten enough of the cake to please his mother, who pulls him out of the highchair and takes him into the bedroom without even wiping him down.

I might be swooning a little too. The whole room tilts like a ferryboat while we watch TV. Everything seems so distant I don't even notice the sound at first. Alberta does. That low gurgling noise I thought was Ricky's sleep apnea isn't coming from my square-headed brother-in-law at all. It's a wet, grinding sound. Coming from Babycakes' room.

"Ricky, go see what that is."

Usually Ricky would scoff and sigh at the prospect of doing much of anything. Something has spooked the old boy though. He's already staring at the dark hallway. I've never seen him look so awake. He's up without complaint and lumbering down the hall in his stocking feet. He disappears around the corner.

The sounds from the other room stop. For a few seconds there's total silence.

Then there are more noises. Something heavy, like a dresser—or a big man—thudding to the floor. A ragged, choked-off scream, cut off by a soggy crunch like a melon splitting. Slurping. A low moan.

"Ricky?" Alberta almost whispers.

Footsteps start from the bedroom down the hallway. They sound like a full-sized man, like Ricky, but also not like Ricky. Not so heavy, or so even. Unsteady like someone who can't hold their liquor, walking like they just learned how.

"Ricky?" Alberta says again. "Babycakes?"

My heart can't keep a steady beat in my chest. My right hand snakes down to my jeans pocket. I can feel the bulge of that plastic pouch of unused herbs. I'd forgotten to put them in the cake. Except I hadn't forgotten, exactly. I'd decided not to. I'd made just a regular old birthday cake with regular ingredients, for reasons I could hardly explain to Alberta, even to myself.

The same house. The same party. The same cake. And Babycakes, always the same. For so long that you can't even remember.

If I thought she would understand, I would tell Alberta that nothing can ever really stay the same. Eventually it's only ever a worse version of what it used to be.

Alberta has just started to push her way up off the couch when the thing staggers out of the dark hallway into the living room. It's so tall its head scrapes against the doorframe. It's wildly disproportionate, as if some parts of it grew too fast and some too slow. A tiny head atop crooked shoulders with long arms and apelike hands. One leg shorter than the other, and its whole pale, naked frame covered head to toe in patches of downy blond fuzz blended with coils of thick black hair. Its jaundiced eyes blink at different rhythms. Its wet mouth hangs open just wide enough for me to see that its teeth are too small, even for its grossly undersized head, but there sure are a lot of them.

Alberta falls back onto the couch and starts whimpering. She looks like a baby herself, there on her back with her trembling arms sticking up to ward it off. She's lost her words too; now, she's just making sounds.

I tip my glass back until every drop of frigid vodka cools my throat and burns my gut at the same time. When I drop my glass on the floor, the ice cubes clatter out like stones. If the room was listing like a ferryboat before, now it's on the verge of capsizing. I almost fall off my chair when I reach down into the cardboard box to fetch one of the plastic party hats, and pull the elastic strap down under my chin.

Alberta's crying has turned to screaming.

Time to celebrate. Babycakes is two.

CRUSADE
By Jason Krawczyk

It's a familiar ache. At every pull, my muscles shudder as if gravity were acting accordingly. There's even a sense of vertigo. Seeing the clouds below me certainly massages my fears away. That unique sense of ease is unsettling. I have to use that. I have to hate that sensation of security and feed it to my rage. I have to keep clawing my way down toward the heat. Dark, black heat.

Experiencing a full life doesn't suppress my awe for this place. The oceans taught me that the deeper the depth, the more crushing the cold. Not here. You can smell the heat intensifying farther down. I found myself taking shorter breaths as deep inhales pierce my lungs with hot and dry pain. My throat sputters a copper flavor as I taste the shavings from the roof of my mouth. I would vomit if I had any hydration to spare. Still, I cannot stop.

I'm enveloped in darkness and can no longer see the sky below me. The time it takes to find a suitable edge for my grasp is humiliating. I do feel slick moisture on the tips of my fingers and toes. My senses have dulled from the noxious heat, but I'm confident the skin has blistered off. How long have I been climbing? Gauging time here seems worthless. I can't even guarantee if there is time here. Time? Should I even give it the luxury of thought? I have my focus, and I will not stray from my goal. I have already given my life, but I can give more.

Sound. Something other than my wheezing. It's faint and dubious, but it's a beacon. Anything. Any form of sensation gives me a place to go. It's a moan. I can't tell if it's from pleasure or pain, but it's from the bowels of the living. There is life down here, and hopefully this life can speak.

Searing shame strikes me down as my grasp slips. How can I crumble into a panic so quickly? This entire endeavor is soon to be lost, but not by a physical failure. My faculties are scattering along with my hope, and tears begin to swell behind my eyes. How has my body found the moisture for tears? It's the moment I feared most: the unknown obstacle that would tackle my fraudulent courage. A nameless variable that reveals the coward underneath. Then my flailing arm finds something: not a grip, but a void. I plunge my hand into a cavern on the side of the rock face. With a grip on the floor of the cave, I pull myself inside.

I'm not sure what direction I will fall, but when I land, my entire body screams. The back of my head ricochets off the surface, and the impact forces the air out of my lungs. If not for my sense of panic, my newly found concussion would have rendered me unconscious. My breath returns to me, but I have to stand. If I lie here, I will find solace. I have to stand. Pain. All I feel is the pain. Standing may take a while.

My joints feel as if they've been shackled from their full range of motion. This agony forces me to press my back against the wall and gently shift my weight upwards. Oh, the wonderment of the floor. It's been so long since my feet felt the sensation of a solid surface. Forgotten impressions return to my spine as I force its arch. My joints rattle as they rediscover their mobility. Has all this time in darkness rotted my mind? Am I using my eyes? A flicker of orange?

Once my legs remember how to walk, I force them to run. The moaning, it's getting louder, and I can almost see the floor. It's not stone like I believed, but perhaps ivory. It's hard to fathom, but it seems to be filled ivory corroded by fire. I stumble at a turn. I can't remember the last time I've spoken, but that silence is broken with the word "fuck." The moaning ceases at the sound of my profanity, and I freeze at the prospect of interacting with something other than myself. Then, after a moment of horrifying stagnation, something explodes into motion. It's not footsteps. Whatever it is, it doesn't have feet. Feathers, maybe? I hear feathers. Feathers and a long, consistent grating sound. I'm about to see something with a pulse. Whatever I witness, I will not allow my mind to plummet into madness. My God. My second word is the same as the first.

Before I can get to my feet, it latches its claws around my shoulders and two of its smaller pincers around my neck. I am hoisted off the ground and carried away like a newborn wrestling his father. Nothing in my life has prepared me for such a visage. Three times my height, with a face similar to a man's, but an eagle's and a bull's head occupying the same skull. Its black bones extend from its appendages and shield its chest, claws, and genitals. I get lost in its coarse wings. I can't count how many protrude from its body, but they each span wider than I am tall. And eyes. Eyes are embedded in every unclaimed patch of skin in this walking nightmare. All of them, drawn on every inch of me.

It hurls me to the ground near a searing heat. There's the origin of the flicker. It's a pit filled with a billowing fire that smells of burning hair. I attempt to flee, but the creature hurls me back to the ground. I rebel, so it clasps me to the floor with an unforgiving might that only strengthens at my attempts to stand. The crushing upon my chest expels the air from my lungs. I yield. I cannot fathom another option.

The monster moves from my sight, but its chaotic shadow reminds me of the futility of standing. Is this it? Am I just at this thing's mercy? The moaning returns. It's not from the winged beast, and there's more than one voice. My eyes find the two wailing mouths and their adjoined bodies. No. Is this a glimmer into my fate? A man and woman, both naked, are seated back-to-back on a mound of charred ivory. By their side was a knee-high spool of ragged brown twine. I'm not confident of the string's building materials, but I fear it justifies the stench of burning hair. I know not where their injuries reside, but rusted blood cakes their bodies.

The walking nightmare of wings looms over the tortured pair. The talons reach the spool and one pulls a forearm length through an ivory needle. I use the word forearm to describe the length due to an unsettling assumption that it was fashioned from one. The other talon grasps onto the male's forehead and pulls him away from the woman's. What I see next causes my muscles to spasm and gut to knot. My eyes are open, but my mind does not allow them to see. As the man and woman shriek, clarity returns to my clouded vision. How? How is this possible? Why would a living thing do this to another?

The demon tears the flesh from their backs, exposing splintered ribs and shredded nerves. I can see billowing desperation from hyperventilating lungs, arteries spraying streams of crimson, and gelatinous red-slicked fat flop out of the hacked skin. The creature has ripped their spinal cords out from their hips and has woven them together. Intertwined, each spine is returned to its rightful hipbone.

With delicate precision, the creature secures the bones back into place with its needle and thread. With braided spines, the man and woman remain in unimaginable agony. The solace of death is foreign here. There is only sentience. Unforgiving sentience.

My second attempt to flee resembles the first. Pinned to the ground, I wail in madness. "Please. Dissolve my mind. I surrender my consciousness to you. Have me not comprehend anything, everything, and nothing. Please. Take me... please."

"I'm sorry."

Words. Not moans or shrieks or screams, but words. Two. Two beautiful words were spoken to harmonize a beautiful sentiment. And a voice. Shrill in the midst of whimpers, but just as wondrous as any hymn. It's feminine. Woman. The creature's gracious enough to create. I knew a woman. I'm a man that knew a woman. I loved a woman. She died. She died, but I followed her. That's why I'm here. I'm not supposed to be here, but I am. I'm here because I loved her. No. I love her. I love her, and I will not stop.

"Get the fuck off!"

Even with the beast clasped to my torso, I stand. Here, strength is not measured in muscle. It's no monster. It's just in my way. It attempts to raise me from the ground, but I grasp onto its wrists and crank. Its shell shatters to reveal a warm wetness beaming with phosphorus light inside. It is its turn to shriek. As the room illuminates from the creature's innards, it collapses. Violence corrupts my mind as I continue to strike, but then I think of her. I can't help but stop. Cracked and chipped, the demon lays in a pool of its light. Life remains, but its will is slain.

"Help us," the woman demands.

Their eyes are still adjusting to the light, but their pain is present in every word.

I run to their aid, but I'm not sure of what to do.

"How? How can I free you?"

"Kill us. Please," the man says in weakness.

"No" comes out of my mouth without a thought.

"Please, before the angel heals!" the woman howls.

"Angel?" I look to the bleeding demon on the floor. "That fucking monstrosity?"

"Death is freedom here. We can't end our own lives, and the constant torture is eternal. You don't belong here. You can defy this place. Please, end us!" the woman pleads.

"But life... I can't. Life is-"

The man interrupts me. "Torture! Torture is life here!"

"Please!" "Please!" they wail on.

What sins have they committed that would possibly justify this misery? Which argument advocates everlasting torment? Their pleas are deafening. I would not believe I had the stomach for such an act, but circumstances challenge values. I too howl as I thrust my thumbs into the man's eyes. His screams end and so does the woman's. She cries in a culmination of relief and fear. I gently place my hands atop her head. She shivers at the contact, but her words reveal otherwise.

"Thank you," she whispers in the midst of sobs.

The second thank you has a swelling fear embedded inside, so I tell her "you are forgiven" and bring my lips to her forehead. I may have seen a sliver of relief, but I will never be certain. Then it's done. The last moments should know kindness.

I crumble to my knees as sorrow overtakes me. It's so quiet now. I was once longing for sound but now am horrified by its revelations. "I'm sorry," says the woman. For whom was that meant? That tortured man? Her words save me with their utterance. The light from the deformed angel is fading. How dare there be a place like this?

"What was that?" a voice that sounds of scraping iron

and singing whales asks. The demon or angel can and has spoken.

I launch to my feet. "Stay down!" I holler with all the intimidation I can muster.

The angel flinches as if my words could lacerate. Its wounds are healing, but it's still crippled. It cowers as it waits for me to act, but I stay waiting. After a moment of silence, it asks again. "What was that?"

"What was what?" I ask.

"You ended their plight. Why?"

"They were suffering, and they asked for help."

Even with its many faces, I can see it can't comprehend the notion.

"But why did you act? What lead you?"

Does this thing even know the meaning of the word I'm about to say?

"Mercy."

Its eyes widen, and it coos in familiarity. With a look of awe, as if seeing an old friend, its lips quiver as it asks, "And why? Why haven't you slaughtered me?"

I ponder upon its question.

"I don't understand." The light-bleeding creature is poisoned with shame, as it asks, "I did you harm and intended to do you more. Why not torment me further? Was it this Mercy?"

???? It's with this question that I realize there's movement in the surrounding darkness. There are more, just like this one, standing just outside of the light. "…and forgiveness." I think that's why. The surrounding life silences in awe of the concept. The angel's eyes stay transfixed upon me.

"Where do I find others that have fallen? The ones that have taken their own life?" Its six eyes never leave mine. "Stay on your path. You'll soon find a land of endless skies and infinite horizons. Whoever you seek will be there. Your search will be arduous."

I respond with a sincere "thank you" and walk off. I hear the rumblings of the words "Mercy" and "Forgiveness" as the creatures congregate. I don't turn to look, but I believe they assist the one I've flogged. If true, it brings me hope.

As I walk, I lose the light of the fallen and am, again, enveloped in darkness. Odd how there is now a sense of comfort in the darkness. Before, I longed for anything other than black, but the darkness never did me harm. I grunt after a hard turn. The light I did not anticipate consumes my person, and even with my eyes shut, it's agonizing. I'm not sure how much time passes with my eyes closed, but more is needed to regain my sight with them open. Oh no. Why?

Meat. The ground is not soil, grass, or sand, but meat. Pulsating wet muscle was sewn together by tendons and splintered bones. This red field goes further than the horizon, and every inch of its terrain is occupied. Like looking upon a colony of ants, I witness a mass of people lumbering atop each other. Moving as one condensed herd, they aimlessly slog with no destination to relieve their warped instincts. Their eyes, lost in the middle distance, reveal empty souls. With exposed infections painting their skin and visible ribs from starvation, these are truly the damned. The clouds are ablaze, and I know not if there are stars above this rotted gloom. Searing orange light seeps through the cracks of this overcast. Only raging fire burns that light.

I march into the crowd. Time is not a factor. If she is one of those lost, then she will be found. I enter the horde, and it takes an extreme effort to fight their current. They move as one, but I refuse to join their mass. In my attempts to slink into space, I lose my footing and shortly after that, my resolve. They collapse atop of me and crawl off to continue their march. Skin. I'm buried in flesh. Every inhale is interrupted by the flavor of warm wet copper. Claustrophobia I have never felt in my life crushes me. "Get off! Off! Now! Off!" I thrash and push and holler my way back to my feet. I don't care anymore. If you're in my way, I discard you with a rage and prejudice that prologues murder. The pain is dull, but I can feel the skin from my knuckles on my wrists, and I can see my contorted fingers as I strike. All of them. I will kill them all. My roar, lost in fury and madness, spews a name.

"Sarah!"

At the sound of my most cherished, the damned stop in their lumbering. They look at me with innocence and astonishment. I am ashamed at the time it takes me to stop fighting, but I eventually calm down. As my breath steadies I see the melancholy in their gaze. With my temper cooled, I took my first step. The men and women part, giving me a passage. Tears start to well as I nod in gratitude. "Sarah!" I hear her name. One of the damned joins my search. "Sarah!" Then another. "Sarah!" Her name echoes throughout this bottomless domain. I can now run as I belt her name. I know not if they know their actions, but this army of lamenting is aiding me.

They're now behind me. A continent of souls gazes upon my back while I gaze upon the horizon... and one lone woman. She's off in the distance, but she could be across an ocean. It does not matter. She's all that matters. I've never been this fast as I barrel toward her.

"No! No! How dare you!"

Blinding light from the sky barricades me from my beloved. Beings start to reveal themselves as the white shine dissipates. They look like the so-called angels I encountered earlier, but elegant, white, and pure. They radiate confidence and power that causes my bones to vibrate. Their leader speaks to me. "Calm your mind good si-"

"Move, or I'll go through you!" I never had a

penchant for subtly. I try to enforce my threat but they strike me down with an appendage I cannot see. "You, sir, have defiled a sanctity that has never not been. You are to cease in your mission." Its voice sings the most beautiful of melodies, and it would be pleasant if I didn't hate its master.

"Do you even remember your name?" The angel asks. I don't, so I don't answer. "Nor does she. You have not entered her mind since her death. She does not, nor will not, remember you."

"Liar! Let me see for myself!"

Its face is comforting, but I don't allow it to be. "You have known this woman for twelve years. Long passed the age you've lived and long passed the eons you've searched for her." Eons? Has it really been? My name sparks nothing in my mind. That is unsettling. "Come home. You've earned your light."

How long have I suffered for her? I attempt to rebel with reason. "No, life does not justify reward or punishment."

"It does. The ones behind you are proof of it. If you were to see her, what would you do? Join this brood of aimless shame? She won't know you. She cares not for you or your actions."

"No!" I fall to my knees and plead, "We'd find a home outside of the light and dark."

As I sob, the angel comforts me. "Ease your mind. Come back to the light. Learn your name."

How can I, knowing she's here? How can I, knowing of the relentless pain here? How? But... I am tired. So very tired. I did not know of my exhaustion until now. Is this just an absolute of the way things are, even after death?

"Yes." the angel says.

It can hear my thoughts. I would very much like to rest. Grappling with their wisdom may be futile. Why am

I so tired? I was looking for her. Did I find her? What was her name... her name... what was it... what is my name... tired... I should sleep... why don't I sleep? I can... I can sleep... I think I shall. Just close my eyes. Close... my... eyes... sleep...

"Mercy!"

My eyes open to see something remarkable: The monster I've sparred with in the pit. It has returned with an army of ones just like itself. Deformed and scarred, they defend me from their pure cousins. The battle rages while I witness strife as old as time. My former enemy stands in front of me. All the wounds I have inflicted upon it have healed.

"Stand! Now! Stand up!" I have little strength as it barks at me. "Look! Look at what you've done!" I turn to see the damned and demons alike, fighting against their enlightened persecutors. "Stand! Now!" it continues to bark. I hear echoes of the words "mercy," "forgiveness," and "Sarah." Sarah... Sarah's her name. That battle cry ignites a loathing in me that would blacken suns. I take the demons hand and it hollers, "Love did this. See it through!" I scream in gratitude as it hoists me to my feet. It rushes back to battle and I truly hope it and its brethren find liberation.

I get a glimmer of my love through this cosmic war. I see her and I shall hold her. I sprint as demons and damned alike defend my every step. Her skin. I can see her skin. Her hair, it's so long and fine and perfect. "Sarah!" She turns as I reach out. Once I see her eyes, I immediately know what I've always known.

"Richard."

Some things can endure eternity.

THE NAME-US GAME COUNTERPOINT
By Cecily Winter

He woke at his desk fully dressed and shook his head to dislodge the fug from his brain. His laptop screen glowed and he tapped it. Weirdly, it blossomed into the police sketch of Star Silver. Her real name was Kim, his first, and he still recalled her silken hair threaded through his fingers. Too bad she broke so soon.

He must've been tripping all night because he didn't recall leaving the house and trolling for the Kim under his motel-standard duvet. Over the years, he'd spent a fortune on bedclothes. DNA was a bitch, and here he was playing the odds when money was short.

A wisp of smoke, visible through a gap in the drapes, told him he'd burned her clothes. He got up and twitched the drapes closed. He didn't want peeping Toms or nosy Parkers calling the cops. On second thought, the smoke could have been from the beach blanket still smoldering after yesterday's rain. If it didn't ash up soon, he'd douse it with gas.

It was barely dawn, and his grandma's stone farmhouse would be chilly until the sun got high. He occupied just three rooms: his easy-clean bedroom-cum-living room, Spartan in the extreme; the bathroom with lime-green fixtures from the 1940s; and the kitchen, about which the less said the better. He'd long ago stopped climbing to the second floor. The roof leaked, and it was a mess, but his dad's mess, and he was long gone. Found facedown and fox-nibbled in the old cornfield. Verdict—heart attack. Maybe the Devil said, "boo."

He entered the doorless bathroom. Like he figured: he'd been way out of it. Had he been roofied? He selected a packaged toothbrush from the vanity drawer, set it beside the sink, then selected one of several plain gray sweatsuits from the closet and folded the pieces on the toilet seat as per usual.

The new Kim tiptoed toward him, stark naked and hugging her arms tight about her breasts.

She asked, "Where'd you put my clothes?"

"Take a shower. You can wear the sweats."

She didn't argue. Baby in the sandbox. He liked them to argue. It raised the temperature.

No lock on the bathroom door, so steam billowed to his laptop where he sat spot-lit by a beam of sunrise making headway through a chip in the blacked-out transom. While he waited, he searched his mind for the place he'd picked up the Kim. He liked a written record, not his own—the essential details were engraved in his memory—but on the website of the National Missing and Unidentified Persons System. Since he'd first logged on to NamUs a while back, a bunch of girly Jane Does had been identified and labeled with their real names.

He didn't care for girlie names—Barbie, Juliet, Tiffany. After his mother took off—she was a Kim if he remembered rightly—when he'd been five, he'd methodically stabbed and dismembered all her Barbie collectibles, then buried their plastic bits in a cornfield grave. Not allowed to strike matches, he dumped their clothes in the kitchen trash. Decades later, the last time he'd been upstairs, his mother's clothes still hung laundered and ironed in her bedroom closet.

He always christened his girls Kim, though not all were blondes or shapely. Why not gorge on the sample pack?

In his memory, he recorded only the dates and cities where he picked them up: Kim/May 14, 2021/Wildwood; Kim/October 3, 2019/Jenkintown; Kim/February 7, 2018/Cape May. He'd been almost 17 with the first in Brooklyn. Her arterial blood messed up his truck—Dad was pissed but he'd avoided major spillage ever since.

He rarely ventured so far these days. Too much stress driving long-distance with hookers or Goodtime girlies doped, dying, or dead. When the site excised people, it meant they'd been identified, found, and returned in body bags to their next of kin or a potter's field. He never followed the news to see where the investigations had stalled but caught a TV blurb last week on the Wildwood hiker. He'd been sunbathing, wind-bathing more like, and preferred to take his time for burial, but a scare from a cruiser siren forced him to leave that Kim exposed to the crabs and gulls between a couple of dunes. He checked her out on the website. Brand new file captioned as a Jane Doe with details of her coloring and approximate age. Only 15, though she'd demanded cash up front.

Cops never once showed up at his door. Dad had taught him the techniques of stealth hunting—squirrel, possum, and crows mainly, but they worked for girlies too and no noisy bang.

He flinched when new Kim's hair brushed the back of his neck as she leaned over his shoulder and her minty breath almost covered the stink of her sweat. Wow. How long would it take to scrub it all off? She must've been on the road a long while. She wore his bathrobe, which swamped her. Why didn't she follow instructions and put on the sweats he left out?

He glanced at the family photo at the rear of the desk—the last one taken in his family. His Barbie-collecting mother with her face scratched out, Dad with beefy eye pouches, and him, aged five, when he was cute as a Disney grasshopper.

"This your hobby," she asked, "helping the cops and families of those missing people?"

Her voice was rich and melodic and somehow familiar like she'd been on the radio or was a chorus girl like Star Silver Kim, there to make his day with her special brand of whoopie.

"Keeps me spinning on the wheel of fortune," he said, catching back a snigger. "I'm drawing a blank on how we hooked up. Where was that?"

She punted the question. "You ever crack a case?"

"You doped me last night?"

"Maybe."

"You could have had me free and clear if you'd asked."

She didn't smile, and he closed the laptop. "Cracking a case isn't the point."

"How's that?"

He had no answer she wanted to hear. "You need joe? I got instant."

"Water's good. I'm parched."

"Sure."

He got up easily, limber as a cougar, and swept the cottage for escape routes. Windows nailed shut, ratty drapes still drawn, and the front and back doors key-locked and bolted high. She could jump out a second-floor window but the rotted floorboards wouldn't hold her weight.

In the steamy bathroom, a corona of soil rimmed the

bathtub drain. The faucet trickled water into a Dixie cup. Faucet was clogged. It busted him up sometimes, how he was forced to live: a sagging roof, fast food on the run, a garbage pile out back the size of Montana. Maybe he'd find a new hunting lodge.

The farm had gone under long before he dropped out of high school. He didn't know how his dad made money but they lived off the grid, not even a phone, and aside from that he'd never wanted for anything. Got a second-hand truck for his 16th birthday. No cake and candles though.

It wouldn't be hard to abandon it. The house, an igloo in winter, a fly-blown furnace in summer, and there was talk of an eminent domain taking for a new highway. He couldn't stick around if the bulldozers got busy. The cornfield was a potter's field of tortured Barbies and life-surrendered Kims.

At his desk, Kim leaned on her elbows, her fists punched into her cheeks. She was engrossed in the screen and didn't flinch when he crept up from behind in noiseless shoes.

"Good with computers, are you?" he asked, crowding her with his body.

"Never used one before, but these faces popped up."

He frowned at the NamUs array on screen. Hadn't he shut it down? Photos or sketches of all his Kims were arranged in a grid like they were about to identify him. It was spooky.

"Who are they?" she asked as he handed her the paper cup.

"Missing women. There are thousands."

She drank the water in one gulp like the night's workout sucked her dry. He couldn't recall a thing about it, and her skin showed no wear and tear. He must have blacked out before the fun hit the fan.

She twisted a hank of hair around a finger. It was wet

and had a silvery sheen. Not that she could be a day over 25. Maybe her hair silvered overnight after a fright. Some lousy john or hopped-up punk giving her the business. Well, she was lucky she'd landed in the hands of a professional. His work was elegant. It was art.

She leaned back in his chair. "You ever wonder if they're dead under a load of farm dirt or alive and keeping a low profile until they figure out a way to get even?"

"The living got better things to do than hiking down Revenge Road and the dead don't care where they're at."

"You ever think about the stuff before? The brutality."

"Philosopher called Hobbes called it when he said, 'life's nasty, brutish and short.'"

"Well, he's a regular Mr. Congeniality."

"He saw the truth and told it."

He yanked Kim up and into his arms—she was a lightweight. He lowered his mouth to nuzzle her cleavage and let a hand slip along her inner thighs. She felt grainy, like damp sand. He was aroused, but she wriggled away.

Somehow, she was way out of reach and staring at him full on with shadow-flecked eyes. Not the eyes of any Kim he remembered.

"I better go," she said. "I'll take the money owed."

"Don't owe you nothing," he said, aware of the curl of his lips, his temper heating up. "You didn't put out. You want cash, you better eat the pillow on that bed."

"I didn't hike across a cornfield for that, but I know enough to speak for Star Silver and a debt you never paid."

Star Silver Kim happened thirty years back. Had she been this new Kim's mom, and the roofie set-up a ploy to even the score? *Wow*. That *was* interesting.

"Convince me about that debt," he said, dropping into his chair. He stretched to grab her and dragged her by her hips onto his lap. With one arm hooked around her waist to anchor her, he worked the cursor to bring up Star Silver's face again. Her flatmate had contributed to the cop sketch and reported her missing but she hadn't known her real name or that her body was six feet down about 200 feet east of the house. He'd never taken chances with photos or videos but he liked having the website's portrait gallery at his fingertips.

"You mean this Kim?" he asked, stroking her image.

"What did you do to her?" she asked evenly.

"You look like the imaginative type. Guess."

She struggled to pry herself off his lap, but he held her down even though she was squishy as a pillow or maybe slippery as if she'd smeared herself in liquid soap or melted lard. His heart muttered up a storm and he went all over clammy.

Performance nerves? He licked her ear. She tasted of clay. "You're going nowhere, honey."

"That so? You think you can hold onto me?"

"I know it."

"Tell me how many you killed, Junior."

"That's not my name but that's my score right there on the screen, barring maybe a couple in the early days."

She quit struggling as if her predicament had upped and slapped her hard across the mouth. She overlapped the center hems of the robe. He didn't like her wearing it. He'd have to burn it when he was through.

She reached to tap the space bar and the portrait array shivered as if to predict a power failure. It was par for the course where he was, but the re-visit had juiced him, and he imagined hurting lap Kim in all the same slow and careful ways as the others. Her skin rose in goosebumps as if someone stepped on her grave, and he relished the dread settling in the pit of her stomach, the fear feeding on her adrenaline.

Brief pressure on his inner thigh made him gasp with pleasure. Until his leg spasmed. He batted away Kim's hand and the razorblade dropped to the floor. His white terry robe flooded with his own arterial blood. She'd hid the blade in the robe pocket, damn her.

"Call an ambulance now!" He shoved her off his lap and she floated from him like a balloon caught in the wind. The pain was a bitch out of hell, but why was he hallucinating? How long did he have? He tried to recall the stats.

Hovering a foot from the floor, Kim faced him and laughed. Only the first Kim had ever laughed at him. He'd been a kid then and a virgin on both counts.

He gritted, "Do. It. Now. Bitch."

She leaned close, stinking of the grave, and tapped the flickering gallery of Kims, who oozed from the screen like gobs of ghostly spittle. He managed to drag himself upright and limped away from them as the spittle solidified into his former playmates, Star Silver included, and some others he didn't even know. He tripped over his shoelaces and fell heavily on his back as his office chair rolled away and the women closed in. Some were matronly, but he'd never interfered with a woman old enough to be his mother.

He sweated buckets, and his tongue clamped to the roof of his mouth. He wished he'd drunk that Dixie cup of water. Ten Dixie cups.

The dead women, most of them naked, some half-dressed in filthy rags, drew about him until their dangling hair and leering faces, and inside the faces, vein and muscle and bone, blocked out the fly-speckled ceiling.

"Thing is," new Kim said over his face, her face translucent as an angel's. But when he touched it with a fingertip, it burned like hot coal.

That voice. Was she sent from heaven to punish him?

"These gals and I," she said, "formed a posse."

Why wouldn't she call an ambulance? He reached weakly for her hand. "Save me. I'll never hurt anyone again. I swear."

"No chance, Junior. We're hunting serials, or haunting to be precise. I used to be a regular Betty Crocker right here in this farmhouse until your dad choked me with a stocking for the last time."

"No way. My whore mother ran off."

"She was wheelbarrowed off, doubled up in a plywood box."

He patched his wound with his hands and watched the blood seeping through his fingers. He was faint. He wanted to throw up. If she were his mother, she had to help him.

"I'd planned on leaving the bastard," she said conversationally as if telling her story trumped his actual damn survival, "and I'd have taken you for sure. But out there so long, I forgot your name, Junior. Once I'd clawed myself out of the plywood and dirt, I sniffed you out, but it wasn't until the others surfaced that I understood what I was dealing with. Just think, if the cops stumble across your remains—you know—from a wake of vultures sniffing you out—you'd become squatter John Doe on NamUs. Or maybe you'd be identified and hit the newspaper headlines as part of an infamous serial-killer duo: the Father and Son Cornfield Killers. Impressive, right?"

Her cold killer eyes were full of shadows and spite.

"Don't be sore. Consider yourself selected out of the dating game." She bent down and extracted his wallet and keys from his pocket.

He made the effort to grab them but fell back with a whimper.

"We need funds for clothes and transport now that we're passing as human. Sorry about that, but we figure you owe a lot of us, and your dad owes the rest."

She squatted to tuck the blade between his fingers. "It'll only hurt a little while. Isn't that what you used to tell them? Now, ladies, give him a chance to do the decent thing."

He breathed easier with a weapon in hand. "Call the cops. An ambulance. I won't tell anyone how you cut me."

She shrugged. "You planning to finish this like a man or what?"

Tears sprang from his eyes. "Mom. Please."

"Looks like I bore his sniveling father's son alright."

The dead crowded him with the stink of rot and blood. They lay their bones and smell over him. They scratched and bit when he'd done the world a favor. Removed a few undesirables only, whores and bitches.

Perhaps he said it aloud, for Allentown Kim, who'd lasted for several pleasurable days, gripped that hunk of slate he'd set over her mutilated face and hammered it against his temple until the crack echoed through his every bone.

Mother Kim said, "It's a hoot, right, the Name-Us game counterpoint?"

From the corner of his functional eye, he saw her shake an admonishing finger at him. He watched her drag a box from under the bed and dress in clothes she'd taken from a bedroom closet—a calf-length skirt, a crisp shirt, and canvas sneakers. At this point, she looked like she'd stepped out of a magazine ad for laundry detergent or hair dye. It was the same outfit his mother wore in the photograph.

His own mother, who'd deserted him by dying, had set up the con and baited the honey-trap. She'd probably yanked the beach blanket out of the fire.

When she drew the drapes and sunlight flooded the room, he saw his blood, a tidal wave over the easy-clean linoleum flooring. His ears rang with screams. His own? The echo of theirs?

Mother Kim floated over his head. "He didn't have

much in him. I'd expected a show of strength. Who'll do the *coup de grâce*? I don't want blood on my going-public clothes."

Star Silver Kim took the blade from his slick fingers and squatted like a toad on his chest, from which position she meticulously gouged his last seeing eyeball from its socket.

"Done," she said.

QUIETUS
By David-Jack Fletcher

Terry woke with a jolt, cold sweat dripping from his body. Hot, thick air burned his lungs. Something had happened. The memory lurked in the shadows of his foggy mind. On the outskirts of his brain, just out of reach. But his body knew. His heaving chest, the panicked hairs on his arms. The pit of his stomach ached, burning to tell him that something was wrong. An intense, heavy force pressed against him from the inside. All he had left was a body trembling with dread.

He wiped sleep from his eyes and sat up. His head throbbed, ripping at the seams, ready to explode. He looked around with blurry vision, unable to decipher his surroundings. The sense of dread rose as he looked around. The memory of what brought him here still evaded him, and his heart pounded against his ribs. A warning that this place—a room, he could tell that much—was the last he'd ever see.

The room was empty. The walls a deep, intense red. He touched the hard surface, smooth and cold. Like concrete, but more organic, with a steady glow. The walls hummed, shallow breaths matching the panic he felt. He tried to adjust, rubbing his eyes as though the action would diminish the overpowering light. The glow seemed to intensify and, with it, a stale heat hit him in waves. The heat and the light and his throbbing head gave way to nausea, his insides churning. Before he could stop, he heaved, splattering the red floor with dark green and brown chunks.

He wiped his mouth, residue of bile a smear on the back of his hand. Vomiting left him breathless, but he knew he had to stand. To make sense of the situation. The walls began to dim, softening the room into a shadowy quietness. The heat dissipated without warning. The low hum almost inaudible, coming from outside the room.

Beyond the red walls.

Holding his pounding head, he tried to ignore the dread and panic surging through his body. He had to focus.

Where am I? Why am I here? How did I get here? Was I kidnapped? Why me?

He thought of his mother, the soldier, using her memory to balance his mind. Her strength always calmed him. The last thing he remembered was tucking his daughter in for the night, and then –

Oh Jesus, Alice! Did someone take her, too?

His seven-year-old daughter had clung to him while they'd said goodnight, a brief peck on the cheek, a token of a parent's love for their child. He'd switched the light off and paused at the door to watch Alice fluff her pillow and sink low into the bed with her stuffed octopus, Mr. Tentacles. Everything had been so normal, so routine.

Then someone had rung the doorbell. He probed his brain for answers, pushed himself to see a face, but nothing came. Now he was here, wherever 'here' was, encased in a tomb of red. Desperation welled inside him, his hands shaking at the thought of Alice in danger.

Stay calm. What would Mum do?

Her military training would tell her to search the area. Find a weak spot, a way out. In one of the walls, he saw a thin outline of what could have been a door, but no handle was visible. His stomach churned again. An organic, instinctual warning.

The outline faded in and out, as though his recovering eyes were playing tricks. He ran his fingers along one of the walls, hoping to find something. Anything. He sensed something beyond the wall. Movement, maybe. The low hum and the stench of his stomach contents his only companions.

He called out, his voice, hoarse and dry. The walls reverberated his weak efforts, and panic rose once more. Everything within him that was rational and calm disappeared in an instant, and his frantic hands searched the cold surface, pleading for an exit, for any crevice or crack he could exploit.

Nothing.

Remember, his mother had told him, *that you never give up. No matter how hopeless something seems, you dig deep and you fight til the end.*

He bashed against the wall where the door ought to have been, but the faint outline had disappeared. He scratched at the wall to no avail, begging for his release. No matter how deep he dug, he couldn't shake the feeling that these walls would be the last things he'd ever see. The feeling that he'd never see Alice again.

Thrashing the wall again, he slipped on the puddle of vomit and crashed to the floor, scraping the skin on his thighs and feet. For the first time, he looked down at his body. He was naked, curled in a foetal position. Terry wept into the chamber around him, distorted and weak. The nudity left him more vulnerable than he cared to admit, even worse than his ignorance of who had taken him, or where he was. Every curve and exposed back hair reinforced his powerlessness.

Naked, scared and alone, he stood up and drew once more on the strength of his mother. He thought of all the letters she sent him. It was what he always did when he was scared, even now, well into his thirties.

Dig deep. For Alice.

He remembered the last time he saw his mother, crouching in front of him at the airport. Her arms tight around him, faint traces of a coconut aroma in her hair. It had comforted him, along with her reassurance that she'd see him soon for his tenth birthday. When most mothers whispered their love before disappearing into some far away war, his whispered strategy and tactics.

He needed that now more than ever before but in that moment the whispered strategies were static in his mind. Her words sounded like a record spinning in reverse, and his breath caught in his throat. He forced himself to breathe. In through the nose, out through the mouth. Slow, steady. The fog surrounding his mind refused to lift.

Despite her efforts to instill him with a sense of bravery, he was only ever brave when he imagined her beside him. Maybe it was because she mothered him from a distance, dispelling advice from across windswept deserts in remote corners of the earth. She had tried to teach him not to let fear consume him for more than five seconds, something he couldn't do without the sense of her presence. He knew her advice was needed now if he was going to find Alice. He reached through time and space to see the words she'd left him in her final letter.

Feel your fear as much as you can feel anything. Know the fear; know what it means to you to be alive.

Her words echoed in his mind, and his breathing calmed. He knew what it meant to be alive. Alice was his whole life. She was his reason for being. Renewed, he continued his search for an exit. Alice was out there somewhere and, like his mother had ordered him all those years earlier, he had to dig deep.

Rising to his feet, ignoring the shameful urge to cover his exposed groin, something shimmered in the corner of his eye. From the ceiling, a liquid seeped. He walked towards the site, anxious, and inspected the liquid as it crept down the wall. One thick stream, spreading like veins, waiting to expose something much larger.

What is that?

Looking beyond the liquid into its origins, he saw no holes or cracks or anything that might suggest a way out, and his chest started pounding again. The liquid continued to seep into the room, its descent matching the rhythmic pulse of his heart. A second stream bled from the walls, pulsating towards him. Thicker this time. Slower in its descent. A transparent ooze that seemed to follow him around the room. He looked closer at the gushing ooze, noticing a slight yellow tinge. It reminded him of the splash when his ex-wife's water broke, ushering Alice into the world.

Alice.

He pressed himself against the opposite wall as the ooze continued towards him. He was petrified of turning his back on the menacing liquid. He remembered his mother's advice. The five seconds was up. The time for fear was over. Fear wasn't the path to finding Alice. Pushing it down to the depths of his stomach and wiping sweat from his eyes, he searched for something, anything that would set him free. He headed back to where the door ought to have been. He scratched and clawed at the concrete, begging the red surface to open. A fingernail snapped. He didn't notice. Ignoring the pain, he scratched harder.

"Let me out!"

He pounded the wall as the ooze approached. Its pulses slow, steady breaths. He looked back to where it seeped from the ceiling. Defying gravity, the ooze ran vertically in his direction, reaching along the wall. Tentacles searching for its prey. It was after him, it *wanted* him, its slow approach taunting him. Dripping to the floor, the ooze paused for a moment to suckle on the puddle of his vomit, absorbing the stomach contents into its opaque form.

The wall stood firm against his bleeding fists. He barged the wall, embracing the searing pain in his shoulder as he stumbled backwards. The ooze shimmered and snaked towards him, its yellowish opaque surface reflecting his own distorted image like a dirty funhouse mirror. The floor and walls were covered now, the ooze closing in on him. He screamed and begged and cried for Alice.

It lapped at his feet, encircling him, tasting him.

"No, no, no! Please, leave me alone!"

The malevolent fluid continued its approach, and he dug deep to find his mother's strength.

She wouldn't accept this. She'd be brave. She'd fight!

With no other options and escape seeming impossible, he turned to the offensive. All he could do was kick at it the way a child does with waves at the beach. He kicked and punched with all his might. It didn't react, but his attacks had nevertheless ruptured a semi-hard surface to reveal a thinner, pinkish liquid within. He kicked again and again, droplets of the ooze remaining on his toes. He tried to wipe them away, clawed at them, but the defiant liquid absorbed into his skin.

Before he could react, the ooze wrapped around his feet, biting at his skin like hundreds of bee stings coming all at once, pulling him into submission on the floor. His mother's advice vanished, sucked into the quicksand abyss just like his legs and torso. He clawed at his feet, tore at his arms and legs, watched in horror while the ooze consumed his chest and arms. His efforts helped its spread as his body drowned.

It crawled across his neck and face, and he sensed its pulsating hatred. It despised him. Thrived on his fear. It took pleasure journeying across his skin. Enveloped now, he was blind. Couldn't breathe, couldn't move as the liquid scalded his skin. Suffocating him in an ocean of boiling water. The world stood still for the longest time. His lungs burned and heaved, desperate for air as the liquid swam up his nostrils and down his throat. Knowing he was going to pass out any second, he tried once more to pull the monstrous ooze from him.

The more he fought, the more it tightened around him, squeezing his body like a snake torturing a mouse. His bones snapped under the pressure. Thousands of tiny sharp teeth gnawing at every nerve inside him.

His empty lungs stopped gasping for breath. The squeezing eased and the ooze began to disappear into him, sinking through his skin. He fought to keep his eyes open, but knew it was no use. Even though the squeezing had stopped, his nerves still screamed in pain, ordering his body into shutdown.

Alice's face was the last thing he saw before his brain switched off. Her round green eyes, jewels glowing from the center of her pale skin. Her flowing blonde hair. He saw her brush it away from her face, as she so often did, and smile at him. He saw her at the beach, running from the cold water as it crashed against the shore. Smiling. Laughing. Full of life.

In the next moment, her face disappeared.

Alice was gone.

***

Terry woke, coughing and wheezing. His lungs devoured the air, sucking it in like an addict desperate for one last hit. Clutching at his chest, he calmed into a steady pant and scanned the room. The ooze was gone, his body free. It hadn't left any traces. No marks or streaks, the way water would while it dried out. He checked every inch of his body, scraping and poking at his flesh. He expected his skin to burst open like a pimple overfilling with pus.

Nothing.

If not for the fact that those red walls surrounded him, he might have thought this whole thing was a bad dream. The room was real, but there was no evidence of any kind of liquid. It was almost like the vicious liquid had never existed. His head was woozy, and his body felt heavy, the way your bones do when forced awake from a deep sleep.

He knew, though, that the liquid hadn't been a terrifying dream. The room was real; the liquid had been, too. And that meant Alice was still out there, waiting for him. He hoped his little girl hadn't succumbed to the malevolent ooze. He knew he wouldn't cope with that.

Dig deep.

His mother's strength grounded him for a moment, allowing him to focus. The ooze was gone, but the threat remained. He was still trapped in the red room. The low hum from earlier was more noticeable now, vibrating under his naked buttocks.

Before he could consider his next move, a beam of white light emanated into the room. He looked towards the source. Part of the wall was rising, gliding towards the ceiling. It was a door, right where that outline had been. Freedom beckoned him, but he shook his head. It was too easy, too convenient.

Alice.

The beam grew brighter, dulling the intensity of the red walls. The door was open now. It unnerved him that all he heard from outside was that low, steady hum. He peered through the glowing white light to the other side, making out nothing but a strange humanoid shape. Tall, thin. Obscured by the intensity of the white light, he saw another one and reached to them.

"Help me."

Ignoring the vibrations coursing through his body, he stood. The exit was so close, a meter or so away. He would leave the room and find Alice, and everything would be okay. He walked towards the door, slow at first, considerate in his movements. Remnants of his mother's training took hold.

After a few steps, he felt a pang. A dull ache, at first, pressing against his internal organs. Another step. The ache intensified. Every inch of him pulsated and he doubled over, holding his stomach in the fear it would burst open.

Alice needs me.

He knew he had to keep going. The figures outside the room didn't notice him as he reached for their help once more.

"Please, my daughter-"

Something was in his stomach, shifting and moving, scratching at his insides.

He stepped towards the door, his stomach throbbing hard against his arms. The part of him that was eager to walk through was overpowered by the other half. The half frozen by fear.

Five seconds.

Pushing through the pain in his abdomen, he drew on every inch of strength he could muster. The pain spread to his chest, suffocating him, squeezing his heart. Fighting for breath, he caught a glimpse of his mother. In the corner of his eye, the hallucination of her spirit urged him along. With her memory by his side and knowing Alice was counting on him, he moved across the cold, hard surface. A lightning bolt of pain jolted through his legs, and he collapsed to his knees, struggling to keep conscious. His legs throbbed, the skin splitting around his thigh and calf muscles.

Survive, his mother's voice rang in his ears.

The pain jerked through him like volts of electricity, but Terry stood once more, determined to reach the exit and find Alice.

You will not fall again. Orders from beyond the grave.

He watched the skin on his feet and legs continue to split open with each step. His torn flesh fell to the side, releasing a thick, black gunk. It seeped from him with each step, like tar in a smoker's lung. The veins on his ankles and lower legs turned black, poisoned by the gunk leaking from his wounds. He slipped on the pieces of his skin and fell back to his knees, unable to bear the pain as the blackness reached his thighs.

Unable to heed his mother's orders.

He was halfway to the door now, kneeling on his calves, now a mess of torn flesh and black gunk. The pain drove him into stillness, his body refusing to move any further, and just like that, the searing pain coursing through him vanished. He braced himself, waiting for the next onslaught, but it didn't come. A sense of relief followed. Relief that he was gifted this moment without pain. A moment when his skin wasn't splitting and his bones weren't crumbling into dust. But in his frozen state, he stared towards the open door.

Towards freedom.

Towards Alice.

He remembered how the ooze had reacted to his movements earlier, tracking him across the room. Through the pained fog in his mind, he guessed that whatever was inside him now operated in the same way.

Any time he moved, the gunk inside him grew stronger. It was he himself that brought the fluid to life. But the exit was right there, and he knew that Alice was close.

Too weak to stand, he dragged himself along the concrete floor, the skin on his face scraping away. He hoped upon hope that safety laid half a meter away and forced himself to keep going. What was left of his feet and legs flaked away into ash, filling the air like pollen. He choked on his own remains as pieces of his decomposing flesh settled on the red floor around him. The trail of thick, black gunk lay behind him, mixing with his remains.

His body disintegrated into ash with each movement, but he was so close to the door. So close to finding Alice. He heard his elbows crack and split apart with the rest of his arms. His blackened fingers reached for the glowing white light, searching for its comforting heat, hoping it somehow held the key to his survival. Yet he knew it was too late. He looked back to see a trail of remains, clumps of organs decomposing amidst the sticky gunk that bled from him.

He lay there, unwilling to let this defeat him, crying for Alice. For what felt like the first time, she cried back.

"Daddy!"

It was she; there was no doubt. His darling daughter was just outside, waiting for him, calling for him. She needed him.

"Alice, I'm coming!"

Half his body gone, the other half seconds from ruin, he gripped the floor with his remaining strength. Alice was somewhere beyond that door, and he'd get to her if it took his last breath. The pain shot through the remnants of his body, while behind him the trail of ruins behind him began to stir.

The black ruins, a mixture of ashes and decomposed

organs, started to take form. Rising from the floor, an arm with misshapen fingers reached to the ceiling. The grotesque being, like wet clay, fighting to hold its shape. An elbow formed and the ruins' arm began to push against the red floor, pulling a contorted head from the ashes. Its mouth was open, releasing an inaudible gasp as the creature found life.

He clawed with all his might, unable to cry or scream. His lungs began to disintegrate into ash, ready to join the creature growing from his remains. Somehow his heart continued to beat. He reached the door, his fingers crumbling to the floor beneath him, reaching for something to grip, something to help pull him along.

His chest rattled, his mouth searched for oxygen that wouldn't come. He looked down to see the creature continue to rise. Faceless and bloody, it wheezed into life.

"Daddy, help me!"

He wanted to call to her, to tell her he loved her. He wanted to hug her and play with her and do everything fathers are supposed to do. But his tongue had fallen away with the rest of his muscles. He would never get that chance now. This was it.

The creature was almost complete now, standing on shaky legs. It would finish growing once Terry's corrosion had ended. The pain was gone now, with no nerves left to feel. In a way, it was a blessing. He could no longer feel the skin on his face split apart or the thick gunk bleed from his eyes and mouth. He didn't feel his lungs dissipate into ash or his heart begin to blacken. He watched through blurry vision as the creature came towards him.

He watched it stretch and take a step.

He watched hair start to form, and pigment appeared in the skin.

He watched the creature turn into him, a mirror-image

of the man he had been yesterday.

The last thing Terry ever saw was the creature grow his face, before the last of him succumbed and broke apart.

* * *

I look at the mess of my birth, remnants of the man scattered through the dusty air. The remains before me nothing but a pile of ash and leftovers of my primordial fluid. Kneeling before what had been his head, I scoop his ashes into my mouth, letting the particles absorb into me. The brain matter was important. Eating the memories will assist the integration. Help to complete me.

Terry. My new name.

Memories start to flood my mind. I have a sense of who this man was and I curl my newly formed lips.

Pathetic.

I step out of the room, unsteady on my new legs at first, but adapting. I look back at Terry's remains and smile. He hadn't realized it, but he was one of the lucky ones. The others weren't being reborn in a greater image than their own. They were simply going to die.

An endless corridor stretches in both directions, filled with birthing suites like mine. Some of the others are already there, waiting for me. I take my place in a queue of people just like me. Born minutes ago, from the same ancient liquid coursing through my fresh veins.

My family.

A young girl stands in front me, her back to me. She turns, smiling, and I recognize her flowing blonde hair. Those green eyes. He has memories of her. At the beach. A tentacled toy. He has lots of memories of this person. They are my memories now.

"Daddy!" She embraces me.

"Alice." The name is familiar on my new tongue.

"Will we kill them all, Daddy?" She looks at me with those big round eyes, hopeful. Moons at the center of my universe.

I give a single nod and squeeze her hand, anxious to get started.

AMBER MAY AND THE NECROTIC WAY
By Matt Martinek

It is unexplainable… this "love" of the dead. Maybe the whole fascination lies in taking what is not yours, or doing what should never be done. After all, the laws of man are fun to break, and taboos even more so. In my case, however, it is something more. It is an urge… innate and very powerful, and it has been with me as far back as I can remember.

Children are supposed to be preoccupied with childish things. And I was, to a point. But when it came to graveyards, I was absolutely enthralled. I could feel the energy from underneath the ground, as well as the resting calm up above. It was a dichotomy of sorts, a certain yin and yang, which left me confused at first, yet very interested and yearning for more. I played in the cemetery. That's what I did. And yes, it was perceived as "weird."

I remember one occasion, in particular, when my urges truly came to light. I was about eleven or twelve at the time, and I was spending time at a cousin's house,

Madame Gray's Vault of Gore

doing some sled riding. Strangely enough, the best hill in the area was, you guessed it, in the middle of a cemetery. It was an interesting feeling… zipping down this snow-covered mound, trying as hard as we could to dodge the granite stones. I should have been focused on the adrenaline of the action at hand, but I was getting off on the feeling of simply being in the cemetery more than anything else. It had a hold of me, and was not letting go.

As we grew tired of trudging up the slippery hill, again and again, we rested for a bit, and something caught my eye. It was a small outside mausoleum, a little past the hill we were currently on. You could clearly see each separate drawer, each separate name of the deceased chiseled into the marbled façade. This idea, too, simply fascinated me… each corpse to its own little compartment… like throwing a dead mouse into your dresser drawer. But the great thing about a drawer is that you can open it up again whenever you need. *So why not just open the drawer?*

I convinced my cousin to run home and retrieve a screwdriver, as he, too, was excited for a bit of the unknown. I was too fearful of choosing an occupied drawer, however. I was more interested in seeing the construction of the vault inside or if we could get the lid of the drawer to move at all. As the sun was setting and the shadows fell, my cousin returned with screwdriver in hand. I chose the empty, nameless, bottom drawer, and began to pry away at the fasteners at the corners of the marble lid. My cousin looked at me like I was crazy, but I didn't care. There was no hesitation, just action. Eventually, the *chink* of the broken metal reached our ears and the lid fell down with a crash, nearly smashing my toes in the process. We jumped like deer off into the woods near the cemetery. I caught a quick glimpse of the black hole of the empty drawer as we bolted for our lives. I instantly started to regret my choice. I should've chosen an occupied drawer instead.

Life moved quickly. The days turned to months, the months to years, and the years to the bored and disgusted 36-year-old man I had become. Those necrotic feelings of old were pushed aside, but never truly forgotten. And one day, just like that, they reemerged from their forced slumber. But instead of finding the confused child, they came across the hardened man, instead... a man who was capable and very, very sure of himself. The dead were calling to me still, and I finally decided to answer.

Embarking on such an arduous task was not taken lightly. Grave robbing isn't like it's portrayed in the movies, obviously. It isn't digging three or four feet and then easily removing the lid of a busted-up coffin made of plywood. That's bullshit. In reality, there is this thing inside the grave called a concrete vault that just so happens to be thick, heavy, and sealed very well to keep the natural world at bay for as long as possible. So my first issue was going to be finding an appropriate target... a grave that was old, rotten, weathered, and somewhat accessible. So I searched and searched.

It took months of research and footwork, but I finally found what I was looking for. It was an old church cemetery on the outskirts of the city, and it looked on the verge of being totally forgotten. The brush and trees were severely overgrown, which would serve me well as far as privacy was concerned. Most of the stones were broken, crooked, or knocked over, and many were barely legible... the letters worn through and weathered by time and nature. Apparently the ground had shifted over the decades, so naturally the positioning of the plots was now noticeably different than it was one-hundred years ago. The rows were no longer rows, but zigzags instead. The place was in total neglect and disrepair.

I spent an entire day there, roaming, taking my time. It had to be perfect... out of sight and as least demanding as

Madame Gray's Vault of Gore

humanly possible. Getting caught was not an option. By the end of the day, I had a few prospects in mind, but there was one that afforded me some opportunities the others did not. It was a small, weathered stone, which had turned green from moss. It read: "Amber May, Beloved Daughter, June 1930-May 1934." A little girl. Better that way. The remains would be easier to move, and hopefully the grave was old enough that the vault would be weakened or broken through already. But the best part about it was the positioning of the gravesite. As I said earlier, the ground had shifted, and this site showed the worst of it. There was a large sinkhole in front of the plot, about three feet down. I assumed the edge of the vault shouldn't be too far away from the severe erosion. In short… there would be much less to dig and less time to spend there.

I did not take action quickly after acquiring my target. I questioned it for weeks… ran through the entire plan in my head, over and over. No room for error, whatsoever. I had been fantasizing about it for so long, the simple idea of actually committing the act was both exciting and terrifying. Because there was no going back. I would forever become a ghoul, and if I got away with it I would probably continue. It would be a terrible secret I would have to keep… I wouldn't be able to tell a single soul, ever. Life, as I knew it, would change.

The moment of decision came to me in a dream. I was there, in the cemetery, knelt down in front of Amber's busted-open casket, holding her remains in my arms as she slowly disintegrated into dust all around me. I was smiling, happy and overcome with the sweetest scent of freshly cut flowers. And so it would be. I stepped over the edge, into the pitch black. For the next couple of days I made a few trips to the graveyard, each time throwing a little piece of the puzzle from my truck into the weeds, about ten feet away from the entrance gate. One night it was a shovel and crowbar, the next a long piece of rebar and a mallet, and on the last night I offered up the final pieces… the sledgehammer and flashlight. It was all ready for me… the tools of my rebirth.

On the night of the disinterment, I was pretty shaken. I had actually taken a few shots of vodka before I left the house. The nerves were just terrible. But, things had to be done. I left my driveway at 9:45 PM on July 22nd, 1988. It was a Friday night… the last Friday night I ever spent as a normal person.

And so I set into motion exactly what I had planned for the last few months. I parked my truck in the shadows, grabbed all my gear from the weeds, and made my way to Amber's resting place. There was not a soul in sight, just as I had hoped. My footsteps were loud and unavoidable… the brush was thick everywhere. Silence was not to be had that night. I was not worried, though. The odds of visitors showing up were slim, indeed. I was relieved at the sight of Amber's stone, as my tools were becoming heavier with each step. It was time.

I set up shop at the base of the sinkhole, near where the foot of the vault should have been. I propped up my flashlight, positioned the rebar, and began to hammer it into the soil. As soon as I broke ground, I knew this would be harder than I had expected. It was such a stony soil, compact from all of those untouched years. I was using the rebar to simply find the location of the vault. I would strike it a few feet in, then move my position, again and again. I began to panic a little after the tenth attempt. I wasn't hitting anything but rock and dirt. I thought about aborting the mission, and just as I was about to give up, I heard the *CLANK* of victory. I had found it.

I retracted the rebar from the dirt and moved on to the shovel. Within minutes, I was soaked in sweat and covered in filth. My heart was ready to burst. I dug with panic and fear, two wonderful allies to keep when time is of the essence. Eventually, I unearthed one concrete edge, then two, until the entire end of the vault was in view. My excitement grew with each shovelful. I could see that the vault was, indeed, cracked lengthwise, which gave me a tremendous sense of relief. I knew the vault would be the hardest part of my task.

I do not know for sure, as time surely escapes a person at times like this, but I believe I spent well over two hours digging feverishly until I could see the entire lid of the concrete vault. I quickly threw the shovel down and lifted the sledgehammer. I knew it would be loud, so I wanted to break the seal within a few strikes. I positioned myself on top of the lid, hoisted the hammer, aimed right for the middle, and brought it down with as much force as my dead-tired arms could muster. Surprisingly, the concrete gave way immediately with a *CRUNCH*. The force of my blow pulled me into the vault, along with the crumbled stone. I was face to face with the wood of the casket.

I must've hit my head pretty hard when I fell, as my entire face was wet with blood. As I wiped the red from my burning eyes, I noticed that the casket was not full size, but instead the size of the child who inhabited it. After I took a few moments to get my bearings, I began to hoist the casket from its resting place. It was not large, by any means, but it was wet, which made it extremely difficult to lift. The weight of the casket, mixed with the unpleasant smell of the moldy wood and rotted corpse inside of it, almost proved too much for me to handle. I took a deep breath, and with all of my might, I removed the casket from the vault and dropped it onto the ground. I fell with it, exhausted. At that moment, it began to rain.

With the muscles of my legs burning terribly, I dragged the rotting wood to the gate of my truck, slipping and falling in the mud the entire way. It was taking far too long, and at this point I simply needed to get the hell out of there. I quickly muscled the coffin into the bed, shut the gate, and proceeded to drive away. In a panic, I forgot all of my tools at the scene, which was not my intention at all. There would be no doubt… the grave had definitely been robbed of its sole possession.

The drive home was nerve-racking, to say the least. There I was, covered in blood and mud (as was the entire cab of my truck), speeding along the highway with a little girl's corpse resting in the bed. I was expecting to see lights at every corner, or hear sirens, but they never came. I pulled into my driveway and just sat there for a while, thinking about what I had accomplished.

Under the cover of a foggy, rainy night, I moved my treasure from the bed of the truck to my basement, where I would uncover Amber's beauty, once and for all. I felt uneasy as I stared at the wooden mess lying there on my cellar floor. *Should there be ritual? Should there be prayer? Decorum, at least?* I, however, was not a God-fearing man, by any means. I beheld the treasure chest for as long as I could before the excitement and curiosity of the moment got the best of me. I began to remove the lid, chunk by chunk, carefully, as the pieces fell apart in my hands. She came into view slowly… methodically, until I removed the final section of wet, stinking wood.

Amber May was everything I had hoped for. The beauty of her rot! What I unearthed was mostly blackened bones and stringy, red hair… but it was more than enough for me to appreciate. She wore what used to be a gorgeous floral dress, but time had not been kind to it. It was withered and filthy and molded… barely in one piece. Most of her teeth had fallen out, and the bones of her fingers were lying in the bottom of the casket near her rotten pink–bootied feet. Her jaws were agape, stuck in seemingly perpetual laughter. Thankfully the insects were few, as there wasn't much of a meal left… I removed those that remained. There was some leftover matter around the body, sprinkled onto the disintegrated coffin lining, which I assumed to be the last vestiges of the girl's flesh. It had the look of moist sawdust. I collected a pinch of it between my fingertips and brought it to my lips. It smelled and tasted of sulfur, but in my mind I was happy and smiling, and all I could recognize was the scent of freshly cut flowers.

From then on, only the ghoul remained.

HOUSE BOUND
By Edward Ahern

There is no living comparison, but perhaps to a mouthful of toothaches, or whole-body shingles, or a non-stop panic attack. I am condemned to be at peace only when without human smells or sounds or sights. I was also human, once, I think, but cannot abide their presence.

And once again they came, spraying energy like acid on me. Pain tore at the tendons of whatever being I am. I lurched free from my dark bed. My stumbles impinged on the physical, causing warped floors and rafters to creak. My keening migrated into sounds like the moaning of wind.

Two. There were two of them. Man. Woman. Even their breathing hurt me. And they talked. Words tumbling like rocks onto me.

"The place really is unsalvageable, Kurt. I'd have been better to get someone to tear it down and build new. I was an idiot to trust your plan. Just like I was an idiot to trust you."

"Look at these moldings, Licia. And the patterned tin

ceilings. We couldn't afford to replicate the marble fireplace, let alone all the oak wainscoting. Cheaper to just strengthen or replace the beams, fix it up. That's what the structural engineer said." There was a forced smile in his tone.

"And, meanwhile, we have to sleep with the mice? No thank you."

"We'll find someplace to stay while the work gets done. Once it's fixed up, I'll find a billionaire technocrat who'll pay twenty times what it cost us to fix up your great grandmother's antique."

"Kurt, I'm discovering that you're not that good a realtor. One burst water pipe and I'm trapped owning Wet Rot Mansion. We won't sleep here, and we'll get two motel rooms. You forfeited your right to see me in underwear when you started sleeping around."

"Don't bring her into it. But, no, listen…"

Their mouth noises cut into me like glass shards. But light still entered the house, and I was captive in the sub-cellar dark. Rage built. Others had come, many winters ago. They'd run out screaming. Except for the one who had died. I wanted to order these two to leave. But could not. I have powers but cannot speak. My loathing must communicate through fear.

They left before the darkness came to deliver me. I moved through the house, wanting to destroy anything that was of them, but found only the stale odors of sweat and deodorant from their passage. I knew they would return. The living are obdurate. I tensed myself for the morning's torture.

But others came first. Poking and prodding at the organs of my housing, and making guttural man words that dropped onto me like bird shit. When the pain subsided enough that I could think, I let myself imagine how I would kill them. But they all left well before the liberating night.

A crew of three men began working in the house every day, ripping out and replacing wiring, sealing leaks, replacing the rotted and warped. Their words and movements dragged barbed wire across my skin, but the repairs were like picking off scabs, without pain but exposing raw, ugly flesh.

One day of dark rain I was just able to abide the dim light and prowl, able to twist a nail gun so it shot two nails into a workman's free hand. But then I could stand no more and, screaming into his ear, dropped back down to my earth.

His scream and mine had mingled, and that fearful living one never returned. But, after another day, he was replaced by an even louder man.

I was, I think, a woman once. But there are few memories left, only vague emotions. I do not know why I am condemned to this torture—what sins I committed, and the injustice of this ignorance adds to my anger. Anger which built, day by anguished day, as the rooms above me were refurbished.

Eventually, the man and woman carried in clothing and personal belongings, and I knew they would be spending nights in my liberated company. Even in my daytime pain, the future choices were delicious: kill or maim, slow or fast, perhaps drive them into trying to kill each other. They already had enough mutual hate.

"If I see even one rat, Kurt, I'm back in the motel."

"Licia, please, we need to do this together. At least for now."

"You just want to stay close to the possible money. Once it sells, I'm walking away. On my own. You should have brought your whore in to stay with you. It's not too late."

His tone was unpleasant. "She's no whore. And, like it or not, we're still partners."

They moved into separate bedrooms, and cooked

separate evening meals, then watched an hour of television together without talking to each other. The words from the television did not hurt me.

That first night, I wanted to scream a lullaby into their ears as they went to sleep, but paused. It had been very long since I'd had a chance to mutilate the living, and I decided I needed to savor them before they ran away or died. I did play a little night music for them, letting the house do my screeching.

That next morning, they ate breakfast together, and their voices cut into me from above.

"Did you hear the creaks and groans this place made last night? Any buyer would sue us after one sleepover."

"Just temperature changes. Licia, I'll get a carpenter in to shim up the flooring. We can begin showing the house next week."

"If I could afford it, I'd move out now. I can't believe you duped me into putting my 401k into this."

His emotion this time was unmistakable—hate that almost matched mine. "Just don't bitch things up when we're showing the house to clients."

"Don't worry. And I'm not going to be your bitch for much longer."

They went off to what I guessed were day jobs, leaving me at peace to plan my performance.

Every house has its little creatures, and I have always been able, without understanding how, to direct them. I marshaled them into the shadowed corners of the kitchen. Centipedes and roaches, ants and fleas, moths and spiders. Many spiders, which I had to restrain from setting up webs for their cohabitants.

The man and woman returned in waning daylight, making mouthings that rasped the skin from my being. The woman reached the kitchen first. I loosed my minions, flying insects first, then the quick crawlers, then the spiders, dropping down from the ceiling. She began screaming, brushing bugs from her hair, and stomping on those slow enough for her to manage.

Unlike words, screams are a balm for me, and I paused to enjoy the relief. Then the man ran downstairs, saw the insects, and began a deeper toned screaming as he found a dishtowel and began swatting. My little companions, now disorganized, scuttled and flew away from the light and noise and death.

The man and woman moved toward each other and brushed the visible bugs from each other's clothes.

"Damn, Licia, I've never seen so many bugs."

"The remodeling probably shook them loose. No way I'm sleeping here tonight, and tomorrow we get an exterminator. I want the whole house killed."

"We're broke."

"Put it on one of your over-extended cards, Kurt. If you don't, I will. I'm leaving, you do what you want."

They left shortly thereafter. The house was blessedly empty the next day, but the day after that, two men in respirators came and began setting up spray bombs. They were quiet, and I was in little pain. Then they left and poison gas filled the house. It couldn't affect me, and killed less than half of my little orchestra members.

The man and woman returned three days after that.

"The place stinks of insecticide, Kurt. Open some windows."

His tone was vicious. "Alicia, open your own damn windows. You're not a princess anymore."

Alicia. The name had resonance, and I wondered if it had been mine. Alicia. Then I wondered if she was a descendent. But I felt as indifferent to her death as his. Act Two would be coming in six or seven hours.

"Look, Kurt, the sooner we unload this place, the sooner we're parted. You open the upstairs windows. I'll take the downstairs."

He sputtered but agreed. As she moved from the

atrium to the study, I was able to muster a breath, and breathed on her. It was, I knew, a foul wind, and she gagged when it enveloped her.

"Oh, what a smell!" she yelled, running out of the room.

The pain from performing under the sun made me recoil, and I held to the sub-basement until after sundown. When I emerged, they had gone, according to their words, to eat in a restaurant. Their absence allowed me to make preparations. Their return was remarkably calm.

"So your great-grandmother, Alicia Wiltington, died here."

"Was murdered here. It was never proven, but the family suspected her husband. He died before admitting to anything."

"How, Licia?"

"Swallowed his own tongue. His body was covered in boils; maybe he just couldn't stand the pain anymore. Inspiring family history, isn't it? Now you see why I want to unload this heap."

There were stirrings, faint but defined. Things that had been buried inside me. My plan altered when I realized how much more poignant my future could be. The bronze bust that I had shifted to the edge of its shelf dropped with a clang onto the floor next to then, denting the oak floor.

"What the hell!" Kurt yelled.

"How the hell!" Licia echoed.

"If that had dropped on my head, I'd be dead."

"Or me, Kurt. Let's get out of here."

"Look, Licia, we're out of cash and the credit cards are maxed. There's no more money for motels and restaurants. We have to stay here. In the same room. No, don't look at me like that. One of us can keep watch while the other sleeps. Believe me, I have no interest in shucking your panties."

Her expression was belligerent, but after several

seconds she nodded. "Okay, the first prospect comes tomorrow early and we have to be here. You sleep on the floor."

"Fine."

Satisfaction filled me. Two open minds to explore and mutilate. I waited, judging time by the shift in the moon, and then went to their bedroom. The man had fallen asleep in a chair. I needed to enter one at a time. I cannot command behavior during human sleep, but over a century and a half I have become adept at making suggestions.

Don't believe what I'm told. She plans to cheat me out of my share, that bronze was meant for me, she will find another way to kill me, she'll inform police about my thefts and put me in prison, she hates me that much.

One verse would be insufficient, so I repeated the mantra over and over, changing words and specifics until his sleeping awareness was suffused with fear and hate. Then I moved on.

I paused to savor the physical sensations of my namesake: pulse, digestion, a minor skin rash, the gentle swell and recession of air, the soft pressure of a filling bladder, the smell of her skin that she no longer noticed. I wanted to be her, but of course could not, and would have to settle for something less.

Did he mean to kill me with that bust? He handles the legal matters and will never let me have my half; he will cheat me out of most of it. Can't let him get drunk and hit me again, he must be stopped, maybe put in prison with what I know, yes, prison and I have control of the funds. Or maybe he has an accident…

Iterating variations on the theme until her hate and fear was as harsh as his. Then back to him.

She's sleeping, kill her now before she kills me, use my pillow, blame her asthma, quick now, it's my last chance.

I prodded the man awake. Kurt shuddered, then sat up. If necessary, I could repeat the urging for several nights, but it was not needed. Kurt grabbed his pillow, stood, and walked over to Alicia's bed. Her arms were under the covers, making a struggle much harder. He fell onto her body and pushed the pillow into her face. She writhed, but the blanket and his weight kept her from kicking or scratching him. After two minutes, she stopped struggling. After four minutes, he lifted the pillow and checked for a pulse.

Before that, I had gone back into her. Dead talking to dead. "Hello Alicia. Yes, he's killed you. No, I'm afraid the police will probably never convict him. But there is justice. Come with me, and tomorrow night will be his turn. That's good dear, just down this way. We can talk about how you will get your revenge. And it will be so nice to have company."

WITH A DEVIL'S STRENGTH
By Dr. Chris McAuley

The artist moves through the city carrying the tools of his trade. The box encompassing them is decorated with an ornate symbol, a golden snake swallowing its own tail. A symbol of infinity, of the darkness that threatens to surround the soul. At times, his thumb caught the gilded edges of the motif and he traced its circular pattern. The chaos that it represented, of a figure endlessly consuming itself, reminded him of his fellow citizens.

This was London at the height of Victoriana and the birth of a mechanized revolution that promised to sweep through the Empire. The artist cut a striking figure as he moved through the cobbled streets, past the pastry shops and the slouching remnants of humanity, their minds lost to the opium dragon or drink. Perhaps both at the same time. His long dark hair and magnificent cheekbones caught many an eye. His exquisite apparel spoke of his taste and means. As his cloak drew up behind him, captured by a stale smelling breeze, his dark suit's golden embroidery came into full view.

Truly he was the epitome of a servant of the arts.

His feet took him towards the docks; as he moved closer to the waters, his nostrils caught the scents of brine and the distinctive odor of fish oil. The artist's pace increased as he glimpsed the perfect subject: a lean ship with sails jutting out like the wings of a bird. The captain looked suitably weather-beaten and had the form of face that could captivate the artist's audience.

Finding a suitable spot to capture this moment, he began to sketch the ship and its solitary crewmember. Lines from Coleridge's *The Rime of the Ancient Mariner* came unbidden to him as his mind drifted:

'The Wedding-Guest sat on a stone:
He cannot choose but hear;
And thus spake on that ancient man,
The bright-eyed Mariner'

From that prose, the artist's mind drifted, imagining the voyages of the lonely captain, his adventures on the high sea to bring bounty inward. His melancholic reverie ever his constant companion.

With a clatter, the artist found himself back in the present. His work ruined. A dog had come to play. It was a golden sort with a joyful expression. It had barreled into the easel; the paints had covered the canvas. The perfect moment was lost.

A white-hot sensation filled the artist's mind. Seething anger came to bear upon this friendly creature. To add insult to this occurrence, the dog proceeded to sit on the now desecrated canvas. As if it had been proud of its action and now demanded a payment of affect from the artist.

In the midst of his horror and anger, an idea struck the painter. It had first occurred to him in a dream state. As he had drifted off a few nights ago, he found himself observing a carousel. Several women in states of undress bobbed up and down on the wooden horses. They were calling out to him, their voices high and light. In that moment, he found a sketchpad had appeared in his hands and he began to outline the vision that had unfolded around him. As he worked, he found it impossible to capture the essence of the moment. He tore page after page in frustration. He desperately wanted to peel back the layers of the scene, to not just portray what his eye beheld, but to project the feelings of the heart.

It was then that the ladies slipped off the horses and made their way towards him. As they came closer, he noted that they had a hungry gleam to their eye and glided in their movements. They reminded him of the serpent which had tempted Eve in the garden, almost hypnotizing him with their hips and gait.

A voice drifted towards him across the inky black nightscape of his dream. It was warm and caressing.

"Unveil us, show to us our true form and, in that, you will demonstrate to your audience who they are too."

This was, after all, the key aspect of art in all its glory. A sweat broke on the artist's brow; he found not a pencil in his left hand but a surgeon's scalpel. In a moment of ecstasy, he lunged forward and, taking the nearest woman in his arms, slashed her throat. He drank in the moment of her death; the blood spurted over his face and hands. In this moment of violence, he had shown the audience and himself what truly lay inside. The blood that flowed over his face and clothes had transformed him into a living canvas.

As he woke from his slumber that morning, he remembered the woman's expression as her life fluids poured from her neck. It was almost sexual, orgasmic, a link between the final moments of life and the need to propagate. That morning, he shaved with feelings mixed between shame and arousal.

Now, as anger and excitement coursed through his body, the artist felt no guilt at the actions to come. Luring the friendly animal to the alleyway had not been difficult. Acting as a friend and companion, he shared his lunch with the golden-haired dog. As he stroked the animal, he felt the effects of the sun on its fur; it was soft and warm. As he lavished affection on the creature, he observed its joy, the tail wagging with contentment. Eventually as the afternoon sun gave way to the evening chill, he led the dog to the dark cobblestone alley.

He held it by its neck. Reaching to his art box, he opened it and drew out a scalpel, much like the one that had been presented to him in the dream. Without a moment's hesitation, the artist drew the blade across the dog's throat. He found that the first cut did not go deep enough; the dog gasped and whined. It kicked against him. Its once immaculate coat becoming matted and stained with the thick blood.

Gritting his teeth, the artist plunged the knife deep into the canine's larynx. He sawed through the cartilage. The cries of the dog transformed into a low moan and blood now projected itself forward. The artist's face and hair became as matted as the dying animal. Laying the dog down on its side, he then went to work on the twitching body.

Cutting and carving through the stomach, his white gloves became stained with the yellow liquids of digestion and the green hues of bile. The artist began to arrange the internal organs; he crafted a tableau, a portrait of the nature of the 'inner dog.' Its genitals were removed and the sexless, mutilated mess of the animal finally met with his approval.

He sketched the scene in earnest; his anger dissipating as he realized that he had crafted a work similar to Bosch. This work was perhaps the first truly creative endeavor that he had undertaken in his lifetime. As he finished his sketch, he paused before leaving the alleyway. Bending down, he touched what was left of the dog's eyes. Finding the ghost of a tear, he licked the salty liquid from his finger with a murmur of satisfaction.

Clutching his sketchpad and art supplies, he moved from the alley to the now darkened streets. His bloodstained clothing and face passed through the dwindling crowds without remark.

Six Months Later

Kathline's back was slammed roughly against the stone wall. Her customer was a heavyset, drunken farmer who had been to the markets that morning. He was spending his earnings on cheap ale and cheaper women. She had to keep her cost low; she needed to attract more customers to pay off the McQueen boys. Lifting her burgundy skirt, she moved her head to the side, trying to avoid showing her disgust as the farmer slobbered over her neck and chest.

"Come on luv, I don't have all night, lots more business to do before daylight comes."

With this admonishment, the farmer grunted. He dropped his heavy woolen trousers and began to stroke himself.

"I have to get meself hard first," he slurred.

Eventually, and with some coaxing from Kathline, the farmer found his stride and entered into her roughly. After a few strokes, he was finished.

Pulling up his trousers, he threw some pennies onto the street. He didn't even turn his head towards Kathline or acknowledge her.

She waited until he had gone back into the pub; the Ten Bells had a back exit, which the prostitutes used on sufferance of the owner. Bending down, she gathered the coins into her hand. There were maybe enough to pay for another night's rent; if she did that, she would have to avoid the McQueen boys for another day. She already owed them ten shillings in exchange for their 'protection.'

A change in the air made Kathline look upwards. A dark figure wearing a top hat and a cloak stood enveloped in the night mists. He had the look of a gentleman and perhaps the purse to match. She had heard of well-to-do men frequenting the Whitechapel area to find solace in drink and a 'bit of rough.' Women who would do things that their well-bred wives would never contemplate. She called out to the figure.

"Allo sir, you see anything you fancy?"

The figure moved from the shadows; the gas lamps refused to illuminate any part of his face. It was as if he was part of the night itself. Kathline began to feel a familiar nervous tingling in the pit of her stomach; she usually experienced this when dealing with the fists of an aggressive punter. Over time, she had learned to listen to that instinct.

As she began to rise from her position, the point of the knife entered her throat. The blade was thrust directly below her neck. Kathline felt the sting of its entry and a feeling of being choked at the same time. Her hands reached up to grab its handle but as quickly as it had entered her, it was pulled away.

She fell backwards, her head striking the hard pavement. She tried to croak a cry for help, her eyes turning desperately towards the pub, hoping for another customer to happen by or for the landlord to change the barrels.

The cloaked figure moved forward. His hands took hold of her auburn hair and he slashed her throat. The blade whistled across her flesh and, before the blackness overcame her, she could feel a pulling sensation.

Jack saw the light go from the whore's eyes, the mixture of pain, terror and incredulity losing its spark and settling into a glassy, eternal stare. Now his work could begin.

The intestines and genitals were opened and placed on display, the thick, sausage-like organs placed around the whore's neck as his masters had demonstrated in one of their rituals. Using the spilled blood, he drew the sacred symbol around her body. Dedicating his offering to the gods who lived below the city. The pentacle star was perfectly traced and conformed to the points of da Vinci's Vitruvian Man.

He had studied the great, artistic master's work at university and, through his lectures on body and form, had garnered a great deal of knowledge concerning anatomy. As he stood to contemplate his work, he murmured a prayer to the angel who had demonstrated the way. In return he could hear a peal of cackling laughter.

Turning and striding into the night, he allowed himself a satisfied smile.

He was, after all, a man dedicated to his art.

PSYCHOSIS
By Shannon Lawrence

Joy wasn't sure when the hunger had started. Whether it was before or after everyone had been confined to their homes. All she knew was that her belly ached as if it would never be filled again. No matter what she put into it, it rumbled and growled and beseeched her for more.

More.

Her sole defense against the cramping agony of her insides was to sleep as often as possible, waking only to stuff more food into her mouth, to push it toward her miserable stomach. It was as if she could hear the echo as the food reached its destination. Only, instead of sound, the waves moved through her entire body in an ecstacy of pain. Her body rejected it. Nothing appeased her hunger whatsoever.

Food no longer had any flavor. It tasted of dirt, of air, of things that shouldn't be eaten and couldn't satisfy. With no other options, she ordered whatever she could get the most of. It had to be cheap and plentious. She no longer attempted to be healthy by eating fruits and vegetables. Instead, she ate the cheapest cuts of meat, most of them canned. Spam, tuna, ground beef, bulk chicken. Rice and bread were cheap, and she ate them hoping they would expand in her stomach, make it feel full for just a moment. Anything to feel as if she'd done something right.

Her abdomen bloated while the rest of her body shrunk. When she looked in the mirror, it was in horror. She'd become so thin, so hollow. Dark circles bruised her undereyes. Her sallow skin sagged, wrinkling as if she were eighty instead of twenty. It jiggled when she moved, a billowing cloud of flesh that strived to be set free from its starving cage.

The change in her appearance was easy to track, courtesy of the images she'd posted on her social media accounts. Before the lockdown, she'd been able to go out with friends, to dine at restaurants, to run to the corner store on a whim. She'd enjoyed life. It showed from the smiles, the fullness of her skin, the brightness of her eyes. She'd had energy, and been able to eat whatever she wanted without gaining any weight. Or losing it, as she was doing now.

Once she couldn't leave the house for anything, it was like she'd devolved. Work switched to remote only. She ordered groceries online to be delivered to her. She couldn't go near her friends in case they were infected without knowing it. Going around other people could mean her death. Or theirs.

Joy hated talking on the phone, and meeting up online was weird and depressing. She wanted company, craved human touch. Without a doubt, she was as hungry for those things as she was for sustenance, and there was no way to satisfy any of those needs anymore. As it was, she wandered around the confines of her home, knowing what a caged animal must feel like. Outside there was sun and wind and rain. There were trees, birds chirping, wildlife scurrying about, flowers bobbing on their stems. Outside there was life, though seldom human. Food deliveries were left on her doorstep, as if magicked there by some sorcerer. Contactless delivery, they called it. Contactless everything. What a nightmare.

So now she wasted away, hungering for food that couldn't sustain her, hungering for interpersonal connection that came direct with body heat and warm breath. She'd never thought of herself as an extrovert, but now it registered that she needed the company of other people. Her street looked like a zombie wasteland, cars abandoned in driveways, no children playing in their front yards. The postal worker came through once a day like clockwork to drop off the mail. Her garbage cans sat empty at the end of her driveway when she got up every Tuesday morning. She couldn't help but want to keep something back from the garbage, to hold onto something that had touched the outside world more recently than she had.

Just the other day, she had stepped out onto her porch, wearing a mask, hoping it would provide the double duty of protecting her from germs, but also hiding her frightening appearance from everyone. When the postal worker walked by, she waved and called out a rusty, "Hi!" He touched his mask as if to check that it sat where it was supposed to before throwing her a quizzical look and a mask-muffled, "Hello." It had taken every ounce of self control she had not to run after him, to grab him and force him to look at her, to talk to her. Anything. But that single hello would have to do for now.

Only, she'd felt something else in that moment, watching him walk away from her in his dark blue shorts and light blue shirt. Something that scared her more than the hunger, more than the wasting away. Alarmingly, what she'd felt was a new stirring of hunger. An anticipatory hunger. As he went on his merry way, unconcerned about her presence other than to question why she'd called out to him, she coveted him. Not in a sexual way. No, the appetite he had awakened in her was one more simple than that for sex. Something even more animalistic.

He'd looked delicious.

She'd caught herself replaying the interaction with him and licking her lips, saliva flooding her mouth. His browned arms and thick calves. So much meat. She'd been hungry this whole time because she wasn't eating the right thing.

Ever since that day, a fantasy had played in her mind over and over. How she took him mattered less than the fact that she did take him. She wrestled him to the ground and ate his raw flesh as he screamed, warm blood pumping into her open mouth in a sensual dance of predatory fulfillment. Or she lured him into the house and slit his throat before chopping off pieces to feed into the oven. Or he willingly brought her a slice of his juicy, well-muscled thigh and coaxed her to eat it however she liked. Or she gutted him and dove in, consuming the soft organs, those delicate sweet meats.

There were so many scenes. The gist of every single one, though, was that she craved the flesh of her postman. It was the only thing that could sate her hunger.

Of course she fought it. There was no possible way this craving could be real. She had groceries at her fingertips. Never had she even thought about cannibalism.

Then someone knocked on her door when she wasn't expecting any visitors.

Joy put her mask on before she went to the door, an almost automatic reflex now, and peered through the peephole. At first, the sight of a stranger on her doorstep brought trepidation, but as she studied his face, distorted by the glass of the peephole, it came again, that mad hunger. This hunger was different because it carried a promise with it: eat this and you'll feel better. The other kind was pure emptiness, a black hole that couldn't be filled. This sensation, though, could be appeased. How she knew wasn't important. She just did.

Any fear at the mysterious presence of a stranger dissipated. She opened the door to find a slightly overweight young man on her sun-bleached porch, his cheeks pink with exertion. He squinted through lightly tinted sunglasses, a wide smile on his face. Though he wore pants and a button-up white shirt, she could make out his heft beneath the clothing. His sunburned, freckled arms alone could feed her for days. When he clasped his hands together, his fingertips dimpled the doughy flesh.

She was so fixated on his hands that his voice caused her to jump. "Good afternoon, ma'am. How are you doing on this gorgeous summer day?"

It took great force of will to tear her eyes away from his hands and meet his eyes. In fact, she was so distracted that only now did she realize he'd come to her door maskless. "I'm good. How are you?"

Normally, she resented any unplanned interruption. No matter what, this young man had to be peddling something, whether it was a product, a service, or a religion. Even before everyone had been shoved into the forced isolation of these last few months, she'd hidden when someone knocked on her door, heart pounding at the anxiety caused by the possibility of having to talk to a stranger. Today she welcomed it. His plump, virginal appearance told her this was most likely a religious pitch, and his lack of a mask only reinforced the idea. After all, as she'd repeatedly been told, God was more powerful than the virus.

She eagerly awaited his reply. He didn't make her wait long.

"I'm wonderful. Have you received the word of the Lord?"

There it was. She looked around with a smile beneath the mask, seeking acknowledgment of her successful guess. It took her a moment to realize her loneliness had made her maybe a teeny bit loopy. There was no laugh track in real life; it existed only in the shows she'd been binge-watching while stuck at home.

"You know what? I'd love to hear what you have to say about the Lord. Come on in." She stepped back and gestured toward her living room. "I'm Joy."

Surprise flitted over his face, but he quickly modified his expression and stepped inside, holding out a hand for a shake. "I'm James." A whiff of soap trailed behind him. He looked back at her for direction as to where to go next. When she waved her hand at the nearby sofa, he dutifully strode over and sat upon it, waiting for her to join him.

She realized she'd made her decision the moment she chose to allow him in the house. Something had to be done about her misery, and this was the only way. Everything else had been tried. Everything else had left her starving, desperate.

Hungry.

It sucked to feel like nothing could fill you up, like you could never be full or even momentarily satiated. This desperate feeling of emptiness had to be eradicated. However, a litany of doubts and questions flitted through her mind at lightning speed: *Can I kill a person? Can I eat a person? How do I even do this? What the hell is wrong with me? What have I become? Do I cook the meat or eat it raw?*

Her stomach rumbled loudly. So loudly, in fact, that surprise registered on the young man's face in a widening of his eyes and a mild double take. She smiled at him and shrugged her shoulders. "Sorry. I seem to always be hungry these days." She settled into the easy chair across the coffee table from where he sat. "Where do we start?"

He took a deep breath and launched into what was

obviously a rehearsed spiel. "I'm here to share the word of our Lord. Jesus long ago told us to bring the word to all people, as in Matthew 28:19. We believe that all can be saved. When-"

"Oh, I'm sorry, but I should have offered you a drink. Can I get you some water or juice?"

He hesitated, but a deep swallow told her his answer before his voice did. "Yes, please. It's hot outside, and I'd love some water."

"Great, I'll be right back."

She hopped up and sped into the kitchen, where she stopped to look around for ideas. He didn't exactly look strong, but any person could pull up the strength to fight for their life against an aggressor. Her knife block stood on the counter beside the sink, shiny black handles poking out of it. The butcher knife would do nicely. It was long and thick, and she'd recently sharpened it. But a knife might be easy to wrest away, or she might cut herself if it slid. They addressed that in true crime shows all the time.

She slid various drawers open, seeking inspiration. Most of it was useless. Each thing that seemed a possibility was placed on the center island. So far, she'd found a meat tenderizer, a frying pan, and the base of her blender. Poison wouldn't do, because it would take time, but also probably poison the meat, which could be deadly to herself.

This last thought made her pause. It was inhuman to think this way. She couldn't really be pondering killing and eating this poor, innocent idiot. Any minute now her stomach would revolt. She kept waiting to feel nausea or a true physical reaction of horror at what she planned. It hadn't come yet, aside from the conscious thoughts she kept forcing on herself. It was the fact that her subconscious seemed entirely fine with it that bothered her now. As if only her intellectual side had an issue with it, but no emotional inhibitions existed.

It was amazing what hunger could do to a person.

"Can I help with anything?" he asked from the other room.

"Nope, sorry about that." Crap, she was taking too long. "I'll be right there."

She grabbed a glass, filled it with ice, then water, and grabbed herself a small glass of orange juice. A quick eyeballing of the items on the counter showed they wouldn't make any sense because it would look weird when she walked into the room holding them. Surely he wouldn't just sit there and watch as she approached him with a butcher knife or the base of a blender. If she'd been thinking ahead, she would have sat him with his back to the kitchen so she could come at him from behind. Instead, his position sat him squarely facing the doorway she'd be going back through.

An idea hit her, and she set the glasses down before scuttling over to the refrigerator. She pulled out some pre-sliced snacking cheese that didn't look moldy, setting it on the counter. She also grabbed a heavy, decorative platter and some crackers. Arranging everything on the platter, she removed her mask long enough to drink down her juice, picked up the platter in one hand and his water in the other, and headed back to where he sat.

"I realized I was hungry, so thought a snack might be a good idea." She set the water down in front of him, then set the platter beside the glass. "Help yourself."

He'd set a Bible on the table, which he now picked up in a tight grip, his hand shaking. The fact that he was getting more nervous instead of less so made it appear this might have been the first time anyone had taken him up on his proselytizing.

Her mouth went dry, which, as soon as she thought about it, made her feel a little better. The fact that she felt guilty meant she wasn't as bad as she'd started thinking she must be. That slight twinge in her stomach backed it up. She wasn't evil, just desperate. Surely there was something in the Bible that would confirm that was a legitimate thing.

His voice squeaked. "Do you have anything specific you're curious about?" He cleared his throat. "Any life questions you want answered?"

Actually, she did. "What if you're about to do something wrong, and you don't feel guilty enough about it?"

He opened his mouth and drew in a breath to speak, but she continued on.

"I mean, you might feel a little guilty about it, but you know you have to do it, that you don't have a choice. If it means your survival, if you'll die if you don't do it, doesn't that mean you have to do it?"

He cleared his throat again, looked at his Bible, looked at her. "Uh..." He opened the Bible and started flipping through it. "Okay, um..."

She waited, thinking that if he came up with the right thing to say, it might save her. If not, at least it might make her feel better about what she had to do. Maybe religion was worth it when you needed to make hard decisions. She saw people praying for all kinds of things all the time: to win a game, to get something they really wanted, to help them with making choices. They wouldn't do it if it didn't work. Someone who was fifty and doing that would have learned by now that their prayers were never answered, which must mean they did get answered.

She waited and watched him as he continued to make little noises and thumb back and forth in the Bible. A wave of red crept up his neck and into his face, his cheeks blazing with it. He kept licking his lips, and he darted looks at her.

Finally, his eyes widened and his posture relaxed. "Here it is. Second Corinthians 13:7. 'But we pray to God that you may do no wrong—not that we appear to have met the test, but that you may do what is right, though we may seem to have failed.'"

She sat back, only then realizing that she'd been leaning closer and closer to him as she awaited his response. "What?"

"It means that if you have faith, you need to test yourself to make sure you're doing things the right way. If you do the right thing, even when you want to do the wrong thing, you pass the test. If you know it's wrong and you do it, you've failed."

"What if I don't have faith, though? What am I testing myself for? I can't fail a test for a class I'm not taking."

"Well, um, I mean, you know what's right, right? You know what you're thinking about doing is wrong?"

"Yes."

"So it's still a test of yourself. You know you should do the right thing."

"But what happens if I don't do the right thing?"

"You…" he started looking through the book again.

Her hunger now gnawed at her entire inside. She'd been distracted by her inner struggle and nerves about the situation, but he was boring her. No longer distracted, all she could do was return to obsessing about her own physical torment. Now that she was paying attention to it, she found her skin even ached. Her nerves were on fire, every single one of them. It felt like she would burn to death, with not even a lick of flame nearby.

Without thinking, she stood up and grabbed the platter in one fluid movement, the food flying into the air, only to land on the carpeting in the same instant the platter met with the side of the young man's head. She felt the *conk* of the contact as much as she heard it, along with the *pomp, pomp, pomp* of the food. The hit was so solid it hurt her hands and spread up her forearms.

He fell forward, but didn't pass out. She'd fully expected it to knock him out completely. Blood pumped from his head where it had split like a seam. He put a hand to it, looked at the blood, and started an insanely high-pitched scream that didn't stop.

She screamed too and hit him in the head again. Blood pattered onto her mask in a tiny parade of droplets.

His screaming stopped, but he remained conscious, blood now pouring from his mouth in a viscous ribbon. Another seam appeared, splitting slowly from his temple and back through his red hair. It formed a bright white chasm in an arc along the side of his head, but then that split filled with vivid red blood. His scalp peeled down in slow motion, flopping over the ear.

Equal parts horror and ire surged through her. This wasn't how it was supposed to go. He was supposed to die with one hit from the platter. It should have been easier.

God damn it, she was so *hungry*.

With a feral snarl, Joy dove for him and slammed the platter into his head repeatedly until he finally slumped the rest of the way to the ground. One of his eyes remained fixed open, the eyelid torn and hanging down the bridge of his nose. The other had already swollen closed, the blood filling every line. There was blood spatter everywhere, including the ceiling, and a small clump of scalp had landed on the couch arm like a small rodent. Blood pooled beneath him, soaking into the carpet.

She sunk to her knees and tossed her mask to the side, warm blood seeping through her pants. Unsure of what to do next, she picked up his hand and put two fingers where she thought his pulse should be. Nothing there. He must be dead. Just to be sure, she shoved his shoulder to see if he'd react, but that one eye remained fixed on her and his body shifted right back to where it had been. It smelled like he'd crapped himself, which definitely wasn't appetizing.

Yet she salivated when she thought about eating him.

First things first, she needed to clean him up. It took her an inordinate amount of time to drag him into the bathroom. Getting him into the tub took almost as long as the rest of it. By the time she'd finished, her entire body ached, she reeked of every possible human body fluid, and she had worked up an even bigger appetite.

She took off his clothes and stuffed them into the garbage can, then she washed him until his skin showed white and clean. With the last dredges of the filth gone, it was time to figure out how to eat him. There was no way she'd be transporting his entire body anywhere else. This had been hard enough. Which meant she either had to eat him here or cut him up. Cutting something off made the most sense.

Joy went to the garage and grabbed a saw. It had belonged to her dad and had sat there, rusting, since his death five years ago. She wasn't even sure what he'd used it for, but thought it should work fine for this job.

Back in the bathroom, Joy started with a leg. She felt it would be nice and meaty, like a steak or a roast. Just thinking about it made her mouth water, and she went to work with the saw. It went through the meat easily enough, but when she got to the bone, she couldn't make any progress. It rasped and scratched in a way that gave her goosebumps, like nails on a chalkboard, but it didn't go through.

She pulled the flesh back to look, but she'd only made a small scratch in the femur. This wasn't working.

Obviously she wouldn't be able to get the whole leg off.

Instead, she sawed sideways, slicing the meat off the top to form a steak-sized cut. She was surprised at how little blood there was. A small amount seeped down from the slab she held in her hand, but nothing welled up out of the thigh where the chunk had been removed. Somehow that made it easier to deal with. She wasn't looking at a human being anymore. It was meat. The same thing available at any store. All meat had once been life.

She walked into the kitchen and slapped the meat down onto her cutting board. Red hairs rose from the freckled thigh skin, and she figured it would be best to trim the outer layer of skin off. As far as she could tell, the muscle part was the equivalent to a steak. She should have cut deeper but, for her first time, a thin steak would have to do. She'd know better next time.

The filet knife cut through the meat pretty well, though there was some resistance, and the cut wasn't straight. Once the skin and hair were removed, it looked... normal. She sprayed the pan down and set it on the stove to pre-heat. Sweat poured down her back, sides, and forehead. The foul stench of body odor rose in a bouquet of nerves and physical exertion. Fear, too, she realized. Fear of what she was doing, of what would happen if she didn't do it. Fear in every moment she had to make a decision and follow through on it.

Fear of wasting away from this hunger.

The scent of hot metal brought her back from her thoughts, and she plopped the steak into the skillet. It sizzled loudly. She seared it, then added seasonings while it finished cooking. The rich smells of garlic, meat, and thyme mingled together and her stomach rumbled yet again.

Outside, darkness had fallen. This had all taken hours, an entire day. She opened some windows to allow cool air into the house. Voices from someone's television drifted in, filling what was an otherwise lonely night with distant company. All this time, and she'd never put on music or turned on the television. Cutting meat was a fairly quiet thing to do except when the saw had hit the bone. The body itself had made a variety of noises while the gases settled within its guts, disgusting noises most of them. Yet she'd ignored them while she worked, lost in some distant part of her mind, various thoughts swirling.

She got like that sometimes. Lost. Plunging deep into her own head.

The steak finished, she plated it, grabbed utensils, and sat down at her table. Finally, she would have relief. She would feel full. As her hope climbed, so did her excitement.

She cut into the tender meat and slid it into her mouth. It tasted gamey. Like deer she'd once eaten when a neighbor gave her some of his kill. Each successive bite tasted worse, but at least she could sense flavor again. Her stomach grumbled angrily, pushing back at the food she forced down her own throat.

This was the answer. This would work.

Only it didn't.

She gagged and threw her fork down, pushing the plate away. Something had gone wrong. She gagged again, but this time it brought vomit up into her mouth.

Joy clapped a hand over her mouth and ran for the bathroom. Kneeling beside the man's body, she threw up every ounce of his meat. The smell sickened her, made her gag again, and she flushed the toilet to get rid of it.

Looking over at the dead body, she realized it must be the raw meat she had to eat. Weakened by the day's exploits and her vomiting, she crawled over and leaned on the edge of the tub. She studied his body to figure out what looked the easiest to eat and the most appetizing. His upper arm near the shoulder looked firm and mostly hairless. The thought of hairs tickling her tongue while she tried to eat made her gag again, and she went for the shoulder.

It was harder to break the skin with her teeth than she expected. She bit as hard as she could and tore at it, bringing a small chunk of flesh with her. It was rubbery and springy, but she chewed nonetheless until it became mashed up enough to swallow it without choking. When she went to take a second bite, she couldn't even sink her teeth in before her stomach forced her back to the toilet to throw up her last bite.

She continued to vomit until nothing remained, not even bile. Then she passed out on the bathroom floor.

* * *

Joy woke up to a room that reeked of vomit and death, and a mouth that tasted the same. Pooling blood had colored the lower parts of the corpse purple. The skin looked to have shrunk, sunken over the joints. The redhead was even paler than before, and Joy's bites stood out starkly.

She climbed to her feet, feeling weak and hungry. Everything hurt, including her stomach. She went to the refrigerator to look for food, but the sight of it left her feeling ill. Maybe this was her punishment for killing someone and trying to eat them. Maybe she'd never be able to eat again, and she'd die from lack of nourishment. She felt so strange, so out of it, like her body wasn't her own. Every movement cost energy she didn't have. Her limbs felt elongated and clumsy. When she held up her hands in front of her face, her fingers looked thinner and maybe a bit longer, but she couldn't tell for sure if she'd changed more.

The doorbell rang. She walked to the door, fighting the fatigue and discomfort draining her body. Through the peephole she saw the postman she'd waved at the other day.

Her stomach growled, her mouth filling with saliva.

So hungry.

She put on her mask and opened the door.

"Are you Joy Desmond?" he asked.

"Yes, that's me."

"Package for you." He held a large box, which he pushed in her direction.

"Can you bring it inside for me?" she asked. "It looks heavy."

"No problem."

She closed the door behind him and locked the deadbolt.

One more try.

THE BLEEDING BOX
By Bryan Holm

Joe had never been to Russia before, and after seventy-two hours there, he hoped to never return. He was a day's drive east of Moscow, in a small copper mining town along the base of the Ural Mountains. The mine had been slowly drying up over the last decade, and the town along with it. The fierce, bitter winter winds wormed their way through the doors of the rental car Joe had slept in the previous night. His current view was one of decay, in both the architecture and the people. Abandoned buildings, broken windows, and emaciated children, without hats or gloves, leaning into the arctic wind as they passed his car.

Joe's breath puffed out in front of him, a frozen fog on the inside of his windshield. He lit a cigarette, sour whiskey shifting in his guts at the first inhale. He coughed harshly, a fire in his lungs. He supposed one of these days he should find some food to eat, and a place to shower. Joe stared at himself in the rearview mirror. He hardly recognized his haggard face, a gaunt ghost of his former self.

Five years ago, Joe had been a successful trial lawyer in Chicago, on his way to making partner at his firm. His long road from there to this desolate city had been a grim one, full of dead ends, frauds, heartbreak, and immeasurable pain. He hoped that today would be different. He had a good feeling about this one. If the rumors were true, his journey might finally be at its end. If it were another disappointment, he was unsure if he could control himself again. Rubbing his knuckles, rough with drying, peeling scabs, Joe wondered if the man in New Guinea had survived. He hoped not.

Joe zipped up his coat as he made his way through the streets, adjusting his backpack as he avoided icy puddles, broken bottles, and withered beggars. Even in the cold, the air was thick with the scent of human piss and shit. A skeletal, flea-ridden dog followed him for a few feet, hoping for a meal, before giving up and limping away. After a block, Joe found what he was looking for.

The brothel was located in a nondescript, crumbling building. It looked to have been a small hotel or apartment complex that passed its peak sometime in the seventies. The front windows and doors were boarded up, an attempt to appear abandoned. The façade mostly worked. Only smoke rising from a rooftop furnace pipe gave it away, a fleeting indication of the desperate lives inside.

Joe circled the building and approached a rear entrance in the corner of a dead-end alleyway. He rapped hard on the rusty steel door. Above him, a small surveillance camera eyed him, its small motor buzzing. A few seconds later, a metal plate scraped to the side, a dark set of eyes peering at him through a rectangle opening protected by a crisscross of barb wire.

"I'm looking for someone…English, you speak English? I'm American," Joe stammered. The dark eyes just stared. Joe pulled a wad of large bills from his wallet,

Madame Gray's Vault of Gore

"I have a lot of money, and I want to spend it."

The opening in the door slid shut, and nothing happened. Joe held the money up to the camera, shaking it back and forth. Joe went to knock again, but the door unlocked and slid open. Standing before Joe was a massive, hulking man, covered in homemade tattoos and piercings.

"Welcome," the man growled.

Joe stared into the dark hallway behind the colossal brute.

"Inside. Quick!" the man barked.

Joe took a deep breath, and stepped across the threshold. The man peered into the alley, making sure it was empty, and slammed the door shut, cranking a large deadbolt into place. The guard said nothing more, and sat down on a wooden stool. The stool cracked under his massive bulk, the legs bowing. Joe was amazed it didn't collapse instantly. The man picked up a dog-eared mystery novel from a TV tray next to him, a cup of hot tea beside it, and proceeded to ignore Joe completely. Joe wondered how many men he had killed. And women, for that matter.

Joe turned, letting his eyes adjust to the dark hallway leading away from the door. As he approached a sharp turn, a red glow broke through the blackness, revealing the true entrance to the brothel. This hallway was lined with bare hanging light bulbs, painted red. Floral, peeling wallpaper lined the walls, the edges yellowed. In one spot, the paper was scorched from a fire that had been hastily extinguished. The hallway was stale, humid, and reeked of cheap tobacco and even cheaper perfume. Ahead of him, an elderly man, so wrinkled that Joe was unsure of his ethnicity, sat behind an ornate, mahogany desk, wedged halfway across the corridor. The man looked up, taking Joe in from behind thick, smudged glasses. He spoke English, with an accent Joe couldn't place.

"First time here?" the man inquired.

"It is."

"Welcome. In this house, we aim to make your dreams come true. What are you looking for? Blonde, brunette, old, young, white, black? We have it all, and so much more."

The old man relayed this to Joe in a bored, monotonous drawl. Joe wondered how many times he had said those lines. How many poor women had he seen come and go through these depressing antechambers? Used, abused, and spit back out into the world when they were no longer of use.

"I'm actually looking for a man…"

The old man cut him off. "No men here! No boys either. You're in the wrong part of town for that."

"Let me rephrase that. I'm looking for a specific man, with a specific gift, and I was told that I could find him here."

The old man pushed his glasses up his nose and sat up in his chair, his demeanor changed. "And how did you come about this information?"

"Maria, she sent me."

"Did she? If that is the case, you must have something for me?"

Joe reached into his pocket, and produced a gold coin, the size of a quarter. He placed it on the desk. The old man grabbed it, studying the intricate spirals carved into each side. He placed it in between his yellowed teeth, and bit down. The solid gold coin absorbed his canines, leaving a light circle of teeth marks.

"Very good," the old man said, "you can't be too careful these days." The old man didn't move; he just stared at Joe intently.

"Uh, what now?" Joe finally asked.

The old man smiled and held out his hand. Infected track marks ran up his arm.

"Got it," Joe reached into his backpack and pulled out a neat stack of one-hundred-dollar bills, ten thousand dollars in total. Joe sighed. "This is a lot of bread. He better be the real deal."

The old man snatched the money, fanning the edge of the stack with shaky fingers. "Oh, believe me, he is. He is as real as it gets."

Joe climbed three flights of creaky stairs, his way lit by more red bulbs on each landing. The steps were carpeted in shag that had been green at some point, but was now blackened and torn apart from decades of foot traffic. Warped hardwood bled through in places, a patchwork of depressing distress. He made his way down the corridor of the third floor, searching for Room 309. As he passed each doorway, moans emanated through the cheap wood. Behind one door, he heard a scream. The door to Room 307 stood ajar, its occupant a young woman, early twenties, thin, pale, lying on a mattress, undressing for someone on her cracked laptop screen. She caught Joe's shadow and said something to him in a language he did not know. He kept moving.

Joe stood before Room 309. It was located at the very end of the hallway, a corner room, the 'penthouse' of this miserable place. The end of the hall felt different to Joe from the rest of the building. A quiet stillness hung in the air, as if the sins he just passed by kept a respectful distance, out of reverence for this room and what it contained. Even the musty smells seemed to have vanished, replaced by a pleasant scent he could not place. Its door was different from the others as well: thick, dark, black walnut wood, newly varnished. The numbers 309 were carved into the center panel, the crevices painted in gold. Joe stood for a moment, his nerves sparking, his guts spinning. He knew, without a doubt, he had finally found what he was looking for. Smiling, Joe raised his hand and knocked twice, softly.

When the door was answered, Joe's doubts immediately returned. Standing before him was a man who appeared to be in his mid-forties, but it was hard to tell for sure due to his massive, gnarly beard. He was tall and skinny, his rib cage poking through a faded, tight, L.A. Dodgers t-shirt. He wore jeans that appeared to be older than he was, and he was barefoot, his feet filthy, toenails uncut.

"Hey man, come on in," the man offered, the hint of a West Coast surfer drawl beneath his voice.

Joe entered his room. It looked like a freshman dormitory. Dirty laundry in one corner, piles of dirty dishes and take-out boxes scattered on the floor. A large, brand new television against one wall, a video game paused on the screen. The room reeked of weed, its source a large glass bong, still smoking on a windowsill. Joe felt his blood pressure rising, he clenched his fists. The man cleared some space off of two chairs next to a twin bed.

"Sorry for the mess, let me tidy up a few things. I'm Phil, by the way."

Phil turned around, and found Joe grimacing back at him. Phil laughed, "Not what you expected, huh? Thinking there should've been an Asian monk, or an old Voodoo lady or something behind that door, right?"

"So to speak," Joe replied.

"Please, have a seat," Phil pointed to a chair, and sat down in the other. "You want any pizza? I got some left."

Joe set his backpack on the floor and sat down, eyeing the soggy pizza box lying on Phil's unmade bed. "I'm good."

"Suit yourself." Phil grabbed a slice of cold pepperoni.

"You're American?" Joe asked.

"Indeed. Born and raised in the great state of Michigan," Phil replied between bites of his slice.

"How did you end up here?"

"That's a story far too long to tell, my friend, at least without a case of beer on hand. Short version, though, I was never much into school, work, anything like that. I went to Mexico for Spring Break, my freshman year of College, and I never went back."

"And you can really do what they say?"

"I can."

"How?"

Phil laughed again, "I sense that you don't quite believe me. And I get it, that's okay." Phil stared at Joe, his raw hands, his weathered face. Phil threw the crust of his pizza slice onto his bed, wiped his hands on his jeans, and leaned forward, placing his hands on Joe's. Joe flinched from the human touch. "I know you have made a long journey of your own to find me." Phil rubbed a thumb over Joe's split knuckles. Joe tried to pull away, but Phil held on tight. "I can see the pain inside of you, the grief dripping from your pores. I'd hate to see the bloody wake your path here left behind, but trust me, your fear, your anger, it's over, as of now. After today, you will be able to breathe again, to move on, to go home and resurrect your life."

Joe yanked his hands away from Phil's. "You're good with words, I'll give you that. But I've heard this routine before, and all that's followed was disappointment."

"Fair enough. Let's just get started then. Let me prove you wrong." Phil stood up and went to a closet.

Joe settled into his chair, trying to keep an open mind, while simultaneously planning his escape if it became necessary. Phil wouldn't be an issue; Joe would enjoy beating his face to a bloody pulp. And it would be easy to get his money back from the old-timer downstairs. There wouldn't be much of a fight there either. The ogre manning the door, however, was another story. There had to be another way out of this building, somewhere. He glanced at the window, looking for a fire escape.

"Ready to start?" Phil had cleared space on a rug on the floor, and was sitting on it, cross-legged. Before him sat a wooden box, roughly a square foot in size. "Please, join me."

"On the floor?" Joe asked.

Phil motioned to the other edge of the rug. "Please."

Joe grunted as he plopped onto the floor, his knees cracking their annoyance at him. He wondered when the last time was that he had sat on the floor like this, pretzel-style, as his son used to call it. Joe knew the answer to that, of course, and his chest tightened as he thought of his sweet little boy, playing with his trucks on the floor of their townhouse back in Chicago. But that felt like a century ago, on another continent, on another planet.

Joe studied the box lying between them. It was made of a kind of wood that Joe had never seen before. It was matte black, but didn't appear to be varnished or painted. Every inch on each side was carved with letters and numerals Joe didn't recognize. On top, an intricate spiral was carved, leading to a small hole in the center, the size of a dime.

"Did Maria tell you much?" Phil asked.

"Only where to find you."

"How is she?"

"Surviving."

"She's always been good at that."

Phil closed his eyes, placed his hands on the box. "This box is my creation, and mine alone. There are no others like it. In all of my journeys, I have found no one else who has broken through the barrier. I am telling you this, not to boost my own ego, but because it's important that you believe. That you believe in me, that you believe in the power inside this box. There are eons of alchemy lying before you, and I don't pretend to understand everything that is at work here. But it does work. That I know. It has taken me two decades to build this, a journey that's included countless countries, ancient tribes, forgotten religions." Phil opened his eyes, staring at Joe. "Are you ready?"

"I am."

"Who is it?"

Joe broke eye contact, staring at his hands in his lap. "My son, Joseph Jr."

"I'm truly sorry for your loss. A child?"

Tears welled up in Joe's eyes. "Eight years old."

Phil smiled empathetically, shook his head. "A tragedy. Did you bring something? A piece of him?"

Joe reached into his backpack and produced a brown leather pouch. He removed a lock of blond hair from inside, held together by a rubber band. Joe began to pass it to Phil, but stopped, "This is all I have left."

"That's all I need." Phil took the hair from Joe's hand, and placed it in his right palm. He stared at it intently, then squeezed his fingers around it tightly. Phil closed his eyes and took several deep breaths. After a few seconds, he opened his eyes, and dropped the hair into the hole at the center of the box.

Phil picked up a knife lying on the rug. He held his hand over the box, and sliced open his palm. Carefully, he dripped his blood onto the edge of the carved spiral. His blood was sucked into the deep grooves, leaving the upper layer dry.

"My blood will slowly make its way towards the center of the box, and when it arrives, your time with your son will be over. It takes about ten to fifteen minutes, give or take, which is honestly about the most that I can handle."

"Okay," Joe responded, transfixed by the slowly moving plasma.

"Just keep an eye on it. Your time will be over before you know it. So say what you want to say, ask what you want to ask, right away. When it's over, I may pass out.

That's normal, just let yourself out."

Before Phil could respond, the lights in the room began to flicker. Phil's eyes rolled up into his head, and then closed tightly. He stayed upright, only his head moving back and forth slowly in a figure eight. The lights in the room went out completely. Joe sat in the dark for a moment, before a soft glow began emanating from the hole in the center of the box, a crimson luminosity that fell upon Phil's face.

Phil's body began to twitch, beads of sweat poured down his forehead. His body was suddenly racked by violent spasms, his breath ragged, choked. His eyes popped open, and he took in his surroundings, fearful, frantic.

"Where am I?" Phil croaked, his voice changed, deeper. Then his eyes found Joe, focusing on him for the first time. "Oh my God!" Phil backed up on the floor with his hands, pinning himself into the corner of the room. Phil's face contorted again. "Who is this? This isn't a child!" Phil's voice was his own again, terrified. "The darkness, the pain!"

Joe looked down at the blood pooled in the box; it was already halfway to the center. Joe removed a handkerchief from his pocket, and pressed it into the groove, stopping the flow of blood. Joe stared at Phil, a grim smile spreading across his face.

Phil's face contorted again, and his fear increased with the change. "Where am I? How did you find me?" Phil's voice was lower again.

Joe couldn't believe it had finally happened. All of his sacrifices, all of them, had actually been for something. All of his pain had been worth it. He was finally face to face with the man who had haunted every waking moment of his life for the past five years.

Joe leaned forward. "Is it really you, O'Bannon, you sick fuck?"

"What's happening?" O'Bannon tried to stand up in Phil's body, but he could barely lift his arms. He looked like a man trying to peel himself from a bar stool after a long bender. Phil wrestled control again. "What have you done?" Phil looked down at the box, the blood soaking the handkerchief, no longer flowing towards the center. "You can't do this, I can't take much more; we can't both survive in my body!"

"I'm counting on that," Joe replied, and stood up, looming over Phil. He grabbed Phil by his hair, and dragged him towards his bed. Phil shrieked, trying to fight, but was unable to do anything more than flop his arms around, as if he were drugged. Once on the bed, Phil's face changed again, a fresh agony, and O'Bannon was back. Phil was unable to fight his way back after that.

"What do you want from me?" O'Bannon asked, tears streaming down his face.

"Just a few moments of your time."

Joe opened his backpack, and removed coils of rope. He tied O'Bannon's hands and legs to the bedposts. Joe flung everything littered on the nightstand onto the floor, and removed a hammer, a pack of razor blades, and a pair of pliers from his backpack. O'Bannon shook his head back and forth as Joe shoved his hand into his mouth, gripping his tongue, and pulling it taut with the pliers. Joe grabbed a razor blade, and slowly cut out his tongue, as close to its base as he could. It wasn't a clean cut, and O'Bannon squealed briefly before his mouth filled with blood, silencing him for good. Joe threw the tongue onto the dirty carpet, and straddled O'Bannon on the bed, sitting on his waist, staring down at him.

"Do you know how long I've been waiting for this moment? You took the easy way out, you know that, you sick fuck? You can't rape and kill half a dozen kids, and then just blow your head off before the cops take even two steps into your house. It's not fair."

O'Bannon attempted to scream through the blood, but could only produce a soft gurgling.

"I was looking for you too, you know. Lotta good the fucking cops were. Three other kids died after my own, my Joey, before they figured out who the fuck you were. Another day or two, and I would have found you first. If you only knew what I have been through between then and now. I even had to dig up your fucking corpse, pull some hair off of your busted-open head. Did you know that? Could you feel me taking a piss on your rotting carcass? That was the only moment of happiness I've had in the last five years." Joe reached over and picked up the hammer. "But that's okay, because I found you now, and we have all the time in the world to catch up."

O'Bannon yelled again, uselessly, a muffled whimper, and Joe went to work.

It was four hours before Joe was done. Exhausted, he slumped onto the floor, covered in gore. He wasn't sure if O'Bannon had finally found a way to escape Phil's body, or if Phil's body had finally just passed away from the cruelty inflicted upon it. Maybe he was still trapped inside of him, a new kind of hell for him to endure. Joe could only hope.

Joe was pleased with himself. He had kept him alive much longer than he had even dared to hope for. Joe stared at the rug in front of him. Phil's eyeballs and tongue were already drying out, a thin crust forming over them. The rest of his organs still glistened, liquid slowly leaving the razor blade cuts he had made into a lung, his liver, his spleen, and a kidney. Phil's genitals lay next to those. That had been particularly difficult for poor O'Bannon's soul. Joe had made that extraction last, almost an hour in itself.

Joe thought about calling his ex-wife, but they hadn't spoken in almost four years, and she wouldn't believe him anyway. Joe eyed the pizza box next to him. Opening it, he found one slice left. It was the greatest thing he had ever tasted. At least this godforsaken city could do one thing right.

Joe made his way down the fire escape, thinking about the wooden box in his backpack. What a waste it had been in Phil's hands. If he could make that much cash from love and loss, just think what one could make from hate and revenge. If he could learn to use it, the possibilities were endless. What would someone pay for a consequence-free hour with their abusive father, the woman that fucked them over, the priest that raped them as a child? Shit, Joe was tempted to have a word or two with his domineering mother, God rest her wicked soul. And could you summon someone more than once? Could he do this to O'Bannon again? Over and over? That would be better than any gym membership money could buy.

Joe sat in his rental car, his mind still racing. He flipped the pages of Phil's passport, noting the exotic locales he had visited. What if he could learn the secrets of the box, and create even more of them? Of course, he would need vessels for them, expendable bodies. Even if the clients didn't always kill the host, they wouldn't last too long, he imagined, harboring the souls of the damned. But imagine, a whorehouse like the one he had just left? A wooden box in every room? The possibilities truly were never-ending. Joe started his car, and scanned the street, wondering which way to go.

THE THORN TREE
By Michael Highgrove

The Thorn Tree had bloomed for the first time in myth or memory.

Word spread quickly. Decades before telegraph or telephones, and decades more before computers or the Internet, the news reached the ears of nearly every villager within an hour of the first idle glance that became a stunned stare.

Whoever first saw it would have looked without thinking. The tree and the tall hill it crowned loomed ever-present, and most ignored it or avoided looking. The tree was their source of comfort and terror. It was their place of judgment, and the tree was never wrong.

One of the last to hear was a brewer. That morning, he was sitting at breakfast with his young daughter when she said she'd seen the Spike Man outside her window. Her father listened and nodded, only half paying attention as he cut her a slice of bread and spread it with plenty of jam, telling her it had just been a dream. The girl shook her head and kept talking. She said a noise had woken her up in the night, and there had been a shadow passing her window. She got up to look and saw it was an old man. She knew it was an old man because his long hair was white and billowy like cotton and his skin was wrinkled and brown, but he wore no clothes and was covered in big, sharp spikes all over. Her father again told her it was only a bad dream and there was nothing to be afraid of. The girl said she had not been afraid; she knew the man was not there for her. For the first time, her father became concerned and gave her a long stare as she happily munched on brown bread, lazily kicking her legs and licking jam off her lips. He asked her what she meant by that, and the girl said she knew she had done nothing wrong. The Spike Man was going somewhere else, so she went back to sleep.

The brewer sent his daughter off to school and cleaned up after breakfast. Word was beginning to spread by then, and he could hear a commotion outside, but the brewer ignored it, too busy with his thoughts. He went to his daughter's room and looked out the window. There was a patch of muddy, bare earth a few yards away, and the more he stared, the more uneasy he felt. A shiver ran down his spine.

He left his simple thatch-roofed home intending to walk the half-mile to the brewhouse. First, he circled 'round the back and stood over the patch of dirt. He felt the shiver again. The footprints could have been from a man, but they were barefoot and the toes were all wrong. Too long and too sharp. Uneasy, he walked in the direction of the footprints, following a straight line and only stopping when he was sure the path would lead to a house. A particular house. Frederik's house. The shutters were still closed, and there was no smoke from the chimney, both unusual at this hour. He was not the first to notice.

Just as news of the tree spread, so did Frederik's absence. That made seven. Seven people gone. No one could blame Edgar for leaving and taking his wife and son—considering what had happened—but now Frederik and Ely and Percy, too, all without warning. And then, of course, there was the stranger, but no one dared talk or even think about him.

The brewer walked quickly back to his house and forced himself not to think of it, but that was impossible. Impossible not to think of what had been done four nights ago, of what happened when those three men—his friends and neighbors—took the stranger up the hill to the tree. A dread had descended on the village since that night, and the cause was obvious. It was something nobody spoke of, but everyone knew. But not everyone knew about his daughter's dream of the white-haired man covered in spikes—or thorns. He thought of her words: that *she* had not done anything wrong.

He was halfway to work, thinking he would be late and that the foreman would be angry. Excited murmurings and dozens of people passing in the opposite direction finally wrenched him out of his head and onto the street. People had come out of their houses and shops, pointing and staring at the same thing: the towering hill at the edge of town. When he saw what had caused so much excitement, a stone dropped into his stomach. He did not want to, but still joined the mass of people heading for the hill to trudge up its steep slope.

Years before, a clergyman with an interest in botany had come to the village. He had heard about the tree and wanted to have a look. When he saw it, he was stunned. He told them the tree was from South America and not meant to grow in cold climates like this, that it had probably died years ago and that was why it did not sprout leaves or flowers or the massive seedpods pregnant with false silk that made its species famous. Back then, the villagers had listened and nodded politely. He asked where it had come from, and they said it had always been there. The clergyman said that was impossible and got shrugs for his troubles.

No one paid much attention to the tree before or after, save for its dark purpose, and then they ignored it even more. Now nearly everyone in the village, save the very old and very young—and even a few of them too, were climbing the hill to see the tree as it had never been before.

The brewer and all the rest stood beneath the tree, gazing into its boughs. Bright green leaves covered every branch, making the tree seem far taller than any had imagined. Pink star-flowers blossomed from the green in marvelous constellations. Heavy pods hung from the branches, split open at the seams to reveal fluffy white cotton within. The leaves were so thick that shadow hid the trunk in a pocket of night. The throng had gathered in a circle. The brewer was in its midst, not close enough to see more than the canopy, but even that was enough to leave him slack-jawed. But something was wrong in the front rows. People ahead of him began turning around and weaving through the crowd, silent, eyes down, making room for others to move up and see. In this way, the brewer came to the front under the eaves.

His eyes adjusted to the dark, and he saw, and he too became quiet. He thought of his daughter's dream and the footprints outside the window and the house they had led to as he looked. He could see three of them clearly—the fourth hidden on the other side—impaled on the tree's thorny trunk, still dripping, turning the grass red.

And he and everyone else knew why the Thorn Tree had bloomed.

* * *

Four nights before, three men met in a pub.
The pub was closed, but that did not matter. Two sat

at the counter, each nursing a mug of dark brown beer. The barkeep busied himself, cleaning glasses that were not dirty, wiping down a bone-dry counter. None spoke. The door opened and another man walked in carrying a black lacquered club, his symbol of grim, inherited authority. He sat at the bar, setting his club down with a clatter that rang through the room. The barkeep poured him a beer, then left by the back door. He would lock up later.

The man with the club, Frederik, took a long gulp of beer and wiped the foam from his lips.

"Where is he?"

One of the other men, a skinny young fellow with an oversized Adam's apple and a large crooked nose, answered without taking his eyes off the beer.

"At my house."

"You sure he won't leave?"

"He's had a few drinks. Won't be going anywhere."

"How'd you get him there?"

"He trusts me."

Frederik nodded and downed more beer. The skinny man, Ely, only took a sip of his own. It tasted especially bitter tonight, and he thought he might throw up.

"You get the belt like I told you?"

Frederik was talking to Percy now. Percy was shorter and heavyset, just the type needed to work the belt and do their night's business.

Percy just nodded. His beer had not lost a drop.

"Go get it. Ely and me will get him and meet you on the hill."

Again, Percy nodded, dropped off his stool, and left through the front door.

Frederik swallowed the rest of his beer in one go and slammed the mug down. Ely jumped and nearly spilled his. Frederik took up his club and headed for the door. Ely followed. He had yet to look Frederik in the eye.

They were alone as they walked the cobbled streets. Not a light shone from any window, their only illumination the moon, half-hidden behind a cloud. The village had silently gone into curfew, knowing that terrible, but necessary, deeds were about to be done. No one would be venturing out tonight.

At first, the only sound was the clack of shoes on cobblestones and the rustle of clothes, but as they neared Ely's house, Frederik's head was filled with the wailing of a child, terrified and in pain. He had been one of the first to find the boy, lying in the mud behind an abandoned workshop, bruised and bloody, his arm bent in impossible directions. Had the boy not been crying, they would have thought him dead.

The doctor came over from town, examined the boy, and said his arm would have to be amputated or he would die. Edgar, the boy's father, refused to let his son be taken away, so the operation was done on the dinner table. The boy lived, but he slept for nearly a week. The doctor said the boy's ribs and skull had been cracked, and that he may never be himself again. The boy's mother silently cried; his father did nothing, and everyone praised his strength and dignity.

The constable came up from town and asked questions of the villagers and Edgar and his family. The child would not speak, and no one saw what happened. The constable did the best he could, but in the end, apologized to Edgar, saying there was little to be done, and left. Everything he said to Edgar was in confidence. In a matter of days, everybody knew every word. There would be no justice for Edgar's boy. At least, none of the usual kind.

* * *

Ten days before the blooming, Frederik went to Edgar's house, carrying the club so everyone would know his reason. He knocked on the door, got a muffled order to come in, and did. They had been expecting him. Edgar was pacing, hands clenched behind his back, looking agitated, angry, and lost. His wife sat in a chair by the hearth, eyes cast down, quiet and meek, holding her son in her arms. The boy nestled in against his mother, burying his face into her breast as Frederik came in.

"Who did it?" No small talk necessary, straight to the point.

Edgar shook his head as he paced.

"I don't know." He spoke through his teeth, eyes on the floor.

Frederik knew better. He had known who it was before stepping across the threshold. There was only one person in the entire village who could have done something so vicious to a child, especially the child of someone as loved and respected as Edgar. Now, Frederik had to get Edgar to agree to his suspicion. They were old friends, and Frederik knew how to convince him.

"What about that new one, whatever his name is—the stranger."

Edgar stopped pacing, his eyes darting side to side as the thought bounced around in his head. Frederik saw a faint glow of relief come over his friend. This would be easier than he thought.

"Could be," said Edgar. He nodded, then smiled and turned to Frederik, his eyes filled with appreciation.

Encouraged, Frederik went on.

"It has to be him. Nobody else would do a thing like that to a child, and everyone knows he drinks. His kind are untrustworthy to start. They came through here months ago and left him behind. What does that tell you? It has to be him."

Edgar nodded, now staring off at nothing, deep in thought.

Frederik knew Edgar would not say what needed to be

said, so he played a dirty trick.

"I can get word to the constable right away. We can have him arrested by tonight."

This snapped Edgar out of it, and he turned back to Frederik, eyes filled now with worry.

"No. That wouldn't do any good. All we have is a suspicion. Nobody saw it or they would have said by now," he said to himself, and then remembered Frederik. "Even if the constable does arrest him, he'll just have to let him go in a day or two. Two days in jail for nearly beating a child to death isn't justice." Edgar's hands curled into massive fists, raw knuckles standing out against paling skin. His eyes, now filled with something dark and ominous, drilled into Frederik.

Frederik shrugged. His friend needed one more push.

"Maybe he didn't do it."

"Maybe," said Edgar, relaxing as he understood. "There's only one way to be sure."

There was a silence then, just the crackling of the fire in the hearth.

"We can do it tonight. I'll get a couple of the others—"

"No!" Edgar stepped forward and placed his hand on his wife's shoulder. Frederik saw her flinch and felt sorry for her. So scared she was even afraid of her husband's touch. It made him hunger for vengeance even more.

"We'll be leaving tomorrow," said Edgar. "Going to the next county to stay with her family. Let the boy recover in peace. If you're going to do it, wait 'til we've gone."

Frederik nodded and left, his friend looking much relieved.

The next day Edgar loaded his family and a few possessions into his cart, hitched it to his horse, and rode out of town.

The day after that, Frederik approached Ely and

Percy, and they made a plan. They wanted the stranger to let his guard down, so they waited, making the necessary arraignments, and steeling their resolve. For Ely and Percy, this would be their first time. For Frederik, it had been too long.

That was when the silent word spread, and everyone knew when to stay in their homes.

The Thorn Tree was waiting, and tonight the wait was over.

* * *

They came to Ely's house, and he opened the door. The stranger was sitting in a chair, head lolled back and snoring loudly, an empty bottle dangling from his limp hand. Ely took the bottle and set it on a table, then they each took an arm and hauled him up. Their charge was not as drunk as he appeared. He groaned and stirred at their touch, looking at them with confused, tired eyes.

"Come along," said Ely, "let's go for a little walk."

The drunkard nodded and mumbled something about fresh air doing him good. His legs wobbled as if just stepping off a ship, and they had to drape his arms over their shoulders to keep him up. Awkwardly, they half-led half-carried him to the door and out. Ely closed it behind them and the three headed down the cobbled street for the tallest hill in the village, and the tree silhouetted at its crest.

The fresh air did do the man good, and as he woke up, he tried to make conversation. Ely made polite responses, but never more than two or three words. Frederik stayed silent, thinking that it was best if the man was awake. It would be more satisfying if he knew what was happening.

They came to the hill. The ignorant accused was holding himself up now, but they still held on to him as they climbed. The hill was steep and their journey a struggle, but a task like this should not be easy, so Frederik and Ely bore it in silence.

The outsider was sobering up, the exercise and cold air winning the battle with alcohol, and he asked where they were going.

"We're going to see about something," said Frederik, and that was the last he said until they reached the top.

The Thorn Tree was a sight to behold: trunk wider than the span of a man's arms, rising tall as a house, narrowing at the top, only to explode in a wild tangle of outstretched branches, a leafless canopy that extended a dozen yards in all directions, out and up. Its trunk, every massive inch of it, covered in sharp, stubby thorns. Percy was already there, the belt slung over his shoulder.

"Hold him," Frederik said, and dropped the man's arm.

Ely grabbed both hands in his and brought them up behind the trusting fool's back, pinning him in place. The stranger was almost dead sober now and getting scared. Frederik had to bend slightly to look the man in the eyes. His own did not blink.

"Has anyone told you about this?" he asked, gesturing at the tree.

The man shook his head, unsure where this was going but not liking it.

Frederik smiled without mirth.

"No, they wouldn't, would they? You being a stranger." He said *stranger* as if saying *plague-infested rat*, which is what he meant.

"I'll tell you, then, if you really want to know."

The stranger did not know how to answer and so said nothing.

"The tree is how we judge the guilty," said Frederik. "It won't hurt an innocent man, you see. But it craves the blood of the wicked. Always has. Your people have strange ways and beliefs, so you should understand."

From the look on his face, Frederik could tell the stranger only thought him mad, but the proof would soon show.

"We don't do this for everyone, you know," Fredrik continued, defensive. "Only when we have no other choice. We go to the law when we can. We come here when we must." He had practiced this last line often. It was his justification, and he held on to it tighter than his club.

"In fairness, I'll give you one chance. Tell us what you did, and we'll take you to the constable, then you can tell him, and the law will do its work." Frederik straightened up, crossing his arms, the black club resting on his shoulder, and glared down his nose. "Well?"

Fear joined confusion, and the stranger just shook his head as if Frederik had spoken a dead language.

"Tell us what you did to Edgar's boy." Frederik's voice was stern now and loud enough to carry to the village below. It did not matter. Nobody would listen even if they could hear.

Understanding dawned on the stranger. He'd heard about the boy and knew the village's anger. He shook his head wildly, protesting his innocence through lips that were still too clumsy from drink to form true words.

Frederik nodded. "Have it your way then," he said. "We'll soon know the truth."

He locked eyes with Ely and jerked his head towards the tree.

Ely dragged the accused man to the trunk. The stranger struggled best he could, but there was still drink enough in his blood to weaken him, and Ely's grip was strong and would not break.

Percy had unwound the belt. Like all devices of torture, it was simple and ingenious. It looked like its namesake: a flat strip of metal, a foot wide and long enough to encircle the tree and more. On one end was a squared loop standing an inch above the metal strap, a small wheel attached to the top that turned a star-shaped gear underneath. The other end had a channel cast into the strap extending three feet up its length, one side flat, the other jagged with sharp, uniform teeth. When the channel end was fed into the loop, the gear would catch the teeth, and every turn of the wheel would tighten it more and more. Perfectly designed for the job at hand.

Frederik set down his club and took one arm, helping Ely pin the stranger against the tree. Percy was shaking and awkward with the belt, fumbling to get it around the frightened man, ducking under and around Frederik and Ely, and shying from the spiky trunk, constantly stumbling over the vast system of roots at their feet. Frederik was irritated with his clumsiness. The fat, useless idiot! Had he not given this night's work any thought or practice? Frederik had gone over this night a dozen times, rehearsing his lines in the mirror, wanting to know what the condemned would see. If Percy ruined it, there would be hell to pay.

Finally, Percy fumblingly got the belt around both trunk and accused and shuffled the ends until they were behind the tree. Once settled, he inserted the grooved end into the loop, turning the wheel until it caught, then kept turning. The belt tightened, pinning down the stranger. Ely and Frederik released their grip. Frederik picked up his club and again bent to look the stranger in the eye.

"If you are innocent, the tree will not harm you." Those final traditional words said, he stepped back. Percy was peering around the trunk, and Frederik gave him a nod. The stranger could already feel thorns press into his back and finally understood. He screamed. Percy tightened the wheel.

The screams echoed from hill to hill and raced along the cobbled streets, making the eaves of houses seem to shake and window glass shudder. Percy tightened more and more. Frederik stood impassively, lightly tapping the club against his knee. Ely looked at his shoes. He had never participated in this ritual before and never wanted to again, even if the stranger did deserve it.

Sweat was streaming down Percy's face, his lips and teeth a tight grimace as he strained against the wheel, tighter and tighter, trying to ignore the unseen man's wailing. Mercifully, the screaming stopped just as the belt would tighten no more. The stranger passed out. His head hung limp and his knees buckled, held upright solely by the belt and the thorny trunk. Without a word, the three executors of justice and tradition walked down the hill. Judgment had been made, and now they had to wait.

Several hours passed and it was still dark. The three returned to the hill, this time struggling under a new burden: a wooden coffin. It was simple, hastily constructed only yesterday by the carpenter. He asked no questions and took no fee. Frederik, Ely, and Percy had dug the grave themselves. It was their duty, for one thing, but there was another reason. The time needed to dig a six-foot hole, six feet deep, was time enough for a man to bleed out once judged by the tree. Frederik knew this well and was happy to teach his companions.

When they returned, the man had not moved. They set down the coffin. Percy took his place at the wheel and started to turn. It resisted at first, then finally gave way and the belt loosened with ease. The body slumped forward, bending over the belt, gradually lowering to the ground as the metal slackened. When the end slipped out of the loop, belt and man dropped. The stranger hit the ground hard and moaned.

The three villagers were frozen and stared dumbly at the prone figure. Gradually, the moans came more and more, and the head lolled side to side. Limp arms soon gained strength and he pushed himself up. A cloud that had obscured the moon's light moved aside. The luminance pierced through the leafless boughs of the tree, and the three could see him clearer now. His back was unmarked. Not a scratch or a frayed piece of fabric. No blood, not even a drop.

The stranger was on his knees now, his head clearing, finally aware that there was not any pain. He reached one arm around, feeling his back all over, then began to laugh.

"See! See!"

That was all he said or could say, over and over through his laughter.

He looked at Frederik, a wide smile on his face as if amongst friends. Tears of joy and relief flowed down his cheeks. He turned to Ely—who looked ill—and was about to say more when the club came down on his head.

He stayed upright for the first two strikes, then fell over for the next dozen. Ely and Percy watched as Frederik's arm came up and down, over and over again, in a blur. Ely could see Frederik's face, and it was a mask of terrified determination like he was killing a poisonous snake.

At first, the strikes were cacophonous, filling the hills and streets with loud percussions, but they soon dampened as skull gave way to brain, which Frederik smashed to jelly. When it was done, all that could be heard was the breathing of three men—two hurried and scared, one hard and ragged—and branches creaking above.

Frederik stared at the body for some time, catching his breath, lips parted, teeth clenched in an insane grimace, gobs of saliva spewing out with every exhaled breath. His arm was sore and shaking; he could barely hold on to the club. When sense returned, he looked up at his companions. Percy was still behind the tree and tried to duck away from Frederik's gaze, but fear kept his feet pinned where they were. A dark wet patch had appeared on Ely's trousers. Both stared in shock.

"We all know he did it," said Fredrik between breaths. "Right? He was the only one." He pointed his club at the tree. "Something must have gone wrong." He pointed at Percy. "You spoiled it somehow. If you'd done it right, the tree would have worked."

He looked back and forth, from one to the other, then down at the still figure at his feet. The only wound on his body had been put there by man. The tree had not left a mark.

"But it's worked every other time, hasn't it?" said Percy.

"Quiet!" Frederik barked, and Percy again hid behind the tree.

Ely swallowed hard, then said in a shaking voice, "I heard that people in India sleep on boards covered in nails but don't get a scratch on them. There's a trick to it, they say. You can lie on a hundred nails and they won't hurt you, but one will. That's what I heard."

All three looked to the trunk and its thousands upon thousands of thorns. Frederik's head bobbed enthusiastically.

"Right, that's it. Has to be. That's why it didn't work. Right?"

Ely and Percy both nodded at the easy excuse, all ignoring the contradiction. If it was so easy for such a thing to happen, why did it never happen before? They all thought this, and all did their best to kill that thought. All failed, but stayed silent.

Moonlight shining through the branches made a mosaic pattern on the ground. The light hurt Frederik's eyes, and his vision became blurry. He rubbed them hard with his free hand and then stumbled as something upset his footing. He brought his hand away and glared down at his feet. He could feel the earth move and was sure he saw the roots shifting. The sound of frantically creaking wood made him look up. The moonlight stung his eyes;

he kept them open, wide now, and watched as the limbs of the tree became like black tentacles, slowly writhing against the bright night sky. He stared up at the wriggling Medusa's head and, through the chaotic mass, thought he could see something. The more he stared, the surer he was. It was a man. Thin, gaunt, covered in long, deathly-sharp spikes, a cascade of white, billowy hair flowing around them, lit up and glowing by the moon's light.

Frederik turned away and shook his head wildly. He still felt a pressure behind his eyes and could hear the branches move overhead and feel the roots undulate underfoot. Finally, in desperation, he brought his club down hard on his shin. The pain spread quickly, and his head cleared. When he opened his eyes again and tentatively looked up, the branches were still and empty, just as they had always been.

"Ely."

Ely and Percy were statues, dumb, mouths agape, staring up at the branches.

"It's watching us," said Percy in a soft, child-like voice.

"Hey!" Frederik barked.

Suddenly, they came alive. Their heads snapped down and turned to Frederik. He watched as their eyes cleared. They stared at each other for a long time, and then Ely pointed at Frederik's leg. There was a red patch where the club had struck.

Frederik ignored it and pointed at the coffin with his club.

"Put him in. Let's bury him and have it over with."

Eager for a distraction—any distraction—the trio went to work. They placed the body in the coffin, nailed down the lid, and carried it to the graveyard. The plot was far removed from the resting places of the good citizens of the village, and would forever be without a marker, just like the rest of its kind, discreetly hidden under the grass.

They buried him without words, then went to their houses, Percy mumbling about returning the belt first, and that was it.

Neither Frederik nor Ely slept that night. Percy's mother said he never came home.

* * *

Three days before the villagers climbed the hill to see the Thorn Tree as they had never seen it before, Frederik went looking for Percy.

First, he went to Ely's house, but Ely would speak to him only through the closed door. He said he had not seen Percy since last night. Frederik wanted him to help look, but Ely said he was feeling sick, and would stay in bed all day.

Frederik searched, asking anyone and everyone, even as they tried to avoid him, but no one had seen Percy. No one looked him in the eye, either, or at his club. Their ardor and bloodlust had inexplicably been replaced by shame in the night. This enraged Frederik even more. He had done what needed to be done—what had always been done—and they had never complained before.

He could not have known or was too wrathful to see that a silent doubt had descended on the village, spreading like pollen to everyone he passed. Deep in their souls, they knew something was wrong, and they were a part of it.

Frederik was eager to take his anger out on someone and searched even more for Percy, but he was nowhere to be found.

The next day, Ely would not answer his door. The neighbors were reluctant to help at first, but Frederik made threats, and the door was forced open. The house was empty. No one had seen him leave, and no one had spoken to him the day before—except Frederik. The silent doubt was a growing tumor, and they avoided him now even more.

Frederik skulked throughout the village, mumbling to himself, occasionally glancing up at the tree on its hill. Frederik knew that they had betrayed him. That coward Ely and that useless fat waste Percy had left, probably heading to the constable, if not there already. He made preparations to leave and planned to do just that once it was dark.

Later, one of Ely's neighbors told her husband about seeing a strange old man outside the window the night before, heading for Ely's house. Her husband told her to be quiet and not to speak of it again.

That night the brewer's daughter had her nightmare, and Frederik disappeared.

* * *

The brewer was not as sickened or as terrified as he later thought he should have been. For some reason, what he saw under the tree seemed right.

There were four of them. Three stood upright, held in place by the thorns. Ely had fallen over, knees and face buried in the grass, his ass in the air. It would have been comical if not for his back—a confused mangle of torn fabric and flesh ripped to carnage. The thorns were red and still glistening. Percy, the shortest and heaviest of the four, had been impaled high up on the trunk. He had slid down during the night, a streak of blood tracing his path. His mother was not there and it was agreed by all to tell her as little as possible. Frederik stood straight, head tilted up, staring at the canopy. One brave villager walked up and got on tiptoes to have a look at his face. He saw the black lacquered handle of the club sticking out between clenched teeth and regretted his curiosity.

The fourth was the most unusual. It was the only one

placed front to the tree, his face buried so deep in thorns it could not be seen. From his build and clothes, though, everyone knew it was Edgar.

Many contemplated this sight and thought of angry yells and pained screams coming from a certain house. They had heard the sounds but ignored them, thinking that a good man like Edgar must have his reasons, and kept to their own business. In truth, no one could account for Edgar the day and time his boy was hurt. No one thought about it then. They were too angry. They would never stop thinking of it after.

They found the belt much later, crumpled up like a piece of paper. It had been tossed aside and rolled down the hill.

One man whispered of hearing footsteps outside his house in the night, and some of the older folk said things about tree spirits and dryads, but they were all hushed quick. Then there was silence, only the wind rustling the leaves. The brewer bowed his head like those before him and made his way back through the crowd, making room for someone else to have a look. Eventually, everyone saw what needed to be seen, and they all went back to the village. There was much to do.

Some went with the carpenter to help him collect materials. Some gathered shovels and made a somber march to the cemetery. The brewer ran straight home and wiped away the footprints in the mud.

Others went to Frederik's house. His door was unlocked. Two large boxes had been hastily packed with clothes and other things. Beyond that, nothing else seemed out of place. There was even a bottle of whiskey and a cup on the table, half full. They left it that way. It would have to be emptied, but later. First, the funeral.

There was scattered chatter about putting a marker on the stranger's grave, but no one could remember his name. One mentioned that Ely would have known. No one spoke of it again after that.

By mid-noon, everything was ready.

The pallbearers made a second trip up the hill. The brewer was one of them. When they peeled Edgar off the tree, his face stayed behind, and they had to scrape it off in bits. They nailed down the lids, then carried the coffins down the hill where a small procession waited. They followed the coffins to the expectant graves. Percy's mother cried. She was one of the few.

On the way, one of the silent mourners glimpsed something odd from the corner of his eye. When he turned and saw what it was, he left the group and wandered, as if in a daze, to an unmarked grave far removed from the resting places of good Christians. Others looked after him, wondering if he had gone mad or overcome with grief. When they saw where he was going and what was there, the pallbearers set down their burdens, and they all followed. The four coffins and their occupants waited patiently.

They gathered around the lonely plot, freshly dug a few days ago, each quietly contemplating what they saw, then moving aside so others may see.

A sapling grew from the dark brown dirt of an innocent man's grave. Young leaves dotted the spindly branches. Thorns covered its thin trunk, numberless and sharp.

HellBound Books

ABOUT MADAME GRAY

Madame Gray, also known as Gerri R. Gray, is an American novelist, editor, poet, and short story writer in the horror and bizarro genres.

She is the author of eight published books, including her popular debut novel, *The Amnesia Girl* (HellBound Books). Her work has appeared in numerous anthologies and literary journals.

A former antique dealer and B&B proprietor, Madame Gray lives in upstate New York in an historic and decidedly haunted nineteenth-century house with her husband and a bevy of spirits.

When she isn't busy creating strange worlds filled with even stranger characters, she can often be found rummaging through antique shops, exploring spooky places, dabbling in the occult or traipsing through old cemeteries with her camera in hand.

Follow her on Facebook at AuthorGerriGray and on Twitter at @GerriRGray.

HellBound Books

Other titles from HellBound Books

Madam Gray's Creepshow

A veritable smorgasbord of twenty-three deliciously terrifying treats, each one simmered to blood-curdling perfection and seasoned with just the perfect amount of gallows humor.

From murder and madness to monsters and the downright macabre, the stories awaiting you within in this superlative anthology push the boundaries of horror to the next level... and way, way beyond!

Featuring stories by: Juliana Amir, Ross Baxter, Norris Black, Matt Bliss, Scot Carpenter, Max Carrey, Josh Darling, James Dorr, Gerri R. Gray, Chisto Healy, Carlton Herzog, Scott McGregor, J Louis Messina, Drew Nicks, Cooper O'Connor, Brett O'Reilly, Lisa Pais, Frederick Pangbourne, Clark Roberts, Rob Santana, Kelli A. Wilkins, and Scott Bryan Wilson.

The Amnesia Girl

Filled with copious amounts of black humor, Gerri R. Gray's first published novel is an offbeat adventure story that could be described as One Flew over the Cuckoo's Nest meets Thelma and Louise.

Flashback to 1974. Farika is a lovely young woman who wakes up one day to find herself a patient in a bizarre New York City psychiatric asylum. She has no idea who she is, and possesses no memories of where she came from nor how she got there.

Fearing for her life after being attacked by a berserk girl with over one hundred personalities and a vicious nurse with sadistic intentions, the frightened amnesiac teams up with an audacious lesbian with a comically unbalanced mind, and together they attempt a daring escape.

But little do they know that a long strange journey into an even more insane world filled with a multitude of perilous predicaments and off-kilter individuals are waiting for them on the outside. Farika's weird reality crumbles when she finally discovers who, and what, she really is!

Gray Skies of Dismal Dreams

Prepare for an excursion into a gloomy world of shadows, where the days are never sunlit and blithe, and where the nights are wrapped in endless nightmares.

No happy endings or silver linings are found in the clouds that fill these gray skies.

But what you will find, gathered in one volume, are the darkest of poems and tales of horror, waiting to take your mind on a journey into realms of the uncheerful and the unholy.

An amazingly surreal collection of short stories and the darkest of poetry, all interspersed with stunning graveyard photographs taken by the multitalented author herself - an absolute must for every bookshelf!

Blood and Blasphemy

If you enjoy your horror dipped in buckets of blood and sprinkled with generous amounts of blasphemy, then you've come to the right place!

Blood and Blasphemy is a collection of over thirty of the most sacrilegious horror stories ever written. Within these irreverent pages, you will encounter a priest that keeps his deformed spawn chained in a root cellar, a convent where a poisonous species of salamander is worshiped, a demonic altar boy, possessed religious relics that kill, blood-drinking clergymen, a Son of God who feeds on sin, an unsuspecting couple who run afoul of religious lunatics in a small town, the divine (and deadly) turd of Christ, and other terrifying tales guaranteed to make church ladies faint and nuns clutch their rosaries.

Graveyard Girls

A delicious collection of horrific tales and darkest poetry from the cream of the crop, all lovingly compiled by the incomparable Gerri R Gray! Nestling between the covers of this formidable tome are twenty-five of the very best lady authors writing on the horror scene today!

These tales of terror are guaranteed to chill your very soul and awaken you in the dead of the night with fear-sweat clinging to your every pore and your heart pounding hard and heavy in your labored breast…

Featuring superlative horror from: Xtina Marie, M. W. Brown, Rebecca Kolodziej, Anya Lee, Barbara Jacobson, Gerri R. Gray, Christina Bergling, Julia Benally, Olga Werby, Kelly Glover, Lee Franklin, Linda M. Crate, Vanessa Hawkins, P. Alanna Roethle, J Snow, Evelyn Eve, Serena Daniels, S. E. Davis, Sam Hill, J. C. Raye, Donna J. W. Munro, R. J. Murray, C. Bailey-Bacchus, Varonica Chaney, Marian Finch (Lady Marian).

The Strange Adventures of Turquoise Moonwolf

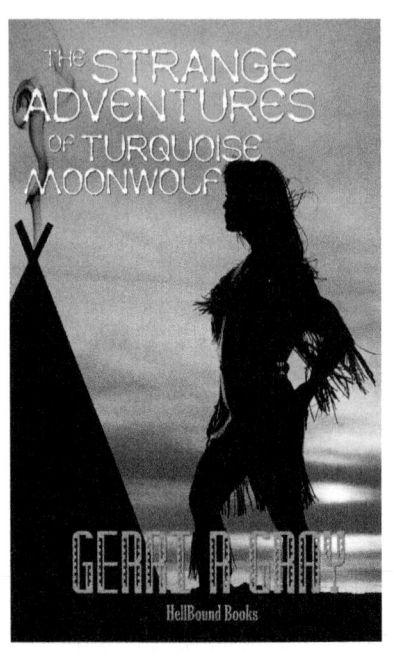

In Turquoise's first strange adventure (Twisted Teepee), a tornado carries Turquoise Moonwolf off in a teepee trading post to a bizarre world of human oddities after incompetent Grandfather Fukowee's rain dance goes awry. Pursued by an evil shape-shifter and accompanied by two escapees from a circus sideshow (one a human ferret and the other a strongman with an abnormally long penis), Turquoise's only hope of returning home is a mysterious medicine man. But a plethora of perils lie in wait along the twisted red road she must follow to get to his reservation.

When Turquoise and an assembly of very weird relatives arrive at the Chateau Catatonia for the reading of eccentric Aunt Uvula's will, sanity takes a holiday. The chaos that erupts in this second strange adventure (Wigwam, Thank You Ma'am) is further compounded by an explosion at a nearby chemical plant that mutates the residents of an adjoining nudist colony into flesh-eating hippies. Wearing nothing but love beads and ravenous appetites, the cannibals run amuck.

Will Turquoise become an heiress of a bed and breakfast, or a menu item of a naked lunch?

In Turquoise's third and final strange adventure (No Happy Medium), Grandfather Fukowee undergoes a bizarre transformation during an exorcism gone wrong and Turquoise is kidnapped by conjoined twins, Russ and Ross Gonzalez, each of whom have changed their first name to Tania after becoming self-brainwashed revolutionaries of the Siamese Liberation Army. However, things get even worse for Turquoise when a wormhole created by a strange comet sucks her into a perilous parallel world.

**A HellBound Books LLC
Publication**

www.hellboundbookspublishing.com

Printed in the United States of America

Printed in Great Britain
by Amazon